Praise for novels by ~~Naomi Kryske~~

THE WITNESS

"A most enjoyable read. There is real depth to the characters, including the firearms officers, and during the courtroom scenes I found myself rooting for Jenny and hoping that the defence barristers would get their just desserts! The interplay between the cops and Jenny is really well thought through, and *The Witness* somehow captured the unique cop's humour, a rare achievement in the literary world. I look forward to the sequels."

BILL TILLBROOK
Chief Superintendent (Retired)
Commander, Specialist Firearms Command
London Metropolitan Police Service

"An American testifying in a British court: suspenseful and surprising! The court scenes are gripping, and the differences between our justice systems add to the drama. Remarkable character development and intense writing combine to make an impressive first novel, which readers are sure to find entertaining."

JOHN-EDWARD ALLEY
Partner (Retired)
Ford & Harrison, LLP

"Masterful portrayal of traumatic stress in a story full of suspense, humor, and poignant moments. I began reading about a victim, a potential legal witness, but got so much more: real, reassuring aids to healing and recovery. The characters are so genuine and some of the situations so vividly written that I'll never forget them. The story really moves, both with regard to plot and the effect it has on the reader."

MARJORIE A. HUSBANDS, MA
Licensed Professional Counselor

THE MISSION

"I was privileged to command men and women much like the characters in this very authentic and enjoyable book. The firearms officers read very lifelike from a professional perspective; indeed their frequent intensity is exactly as I have seen from the longer-serving more experienced staff. And Kryske was also able to spring a couple of surprises on me!"

BILL TILLBROOK
Chief Superintendent (Retired)
Commander, Specialist Firearms Command
London Metropolitan Police Service

"Spot on! Portrayals of police ops were accurate and realistic. This American author has done extensive research. Realistic characters as well; some of them even reminded me of officers I knew on the Job. Good storyline. A really good read!"

IAN CHADWICK
Specialist Firearms Officer (Retired)
London Metropolitan Police Service

"A heartbreaking yet ultimately hope filled story, *The Mission* chronicles the trauma and recovery of sudden grief, something the author clearly understands…Intense, moving, profound."

MARJORIE A. HUSBANDS, MA
Licensed Professional Counselor

THE HOSTAGE

"The hostage rescue description is really accurate. I've been on similar missions during my time in police service, and my heart rate actually went up as I read it. The post incident procedure is exactly what happens. These and other realistic scenarios add to the impact of the book. And the court scenes were the best I've read, gripping and yet humourous."

IAN CHADWICK
Specialist Firearms Officer (Retired)
London Metropolitan Police Service

"An emotionally engaging novel! Brian is a superbly constructed character, and he functions – alongside of Jenny – as a compelling protagonist. I absolutely loved the diary entries of Elspeth. She bridges the past, present, and future in a very powerful way, and her story is wonderful and original. Finally the representation of miscarriage and infertility – rarely tackled in literature – was a great strength of this book."

ANNA HALL-ZIEGER
Professor, Creative Writing
Texas A & M University

"The story begins with a crime and then proceeds to highlight the effect it has on multiple characters. As the police procedure evolved, I actually felt a part of the plot. The characterisations – major and minor – and the technical details were all absolutely spot-on. Perfect! A fine ending to an engaging trilogy!"

BILL TILLBROOK
Chief Superintendent (Retired)
Commander, Specialist Firearms Command
London Metropolitan Police Service

THE HOSTAGE

A Novel

ALSO BY NAOMI KRYSKE

The Witness

The Mission

THE HOSTAGE

A Novel

Naomi Kryske

HOMEPORT
publishing

Cover Design: Joni McPherson and Larry Kryske

Trade Paperback ISBN: 9780578944548

Library of Congress Control Number: 2021915396

Printed in the United States of America

In honor of

the two MPS firearms officers whose experiences inspired this book

and

the one MPS firearms officer whose advice and counsel
made the trilogy immeasurably better

AUTHOR'S NOTE

LIKE *THE WITNESS* AND *THE MISSION, The Hostage* is written in two languages: British English (including spelling and expressions) for the British characters and American English for the American characters.

Thus you will note, for example, "realise/recognise" for "realize/recognize" and "colour/honour/neighbour" for "color/honor/neighbor."

British English sometimes omits or uses fewer or different prepositions, such as "in hospital" for "in the hospital" and "different to" for "different than."

In addition, their past tenses may be unlike ours: "learnt" for "learned" as well as "travelled" when we would write, "traveled." However, "focused" remains "focused."

PROLOGUE

THE METROPOLITAN POLICE SERVICE was created in 1829 by Sir Robert Peel, Home Secretary for Great Britain. The officers were therefore affectionately – and sometimes not so affectionately – called bobbies or peelers.

Peel introduced the concept of policing by consent, in which police officers were considered "citizens in uniform" and relied on public cooperation and approval to carry out their duties, one of which was to engage in the prevention of crime. Physical force was seen as a last resort, and even then, only the minimum amount necessary to achieve the objective and keep the public safe was recommended.

Although bobbies in the nineteenth century had firearms available to them, they patrolled routinely with only a truncheon for self-defence and apprehension of criminals. In the 1880s constables were permitted, although not required, to carry revolvers, called "comforters," during night-time patrols. In the mid-1930s this permission was revoked. Revolvers were kept locked at the station unless a constable had good reason for having one.

The first unit of armed officers was formed in December 1966. Since that time, the firearms unit has been renamed and reorganised on several occasions, one of the most recent being in April 2005, when it became known as part of Central Operations or CO19. However, the MPS is still largely an unarmed force, with more than ninety percent of its officers never having handled a firearm and not wishing to do so.

Police officers who complete an initial firearms course but who do not carry a weapon in their day-to-day duties are called

Authorised Firearms Officers (AFOs). They may be called out if an incident requires the assistance of a large number of officers.

Officers who pass the Armed Response Vehicle (ARV) course as well as an advanced firearms course are full-time firearms officers and the first to arrive on a crime scene. Each ARV carries a driver, an operator, and an observer. Officers may stop and search suspects, their vehicles, and their premises. They control and contain armed incidents and handle approximately one thousand calls per month.

If an enhanced firearms capability is needed, Specialist Firearms Officers (SFOs) are deployed. These individuals are abseil and shotgun trained and have graduated from the Specialist Firearms Officers course. They also serve on a full-time basis, conducting over fifty preplanned intelligence-led operations each month, including hostage rescue scenarios and response to chemical, biological, and nuclear threats. They are held to the highest standards of accuracy. SFOs are available round the clock.

All London Metropolitan Police firearms officers have extensive kit available to them. Two types of Kevlar body armour, digital encrypted radio with handset and microphone, chemical, biological, radiological, or nuclear (CBRN) kit with two respirators. Amphibious kit. Personal abseil harness.

Flame retardant overalls, hooded Gore-tex jacket, blue nylon bomber jacket. Combat helmet, blue baseball cap or balaclava if identity needs protecting. Britton boots, personal sleeping bag, Gore-tex bivvy bag. Telescoping (expandable) baton. CS gas, a nonlethal component of tear gas. Pressure bandages. Plasticuffs.

Weapons include Heckler and Koch 9 mm single shot semi-automatic carbine rifle, H&K G36 assault rifle, 7.62 Styr sniper rifle, and Glock semiautomatic self-loading pistol. Tasers. Ammunition.

Officers train every six weeks: To maintain the level of authorisation and familiarity with the equipment. To identify weaknesses which can then be corrected. To develop patience. To generate alternatives, particularly deescalation. To learn what to say and how to say it so that commands are clear. To weigh cover versus concealment. To decide how and where to aim and when or if to fire. How to maintain focus and accuracy whether moving, standing still, or in a compromised position. How to prioritise when there is more than one target.

Scenario after scenario, in all sorts of weather, at all times of day, whether weary or wide awake, until movement is nearly instinctive. No hesitation. Nothing but rapid, seamless, decisive action. Feelings set aside. Only the cold hard facts of a mission determine the response.

On the Job thousands of calls and hundreds of operations take place, and rarely is a round released.

Hence the endless planning and training. With the hope that their expertise will be unnecessary.

PART ONE

August 2005

The Incident

"What is character but the determination of incident?
What is incident but the illustration of character?"

Henry James

CHAPTER ONE

SERGEANT SIMON CASEY, a specialist firearms officer with London's Metropolitan Police, frowned slightly when his mobile buzzed. His wife, Jenny, rarely rang him whilst he was on duty, knowing his phone was shut off during firearms operations. Today, however, no ops were scheduled for his team. He was in a briefing room at the Leman Street base reviewing tactics for an upcoming raid. He flipped the phone open, a question on his lips, but she was already speaking, and it didn't sound as if she were speaking to him. He waited, saying nothing.

" – still hurts."

He frowned again. He could hear pain in her voice. Where was she? Was she all right?

"Why did you bring me here? I don't know you."

He heard a muffled scream.

"Why did you hit me? Don't you want to help me? I need a doctor!"

Covering the receiver with one hand, he strode to the door of the briefing room, simultaneously signalling silence and gesturing for the man in the corridor, Police Constable Brian Davies, to join him. Casey set his mobile carefully on the desk and muted it whilst rummaging for a notebook. He didn't want anyone on Jenny's end to hear noises in the room nor did he want to have any difficulty in hearing her. He wrote, *Jenny. Trouble. Need to record this.*

"Please call an ambulance. I need medical help. My head hurts so much I can't sit up."

Severe head pain, Casey wrote.

Davies, a member of Casey's firearms team, located a tape recorder, inserted a fresh tape, and pressed the Record button. A huge bear of a man, he towered over Casey even when seated next to him.

"That lamp is so bright. And could you speak softer?"

Sensitivity to light and noise.

Both men heard a gasp and a sputter, then retching.

Nausea.

"Stop moving! You're making me dizzy."

Dazed.

Her voice was difficult to hear, and the other individual – or individuals – couldn't be heard at all.

Additional officers began to enter the briefing room. Davies stationed one at the door to maintain quiet and instructed another to ring the Information Room at New Scotland Yard.

The faint voice continued. "I remember Caledonian Road. A church. How did my clothes get torn? And wet? Did I fall? Is this your flat? It's cold. Is that why you're wearing that hoodie?"

Confusion. Possible shock. Casey looked at the symptoms he'd recorded and added, *Concussion probable. Loss of consciousness unknown.*

The voice on the mobile whimpered, "No, stop! Why are you pointing that knife at me? Don't you understand? My name is Jennifer Casey, and I need help. Who are you?"

Davies watched Casey. At 38, the ginger-haired sergeant was an experienced firearms team leader with unusual discipline and focus. Had he held a pencil, however, the force of his grip would have snapped it in two.

"Sorry! You don't have to get mad! No, of course you don't need a gun. I just need to know – your name." There was a pause. "Why? Because I'm – mixed up. Would you tell me anyway?"

Davies placed his hand briefly on Casey's shoulder as they listened to Jenny's ragged breathing and slow speech.

"Roy…that's a good Texas name…I'm from Texas…you're tall like a Texan. Are – are you from somewhere near the States? Jamaica?"

Jenny's voice was fainter, and the men struggled to catch the words: "Why do you keep calling me Tanya? Oh, no...there's blood in my hair...my head...I think I'm going to be sick again..."

Casey's penmanship deteriorated. *Speech slightly slurred,* he scribbled.

"I'm so tired...let me rest...please..."

They heard a sob.

"Jenny, not Tanya...oh, help..."

Nothing. Casey suspected the battery on Jenny's mobile had gone dead. No matter how often he admonished her, she rarely remembered to keep it fully charged. He broke the hush. "Some bloody nutter's got Jenny," he said, unable to keep the anguish from his voice, "and I've just lost the connection."

CHAPTER TWO

SIMON CASEY, headstrong as the saltwater fish he liked to catch, had lacked supervision as a lad. It had taken military service, first in the Royal Marines and later as a Commando and then a Special Boat Service medic, to settle and season him. None of it, however, civilised him. War was controlled violence, and he was very good at it. He got used to being uncomfortable and worse. As a consequence of the stress of training and missions, some SBS members returned to base with more than grit and mud on their bodies. They laundered themselves as well as their uniforms. When the missions were over, however, SBS recreation rituals could be nearly as dangerous because there were fewer rules. Time on leave was the only true period of relaxation. He enjoyed his pints as much, if not more than, the next man. Although he left the intensity behind, the discipline remained.

The transition to specialist firearms officer with London's Metropolitan Police was more difficult than he had anticipated. First, the police academy. Not the sort of instruction he preferred – committing to memory long passages of law – but a necessary procedure. Then came a long two years patrolling with only a collapsible baton, a whistle, a radio, and handcuffs. Domestics where the female wouldn't press charges; drunks who assaulted responding officers and then resisted arrest; witnesses who couldn't identify their attacker; people who spent all their money on drugs and then stole food; addicts who neglected their children; bedsits where just making entry was a risk to an officer's life.

He was a fish out of water, and at times he had questioned his course. The discipline was, in his view, sometimes too relaxed. He wasn't glib with the members of the public he encountered. He could take charge quickly in a situation but didn't like turning the scene over to officers who had, as they so cheekily said, more resources. His training and experience with firearms had been extensive, and he wanted to use them. Hence he volunteered for the specialist armed officers unit as soon as it was allowed. Upon acceptance a camaraderie similar to his SBS team began to develop with the other armed officers. He welcomed the additional professionalism of the armed units, and he found the weapons and the humour familiar and comforting. Qualifying for their elite division also assuaged some of the anger he'd felt when an injury suffered in combat rendered him unfit for further military service.

He played hard and sought women who did the same, who weren't looking for attachments, and the brief nature of their couplings didn't disturb him. He didn't promise future assignations, and at times he was more concerned with meeting his own needs than theirs. Then he'd been assigned to protect a witness, a severely injured young woman critical to the government's case against a vicious serial killer. He'd not wanted it. Months of inaction did not appeal to him. Looking after a survivor who was fearful and tearful appealed even less.

From military ops to armed police actions to being a minder? A step down, in his view. He felt pressurised to take the assignment but overcame his reluctance by telling himself that the other officers on the protection team hadn't his background. His medical training as well as his security skills were needed. Perhaps guiding the physical recovery of the witness would be a short-term exercise.

Young, American, and obstinate, she hadn't wanted protection any more than he had wanted to provide it. At first her fear had frustrated him. On occasion she'd felt that she had to defend herself against him and the measures he mandated to ensure her safety, but he'd come to consider her opposition and defiance of his authority as signs of healing. He had not anticipated being touched by her courage and dogged determination to overcome every setback. He learnt that she was slight only in stature.

His respect for her had come gradually and grudgingly. The day he realised that his feelings for her went deeper was one of conflict. He told himself he wanted no entanglements, but her engagement and marriage to another more senior officer hit him hard. He was glad for long hours on the Job, for pints with his mates. Then he'd hear her name or see a woman who resembled her and remember. He resolved to move on. He tried to do.

She'd been married less than two years when the other officer, a posh detective, had been killed in a terrorist attack. He'd seen how bound she was by shock and grief, but he'd kept in touch, a flickering spark inside him hoping. Over time she had come to rely on him and then to love him. They'd been married for just over eighteen months, and he believed that she was happy.

He'd left his expletives behind, but now he swore silently. He faced losing her again, Jenny, his wife, the woman with the small, shapely body and soft, perfumed skin, the woman who surprised him still with her verve and humour, the woman carrying his child.

CHAPTER THREE

THE NEWS WAS SPREADING. On the advice of his ops officer, Simon Casey moved to one of the inspectors' offices not far from the SFO briefing room and waited for the suit from New Scotland Yard. The briefing room was not sufficiently private for the interview he knew was coming, and the space would be needed by other specialist officers preparing for upcoming operations.

Was Jenny's mobile operable? Was the risk in ringing her back acceptable? Yes, more information was essential. He punched the numbers. Nothing. That was it then.

He walked to the window. Jenny was out there somewhere in the vast city. Did she have a window where she was? Could she escape through it or at least discover her location?

Where was the NSY man? It was past time to get on with it. He checked his watch. 17:45 on Thursday, 25 August 2005. With British summer time, it was still light, but night would come eventually, possibly increasing Jenny's danger and certainly magnifying her fear. It was a dark point of view, but he was in a dark mood.

Not for the first time, he raged internally against the Met's careful adherence to procedure. All they needed was a location, and they could be on scene within minutes.

His thoughts were disturbed by a knock on the door. PC Clive Croxley introduced him to DCI Evan Cunningham. Casey didn't think Croxley should have been permitted on the SFO team floor, even as an escort. He'd made grievous errors in judgement as an Armed Response Vehicle (ARV) officer before failing to qualify for specialist duty. He shook his head. He couldn't allow himself to be distracted. He had to focus on Jenny's situation now.

"I'm from SCD7," Cunningham said. "As you may know, the Serious and Organised Crime Command is a part of the Specialist Crime Directorate, and we will handle the case until the appropriate borough is determined."

Cunningham was younger than Casey would have expected for a detective chief inspector. No doubt one of the Met's fast-tracked officers, his rumpled suit and loose tie gave him an owlish appearance somewhat at odds with his square chin and stocky shoulders and belied the gravitas he was attempting to project. Casey hoped that he had retained enough information from his multiple training courses to lead the investigation effectively. Not inclined to be impressed by rank or titles, Casey simply indicated the empty chair across from him and waited for Cunningham to puff up his feathers.

"Sergeant Casey," Cunningham began. "I understand that you received a call from your wife some time ago and that you recorded it. Is that correct?"

Casey nodded.

"In investigative terms that makes you a witness."

Casey was silent.

"You'll need to notify your operations supervisor that you'll be sidelined for a while."

"Done."

"Let's hear this tape of yours then and see what we can learn, shall we?" Cunningham, seemingly unaffected by what he was hearing, took notes whilst he listened. "Your wife has given us more than enough to start," he said when the recording concluded. "She thought to ring you. A most resourceful action. It appears that she has been taken by an irrational man – on impulse – but I must ask if there is any possibility that you are the reason for this."

"None, sir," Casey assured him. "As a specialist firearms officer, I'm essentially anonymous outside these walls."

Cunningham consulted his notes. "Roy – Tanya – do either of these names mean anything to you?"

Casey shook his head.

"Let's recap then. The hostage taker has committed at least one violent act, perhaps more, since your wife has a head injury and her clothing was torn. He is armed with a knife. We do not know if he has a firearm. He is tall, has dark skin, may reside somewhere near Caledonian Road, and has confused your wife with someone else. What time did her call come through?"

"About 16:00."

"Why was your wife in Islington?"

"She had a 13:30 appointment at the Caledonian Road Methodist Church. She wrote a book on grief and planned to deliver some copies there."

"We'll check to see whether she arrived and if so, when she departed," Cunningham said. "In the meantime I'll contact the Islington nick. We'll need them to assign a detective and provide some uniforms to aid in our investigation."

"Sir, she's expecting. Nine weeks gone. She may have been unconscious for a time. And a possible concussion complicates things." Casey showed Cunningham the list of symptoms he had recorded.

"You have medical training, Sergeant?"

"Yes, I was a combat medic before joining the police." He spoke again, his voice hard. "It's nearly six now. You'll not have her out before nightfall. She'll have to stay over with that bastard. And I'll have to give the news to her parents."

Cunningham had learnt early on to insulate himself from the feelings that affected others during an incident. He was a police officer, not a psychologist. Procedures that led to a positive result were what mattered. "Sergeant, I understand your concern. We have a duty of care to your wife. We'll proceed as quickly as we can, but we cannot move forward without more information than we possess at this time. Have you received a ransom demand?"

"No."

"Is your wife wealthy? Is her family?"

"No."

"Then we'll consider this an abduction, not a kidnap. It's an informational issue," Cunningham explained. "A hostage negotiator will need to know that money's not a motive." He made a note then looked up. "I suggest that you stand by."

The distinction didn't signify to Casey. Either way she was a hostage.

CHAPTER FOUR

STAND BY. Casey had used that phrase himself on occasion, but in the space of one evening he'd come to hate it. He did, however, as he was told, ringing a neighbour to look after Jenny's dog Bear, named for a period in her life when her depression had been large and frightening. Fortunately the dog wasn't.

Unaware that his feet had found a pattern, he paced, toward the window, away, toward, away, until the darkening shadows dimmed his view of what lay outside.

The dinner hour came and went as he waited. He ate a few bites of the meal Davies brought him from the canteen, wondering whether Jenny was able to eat. Whether her injuries were severe. He would not allow himself to think beyond that. A pint – or more – was in order, but that had not been supplied.

A knock. Croxley again, probably restricted to base duty for the recent negligent discharge of his firearm. This time he guided a crowd, Cunningham and two others. The woman shrugged out of a tweed jacket much too colourful for the occasion. She brushed her straight hair away from her face. Not deeply lined, so she was probably closer to forty than to fifty. A lanky man with a greying beard and a long face accompanied her. Casey's heart sank when he saw them. Jenny's life rested on this garish individual and her world- weary colleague.

"Sergeant, I'm Detective Inspector Clare Thoms," she said, extending her hand. "My sergeant, Timothy Riley."

Casey stood and clasped her hand briefly before reseating himself. He nodded at Riley, who took out his notebook.

Thoms noted Casey's reddish-blond hair and average height and estimated his age at mid to late thirties. These were the only neutral features about him. Fit, but then they all were, weren't they? And intense. Tightly coiled and ready to spring. She simply wasn't going to let those icy blue eyes or clenched fists anywhere near the details of her investigation or the displays that would be visible in the incident room. "Tell me about your wife. Expecting a baby, is she?"

"Yes. She's in the first trimester. Nine weeks. Half nine, actually."

"Her call on your mobile was the last contact you had with her?"

Casey nodded.

"Normal pregnancy so far?"

"Morning sickness and fatigue, but only what's expected, according to her doctor."

"First child?"

"Yes."

"None to worry with at home then," Thoms concluded.

A stab of anger at her coldness caused Casey's heart to race. He forced himself to take several slow, deep breaths to restore its normal rhythm.

"Based on your notes, you believe that concussion may be a complicating factor, is that correct?"

Casey detailed the symptoms he'd recorded. He saw Riley enter them in his notebook. Another notetaker, like Cunningham. The Met must have an entire swarm of them. He couldn't envision either of them taking meaningful action of any sort.

"Are you happy in your marriage, Sergeant?"

He should have expected the question but still resented it. He answered in the affirmative.

"Then why did your wife write a book about grief?"

Casey hesitated.

He's uncomfortable, Thoms realised.

"Her first husband was killed suddenly. She wrote about her grief experience as a way of helping others." He considered, only briefly, mentioning her role as a witness in the trial of serial killer Cecil Scott.

Thoms waited. He's not disclosing everything, she thought, but they never do. That was the trouble in most interviews. "Are you acquainted with a man named Roy?"

An abrupt change of subject. A device detectives often used to gain a result from interrogation. His resentment grew. "No."

Thoms heard the edge in his voice. "Any possibility that your wife knows him? Misjudged his character and went off with him?"

"None. No." He spit out the words.

"You work long hours. Could she have sought a way to – occupy her time?"

He was on his feet before he realised it. His voice was dangerously soft. "She'd. Not. Do. That." He reseated himself, a spasm in his shoulder the only indication of his tension.

Thoms changed focus. "Here's what we know. The church is at the intersection of Caledonian Road and Market Road. We've made contact with them. She left at approximately 14:50 but not through the same door she entered. It's only a short walk to the tube station at Caledonian Road. However, the sign for the tube station can't be seen from the church's side door, so she'd have had to change directions. It was raining at the time. Not many people on the street, unfortunately, so fewer potential witnesses for us." She paused. "Where do you live, Sergeant?"

Hurry up! he thought, gripping the table with his hands. "A flat in Hampstead," he answered in as even a tone as he could muster.

"Hampstead? On a copper's salary?"

"My wife owns the flat."

"She has her own source of income?"

"She inherited the flat from her first husband."

Interesting. Relevant? Hard to say. "Which trains would your wife have taken to get home?"

Another change of enquiry. Was she being thorough or trying to unsettle him? Let her try. Only Jenny's situation unsettled him. What Thoms considered interrogation was child's play compared to what he'd been subjected to in Special Forces selection. "The

Piccadilly line. Holloway Road or King's Cross St. Pancras. Then a change to the Metropolitan line."

"Estimated arrival time?"

"She'd have wanted to be home before the trains became crowded."

"Let's review. The call came to you at 16:00. Over an hour after she left the church. Considering total travel time – including walking to and from the stations – and the fact that she may have been unconscious, even briefly, I rather doubt that she completed her trip. We've not heard of any incident or disruption on the lines, but we don't know when in the abduction the assault occurred. We'll be checking closed-circuit television to see if she entered the station, but until then we'll not rule out the possibility that she got on the train and was forced off early on."

"She wouldn't have gone with him."

"Can you be certain of that?"

He leant forward to make his point. "Positive. She would have resisted. No matter what it took."

"How do you know?"

Casey did not respond immediately. He closed his eyes momentarily, remembering what Jenny's lack of resistance had cost her in the past. When he'd collected himself, he opened his eyes, the force of his gaze causing Thoms to lean away. He made no effort to disguise the edge in his voice. Why didn't they know this? "Some years ago she was drugged and abducted. When she woke, she was nearly beaten to death. And more. Over time she healed, but given any choice, she'll never allow herself to be that helpless again. The offender was Cecil Scott. You may recall the case. She was the Crown's key witness."

Thoms tried not to let her surprise show. The trial had been the focus of press coverage for weeks. "Did you know her then?" she asked.

"I was one of her protection officers. The Met kept her under wraps until her testimony was given."

Thoms was silent, wondering whether his wife's previous experience made her more or less resilient in the current situation. "Thank you. Let's move on. Have you a recent snap?"

Casey took a photo of Jenny from his wallet and held it up. "Five feet, two inches tall, approximately seven stone. Dark brown hair, a bit longer than shown here. Brown eyes."

Thoms appreciated the law enforcement description. "Did you get that, Sergeant?" she asked Riley.

"Yes, ma'am."

"She has a scar on her face?" Thoms asked, leaning forward to examine the photo which Casey still kept. "And you didn't think to mention it because – ?"

"I no longer see it." He pocketed it, stood, and moved away.

Thoms did not break the silence. She decided against pushing him. She needed him cooperative, at least for now. She watched the muscles in his back tense and relax, tense and relax. When he returned to his chair, he rubbed the sides of his forehead, but his countenance was firm.

"I'll have the photo now," she said, noting his dilatory behaviour in producing it. "Her age?"

"Thirty." He recalled Jenny's point of view on her birthday. What had been a lighthearted memory was now painful. Three decades, she'd said. I feel ancient.

"She's from the States? Sergeant?" Thoms prompted.

"Yes. She's the oldest of three children. Her parents live in Houston. That's in Texas."

"What was she wearing?"

"She wasn't dressed when I departed. We had early turn today." She hadn't been awake. He had kissed her before he left, his usual practice. Thoms' voice brought him back to the present, and he disliked her for it.

"What's she like as an individual?"

Was that relevant? "Intelligent, quick thinking, determined."

"And you, Sergeant?"

"Sorry?"

"Like it or not, you're a principal in this case. What do I need to know about you?" She saw his jaw tighten. A sign of impatience, not unusual in the circumstances.

"That bastard's hurting her and likely hurting my baby as well," he hissed, "and you're asking about me?"

"We don't know that, Sergeant."

"That's the point, isn't it? You don't know."

"Sergeant?" Thoms pressed.

"I'm from Cornwall. I was in the Special Forces before I joined the police."

Thoms waited, but he gave no details. No matter. She could fill in the blanks later if necessary. "Faced with a paucity of evidence to the contrary, we'll work from where she was last seen, Caledonian Road," she decided. "I've quite a list of investigative actions, many of which can be conducted concurrently. None, however, can be initiated before first light. I'll be sending out uniforms to look for any sign of her and querying the PCSOs, since they're the ones most frequently on the ground."

She turned to her detective sergeant. "Ring Gardner and Caruthers. Tell them I need them first thing."

For the first time Thoms referred to Cunningham, who had remained silent during her dialogue. "I'll have our colleague here arrange for a hostage negotiator. It usually takes some time before the negotiators present themselves, and I want to be ready to avail ourselves of their services as soon as we've located her."

Casey tried not to wince. In his experience negotiators viewed time as an ally. He did not, and he'd never been on an assignment where the X-ray – the hostage taker – came out quietly. Despite the DI's positive comment, he knew they could be facing a siege.

"Sergeant, I suggest that you go home and look after yourself. Your wife's going to need you when she comes out of this. Report here in the morning, and I'll ring you."

Casey watched the three depart, Cunningham with the rank, Thoms, nominally in charge, and Riley, tired and taciturn. The modern Met, dispensing patronising advice. Experts at invasive and irrelevant interviews. And police community support officers? Why did Thoms think that those with minimal training could assist in any significant way?

He understood that Thoms wanted to keep him at arm's length. His faith lay in operations. Her currency was information, and she would deal with him on a need-to-know basis. He might as well have been a civilian.

CHAPTER FIVE

WHEN CLARE THOMS joined the police in the early 80s, she entered a man's world. Margaret Thatcher was prime minister at the time, but that didn't make things better for women in other careers. At first it didn't deter her; she'd grown up with brothers who treated her as one of the boys. Her parents didn't coddle her – or indeed any of them – but they were fair. When she did well, they acknowledged her for it. School had been the same, the grading system equitable, and the subjects made sense to her. The practice of policing, when she considered it, built on these, enforcing order and providing consequences for those who participated in disorder.

It was in the world of policing, however, that she experienced prejudice for the first time. Not being a man was a distinct disadvantage. The sexism was institutional and required stoicism, sacrifice, and silence on the part of the women who signed on. Her rank wasn't simply PC for police constable; she was a WPC, woman police constable, or "wop-see." Male officers didn't have to suffer the indignity of being called MPCs or "mop-sees." No form of differentiation was required for them because PCs were assumed to be male. Women were regarded as the exception to the rule, which she found demeaning.

Her uniform also segregated her, because skirts were required, which made pursuing a suspect difficult. All officers were good at concealing their feelings, but emotional displays, however mild, by females caused them to be labelled as weak, regardless of the circumstances. Vomiting was the exception. It received no criticism because the men had all done it when they'd seen their first mangled body or attended their first post-mortem.

Women were expected to walk the same, talk the same, and drink the same as the men, but they stayed unknown. When she made detective, she thought she'd left the uniform behind, but in practice it had simply changed. White blouse, dark skirt, dark, sensible shoes. Hair short and neat. To avoid any suggestion of impropriety, she wore little or no makeup. The male officers didn't see the individual wearing the clothes. She was still anonymous.

At one of her early assignments, she'd been told in no uncertain terms that she wasn't wanted. Nor were any complaints that might result from the behaviour of other officers toward her. Inwardly she railed. She wasn't seeking special treatment, only the same. She hadn't become a police officer to keep her head down, particularly with those she considered her colleagues.

Learning the protocols was the easy part. Working harder didn't help her to advance. Developing a tough exterior didn't help her to be accepted. Senior officers didn't even know her name. Find another career? No, she liked the order that came from enforcing the law. She liked the connections with the community. Resigning – failing – was not an alternative.

One cool morning she wore a colourful scarf round her neck. Most of it was tucked inside her blouse, but she didn't remove it indoors. No one commented. The next day she allowed a bit more of it to show, and one of her fellow PCs referred to her as "the one with the scarf."

"DC Thoms," she said, loudly enough for everyone to hear. As the days passed, she varied her scarves and the ways she wore them, tied to her ponytail, twisted into a French knot, under the collar of her blouse. She used accessories to establish her identity.

Years passed. She volunteered for extra duty, attended courses to increase her knowledge of specific issues, and took the exams required for increases in rank. She no longer feared making a mistake. Behind her were the years of worrying that when the gents laughed, she was the reason. Over time she graduated from colourful accessories to colourful blouses, feminine shoes. She modified her leadership style. Sometimes toughness was necessary; sometimes it wasn't. The same approach wasn't equally effective with everyone. She learnt to use patience and to let sympathy show. Respect was slow in coming, but it did come. The environment of policing hadn't changed much, but she had succeeded in spite of it. These days male as well as female officers worked for her. They all had to accept her authority, and they all knew that she abhorred bias.

CHAPTER SIX

ON HIS WAY HOME Simon realised that although his name as well as hers was on the paperwork, he still thought of the flat as Jenny's. Bear met him at the door and whined softly when she did not enter with him. "She'll not be coming home tonight," he told the dog. The flat was dark. He felt a bit like whining himself. Kneeling to ruffle the dog's ears, he decided to go for a run to clear his mind. To delay the inevitable. He took Bear with him.

At first he felt some frustration with the dog's inability to keep up. However, Bear wasn't accustomed to his rapid pace. Jenny didn't run with him; she walked, and not at night.

Jenny. He stopped and bent over, not to regain his breath but to establish focus, because the exercise wasn't having its desired effect. His mind was no more centred than when he'd begun. And he hadn't delayed long enough to avoid the phone calls he had to make.

He had kept to the periphery of the Heath, not afraid for his own safety but needing the glow from the homes and street lamps on the border to guide him. The interior of the park would be peopled with couples or soon-to-be couples, transitory relationships the police were aware of but ignored.

Now he straightened and resumed his route, slowing his pace for Bear and glad for the companionship of the dog's presence. At least he hadn't been alone with his thoughts. Finally, having tempered at least to a degree, his anger and concern, he returned to the flat. He could no longer postpone what he had to do.

The flat was spacious, the lowest floor with guest accommodations, the main floor with the public rooms, including the kitchen, dining room, and sitting room, and the top floor with a master bedroom and bath and two smaller bedrooms next to it. Tonight without her it seemed even larger.

He mustn't think on that. It was still not late in Texas, where Jenny's family lived. He had to ring them. He could imagine her saying, "Tell them, but don't scare them." Informing without alarming was perhaps not possible in this case. Nevertheless when he spoke with her father, he kept his recitation direct and brief, omitting details which could be inflammatory whilst recounting what they knew and acknowledging that it was precious little. He then listened to Bill Jeffries' shock. The call was difficult but mercifully short because he had no assurances to give. Jeffries didn't mention Jenny's pregnancy, which was puzzling. She had been so excited by the news that she'd rung her parents straightaway. Now Jeffries' request for updates came as a command. Casey assented before ending the call.

It was nearing midnight. He debated ringing Father Neil Goodwyn, the former British Army chaplain who now worked for London's Metropolitan Police. He had counselled Jenny previously, helping her to regain her faith and equilibrium after other trying experiences. Goodwyn had served in the Middle East where the sun had bleached his hair and darkened his skin. His body had been whipped by the wind and the stinging sand. "In the Middle East the weather was an adversary almost as difficult to overcome as the enemy," he had said.

Regardless of the hour, Jenny would want him to notify the priest. He paused for a moment, realising that he also wanted to ring him. He respected him, and he needed to speak with someone without the impersonal, objective tones he'd heard all evening from the investigators and the judgemental point of view Jenny's father had held.

Goodwyn answered on the second ring. He didn't sound as if he'd been sleeping. Casey gave him the full, unadorned picture, from the phone call that had alerted him to her predicament to the meets with the detectives, even expressing his frustration with the interview process.

"Don't give up hope," the priest advised, "because she won't."

"She'll not be able to defend herself physically," Casey argued.

"Perhaps not, but she has an agile mind. She'll be looking for a way either to resolve her situation or to escape from it."

"She'll be expecting me to do something."

"It's always difficult to leave the action to others, is it not? But in this case you must."

"When she's pregnant and has a concussion?"

"Even then. She's intelligent, capable, and creative. I'll pray for those qualities to assert themselves whilst the detectives do their work. Is there a place I can wait with you?"

"I don't know where I'll be," Casey answered.

"You'll keep in touch then?" Goodwyn asked.

"Yes." Casey put the phone down.

The flat was quiet. He missed her voice and surprisingly, her inquisitiveness. In their early days together, she had peppered him with questions when he came home, confessing that she wanted to know everything about him. When did you learn to fly kites? How can you like mussels? Do you wish you had a sister? Will you teach me to snow ski? Would you still love me if I started smoking? Have you ever donated blood?

He'd responded to most of her enquiries and sometimes asked her the same: What is your favourite colour? How do you want to celebrate your birthday? Where do you want to travel? Over time he looked forward to the questions. Some of them initiated good conversations; others made him laugh. On occasion, however, he was knackered and called for a full stop. He hoped that if she had a moment to catch her breath, he'd be able to catch his.

Once she asked if he'd ever delivered a baby and if not, did he know how. He'd paused and then smiled. I know how to make one, he'd countered with a chuckle. She had hugged him and whispered, "Show me." And he had.

Tonight he would have been glad for her curiosity, whatever the result. He would have even welcomed her customary question, "Did anybody shoot at you today?" Not wanting to feed her anxiety, he always replied in the negative, which was usually true.

Sitting with a beer in his hand and the dog at his feet, he considered the questions he had for her. Are you still alive? Where are you? Where? What has that bastard done to you? Are you seriously injured? Is the baby all right? Are you captive in the dark? He didn't need to ask if she were afraid.

Everywhere he looked he saw evidence of her, everything a reminder that she was not there. Her shampoos and nail polishes on the counter in the loo. She liked trying new fragrances and shades, and a trace of her peach-scented soap lingered. Some disarray here and there – a sweater draped over the arm of a chair, items from the cleaners she hadn't put away yet. A photo of the two of them on the chest of drawers. Taken at the wedding, when her smile had eclipsed everything else. Standing next to it, a second snap, taken on their first anniversary. Only two photos. Not enough. If she came home, he'd remedy that. No, when.

The desk in the corner was piled high with books of poetry. She'd made several visits to one of the schools in Highgate, just north of Hampstead. The head of the junior school, in which children aged seven through eleven were registered, had been looking for a part-time instructor to increase the interest of the students when they began their study of poetry. He'd been charmed by Jenny's American accent and thought that the children might be as well. Her educational credentials had been more than acceptable, and her willingness to work without a wage had made the arrangement worth trying.

"You're my first victim," she'd said when she practised her presentation with him. So he'd listened whilst she explained about the different types of poems and how each written work was derived from a background or context. To his surprise he'd been intrigued when she explained the elementary rules of American baseball and then read a portion of the narrative poem, "Casey at the Bat," which told the story of a legendary hitter who bore the same name that he did.

She'd stopped before the end of the poem and asked, "Do you want to know what happens next?"

He did, of course, but he wanted to needle her a bit, so he'd remained silent.

"Simon, you're supposed to raise your hand!" she'd exclaimed. "Because that's my punch line, to show them that they're interested in poetry even though they didn't think they would be!"

He'd then raised both his hands, which had made her laugh. "You'll be well received," he'd predicted, and she had been.

Now he turned away from the desk, taken aback that his memory of that encounter was still so vivid.

On her nightstand rested a paperback book with a bookmark from the Gaucho Restaurant where they'd eaten the night she decided she was ready to start a family. Glancing at the neatly made bed, he reached out to touch her pillow then drew his hand away. He didn't want to sleep there. He headed to the kitchen, where he saw a grocery list she'd begun. He found some leftover food in the fridge to warm through, let the dog out, and slept on the sofa.

CHAPTER SEVEN

WHEN NEIL CHAUNCY GOODWYN was young, not yet a teenager, he ran away from home. Unfortunately he chose a rainy night, and when he sought shelter in a doorway, he was propositioned by an intoxicated man. The first avenue of safety belonged to a church, where, soaked and shaken, he fell asleep on one of the pews.

In the morning a man's voice startled him, but the grey-haired individual wore a priest's collar and had stationed himself a respectable distance away.

"Hungry?" he asked. "If you'll join me in my office, I can collect some doughnuts for us. By the way, I'm Father Giles."

Neil followed, wary but famished.

"Coffee or tea?"

Tea was an unhappy reminder of home, and the aroma of the coffee enveloped him like a hug, so he held out the cup. Father Giles filled it only halfway, adding cream to top it off and explaining that he liked creamed caffeine. "This way it's never too hot," he added. He offered sugar, which Neil accepted. Neil took a tentative sip.

"May I know your name?"

"I'm Neil. Neil Goodwyn."

"And you're here because – ?"

Neil paused. Father Giles' office was small and cluttered, but he had left the door wide open. There was a cross on one wall. "Are you going to call the police?" he asked.

"No, son. Not without your permission." Giles moved his chair away from the telephone. "Of course, if someone's hurt you, I'll hope that we can contact the authorities together."

The coffee was bitter and sweet at the same time. The doughnut had more appeal. "My parents – they don't notice me."

The priest waited. He noted Neil's clothes, rumpled after a night on the pew but of good quality. His hair was cut short, and he hadn't appeared to have any tenderness when he moved. If neglect or abuse were present, it was emotional, not physical.

"I have an older brother and a younger one. My father's a doctor, and he's gone a good deal. My mum teaches psychology. She helps my brothers but not me."

The middle child, Giles thought. Developmentally the one with the most difficult route to adulthood. Evidently this child hadn't acted out to gain attention; he'd just left. But his need, if not addressed, could make him vulnerable in the future to bad influences. Perhaps in this case it was not too late to correct the imbalance. He continued his gentle probe. "You do well in school, do you?"

A nod. "School's easy. Except for sport."

"And discipline – any problems at home or at school?"

Neil shook his head. "No demerits," he said. "I know not to talk out of turn."

An odd choice of words, Father Giles reflected. He leant back in his chair. "Sometimes, son, we have to speak up a bit. God knows our hearts, but others may need some prompting. Your mum and dad – they'll be missing you. When you're ready to go home, I'll accompany you. I want to reassure you as well. You're important to God, and you're important to me. You have a purpose in this world. I believe God will find you when the time is right."

No one at home talked much about God, but Neil liked the kindness of the priest's words. He accepted his offer to walk with him. Neil's dad had had early morning presurgical rounds at hospital and hadn't known he was gone. After thanking the priest, his mum raised her eyebrows at Neil's draggletailed appearance and said only, "Your rebellion's come a bit soon."

So it was back to school the next day, although from that time on, Neil made it a practice to visit Father Giles on a regular basis. When Neil confessed that he was confused about his future, the priest encouraged him to keep at it. "Things will become clear," he said. "Life is a puzzle for most of us at one time or another."

So Neil did. Science, maths, languages – he scored well in all of them in spite of his lack of focus. He had a good memory, and he could understand their practical relevance. The application of heat could cause items to liquefy, steam, or burn. Goods had a price, and it was helpful to know if you could afford to buy them and how much money you'd have left if you did. Useful to know but not profound. Like a ship without a rudder, he drifted through his classes.

When Neil's older brother left for university and Neil began to receive a bit more attention from his parents, he was bitter. "Try to accept with grace and not judgement," the priest advised. "They are giving what they can."

Finally Neil was old enough for university, where he took a class in religion, and everything changed. The thesis of the professor was that religion was a result of man's need, but Neil didn't think so. He didn't believe that men satisfied their own spiritual needs. Even in his limited experience of life, he saw that nothing that men made kept them happy for very long. Their creations were transitory. So he began to consider that there was a plan. His imperfect understanding of that plan did not negate it.

In the context of a plan, education made sense. Mathematics, the "what," gave order to a disordered world. Science, the "how," laid down laws which governed the way things worked. History was the "who," a record of man's aspirations, his successes and failures. Language ensured that communication between men was possible. Religion, first an impersonal study that led to fascination with theology and the questions of the universe, became a personal belief in God, because Someone had created the plan. Religion was the "why."

Art and music were man's response to God's world, inspired by God. God's response to man? To address his hopes and fears. Age, gender, ethnicity, level of education, geographic location – nothing seemed to be of significance to this God save need.

He had known then what he wanted to do with his life: serve this God who served people. Consequently there were more classes, papers, and treatises. Exams to pass and qualifications to meet. And how better to serve this God than to serve those who served? So he found himself a British Army chaplain with forces in the Middle East, hoping that his presence spoke more clearly of his assurance of God's love than his words did. Could he give extended discourses on theological principles? Yes, but it was more important to demonstrate his devotion than to delineate it.

Father Giles, now Stephen to Neil, had received the news with quiet pride. "I never believed it was solely circumstance that brought us together," he said. "And wherever you are, we'll not be separated in spirit."

Courageous words, Neil thought, for a man whose body seemed more frail even as his faith seemed more robust. The priest's resonant baritone had thinned as well, almost as if the sustaining confidence he'd given Neil, and not just the passage of years, had consumed him. They had both been changed.

In military service Neil was at war with the elements, with the enemy, and with his own inadequacy in the face of injury and death. He saw soldiers, some younger than himself, walking hand in glove with fear and courage, sometimes mercifully unscathed, sometimes sadly not. He made himself accessible to all of them, and in his tent there was no rank. He was humbled because he knew that any good that resulted from his efforts came through a power greater than his own. His faith was enlarged, not diminished, in spite of the obstacles they faced. It was a baptism of sorts, an experience which transformed him. Without it, he would never have become the man his wife loved.

Laurie had been a flight attendant, and as their relationship progressed, she wanted less travel for herself and fewer deployments for him. She wanted a permanent commitment and a stable home. So the transition from military to civilian life had taken place, and he had a new allegiance, to serve the law enforcement community by accepting a position with London's Metropolitan Police.

He was now an earthly father to two girls who had been blessed by Stephen in one of his last official acts. Neil also felt blessed, although he was a less holy father than he wished to be.

"Pray each day to be worthy of the responsibilities entrusted to you," Stephen had said before he died.

As he had in so many other instances, Neil followed his advice.

CHAPTER EIGHT

HER CONSCIOUSNESS DAWNED SLOWLY in the dim light, a single bare bulb the only source of illumination. Jenny woke with her cheek on a cold tiled floor. A bathroom, small, with no tub. A sense of foreboding crept over her, its weight pinning her down like a butterfly on display. Her breaths were so shallow she couldn't hear them. Her throat was dry and sour. The floor was sticky, and the smell would have turned her stomach even if she weren't pregnant. When she sat up, she had to close her eyes to stem the dizziness.

How had she gotten here? And where was here? And when was it? Was it still Thursday? Gradually bits and pieces of memory like summer fireflies began to accompany the pounding in her head.

The day had begun with such innocence. An upset stomach, which she had countered with crackers and small sips of Sprite. A few minutes petting Bear, who liked to nudge her with his nose until she responded. A light lunch, then off to the Methodist church to deliver copies of her book. Because she was encumbered with a bag of them, she'd left her purse at home, putting two twenty-pound notes in her pocket next to her travel card and mobile phone. Several of the staff had met with her, and all had been simultaneously sympathetic for her loss and receptive to her written message about healing.

What else? She tried to think. It had been raining when she left the church and walked toward the tube station. A tall man had hit her. Then – nothing until she had woken on a carpeted surface. Nearby was the man, who had a sallow, stubbly face, a reedy voice, receding hair, and – a knife. The man with scruffy clothes that looked too big for him, who called her Tanya. She had fallen and felt sore all over, but the man wouldn't let her go, wouldn't call a doctor. The man named Roy who insisted on treating her himself, rubbing the wound on her head rather roughly with a gauze pad with alcohol on it. He'd given her crackers, stale, which she had thought she could keep down, and canned soup, which she hadn't thought she could. And weak tea, diluted with milk that was nearly sour. She hadn't wanted the caffeine because of the baby, but she didn't feel she could refuse. Maybe small doses wouldn't hurt.

Now she recalled his outbursts when she told him her name. When she claimed she wasn't Tanya. When she cried. He was unstable, his mood swings extreme. He had threatened her with a knife. She had been afraid for the baby. Except for the nausea, she had no discomfort in her abdomen, but was nausea late in the day normal? Was that why she'd sought refuge in the bathroom? A bathroom with a door that was shut but wouldn't lock – in reality she was vulnerable in this room. There was no guarantee that Roy would respect a closed door. She needed help.

She remembered! She'd tried to call Simon on her cell phone, but she'd never heard his voice, so she didn't know if he'd received her message. She checked her phone. It was dark. The battery must have died. How long had it been that way?

She looked at her watch, an Italian design with a red leather band and small glass flowers encircling the face. Simon had bought it for her on their second honeymoon, to Italy. They had married in January, when it was too cold to travel there, so immediately following the wedding they'd driven to the southern coast of England. It was frosty there, too, of course, but neither of them had minded. They'd bundled up when they left their room at the hotel and unbundled each other while in it.

As soon as the winter weather receded, he had kept his promise of an Italian trip. Eschewing the crowds in the big cities, they'd stayed in several small hotels along Lake Garda. She didn't know when she'd felt so relaxed; they had no concept of time. They took walks with no destination, laughed at their attempts to communicate in the language, and ate far too much pasta. It hurt to remember something that seemed so long ago, something that took place in another life, to another Jenny. Even yesterday she was a wife whose husband still held her hand, still kept his arm around her while she slept. Now if she reached out, her hand would touch nothing. The emptiness filled her, and she began to cry.

Through her tears, she looked again at her wrist. The watch was pretty but useless. At the very least she needed a timepiece with GPS. One with a built-in weapon would be even better, a button she could push to release a burst of paralyzing gas or a miniature poisoned dart.

She tried to tap SOS on the bathroom wall. She couldn't remember whether the sequence was three longs/three shorts/three longs or the reverse. She tried both combinations, waiting several minutes between, hoping that the bathroom backed up to a living space in another flat where someone could hear her. No response came. Should she pound on the wall instead? No, Roy might hear it.

She took a deep breath to calm herself but it didn't help much. It was night. If she turned off the light, she wouldn't be able to see danger coming. And she couldn't face being entombed in the dark.

Simon would know she hadn't come home. He would have alerted his team and others that she was missing. But how would they find her? She didn't even know where she was, and all she had been able to give him was a man's first name. If her call was received. If not, then he had no clues at all.

He had Special Forces buddies who would help, no questions asked. She'd met some of them. Simon warned that Marchetti looked a bit rough, tattoos notwithstanding. When she'd winced at the sight of his inked designs, thinking of all the needle punctures he'd endured, he'd laughed. "No worries," he'd assured her. "I felt alive." Cooper had few social skills and a gravelly voice which he never raised, as if he knew how frightening it would be when loud. A beard might have softened the firm set of his jaw, but he had been unfailingly courteous. She would welcome their toughness now.

She was on her own. She had to take stock of her situation, assess it, Simon would say. Then develop a plan of action. No, plans. It was possible that she would need more than one. She had to be able to seize on any opportunity that presented itself. But what could she do? She was in no shape to do anything. She couldn't even brush her teeth. Rubbing them with soap turned her stomach, but there was no toothpaste.

She was cold. Her lightweight sweater wasn't enough to insulate her, but at least it was dry. She wished she'd worn slacks for the warmth instead of the denim skirt with the relaxed waistline. Her red tennis shoes should have made it easier for her to run, but clearly they'd had no power to transport her. She wiped her tears with a towel, then folded it into a pillow, cradled her arms across her belly, and waited for morning.

CHAPTER NINE

WHEN JENNY WAS YOUNG, all she wanted in life was to be big. To be grown up. To be important. She was the oldest child, but the birth of her two brothers suggested that she didn't matter as much as she thought she should. Her parents were strict, and she was always trying to measure up to the high standards they set for her.

She looked for ways to stand out and discovered both reading and scouting. She digested books as fast as they were fed to her, winning every summer reading roundup the library offered by being the first to complete the list of books in each category. Scouting was more difficult, requiring practical skills and interaction with others, but she reveled in the chance to earn merit badges, as if the round embroidered patches could convey some kind of lasting value. These successes, however, were glossed over by her parents, as was her performance in school, since her scores might have caused her brothers to feel less than accomplished about theirs.

In college she met Rob. He came from a large family, and she heard another point of view. Parents who loved their firstborn often wanted more children as a result. They became more comfortable in their role as parents. Rob wasn't the oldest or youngest or the only boy, but he wasn't envious of his siblings. There was room for all of them to be recognized. Enforcing rules for behavior was a simple necessity. If my parents hadn't taught me, he'd laughed, the police would have. I favored the gentle touch! Besides, they started with a gem, as yours did, and only had to shape and polish me.

As their relationship progressed, she began to see herself in a new way. Rob was supremely assured in everything he did, shooting the basketball too far from the basket, driving too fast, responding with a laugh to every dare. His confidence was contagious, and in his presence she felt not reduced but enlarged. Their personalities complemented each other like macaroni and cheese, he always pushing the envelope, she the sturdy one, but with a descriptive way of speaking that left him speechless and an extensive vocabulary that he swore improved his essays. She felt comfortable expressing her thoughts, and he seemed impressed by them. You're only Lilliputian in size, and because of you I can influence others with my literary *savoir faire,* he teased.

As she went from one college class to another, she skipped instead of walking, and the future seemed as ripe with possibility as a newly picked apple.

Since she preferred fiction to fact in her reading, she settled on a major in English literature, and with Rob's encouragement, decided she would teach. She would make a difference. Each year she'd have a classful of young minds she could impact. Then the unthinkable happened, a fatal car crash. A headline with Rob's name. His zest for life had seemed unconquerable. How could he be gone? And had he been only five feet, eight inches tall? Had death diminished him? His death diminished her; her confidence began to unravel, and she found herself adrift on a wide sea. Alone in her grief, she couldn't concentrate. She dropped several classes from her course load and took an extra year to graduate.

London: She came to evaluate graduate schools, a way to move forward on the treadmill that was her life after Rob. Had the madman who raped and nearly killed her sensed she was already dead inside? Had shock robbed her of a healthy awareness of her surroundings? Had that made her easy prey for him?

Detective Chief Inspector Colin Sinclair of New Scotland Yard was at her bedside in the hospital when she woke, broken, battered, bruised, and saturated with pain. He was gentle but persistent in his investigation, requiring her to describe the sexual assault and beating when what she wished was to be mute. To convince her to testify, DCI Sinclair told her how powerful she would feel, as if he knew that was the single thing she needed most. She didn't want to do it. She just wanted to run and hide. It had been a vicious attack, and she carried scars from it.

To keep her safe until the trial of the man who had attacked her, she was placed in witness protection, guarded by London Metropolitan Police firearms officers. The man in charge was a sergeant with a hard face and an unforgiving expression. He was tasked to provide medical care for her, but his uncompromising demeanor scared her at first, and she knew TLC would not be a part of her treatment. Isolated in a flat in a foreign country, far from her family, still consumed with fear and in pain from her injuries, she despaired. The sergeant, Simon Casey, surprised her by listening and not judging when she tried to make sense of what had happened to her. He understood how violence had changed her, how issues she thought she had resolved had been resurrected. The other officers were patient and encouraging. They were always ready for a conversation or a game of cards. They seemed to respect her.

DCI Sinclair knew it took time to rebuild a life. He brought a psychiatrist and then a priest to counsel her. From them she learned that a big difference existed between who you were and what happened to you, the internal and the external. It was best not to confuse the two. Memories, however painful, were in the past.

Months of mind-numbing monotony passed while they waited for her to heal from her injuries and then for the legal process to advance. Against all odds, the flat turned into a refuge for her, because the men became supportive, responding to her needs with thoughtfulness and reassurance. She learned to trust them. She found that she was fond of them. Sergeant Casey, who had been the most frightening at the beginning, helped her, offering advice when she asked. She saw him in a new way, with strength instead of severity in his face. His rare smiles showed sincerity not artifice. At times she felt a connection with him that was almost a glow.

As the trial date approached, respites came in the interview process. Colin visited her regularly, and she saw glimpses of a human being inside the professional manner. He was educated, elegant, and lonely, a gentleman both by birth and behavior. He needed to matter to someone, and she appreciated how important that was, but until her legal obligations were over, she didn't realize that his intentions were serious. She didn't recognize that his love had given her heart a new rhythm. What began as a trickle became a flood, a torrent of thoughts and feelings. He proposed marriage and she accepted, entering into wedlock with love, hope, and a new confidence. She had overcome horrifying experiences. The road ahead was clear.

She settled into Colin's flat in Hampstead, a quaint yet charming suburb northwest of London. She learned about pounds and pence and tubes and trains. She became accustomed to cooking with British weights and measures. She was proud of herself and thought Colin was too.

The climate of terrorism notwithstanding, everything about Colin's death had been a shock. He didn't have a dangerous job. The incident which took his life wasn't part of a police action. It had taken only one man with an explosive, and Colin was gone. She was shaken to the core. They were still newlyweds. They hadn't had time to start a family.

Day after day of inertia followed, in which she was unable to dislodge the heavy mantle of grief. She longed for what she could not have, a life with the man she loved. She dreamed about him, disjointed dreams, as if each time she moved in her sleep, it was because a puppeteer jerked the strings. First she saw Colin in sharp relief, then fading. He was next to her, close enough to touch, then too far away for her to reach. She hid herself in slumber because there, at least some of the time, Colin was alive.

When her grief was at its worst, Sergeant Nick Howard intervened. He had been one of the substitute officers on her witness protection team, a stern and uncommunicative man she'd never been able to engage in conversation of any kind. He challenged her to justify Colin's belief in her. Grieving didn't mean giving up on life, and healing wasn't a betrayal of her love for her husband but a way to honor him, to show that he had chosen a wife who was strong and resourceful, courageous enough to go on alone. She had only to face one day at a time without him. And then another. And another.

Recovery, however, didn't occur in a vacuum. Learning to accept life without Colin didn't mean rejecting help from others. She welcomed visits from the priest, Father Neil Goodwyn. She scheduled appointments with the psychiatrist, Dr. Theodore Knowles. How many times would she have to start over? As many times as it took. There was no guarantee of stability. Preparing for the unexpected was the name of the game, and resilience was the key element in winning.

When Simon Casey revealed his feelings to her, she was stunned. He had been faithful in friendship but had never, either during witness protection or after, indicated that love was a consideration. She wasn't looking for love or second chances, only for healing and wholeness, and the vestiges of her grief for Colin made it difficult for her to know how she felt. Simon was reticent, a man who wanted his actions to speak louder than his words. He was patient. He gave her time to clarify her emotions. His hours on the Job were long, and they spent more time apart than together, but she began to miss him when he was not with her. Desires she thought were dead, rekindled. She trusted him, and the closeness she'd felt while in witness protection deepened and flourished. Underneath his tough exterior lay a man capable of deep commitment and love. She ignited slowly, and time fanned the flames. The day she realized that she loved him, she rejoiced. He was the rainbow after the storm.

When she looked back, she realized that her traumatic experiences had tempered her. Hoping to share with others what she'd learned, she wrote a book on traveling through grief, a kind of workbook, and had copies printed which she could distribute. She wanted to give meaning to her tears and healing to people who were still shedding them. The person she had been had disappeared. Her scars had made her stronger. She had been assailed but not defeated, wounded but not crushed. She had matured.

CHAPTER TEN

JENNY HAD SLEPT FITFULLY. She was stiff, her head still ached, and her stomach was upset. Morning sickness. Eating something would ease it, and she debated coming out of the bathroom versus staying in, sick but safe. Could she hold on a little longer? Her stomach turned over again. Not a good sign, but to be truly safe, she needed to escape. She opened the door and peeked out.

He was not in the living room. The kitchen was just beyond a small dining area, and even in the dim light of the cloudy day she could see dishes stacked on the counter. A toaster. A drinking glass next to a cluster of pill bottles. She listened. It was quiet, all quiet. She couldn't hear him moving. Could he hear her? Her breathing and heartbeat both seemed unusually loud. Her stomach notwithstanding, this was her chance. The front door was just to her right. She ran to it, removed the chain from the guard, shifted the latch handle from right to left, and grasped the doorknob. It wouldn't turn. It was locked. She felt his arms around her waist, and as he pulled her back, she screamed for help.

He half carried, half dragged her to the sofa. "No! You left me once, Tanya," he fumed. "Try that again, and I'll slice you open!" Grimacing, he pressed his fingers against his temple.

Did his head hurt, too? And where was the knife? It was too big to fit into his pocket. She took a shallow breath, trying not to aggravate her stomach.

After a few minutes, he spoke more calmly. "I'm not going to let you leave me, am I? I want you with me. I'll make you stay if I have to do."

Her heart sank. "But I don't know you," she insisted in a shaky whisper. "You hurt me and brought me here. You have to let me go."

"Don't mess me about! It were an accident! I didn't mean to harm you. I wanted you to come nice-like, but you wouldn't."

Should she continue to disagree? Not at the moment – her unsettled stomach reclaimed her attention. "I need something to eat. Crackers. Toast." She watched him move into the kitchen, his long spindly arms and legs like a mantis' extremities but with surprising strength. When he'd caught her, it was a hard grab, and his height had allowed him to get to her quickly.

He returned with bread he'd warmed in the toaster. It had seen better days, but she managed to get it down. "Tea. Please."

When he brought it, he shifted the checkerboard to the side and placed the cup on the coffee table, its finish marked by spills or hot cups with no saucers. His fingers were thin, with knobbly knuckles.

No newspaper. Nothing to ground her, to tell her that her imprisonment was not as endless as it felt.

"Are you ill?" she asked. "Do you need to see a doctor?"

He gave her a puzzled expression and did not reply.

She tried again to establish a connection. "Are you taking a sick day from your job?"

This time he stared.

"Have you lived here a long time?"

He slammed his fist on the table, knocking the checkers askew and spilling the tea. "You know all this!" he thundered.

His volume made her head pound, but she responded in kind. "You're right – if I were Tanya, I would know it. Don't you see? I'm not who you think I am!"

He thrust himself to his feet and backhanded her. "Stop trying to trick me! I know exactly who you are and what you've done. Left me when I needed you. I'll not let that happen again." Using some kitchen twine, he bound her wrists.

The day wore on, Jenny trying to push past nausea, head pain, and overall fogginess to convince him of her identity, to force him to use her name, to see her for who she was. Nothing succeeded. He was angry all the time, mumbling to himself and raising his voice to her when he hit her. Whatever his medicine was for, it didn't help his mood. She couldn't get through to him, and when she suggested that they go out for groceries or to take a walk, he located the knife and kept it in his lap.

Being Jenny was dangerous. She began to worry that he would assault her if he saw her wedding ring. She transferred it to her right hand. The necklace Simon had given her as a wedding present – a simple gold chain with two connected hearts – was under her shirt. She could feel it through the fabric, but Roy couldn't see it.

Her thoughts wandered to happier times. In their wedding discussions, Simon had said that the "where" didn't signify. Neither did the "when," although he preferred it to be soon. For the rest, he wanted what she wanted, although when she queried him about the honeymoon, he promised to make all the arrangements. She'd been intrigued and thought that his desire to take charge was surprisingly romantic.

A sudden sharp pain in her upper arm and an angry voice jarred her back to the present. "Answer me!" Roy demanded. "I'm speaking to you, aren't I?"

The cold flush of fear made her blood feel warm against her skin. Not paying attention was hazardous; she had to discipline herself, no matter how distasteful it was.

She sat at the table in the dining room while he made dinner in the shabby kitchen. The window overlooked a courtyard bordered by other blocks of flats whose front doors opened onto a sidewalk with a railing. The courtyard looked deserted except for the litter, now wet from the rain. From her perspective Roy's flat was on the third floor. Too high to jump from even if she were able to distract him long enough to get the window open. Nor would she have time to attract anyone's attention.

She watched and waited. He put cheese and fruit on the table and served soup again. Soup. She had learned to make soup – many different soups, in fact – because she could warm them while Simon was on his way home. And if he were hungry more for her than for the soup, she could turn off the fire and reheat the soup later. When they'd started trying to have a family, he'd encouraged her to rest in place after lovemaking to increase their odds of success while he readied the soup. She forced herself to think about making soup, each step with each ingredient, not out of the can the way Roy was doing, the knife always within his reach.

"You dyed your hair, Tanya," he said whilst he ate. "I was liking the lighter colour, but you can keep it dark if you want to do."

"No, I'm Jenny. This is my natural color." She nibbled on the fruit, hoping the natural sweetness would calm her stomach and wishing he'd untied her hands before they ate.

His eyes narrowed. "What's wrong with you? You weren't so stroppy when we were together before."

"I've never been with you. We've never even met!"

He took hold of the knife and thrust it in her direction, grazing her hand. "You can't cross me!" he screeched. "I'll teach you!"

She stifled a scream. Her approach had backfired. After dinner he didn't let her out of his sight. When the overcast day turned into night, the flat seemed to shrink and hope with it. Her requests for him to speak more softly were ignored. When she asked if she could sleep on the sofa, he exploded, saying he didn't trust her. He pushed her into the bathroom and wedged something against the door. She was glad her only other possessions – mobile phone, travel card, and money – were still in her sweater pocket.

She was safe for another night, but what would the morning bring? More anger? More violence? She couldn't fight back – she had no weapon, and she was weak and sick. She picked at the knots that held her wrists together but was afraid to do more than loosen them. Do anything to preserve your life was the rule, but that didn't tell her what her strategy should be. Already she had bruises on her arms and chest as well as puncture marks from the times when his gestures with the knife had come too close. Once, when he lost his balance as he was walking toward her, the knife pierced her thigh, and his elbow hit her in the stomach. The baby, she'd thought, but held her tongue. He must not discover that she was pregnant. If he thought she was Tanya – and pregnant – he would be even angrier.

For the first time in her life, she had something to protect besides herself. Only nine weeks along, and already her priorities had changed, from counting the days until she reached the end of her first trimester to preserving another's life.

She sobbed in fear and exhaustion. Had it really been only yesterday when she'd visited the church? There had been no contact from the police.

CHAPTER ELEVEN

BEFORE THEY MARRIED, Jenny and Simon talked about having a family. They both wanted children, but because she hadn't been able to conceive with Colin, she was afraid she wouldn't be able to have any. After they married, she was reluctant to try, postponing the subject each time he raised it.

He reassured her. He asked only that they take one step at a time. Make love without birth control, he suggested. A commitment to start the process wasn't a commitment to undergo the painful and invasive infertility tests she'd experienced before. She promised to think about it but didn't, and the issue was between them every time they made love, whether they said so or not.

Finally his anger surfaced. "Delay long enough, and it's the same as denial." He demanded to know why she'd been willing to proceed with Colin but not with him.

"Because you aren't the one who has to lie on the examination table! Don't you understand? I had the tests, and they didn't accomplish anything. I went through all that for nothing!"

"I'm not asking you to have any medical tests, just to remove the barrier."

"But you will!" she exclaimed. "When I don't get pregnant, you will!"

"You knew when we married that I wanted a family."

"You knew I might not be able to."

"You've not tried." With effort, he corrected himself. "*We've* not tried. Would you have us give up before we've tried?"

"Simon, I was ignorant then. I didn't know how bad the tests would be. And each month hope turned into crushing disappointment. It's an emotional roller coaster I don't want to ride and don't want you to, either."

He held and soothed her, but she knew nothing had been resolved.

Then one night he stayed over at the base, and she began to worry that his feelings toward her would change. Wanting to reconnect, she suggested when he came home the following afternoon that they have dinner at the Gaucho, an Argentinian restaurant on the High Street with cowhide-covered chairs, Texas-sized steaks, and margaritas poured over crushed ice and served in cocktail glasses.

They were more than halfway through their meal when a young couple with a small baby was seated next to them. When the infant started to fuss, the mother took him out of the carrier and, leaning forward slightly, slipped one hand and then the child under her blouse. Even in the dim light, her happiness as she nursed him was unmistakable, and Jenny was moved.

"Simon, do you see the radiance on her face?" she asked. "I've let fear overwhelm me, and I don't want to do that anymore. I want to feel what she's feeling. I'll do anything. I don't care what it takes. Let's go home." And they had.

Once committed, she was more frustrated by their lack of success than he. And frustrated with him, because she felt that his long hours were a factor. When he was on early run, scheduled to begin at six in the morning, he was required to report the night before in order to allow time for multiple briefings and then a raid that took place before dawn. On most days other operations followed. She went to bed alone and woke up alone. On weeks when his team was on a different rotation, there were still huge gaps of time when she did not see him. Finally she erupted, asking, "How am I supposed to get pregnant when you're never here?"

He didn't respond with anger. He simply said, very quietly, "We have to use the time we have."

"Now?" she yelled. "It's three o'clock in the afternoon, and we're fighting!"

"We don't have to be."

She seethed. He wasn't going to engage at the same level, and that made her even angrier. "Why aren't you mad?"

"Because it's difficult for me also. And your upset isn't unexpected. I know you're unhappy with the hours I work. We all struggle with that, but our loved ones most of all."

His understanding tone told her he was hurt by her comments. He had no control over his schedule. "Simon, if I fell and skinned my knee, would you help me up? Even if we're upset with each other?"

That earned a partial smile. "Every time," he said. "And more besides."

"It's all because I miss you," she admitted.

"Then come to me," he said. "Now. In the middle of the afternoon."

"Before you have to go."

"Yes, before I have to go."

"How much time do you have?" she asked.

"Enough."

She hesitated only briefly. If she didn't take advantage of this opportunity, she'd miss him even more when he was gone.

As it turned out, she conceived before tests were necessary for either of them. She was relieved and happy, making him smile by recalling the slow, intense lovemaking they both preferred and wondering aloud whether their baby had been conceived in one of those sessions. If so, would their languid circumstances affect him? Would they forever be urging him to hurry up?

For his part, Simon established a new ritual. On the evenings when he was home at a decent hour, he bathed her and marvelled at the healing that had taken place in her body. She, who had been near death, now carried life. The breast her attacker had slashed would nurture a newborn. He was fascinated by what he knew was growing inside her but could not see. And just a week ago, he had been on leave and had gone with her to her checkup. They had heard the baby's heartbeat for the first time. He'd been unable to restrain his smiles, and the spontaneous hugs he had given her had multiplied almost as fast as the cells in her womb were dividing. The baby was only the size of a postage stamp, but their love for him or her felt infinite.

CHAPTER TWELVE

A MOST PRODUCTIVE INVESTIGATION THUS FAR, DI
Thoms thought, although she doubted that Simon Casey would
agree with her. In her Friday morning briefing, Emily Gardner, one
of her PCSOs, had responded to Jenny's description of the hostage
taker, identifying him as Roy Wilkes, who lived at the nearby
market estate. She knew that he was currently on medical leave
from his job. He had a partner, but she hadn't seen her recently.

Another PCSO, Stephen Caruthers, had chimed in with the
information that some of the older units where Wilkes lived were
scheduled for demolition at the end of the year or early the
following. Many residents had already moved out, discouraged by
the high incidence of crime in the area and the deterioration of the
housing units.

Thoms smiled. Both officers were a bit keen, but she
appreciated their enthusiasm. Perhaps some of her more
experienced subordinates would be infected by it.

She sent uniformed officers to query the building manager,
both about Roy and his partner, to request a floor plan of Wilkes'
flat, to establish the location of the flat within the block, and to
identify the occupants, if any, of the neighbouring flats. This
information would allow her to use uniforms to provide
containment until specialist units arrived. House-to-house
enquiries would be necessary only to evacuate residents close to his
flat and to alert others of the police presence.

It would be necessary to confirm that Mrs. Casey was indeed
Wilkes' hostage. Unfortunately there was no CCTV on the side
street near the Methodist church, so a visual of the abduction, if it

had indeed occurred there, would not be available. She sent uniforms to search the area and requested CCTV of activity near the tube station.

In the meantime internet searches had yielded background information on Mrs. Casey and her husband. She was an American citizen, originally from the state of Texas. She had indeed been a witness in the case against Cecil Scott, her testimony linking him to serial crimes and thus to his conviction and incarceration. She had married Colin Sinclair, a detective chief inspector with the Met, in December 1999. He had been killed in February 2002. She had married Simon Casey in January 2004.

Casey was born in Penzance, Cornwall. He had joined the Royal Marines and qualified for service as a commando. Further records of his military service were classified. He had been medically retired from the military prior to joining the Met and had applied for the firearms unit following his probationary period.

By noon she had reported to Casey that a suspect had been identified. "Where is my wife?" he had demanded. "We don't know yet," she had replied. "Steps are being taken to verify his location. And hers."

By early evening CCTV reports had been examined which showed no record of Mrs. Casey entering the tube station. The estate manager had given them Wilkes' address and reported that his was a second floor flat at the end of a walkway. The neighbouring flat was unoccupied. Although her name was not on the lease, his partner had been named as Tanya Hanson. She would be located and queried regarding Wilkes' medical and psychological condition.

Although they had no proof that Mrs. Casey was being held in Wilkes' flat, they would proceed on that basis. It would be the job of the hostage negotiator to initiate the first contact with the suspect and to establish her presence. Containment would be provided before nightfall, but the negotiator would not be on the scene until morning, when the specialist units would arrive to relieve the uniformed officers on site. At that time the negotiator would report to the command centre, currently being assembled.

DCI Cunningham was Gold Commander for this operation as well as SIO (Senior Investigating Officer). These responsibilities gave him the authority to develop the strategy for the investigation, which included identifying the resources necessary for the successful resolution of the incident. As a result he would secure the services of a hostage negotiator and consult officers from the firearms unit.

Thoms was Silver and would determine how the strategic plan would be implemented. Others, as circumstances unfolded, would assume the roles of Bronze, those on the ground taking the prescribed actions. In this case uniformed officers attached to the Islington police station would carry out enquiries and other steps needed to gather essential evidence.

She rang Casey and was not surprised by the anger and impatience in his voice. "We have as yet no hard information that your wife is being held by this suspect," she told him. "The hostage negotiator will be gathering that data. I realise that you're uncomfortable with our progress, but I trust the professionalism and expertise of our officers, and you should also." She ended the call.

CHAPTER THIRTEEN

SIMON CASEY spent Friday assisting other firearms teams on planning, waiting for news of Jenny, and worrying on her. The call from DI Thoms didn't ease his concern. She couldn't be certain the suspect – whose full name they now knew – had Jenny. Wasn't the tape sufficient evidence? But that was old news now; if Thoms' investigation hadn't confirmed Jenny's presence, it meant they hadn't been able to discover whether she was still alive. What Thoms considered progress, he deemed insufficient, as did Jenny's father when he spoke with him. Although it had never bothered him in the past, today Jeffries' laconic manner perplexed and disturbed him. A college professor, he was accustomed to giving extended lectures, but their conversation was terse. He was perhaps partially to blame; he'd sounded like a bloody press officer. In contrast, when he updated Goodwyn, the priest remained steadfast.

Thoms' reasonable attitude irked him. Time was critical. If he contacted a couple SBS mates, could they help? If word got out, he'd be dismissed, but it would be worth it if Jenny's life were saved. Even as he had the thought, he ruled it out. A rash action born out of desperation was contrary to all he'd been taught and had little chance of success. Although at the least his mates would be glad to lift a few pints with him, he could not do. If anything changed about Jenny's situation, he would need to have his wits about him.

He thought again on what they knew. Not enough by a long chalk. Before his firearms team had an op, they had multiple briefings. Detailed briefings. They would not set foot outside the base with so little information.

He'd been on missions where winning over hearts and minds was the goal. It was always difficult to win both, and now he understood why: because they could be in conflict with each other. In this case his rational mind would win out, but his heart would be looking, always looking, for a way.

He wondered if Thoms' approach were affected by recent events in London. On July 7 terrorist attacks had shaken the nation. Three bombs had been detonated in underground tube stations, and a fourth had blown apart a bus, all timed to explode when usage was at its height. Public transportation was essential in London. Trains starting and stopping were the pulse of the city. The message that travellers were not safe affected everyone. United in outrage and grief, citizens had shown universal regard for the police officers and first responders who had worked in horrific conditions to rescue the injured and identify the deceased.

Second attacks two weeks later had been unsuccessful but had upset the courage which Londoners were determined to display. Then, a day later, Jean Charles de Menezes had been mistakenly identified as a terrorist by surveillance and other officers and killed by gunfire. No officer would ever forget the name. All wanted the summer to end, for the passage of time to give them a respite. Worn thin by the shock, the devastation, and the extra hours on the Job, it was more difficult for officers to leave the stresses of the Job behind when they went home.

Now all firearms officers – and their operations – were under unending scrutiny, even suspicion, on the part of some. He didn't anticipate the actions of his mates on the Job being affected, but those in senior positions could be more wary than usual in employing them. It was grossly unfair. Restraint was already an integral part of their training.

So Jenny would spend another night in danger. He'd never known her to give up, to quit fighting, no matter what she faced, and he thought she'd come out of each previous encounter stronger. Physically, however, she was at a disadvantage, weakened temporarily by the pregnancy and concussion and possibly unable to get sufficient rest or food. The hostage negotiator would be focused on establishing good communication with the hostage taker. He wouldn't be inside the flat, where he could assess Jenny's condition, and asking too many questions about her could be counterproductive.

Early on she'd had some reservations about starting a family. Once she had overcome them, she'd been committed 100%. That was her way; when she was in, she was all in. Some mornings she asked for a rerun, even when they'd made love the night before. And once she had asked if he had time for the second verse, and it had taken him a moment to realise that she wasn't talking about music. She had baffled him when she requested some southern comfort, and she had to explain that she wasn't referring to the brand of bourbon her father drank but to the physical comfort that he, Simon, gave her. Love, humour, and playfulness infused her.

The positive result on the home pregnancy test had brought them both joy. He hadn't known that the news would affect him so deeply so soon, but his protective instincts had kicked into high gear. It struck him how doubly vulnerable she was and how powerless he was to help her. Was it possible that they would come so close to everything they wanted, only to lose it all?

He rubbed his hands against his trousers. He could fast-rope, use his own strength to support the weight of his body during a rapid descent into action. Simple, then, to use his strength to control his fears. No, the mental challenges were always more difficult. Damn. His palms were still sweaty.

CHAPTER FOURTEEN

FOLLOWING HIS BRIEFINGS, Inspector Marc Coulter, the hostage negotiator assigned by New Scotland Yard, entered the mobile command centre van and studied the status boards mounted there. The incident had begun on Thursday, two days prior. He wished that he had been involved nearer the outset, when the offender was often uncertain about his actions, not entrenched in them. Procedure, however, rarely allowed for early intervention.

The chronological board was empty since negotiations had not yet begun. He turned his attention to the suspect's profile board. Their initial description of him, provided by the victim herself in the phone call to her husband, had been amplified by information gathered by the Islington detective team. Roy Wilkes, age 52. Nearly a decade older than himself. Ethnicity: IC3, or black, according to the hostage and confirmed by the PCSOs. Recently separated from his partner. Medical history: Diagnosis of inoperable tumour resulting in medical leave from Tesco's, where he had been an assistant manager. Narcotic painkillers had been prescribed, according to his employer. The next of kin line was blank.

"Wilkes is in pain," Coulter commented. "Let's see if the National Health Service will tell us what other symptoms he may be experiencing."

Everyone has a story, and Coulter was aware that he had only a small part of Wilkes'. Sometimes a part was enough; usually it wasn't. The more he knew about a hostage taker, the better. He consulted the board again. Criminal background: Wilkes' record was clean. No drugs offences, in fact, no offences of any sort.

Religious affiliation: None. Deadly weapons available: Knife. Presence of firearm not known.

Coulter's first order of business: establish the existence, identity, and health of the woman in the flat. Officers had interviewed the staff at Caledonian Road Methodist Church. Mrs. Casey had kept her appointment with them, leaving shortly before 3:00 p.m. She had not appeared to be anxious or tense, laughing when they congratulated her on her pregnancy. Her "invisible" baby, she'd said, because she wasn't showing yet. Three lives depended on his efforts then, not just those belonging to the two adults.

He nodded at the intelligence coordinator and the firearms officer but spoke only to the secondary negotiator, Patrick Byrne. Byrne was younger than he and a bit too eager to be a primary as yet. He kept his curly hair styled, as if he wanted to be presentable in front of a camera. His language when speaking to suspects was too concise. More experience as an officer could give him a more conversational and less terse tone. His exacting nature, however, made him a good secondary.

To avoid distractions, Coulter generally paid little attention to the other officers in the van. He was aware that firearms teams were on the scene and that even as he sought a peaceful conclusion, a parallel approach was being prepared to deal with the incident if negotiations failed. He wouldn't be given the details, but he knew from experience that it would be there.

The lack of visual cues made his task more difficult, but his course of action was the same. Start talking. Keep talking until the hostage taker does. Then listen. And listen.

"Indicate in the log that the first phone contact was initiated at 10:32 a.m., Saturday, 27 August." He picked up the phone.

Byrne made a notation on the white dry-erase board with a dark marker.

"Hello?" answered a raspy voice after the third ring.

"Mr. Wilkes, I'm Marc Coulter with the Metropolitan Police. We understand that your neighbours haven't seen you in a few days, and I'm calling to be sure you're all right." He purposely did not identify himself as a hostage negotiator because the word "hostage" was never used.

"You're police?"

"I work with the police, yes. Have you ever had any experience with police?" If not, his job was usually easier. No negatives to overcome.

"No, and I've got no need for you now." He hung up.

"First telephone contact terminated by the suspect," Coulter said. The police term for a hostage taker was "X-ray," but Coulter felt the word dehumanised the individual and therefore declined to verbalise it.

Byrne added to the log whilst Coulter redialed. "Mr. Wilkes, Marc Coulter again. I'd like to chat."

"I didn't ask you for this. Go away."

Defensive already, Coulter noted. "I can't do that, mate. I'm concerned about you. I'd like to invite you to come out." It never hurt to ask, even at the outset. Some suspects capitulated quickly after interest was shown in them.

"Not coming out. No reason to. I'm here with Tanya."

"You both all right?"

"Of course we are! Tell him, Tanya!"

An unusual move by a hostage taker, but the unexpected didn't worry Coulter. He had trained and prepared for it, and the possibility kept him on his toes.

"Hello?" A female voice, trembling.

"I'm with the police," Coulter said hastily. "For your safety, please answer only yes or no. Is your name Tanya Hanson?"

"No." Coulter heard emphasis, but subdued.

"Jennifer Casey?"

"Yes." A sob barely contained.

"Has he threatened you?"

"Yes."

"Have you been injured?"

"Yes."

"Seriously?"

"No..." The tone was tentative.

"Are you in immediate danger?"

Coulter heard the pause and didn't wait for her to continue. "Not at the moment but your situation could change quickly?"

"Yes."

"Don't give up hope. I'll do all I can to help you."

"That'll do!" It was Wilkes again. He must have grabbed the phone away from her. "Enough for you? We don't need anything. We've enough food, clothes, and the like."

"You've both got clothes?" Coulter asked.

"Tanya even more than me, yeah," was the response. "We've no needs."

"No needs at the present time," Coulter repeated. "That's good news, Mr. Wilkes. I'll just check back with you in a bit." He ended the call. The time was entered in the log with the notation, "brief but satisfactory."

"Notify the incident commander that Mrs. Casey is alive and in good condition so far," he instructed the intelligence officer. "Further efforts to locate Tanya Hanson need to be made. It's not a good sign that her clothes are still in the flat. Most women wouldn't leave personal items behind in a voluntary separation. And if he has a new 'Tanya,' where is the old Tanya?"

He stood, stretched his legs, and stared at the photo of Jennifer Casey on the profile board. Jenny, she was called, the wife of one of their own. A lovely woman, even with the scar on her cheek. Evidence of an earlier trauma, perhaps, but she was smiling in the picture her husband had provided. Coulter knew that if he couldn't resolve this incident quickly and peacefully, she could carry scars from it as well.

Win and lose as a team was the preferred attitude in these situations, but he still took the losses personally. How could he not? It was his hair that was prematurely grey and his sleep that was fraught with endless replays. He sighed and ran his hand through his hair, which he kept short to make the grey less evident. When his moustache turned grey, he had shaved it off. His wife had ribbed him a bit, asking if his extra weight were premature as well. A result of his sedentary lifestyle, more likely. He stretched again, bending over to touch his toes or as close to them as he could reach. The van was stuffy, with no smell of coffee brewing. Teapot One, the Met's on-scene catering service, was providing snacks as well as beverages.

"Keep him talking, keep her alive," Coulter said, repeating one of a negotiator's mantras. The greatest danger to the hostage, or "Yankee," occurred early in the negotiation process. He punched the numbers of Roy's phone. "Mr. Wilkes? Marc Coulter here. It just occurred to me that the lunch hour is approaching. Anything you'd like me to send in for you?"

Coulter's philosophy was to create obligation and need, in other words, send something, possibly more than once, but not too much at any one time. He didn't mention that the officer delivering the food would be covered by a marksman until he had left the meal and moved safely away.

This time Wilkes' tone showed suspicion. "I've told you, I don't need – " He was interrupted. "Tanya wants a Coke. Her stomach's upset. She's always wanting sodas, but I don't have any."

That was an opening Coulter needed. "Is she all right otherwise?"

"Not behaving like herself so I've been firm, haven't I? Tied her hands."

"Anything else?"

"Cries over the least thing. Like a whinger. But it could be the sick."

Coulter made a conscious effort to keep his voice calm. Hostage Negotiation 101: Focus on the hostage taker, not the victim. However, focus or not, the hostage was depending on him. He had to determine if Wilkes knew of Mrs. Casey's pregnancy. If so, she could be in even greater danger. "I'm confused. What do you mean by that?"

"The bump on her head, that's all. Says she can't wash her hair because it might bleed. She's making too much of it, she is. She can manage."

"Any other medical problems I need to know about?"

"Mine, but you've no need to know."

"Thank you for your honesty," Coulter said. "I'll send Cokes, but I'll include something for you as well. It takes time to arrange these things, you understand. When the food is delivered, the officer will knock twice and then leave. You needn't have any contact with him. We'll chat again soon."

"Sir, let's send caffeine free cola," Byrne suggested. "She's pregnant, but she can't ask for anything without caffeine and risk prompting questions."

Coulter nodded. Byrne and his wife had a new baby. He'd know current medical advice for women who were expecting. "Good start otherwise, I'd say. He seems sober. No violence or threat of violence so far. He's restrained her, and that's worrying, but it doesn't appear that substance abuse is involved. Small positives count. Over time they can add up to large ones. And let's send food he'll have to prepare. If we keep him occupied, we keep Mrs. Casey safe for the time being."

CHAPTER FIFTEEN

MARCUS AARON COULTER, Mac to his friends and family, Marc to everyone else. Crisis negotiator when called upon professionally, but really "negotiator" could have been his middle name. He'd always been able to see both sides of an issue. Those who were more definite and outspoken had accused him of being indecisive, but privately he felt that his careful consideration of issues made him less likely to judge. He had opinions; he was simply the last to offer his.

His wife Jeanne had come from a family of porcupines. To hear her tell it, they disagreed on everything, rarely backed down, and held grudges. She had indeed been prickly when they met, feisty and defensive, but his unforced responses had resulted first in relief on her part and then in trust. He listened before answering, whilst in her family she'd rarely been able to complete a sentence. When he apologised for an action or a slight, she waited for the "but" that would negate it, the qualification she was accustomed to. Sorry, but you heard me wrong. Sorry, but you shouldn't have overreacted. Sorry, but you shouldn't have spoken out of turn. These statements in effect placed the blame on her. Her family was offensive in wrongdoing and defensive in regret. In contrast, Marc's apologies, when they came, were unfettered and sincere. He and Jeanne were a good match. He appreciated her strong convictions, and she valued his even temper.

His parents were well read and kept themselves abreast of current events. They had encouraged open discussion, but he was quieter and more restrained than his brothers. He was given credit for "choosing his battles," which he understood to mean, fighting over only the most important things, but in practice he preferred not to fight at all, just to let the sparks fly between his older and younger siblings. To their surprise, after a slow start, he had excelled on the school debate team. He had no difficulty arguing the affirmative position, whether he led with the opening statement or participated in the rebuttal or the closing. However, his teachers liked to use him on the negative because his attentive listening to the other speeches gave him an advantage in preparing his points.

In the world of policing, he was comfortable with diversity and not disturbed by conflict. When he gained sufficient rank to register for the crisis negotiation course, he applied. The components had been comprehensive, but no classroom or exercise could duplicate every situation or every type of individual a negotiator might encounter. Sometimes he felt a chameleon because even within a single incident, circumstances could change quickly. He had to be prepared to adapt. The same was true in what he considered his day job, in the area of covert policing. Developing methods of gathering evidence and providing surveillance on criminals and their cohorts occasionally required thinking outside the box as well.

He'd had some significant successes, of which his wife maintained teasingly that she was one. Her view wasn't entirely untrue. Negotiation had been a factor in their courtship, although he hadn't recognised it at the time. What was negotiation, after all, but the influencing of another person to gain a desired result?

Marriage was not dissimilar. He and Jeanne didn't always want the same things at the same time. He was fond of outlining options and allowing her to choose, without shading the pros and cons of each choice according to what he wished. At the end of the day, they were closer.

Negotiation – glorified manipulation? He didn't think so. Manipulation was far too one-sided. Negotiation meant working with people to seek, if possible, equitable solutions. There was always more than one way to look at a situation.

He kept a travel bag to hand with toiletries and several changes of clothes, since he often didn't know in advance where he'd be sited during negotiations. When the Job required him to be away from home for several days, he relied on Jeanne's understanding and strength when he returned. It wasn't possible to overestimate her importance in his life.

Hostage negotiation was the most difficult scenario he faced. Many hostages were women or women with children. It was his job to develop a non-judgemental conversation with the man or men who had taken them. He could do it; he had even been told that he was good at it, although he wondered sometimes what that said about him. The ability to achieve rapport with villains was not a skill many would care to emulate. It meant seeing an incident from the suspect's point of view. And there was a cost to forcing himself to sound accepting and respectful when he wanted to scream that they had put innocents in danger. Some days he felt so tainted by the contact that he showered before embracing his wife and children, although he was never able to remove the dirt that got under his skin.

CHAPTER SIXTEEN

CHIEF INSPECTOR DENISON, in charge of all firearms operations, had kept Casey informed of developments. Consequently he knew the suspect had been identified and located and that negotiations had begun. He also knew that Jenny had somehow survived a second night in captivity. No other information was forthcoming, which was unacceptable. In addition, he'd been stood down from his team and given a minder. Not an unusual procedural step, but he still chafed at Denison's authority in this instance.

"This officer has been assigned to you," Denison had said, referring to Russell Kelly, a burly PC with thick hair who was relatively new to the firearms unit but not to policing. "He'll be with you for the duration. He will be the recipient of any information that becomes available and will pass it on to you. The two of you will be stationed inside the outer perimeter and well away from the press. Kelly's been briefed on the location. If I find you any closer, I'll bar you from the plot. And don't think on arming yourself. It's not your operation, and you're not authorised. Am I clear?"

Crystal, Casey thought, but the restraints still rankled. He turned away, muttering under his breath, but the CI's voice followed him.

"Think, man!" he exclaimed. "They've got the investigative skills and resources. Like it or not, we've got to rely on them. *You've* got to rely on them. I'll support you in every way I can, but I'll not allow you to go rogue. Attempt to make contact with the negotiator or any member of the tactical team and I'll have you home!"

Kelly glanced at Casey and waited a moment before responding for both of them. "Yes, sir."

They relocated, leaving the Leman Street base with Kelly driving. From their site Casey could see the mobile command centre and beyond it, the run-down estate. He hated to think of Jenny being held there. From his many ops with the firearms unit, he knew what the conditions would be like.

The hours dragged, initial updates revealing little, even from the tactical teams' surveillance. Casey exited the vehicle from time to time to stretch, as did Kelly, whose bulk made him uncomfortable behind the steering wheel. However, Casey heard no whingeing nor was Kelly the chatty sort. He offered no platitudes. Casey didn't want to be distracted from his thoughts of Jenny. How seriously was she hurt? Was she well enough to try to get away? What was she experiencing? He wished he had something positive and concrete to report to her family and to Goodwyn as well. He had become accustomed to her father's curt responses. Goodwyn, however, asked after him as well as Jenny.

Over time he thawed toward Kelly, who sought updates on a regular basis, brought tea and food at appropriate intervals, and managed to keep his thoughts to himself.

He did not consider himself an impatient man. Waiting was an inherent part of the work he did, although he had never learnt to like it. Periods of inactivity had dotted his military career and his police service. He had waited longer, however, to make Jenny his wife than anything else in his personal or professional life, and he still thought the sweetest word in the English language was her "yes." The waiting he experienced now was more difficult than any that had come before because he had no role to play in her rescue.

He trusted the skills of the firearms teams on site. They would recce the area and provide information that was critical in formulating a workable response. They would prevent the suspect from escaping. They'd observe him, continue to gather intelligence, and establish arcs of fire. He had led one team and trained one week in every six with several of the others. No mission survives intact, but their experience had taught them to expect the unexpected and to find a way to make it work. He had less faith in negotiators. They talked, an ineffective weapon in his view. He had far more faith in action, which he was not permitted in this case, and his feeling of helplessness frustrated him deeply. Jenny's ability to defend herself against the bastard who had taken her had been compromised, how seriously he did not know.

He ran his thumb over his gold wedding band, to his mind just as binding as Jenny's, although far simpler. Hers was a ring of intertwining yellow, white, and rose gold. Their short engagement hadn't given them time to select a separate ring to celebrate it, a condition he still wanted to remedy, although she insisted that it wasn't necessary.

He resolved to wait constructively. He had never been particularly concerned with physical comfort, the mission, to his mind, always superseding personal considerations of any sort. Today, however, his mission was to be ready to support his wife in every way possible when she was rescued, and that required him to take note of his physical needs. He would eat enough to keep his strength up but not enough to dull his senses. He would avoid dehydration but consume no alcohol. Alternating short periods of exercise with power naps would help. It was a different sort of combat, disciplining himself to keep focused when he was not on the front line. Fortunately distractions were minimal, the uniformed officers having restricted traffic around the area.

"Your wife's reportedly spending a good deal of time in the loo," Kelly said. "The negotiator suspects that she may be exaggerating her symptoms somewhat to keep the hostage taker away from her."

That was a bit too optimistic, Casey thought. The negotiator could not know. The full effects of a concussion wouldn't have receded yet, and she had morning sickness. Stress could exacerbate both conditions. She'd be weak. It was unlikely that she was eating sufficiently. Was she seeking safety or was she ill? He could only hope that she was well enough to be playing for time and looking for a way out. If not, she'd be waiting for officers to come in.

"The suspect is relatively calm at the moment," added Kelly. "The negotiator has chosen not to challenge his belief yet that your wife is his partner. Woman by the name of Tanya Hanson. The negotiator wants to create a strong relationship with the suspect first."

Outwardly Casey did not react, but inwardly he fought anger. Jenny was pregnant, sick, and frightened. Delay would work against her. Was there no way to move this process along? Clouds that had been low in the morning were now releasing drops of rain that struck the windscreen and then bled down the glass. As a result the buildings in the distance were blurry at a time when every detail was precious to him.

"Just want you to know, mate," Kelly assured him, "we'll stay each day as long as you need."

He'd got that right.

CHAPTER SEVENTEEN

"SPAGHETTI?! That's what they sent?" Marc Coulter erupted.

A sheepish intelligence officer tried to justify the choice. "He had to cook the pasta," he said, "and warm the tomato sauce. And the garlic bread."

Better than my fare, Coulter thought, but the offering had produced no appreciable gratitude from Roy, as Mr. Wilkes was now allowing himself to be called. The marksman who'd seen Roy open the door reported that he'd used one hand to manoeuvre the food inside and the other to hold the knife. Although Coulter was fond of saying that each suspect's "No" was only one step away from resolution, he had to admit that the rest of the afternoon had proved unproductive as well. Roy had embarked on an extended discussion of fishing tackle and techniques but had refused to come out of the flat when a session of fishing at dusk was suggested. Responding to his wistful tone, Coulter had asked for more details of past fishing expeditions.

"Did you usually go early in the morning? Did Tanya accompany you?"

"No, I was always wanting to go alone," Roy admitted. "But she liked how I cooked what I brought home. These days I don't feel up to it."

"Not up to the fishing or the cooking?"

"The fishing. I'm sick actually. Tumour. And cooking's not fun when you've no one to cook for."

"It sounds to me that you were lonely before Tanya came."

"Yeah, but that's over now, isn't it?"

Coulter then showed repeated concern for Roy's physical health, expressing sympathy for his exhaustion and pain. "Sometimes it helps to talk things through with someone," he said, but Roy didn't respond, their conversation being disrupted by his shouted commands to the hostage.

"Don't go in there! Stay where I can see you!"

The call was disconnected. It took several tries before Coulter was able to reach him again. When queried, Roy confessed he had a hunting knife that had belonged to his father, one he'd used in the past to gut the fish he caught. Usually information gave Coulter an edge and perhaps an angle to pursue, but in this case the more he found out about Roy, the less confident he felt. Yet it was still his job to reason with a man whose reason had left him.

"I need it. I still don't trust her. That's why I've got her hands tied. But I can talk more now," he said. "She's resting on the sofa."

In spite of his shock at Roy's disclosure, Coulter kept his voice calm. "Sleeping?" he asked.

"She says she can't stay awake. She never used to be a slacker, but when I raise my voice, she gets up quick enough."

This incident was following the pattern of domestic violence, with one notable exception: Roy's violent expressions were not alternating with periods of remorse. "Roy, I'm concerned when I think of you shutting yourself off."

"I never had many friends, but now I've got Tanya to lean on, don't I?"

"I'd feel better if I knew you'd see a doctor," Coulter said. "For a second opinion or to see if your medication can be adjusted to make you more comfortable. I can arrange it for you. If you're not sleeping well, they can help you with that also."

"No!" Roy responded with anger. "Don't like doctors. They only say what they can't do."

"Your diagnosis was difficult, I see that. It doesn't seem fair, does it? But it worries me that you won't give the doctors a chance to help."

"They've done their bit! I'm not coming out to see a doctor! Don't want to leave Tanya!"

"You could come out together then," Coulter suggested. "Good medical care can be provided for both of you. You may be needing some of your medications to be adjusted or replenished. I can assist you with this."

Roy severed the connection.

Coulter then changed his approach. "Perhaps," he said when the next call went through, "it's the flat which has you so discouraged. Most of the ones in your block are in disrepair. Come on out, and I'll help you find a better place. Many of your neighbours have relocated, and I can help you do the same."

Another hangup. The hours crept by, Coulter reestablishing the connection again and again and Roy terminating it. His dependence on Tanya showed a need for affection. What could Coulter offer? Respect. So he listened to Roy's ramblings about topics unrelated to the incident, occasionally uttering a "yes" or an "ok" to encourage him. There was no such thing as small talk. What sounded like just a conversation could amount over time to much more. In fact, all talk could lead to rapport, so Coulter continued to be patient. He had few other options. The moderate weather – with temperatures ranging from ten to nineteen degrees Celsius – precluded terminating utilities to force him out.

Meanwhile the chronological board was crammed with contact times, topics, and estimates of success. So far, Coulter hadn't told any lies, but if he did, they would be recorded on the board, since it was essential to keep up with them.

Roy's employers and coworkers had been questioned. Most expressed surprise at his action. Although he had kept himself to himself – never mixed socially – no one disliked him. He knew his job and had on several occasions been given more responsibility. These additions had been made to his profile board. Both parents were deceased. No siblings. Symptoms of his condition included fatigue, irrationality, paranoia, volatility, memory lapses, lack of balance, and difficulty concentrating. None of these boded well for Mrs. Casey. Coulter's skills were needed more than ever.

In addition, the profile board for Tanya Hanson was being completed. She was Caucasian, age 47, with light brown hair and brown eyes. Height approximately 5'7". Weight between ten and eleven stone. Older, taller, and heavier than Mrs. Casey, Coulter noted.

She had given notice at her place of employment but had not finished working the remaining days nor left a forwarding address. No charges had appeared on her credit cards. She had not been located, although further enquiries were being made. Coulter had no intention of using her as a third-party intermediary – in his experience, TPIs could never be made to follow a script and often caused a situation to worsen – but it worried him that she was not available to provide information about Roy.

"Rest or continued contact?" inquired Byrne.

Coulter consulted his watch. They had not sent Roy an evening meal, nor had he eaten. It was long past his assigned time, but it was his practice to come in early and work late. No matter how hungry and tired, he found it difficult to let go with so much still unresolved. "He's made no substantive demands. He doesn't have a cause. He's sick, and his main fear is abandonment. His only expressed goal is to be left alone, which I can't agree to do, of course."

"He keeps taking your calls," Byrne commented.

"Yes, but I've not been successful in persuading him to come out. His mental delusions concern me the most. The victim was chosen specifically, and his emotional attachment to her is very strong. Consequently it could very quickly become dangerous. The setting is confined. The man's physically unwell, which is another complicating factor. The symptoms of his condition, particularly the volatility, aren't under control. I purposely didn't allow him to rest today, but further exhaustion – caused by continued contact – could destabilise the situation. Antidepressants would balance his emotions, but we've no indication that he's taking any. He has a deadly weapon. My hope is that if he is compelled to rest, Mrs. Casey will be able to as well. Although my focus must remain on him, I can assure you I'm considering Mrs. Casey's condition also."

"Sir, I believe the risk of violence is still high," Byrne said. "Don't incidents that begin with violence usually turn out to be more violent?"

"That possibility exists. He's had multiple recent stressors, after all. But we've bought Mrs. Casey some time. I consider the risk overnight to be low. Tomorrow is another matter entirely. When I begin to question the identity of the woman who is with him, the risk may escalate exponentially. But I've no choice. For Mrs. Casey's sake, I've got to find a way to move this situation forward."

CHAPTER EIGHTEEN

A LATE DINNER – if the food Roy scraped together on Saturday could even be called that – because the spaghetti was gone. She'd liked the pasta, but Roy had eaten most of it. Now she faced a third night of confinement in the cramped bathroom. She hadn't dreamed about being a prisoner, however. She'd dreamed that Simon was timing the gap between her contractions and asking her for the thousandth time if she were packed and ready to go to the hospital, all his calm and objectivity gone. Waking gave her an overwhelming sense of loss.

She was hungry, but breakfast didn't help. She had never adjusted to the British custom of beans for breakfast, and now the idea was revolting. She couldn't keep anything down except the Coke, and when her stomach rebelled, her head did, too. It was Sunday morning; she missed her Sunday mornings with Simon and the chocolate croissant he'd bring her after her tummy had settled. She missed Bear's wagging tail when he knew she was fully awake.

The negotiator began calling shortly after breakfast. The first conversation seemed to encourage Roy. She heard him agreeing that he'd coped well in the past. He expressed pride in his job. In the second call his tone changed.

"I'm not hearing you right," Roy said, holding the phone in front of him and glowering at it. "Say again?"

The voice of the negotiator was clear. "My boss thinks there may be some confusion about Tanya's identity. Would you mind having a look at her and then describing her to me?"

"Roy, you don't have to do that," Jenny said quickly, fearing his anger. "You know what Tanya looks like. Just tell him."

Evidently the negotiator couldn't hear Jenny. He was still speaking. "The thing is – I'm looking at a picture of Tanya, and I'm wondering if an error has been made. If so, I can help you with this."

"You don't know anything!" Roy yelled.

"Hearing you so angry really scares me, Roy."

Hearing him yell at the negotiator scared her, too. Roy placed the phone on his lap and clutched the knife with convulsive pressure.

"Take a couple of slow, deep breaths," the negotiator advised. "Let's talk this through. You sound stressed. I'd be stressed as well. I know you've been going through a rough patch, but I need your help. There's a young woman missing in the area, you see. I've got a description of her here, and there are some big differences between her appearance and Tanya's. That's easy enough to check, isn't it, mate?"

To Jenny the flat seemed to be shrinking and the light dimming. Her initial insistence on her identity had made Roy mad. She was willing to try almost anything to defuse his anger, so she'd decided to stop contradicting him when he called her Tanya, although that felt like climbing out on a weak branch. The only positive result was that he had untied her hands. Now if she could just get him to relax, maybe he wouldn't stay so close. But the negotiator had created a storm, and she was in the middle of it.

Roy's time on the phone had allowed her to get a better sense of her surroundings. The flat consisted of a living room with a painting of a mountain scene over the sofa and two armchairs, one of them near a series of bookshelves, mostly empty except for a collection of board games, Monopoly, Scrabble, Labyrinth, and some with British names she didn't recognize. Otherwise just a few decorative boxes, glass figurines, and a candle were on view. Not many books.

She wished for more decoration on the walls, for something to distract her from the stark conditions and the grime absorbed by them that was almost an illustration in itself.

She could see only two windows, one near the front door with curtains and a larger one in the dining room with no drapes. A small breakfast room bordered the kitchen, which had a pantry but no door to the outside.

She'd spent each night on the floor in the guest bathroom. Roy's bedroom – which she didn't want to enter – was opposite a second smaller room that appeared to be a sewing room. She could see a sewing machine on a table, fabrics, hangers. A woman's jacket hung on the back of a chair. Had Tanya left all this? Where was she?

"We have a problem, but we can find a solution together."

"You'll make off with her! I can't bear it!"

Roy stood suddenly, startling Jenny, who couldn't restrain a scream. The phone slipped to the floor, where they both stared at it.

"We're done," Roy said and leant over to disconnect the call.

She blinked rapidly, looking down so he wouldn't see her dismay.

****

Coulter sighed. One scream, although alarming, wasn't sufficient for a firearms team to make entry, but they'd move from a more distant lying-up point closer to the flat, if they hadn't already. He watched the firearms officer leave the van to report to the senior firearms commander on site and then up the chain of command. He redialed immediately. Part of his job was to get the suspect to acknowledge that there was a concern. Then the real work of negotiation could begin.

"How is everyone doing?" he asked. "Still all right?"

He paused to listen. "What was that? Roy, if you could just slow it down a bit, I'd have a better chance of understanding you." He consciously slowed his own speech. "Roy, are you telling me you feel stuck? You're not ready to deal with this?" He was quiet for a moment. "A lot of people in your situation would feel angry and depressed. I know I would, but I've found that it helps to keep talking. Can we agree together to do that?"

He heard a grudging assent from Roy.

"All right, yes. That's good. We'll sort it out, you and I. You have my word on that. Let's start again. I'm listening. Tell me what you're feeling right now."

He wanted Roy to know that he understood him, so he repeated some of his phrases. "You need her. She's very important to you, I can see that. As my wife is to me." Hoping to lessen the chances that Roy would hurt the hostage, he added, "I appreciate your taking care of her. Tell me about her."

"She's bonnie, younger than me, with brown eyes and a nice smile."

The description he gave fit both women. Was Roy speaking in general terms to conceal relevant differences or was he sincere in what he saw? It would be more difficult now to elicit salient details. "I'd like to meet her," he said. "All you have to do is walk out together. I know you want to do the right thing, and the right thing is to throw out any weapons you have and come out."

"I'm not doing that, am I? You're the filth, and you'll hurt me!"

"Roy, it's not like the telly. Nobody's going to get hurt. I've been concerned about your safety from the start, haven't I? We've communicated. I've supported you. I've sent you food. I've kept all the officers out. I'll continue to do that. I'd just like you to keep things quiet in there. Can you do that?" He waited for Roy's response. "Roy? I'm still here and willing to hear whatever you have to say."

He heard only the hangup.

Coulter was frustrated. Their rapport hadn't led to any change in Roy's behaviour. He stood, extended his arms, and clasped his hands behind his head to relieve the tension in his shoulders. He had been a negotiator long enough to have had some successes as well as failures, and he could never predict at the outset of an incident what the resolution would be. In this case, however, Roy's isolation concerned him. None of his coworkers had kept in touch with him after his diagnosis. Because his dependence on Tanya was extreme and unhealthy, it would be difficult to convince him to let her go.

The craft of negotiation contrasted with the public's view of police work. Citizens heard the sirens and saw the blue lights flashing and assumed that what police did was exciting. His brief was to slow down the action, make it boring, keep it calm. His pulse and blood pressure were the only indicators that what he did was exciting for him. He had never disclosed it to anyone, but he thought of himself as a sort of warrior. He didn't fight physically, of course, but he did engage in a war of words. He fought for the priorities of life – the hostages, the officers, and even the hostage takers. "It won't hurt for us to have a time out," he said. "Let's eat whilst we can."

CHAPTER NINETEEN

JENNY'S STOMACH WAS STILL at war with itself. Today, the fourth day of her captivity, nausea had triumphed over hunger. Her residual headache added shards of panic. Shouldn't she be feeling better? She was tired, too, because she didn't sleep well at night. What impact was all this having on the baby? The doctor who had confirmed her pregnancy had mentioned that she might need extra rest. He'd added that less stress would be wise. She was supposed to be eating for two but had barely consumed enough to sustain herself.

She sat down on the sofa. When the negotiator had made contact with Roy on Saturday, she'd been elated. He was a police officer. Once he was involved, other police would be on the scene, too, wouldn't they? Was Simon one of them? Would they allow him to lead his team? If not, who would rescue her?

Did they have to wait for the negotiator to call it quits? Sunday was only the second day he had been calling. How long would he continue to contact Roy? To establish a connection with him, to cajole him, and to attempt to convince him to come out? Didn't they realize how precarious her situation was? The negotiator was occupying Roy but also inflaming him, which made him more dangerous, and physically she was deteriorating. None of them were in the flat with her. She was on her own. What would Simon tell her to do? Keep your eyes in the boat, as he had when he'd been in the Special Boat Service. The phrase was his way of emphasizing the importance of focusing on the immediate, and her immediate problem was how to stay safe – and keep her baby safe – with a disturbed and armed man only a few feet away from her.

"Tanya, why haven't you changed your clothes?"

She didn't know what to say. He hadn't changed his; he was wearing the jeans and shirt he'd had on the day before and the day before that. Why had he noticed her clothes and not his own? She was too scared to ask. She'd sponge bathed in the little bathroom at night, trying to keep all the wounds made by the knife clean, but had been afraid to remove much of her clothing at any one time. "I haven't felt well enough," she finally said. "And these clothes are new, so they're my favorites right now, even if they are a little rumpled."

He sat next to her. "You didn't have this before," he said, running a finger over the scar on her cheek. "What's happened to you?"

She froze. She had hoped only for the absence of anger. She had not expected to deal with displays of affection. She had accomplished nothing, only traded one treacherous situation for another. She wanted to wrench the knife away from him to protect herself but dared not try. "It's – it's a long story," she stammered. "I don't want to talk about it. It doesn't affect us." She glanced at her watch. Would Roy realize that it wasn't Tanya's? Should she have removed and hidden it? She slid it under her sleeve. The negotiator hadn't called recently. Was he taking a break for lunch? Could she distract Roy by mentioning it? "What's for lunch?" she asked.

He moved away, taking the knife with him. She heard him rummaging in the kitchen. He returned with a can of tuna, two forks, and crackers. He put the knife on the table within his reach but not hers.

"When I saw you on the street," he said between bites, "I knew you were coming home." He patted her knee.

Her stomach turned over. She remembered throwing up once when she was in the shower with Simon. He had chuckled, gotten her in bed quickly, and brought her Sprite and crackers. Perhaps if she threw up in Roy's lap, he wouldn't sit so close to her.

****

Coulter's next conversation with Roy found him calm and talkative.

"I'm winning her back," Roy reported. "She knows I'm wanting to do anything to make her happy."

"How are you planning to do that, Roy?" Coulter asked.

"Women like shows of affection, don't they? I'm thinking a little cuddle later."

Coulter's concern for Mrs. Casey's welfare multiplied. Mood changes, which included verbal outbursts and sudden increased interest in sex, could occur at any time in men with Roy's condition, often for no apparent reason. Could she resist his affection without angering him? It's possible he wasn't capable of sexual activity, but Mrs. Casey wouldn't know that. Any action he took would be frightening. If he failed to perform, his wrath would boil over, and Mrs. Casey would suffer the consequences.

"It's time for us to tell the truth to each other," he stated. "Are you ready to hear the truth? If you don't choose to come out, other officers may want to take charge."

"Stop trying to trick me," Roy instructed. "I know the truth. Tanya's back. She's here. I don't need you. Any of you."

"Roy, I'm sorry to hear that. I appreciate your point of view, but I'm not leaving you," Coulter said. "I'd just like to know what has brought about this change."

"That's my business and none of yours. But I've got a checkerboard with all the pieces. Tanya wants me to teach her to play. She was never interested before."

Coulter was taken aback. What was going on in that flat? He gestured wildly at the secondary negotiator for a suggested response.

Draw him out, Byrne scribbled on a pad.

Coulter nodded. "Checkers," he said slowly. "Have you been playing long? How would you teach a beginner?"

"It's all about the right moves," Roy said. "Get the joke?"

"Roy, I'd take it easy," Coulter advised. "Sometimes women aren't ready to move as quickly as we are. And if Tanya's hurt or still feeling sick, she might not be able to respond."

"Ta," Roy responded and hung up.

Coulter's next call went unanswered.

****

Jenny was shocked. She hadn't encouraged Roy; she simply hadn't discouraged him. Had he forgotten his initial violence toward her? And playing checkers wasn't proving to be the distraction she had hoped. It was quiet in the flat, the silence broken only by the thudding of her heart and the ringing of the phone, which Roy was ignoring. Surely, she thought, if the police were outside, she'd hear them. She felt her hope slipping away like water at low tide. He was not rational. It had been crazy to think that anything she did would affect his behavior. His hand was on her thigh and his eyes on her breasts. "Roy, I think I need some time," she said.

"You're not going to turn into a cold fish, are you? You never were before."

"This seems sudden."

With one backhanded motion, he swept the checkers to the floor.

"Please don't be angry," she pleaded. "Doesn't this need to be right for both of us?" How could she stall him? "We could rest, have a nice dinner. Why don't we go to one of the places we used to go? It would be more romantic." She tried not to let her distaste show.

"You used to like it when I cooked for you," he remembered. "I'll find something in the freezer. You have a nice lie-down." He smiled at her. "Things are working out for us. I knew they would."

CHAPTER TWENTY

LUCK HAD ALWAYS PLAYED a part in Roy Alden Wilkes' life. At least, his mum had always said so. He'd grown up in Scotland, where she had taught him to see the natural beauty all round him. As an only child, he'd got all her attention and very few restrictions. He could go where he wanted, when he wanted, and he enjoyed the special treats she took from the kitchen and packed for him when he wanted to explore.

At school he'd found it difficult to settle, and the wealthier students teased him about being the wrong colour and the wrong class. His father worked on one of the large estates, where he learnt to hunt and fish. But if his dad had had a town job, he'd never have been permitted to play near the rivers and dales. There were good places to hide, places no one else knew or went to. His mum never tired of hearing of his discoveries. He could relax, stop looking over his shoulder. Use the rod he'd got for his eighth birthday.

It was a blow when his mum was killed in the car accident, but he'd been thrown clear. He'd been a bit muddled for a time, missing her encouragement, so the squire had provided a tutor for him and allowed him to work with his father, setting the traps for small game and checking on their success. When he returned to school, he was taller and more muscular, and the other boys left off harassing him.

He hadn't excelled in his schoolwork. Eager each day to leave the classroom behind, he learnt just what was required. As soon as he was old enough, he headed to London, where diversity was the norm. There his lack of advanced schooling didn't matter; there were all sorts of jobs for blokes who were willing to work hard. He'd done a bit of this and a bit of that before starting at Tesco and making his way up. Some of the managers there weren't any more educated than he was, and they all agreed that he knew his seafood. That always made him smile, because the fish he knew best didn't come from the ocean. He never corrected them, however. He stayed quiet. He determined to make himself reliable. Over time, fate would favour him.

He'd met Tanya at his local one night when he was drinking by himself. She'd served him his pint and seemed charmed by his Scottish accent. He hadn't thought he had much of one, his mother not being Scottish after all, but since she liked it, he'd exaggerated it a bit. Rolled his r's slightly. Drawn out his vowels. Glossed over some of his consonants. Talked about what a nice evenin' it was and how much he liked drinkin' the pints she brought. Her smile put him in mind of his mum's, and her tales of rowdy customers gave him a laugh.

Amongst his childhood pursuits, only his love of fishing remained. When he left for London, his father had given him some tackle – hooks, lures, and the like – and a knife, and he'd saved for the rest of what he needed. He found places to go in Hertfordshire, Shropshire, other counties. No one could ask anything of him when he was fishing, even the fish. On the contrary, he was asking something of them. The odds of catching were always against you, but he'd had success. Pike, perch, carp, bream. Tanya was less keen on the early mornings, but she liked eating what he caught.

They'd done well together for a long time. No bairns, just the two of them, but they had enough money to enjoy their holidays and an occasional extra. Yes, the years were good until his diagnosis. Knocked for six then, he had been. He continued to work for some time, although he had more anger than energy. He didn't like how the meds made him feel, but there was no arguing with the doctors. He'd been short with Tanya sometimes, he admitted it, but wasn't that normal in his situation? He always regretted his temper, which was the important thing, whether he said so or not. But he'd seen puzzled expressions on her face, and she wasn't as much for chat as she had been. Once she told him she was frightened, which made no sense at all. She'd only ever been the one for him.

Then came her admission that she might need some time away. He'd not seen any reason for it and had argued with her strongly. The next morning she was gone. For the first time he wondered about his lot.

But then a chance meeting. There'd been some resistance on her part. She'd always had a bit of an independent streak. He'd had to insist that she come with him. Then she hadn't wanted to stay, which he didn't see the reason for at all. Miffed, most likely, for not having got her way. But he'd never claimed to understand women, had he? She had changed, but he pushed the thought away. She was back. She was coming round. He could count on destiny's goodwill.

CHAPTER TWENTY-ONE

REHEATED CHICKEN FROM THE FREEZER. Roy had put it in some kind of sauce, which Jenny suspected was soup he thickened somehow. Canned peas. Canned potatoes. None of it was her idea of a nice dinner, which didn't matter, but it didn't take him long to cook it, which did matter, and he kept glancing at her while he was cooking. He was still taking medicine, but not many pills were left in some of the bottles. What then? The knife was next to him on the counter. She was closer to the door than he was, but she didn't think she'd have enough time to open it and get away before he caught up with her.

Where were the police? When she looked out the dining room window, she couldn't see anybody. If she waved or tried to signal, only Roy would know.

She ate slowly. Everything except the potatoes sickened her, but she was hungry. She took small bites, wanting to prolong the meal. She watched him mash his peas on his fork. The phone rang periodically, the silence between the rings oppressive. Roy had answered twice with an emphatic "No!" before ending the connection.

"Maybe you should answer that," she suggested to him when the calls continued. "He only wants to talk." She felt sorry for the negotiator. At least he had tried. Now there was no one. The flat was quiet otherwise. If the police were outside the front door, she couldn't hear them, but the rain and occasional gusts of wind would cover many sounds, and she thought that officers would be unlikely to advertise their presence.

Another ring. In desperation she grabbed it, asking, "Where are you?" before the caller had spoken. Roy had wrenched the phone away, and now he kept it out of her reach and didn't answer at all.

"I need to lie down," she said. She went into the bathroom – so far he hadn't followed her there – sat down against the wall and cried, removing her sweater and sobbing into it so Roy would not hear her.

It didn't seem that help was coming. The rising fear gripped her chest. Was this what terror did? Made it hard to breathe? She had to try again to escape.

****

Coulter had heard Mrs. Casey's strangled question. It was dangerous for a hostage to challenge a hostage taker. She must consider that risk lower than the risk of not speaking. It pointed to the deterioration of the process. The firearms officer had left the van. Byrne was silent. Roy was more unstable, and Mrs. Casey must be beyond hope. He wished he could reason with Roy face to face, but that wasn't possible. He wished he had eyes inside the flat, but sometimes that information proved counterproductive. The stakes were high, as they always were. He'd try again. He wasn't seeking personal success; he simply recognised the cost of failure. A life – or lives – could be lost. Consequently he never participated in post-incident banter. But this wasn't over. Not yet. He dialed.

****

"Your wife's agitated," Kelly reported to Casey.

As am I, Casey thought. An understatement actually.

"The X-ray has stopped answering the negotiator's calls. Your wife picked up once but didn't have a chance to say much before the phone was taken away."

A sign of the grave nature of her predicament.

"No one's quitting, mate," Kelly continued, losing his reserve, "but the teams have moved into position. The negotiator has requested additional time, and it's likely he'll be given it. I debated telling you, but – " He stopped when he saw Casey's face darken. "But I think you've a right to know," he stammered.

Casey turned away, his jaw tightening.

"You can't make entry, mate," Kelly said, his voice shrill. "I'd have to stop you."

"You'd not succeed!" Casey erupted.

"You don't know the exact location," Kelly reasoned, still trying to cap the volcano. "You've no weapon. You've got to trust the teams and wait."

Casey was nearly bent double with tension, feeling as if something had struck his chest. He was a man of action, and he had been called upon to *wait.* Trusting the teams was not an issue; he had trained with most of them. Trusting the senior officers to give the "Go, go, go" was another matter. Nothing in his life had been as difficult. He clenched and unclenched his fists. He gradually straightened. He nodded.

****

"Tanya, get in here!" Roy yelled.

Jenny cringed. She didn't want to leave the bathroom, but if he came in after her, she'd be cornered. She had nothing she could use as a weapon. She returned to the living room. "Is there something we could watch?" she asked, catching herself before calling it the TV. Tanya would have called it the telly. Roy had set their plates aside but showed no sign of intending to clean up. "We could turn the volume up to drown the sound of the phone."

He frowned, his face sinister as he located the remote. He found a nature program, and she prayed that it would last longer than thirty minutes or an hour. The knife was still in the kitchen on the scratched countertop that reminded her of her skin.

Occasionally she made comments about the program to focus his attention away from her. He didn't respond. She was running out of time. To prevent panic, she tried to remember how to count in Spanish, French, and Italian. During one commercial break, he leaned over to kiss her and pushed one hand under her skirt. She shuddered. "No!" she said too sharply.

"You will no' refuse me," he warned.

"Roy – Roy – I just need to relax. Why don't we have some tea? I'll make it. You've done everything else."

He followed her into the kitchen and watched while she brewed it. He had one hand near his crotch, and she doubted that she'd be able to get him to drink any of the tea. The saucepan wasn't large. To give herself time to think, she filled it to the brim with water, and while she waited for it to come to a boil, an idea began to simmer in her brain. Maybe she could hit him with the pot. But if she didn't strike hard enough, her action could backfire. She watched bubbles form on the edges of the water, evidence that it was now scalding, sufficient to brew tea, but what if it were hotter?

"It's ready," he said.

Almost, she thought. When she saw a rolling boil, she put both hands on the handle, and using all her strength, swung the pot in his direction. The saucepan gave his chin only a glancing blow, but the bubbling liquid hit him in the face and chest. As he roared in pain and rage, she ran toward the door. "Help! Help!" she screamed.

He came after her, knife in hand. "I'll kill you! I'll kill you!" he shouted over her cries. She'd barely reached for the latch when she felt his arm around her waist, pulling her back with such force that she doubled over. Something struck the door hard, once, twice, then she heard the sound of splintering as the door gave way.

A cacophony of men's voices: "Armed police!" "I'll kill her!" "Drop the knife!" Gunfire, very loud and very close. She felt Roy's grip loosen as he fell behind her. She fell, too. Large boots surrounded her. They belonged to men in dark clothes with covered faces, men who seemed to be everywhere. Someone scooped her up and moved toward the door, through it, outside. Her chest was heaving; was she still screaming or simply gulping the freshness of freedom? The air slipped by them, because the officer was moving quickly, along a walkway with an iron railing, then down, down steps. The accessories on the front of his vest dug into her.

She couldn't hear anything except a distant roaring. She covered her ears to shield herself from the sound, but it didn't help. Was it thunder? No, the sky had cleared, and the rumbling was inside her head. She yawned to make her ears pop, to no avail. She tipped her head to the left, then to the right, as if she could pour the buzzing out like the water in her ears after a swim.

Ahead she could see the double stripe of green and yellow squares of a London ambulance, so different from the red rescue vehicles American paramedics used. The rear doors were open, and her carrier set her down, as if he knew that her legs would not support her, and squeezed her shoulder briefly. A lean man in street clothes approached her, holding up his warrant card, his lips moving. A paramedic, his dark green uniform dotted with badges and other insignia, reached for her with white gloved hands. She looked for the man who had delivered her, but he was nowhere to be seen. Where was Simon? She was out, safe. Where was Simon?

Part Two

The Investigation

"My object in enquiring is to know."

E. Housman

CHAPTER ONE

PC BRIAN DAVIES rang his wife. "Bethie, I'll be on my way home soon. Are Meg and Robbie asleep? I know it's late, but I need to have a word with you. I'll explain when I get there."

He didn't tell her that a fellow officer was driving him and why. In his numb condition, he couldn't have said whether the car was moving fast or not, and nothing they passed registered. His eyes were open but he'd lost focus.

He didn't want to relate any of the evening's events until he was well away from the firearms base and able to see her face to face. He was counting on her ability to remain calm in difficult situations. Fortunately they'd been a bit older when they married. She'd completed her university courses and been settled in her teaching job when their relationship became serious. He'd been well past his probationary period with the Metropolitan Police and a qualified firearms officer for several years. Her teaching lent stability to their marriage, and she had a realistic understanding of the physical exertion and mental concentration needed for him to perform his duties safely and effectively.

The years when Paul Condon had been commissioner of police were rough. All specialist officers had been required to rotate away from their duties and serve in other capacities. He'd had slightly better hours but hadn't been as happy. He'd begun as a regular copper – they all had – but once he'd had specialised training, training he was proud of, he found he wasn't as suited to regular policing. The firearms unit was where he belonged. Now that could be called into question.

The house was dark and quiet when he arrived, the only illumination coming from the lights on the porch and in their bedroom. Most nights that would have brought a smile to his face. Most nights he would have anticipated the children climbing in his lap for kisses before bed and Bethie doing the same after the kids were asleep.

She was waiting for him in the bedroom.

He embraced her. "Bethie, I – I don't know where to start."

"Rough day?" she asked. "Were you still on one of the hostage rescue teams?"

He nodded. "Negotiations had broken down, so we moved closer to the flat."

She waited.

"I heard Jenny screaming for help. I took the decision to make entry, and he had a knife. His hand was moving. I had to stop it. That's it."

"Brian, what are you telling me?"

He paused. "That I killed a man today. The man who had Jenny."

Her face paled.

"You've got to understand. I had to do it. If I hadn't responded, he would have killed her."

"Sit," she said. "Here, next to me." Her normally calm husband was shaking.

"I was prepared to do it. We all are, but I never thought I'd have to do. I've already reviewed my actions over and over, but there's nothing else I could have done. Nothing else I should have done."

"Are you certain he's dead?"

"No doubt. There wasn't time to aim, but I didn't miss. Centre mass. But it didn't have to end the way it did. His call, not mine."

The import struck her – not just of the nature of what he was disclosing but that he was disclosing anything at all. He rarely spoke of what he did on the Job. "Is Jenny all right?"

"I think so. Injured but not seriously. We got her out of there straightaway. The ambulance took her to hospital for evaluation."

"Then you did the right thing," she soothed. "You did."

"If I did the right thing, why do I keep seeing – seeing – Beth, I'll not tell you." He blinked hard. At a glance his eyes had taken in the starkness of the surroundings and the blood of a man dead not from disease but from the ammunition in his gun. "Do you hate me, Bethie? I pulled the trigger."

"Hate you for saving Jenny's life? Of course not!"

"But I wasn't angry. I killed without anger. What does that make me?"

She hesitated, knowing that her words mattered and wanting to say the right thing, for both of them.

"Bethie?"

"Bri – you're – you're a good man. The sort of man who tries to make the city safer. Who is ready to risk his life to save someone else's. I'm proud of what you do. I'm proud of *you.* You're brave and strong. The best husband any woman could have."

He was silent.

"Brian, listen to me. You did what had to be done. Responded when urgent action was needed. For Jenny. I'm so glad you were there. As she must be."

She was relieved to see him nod and then reply.

"My mates are glad for what I did. And the Chief Super told me to rest and relax. Not to pay attention to the press or watch the telly. Not to doubt myself. Not to have much alcohol. The incident will be on the news, but not my name." He stopped. There must have been additional instructions of some sort, but try as he might, he could recall nothing more.

"What's next?"

"An investigation. I've already given a short statement. Just notes really. And Howard, our team leader, did as well. They've taken my MP-5 with all unused rounds. And my Glock, which I didn't use at all. The clothes I was wearing. They swabbed my hands for gunshot residue and took a blood sample to test for alcohol and drugs. I'll have to make a full statement later on. I'm suspended from operations. Beyond that, I don't know."

"That's good news then. For the first time since you joined this unit, I won't be worried all the time. I'll know that you're in one piece and that you'll be coming home at night. For now, you're exhausted. We'll both rest. But there's something we need to do first." She took his hand and led him to the children's room.

He saw his daughter Meg, not yet five, her dark curls like his wife's, graceful even in sleep. Robbie, barely two but almost Meg's size already. Sleep held his energy in check but only just. Brian recalled how he and Beth had furnished this room – bit by bit whilst awaiting Meg's birth. The larger Beth's belly became, the more filled with furniture the baby's room. Then Robbie had arrived. Now, with toy boxes and book shelves, clothes on hangers and in dresser drawers, the space seemed occupied by more than their two children. Other personalities, Thomas the Train being only one example, populated it.

"Look what we have," Beth said. "I love you more than ever. And that's not going to change."

He felt the beginning of a smile creep past the lump in his throat.

CHAPTER TWO

OUTSIDERS WERE INTIMIDATED by Brian Allen Davies. Within his family, however, he was the youngest, smallest, and most restrained. His boisterous older brothers, and even his sister on occasion, had given him punches to prove a point or end an argument.

They were all tall, but his height seemed no advantage in their company. Outside the family, however, his dimensions alone gave him power he sometimes felt he did not warrant. People took notice even when he spoke softly. If he raised his voice, they were afraid. Coaches drafted him for their teams, hoping he was as aggressive as his brothers. He may have been physically suited for an athletic career, but he didn't prefer it.

Beth, however, had never been intimidated by him. The oldest in her family, she had grown up on a neighbouring farm. She had always seen through his size and into his gentle spirit. "If you had fur, you'd always be a puppy," she teased. "You're so much more than muscle and bones."

The incident which defined the course of his life had occurred one afternoon when he was walking home from school. He was thirsty, and although the petrol station was not on his route home, he knew he could buy a soda there. Coming out with the drink in his hand, he bumped into a man hurrying through the door. The man pushed him out of the way, then followed his shove with a blow, as if to ensure Brian kept his distance. Brian didn't, responding instead the way he did with his brothers. They traded punches, but this time his had more effect, and the individual fell to his knees. Brian picked up his soda, shook the can to see if any liquid were left, and walked away.

A police officer stopped him before he reached home, the car coming to a halt in front of him. "I'm Constable Laine. What's your name?" the officer asked after he exited the vehicle. He approached warily, his hand on his truncheon. The young man who fit the description given by the victim at the petrol station – brown hair and eyes, dark trousers and light shirt – was both taller and broader than he was.

Brian told him. His voice was pitched slightly higher than Laine expected. He had blood on his chin from a cut lip.

"May I see some identification, please?"

"I don't have any."

"No driving licence?"

"I don't have one."

Did he have below normal intelligence? Or was he irresponsible? "Lost it already, have you?"

"No, sir. I'm not old enough to drive."

"How old are you, son?" Laine enquired.

"Twelve, sir."

It made sense. The pudgy cheeks, smooth skin, awkward stance. He hadn't hit puberty yet. The male victim had mistaken his bulk for age. He rather thought he could persuade him not to initiate legal action against a child. Still, he had a report to file. "Did you assault a man at the BP station?"

"I bumped into him on accident. I said sorry, but he came at me and pushed me. I pushed back."

"Why did you leave the scene?"

"To walk home."

Laine paused. "I'll take you home, son."

Not long after, PC Laine visited and spoke with him in the presence of his parents. "If you continue to grow, you'll be more than a match physically for any man you meet. Your challenge is to be stronger mentally. There is always more than one way to resolve conflict. If you're wise, you'll decide now what will govern your actions: good or evil." He had been clear and strong in his words, but he had never raised his voice.

Years later Brian remembered both the consequences of his lack of control and, though he hadn't seen him again, the considerate way the policeman had dealt with him. The repetitive nature of police training appealed to him, and the caution that infused every action that firearms officers took had become a part of him. He could be accused of many things but being reckless was not one of them.

CHAPTER THREE

EVEN BEFORE THE AMBULANCE WAS MOVING, the paramedics were busy as bumblebees, taking Jenny's pulse and blood pressure, looking in her eyes, asking her questions she couldn't hear over the roar of the engine and the rumble in her ears, starting an intravenous drip. The man in plain clothes was on his radio.

She'd gone from being in a flat with a strange man to being in a van with male strangers. The difference in their intent notwithstanding, their actions were still invasive. She wanted to curl up and shut them all out. Where was Simon?

At the hospital she was wheeled past a uniformed police officer and into a room where a woman in a dark suit and a neon orange blouse waited. Not a nurse then. The storm in Jenny's ears had subsided somewhat, into a murmur that was more irritating than painful. She saw the woman hold up her warrant card and mouth "detective" before appearing to give instructions to the medical personnel who entered. Her clothes were removed one piece at a time, in spite of her tears, and placed in evidence bags. She was given a hospital gown.

"Any other belongings?" the detective asked, slowly and distinctly.

"Simon – I need Simon – "

"He's been notified. He's on his way."

The Accident and Emergency doctor worked quickly, making an overall examination before itemising the multiple abrasions and contusions. He did not suture the lacerations. The nurse followed behind, cleansing and medicating the places where the knife had broken her skin. She and the doctor conversed as they worked, but Jenny found that if she closed her eyes, she could tune them out by focusing on her internal humming.

"Mrs. Casey." The doctor touched her shoulder. He must have addressed her more than once, but how did he know her name? What was his name? Had he told her?

"You've got a rather large lump on your head. Still having headaches?"

His accent reminded her of Roy. She tried not to panic, giving a quick nod.

"And feeling pressure?"

"Yes," she managed to say.

"How many fingers am I holding up?"

"Not more than five," she answered, trying for a joke and evidently failing because no one smiled.

"No cause for concern then," he said briskly. "Difficulty concentrating and occasional nausea may be present, but these symptoms usually go away on their own with time. I see you're expecting. We'll monitor that. For now, the police want to have a word with you."

More than a word, Jenny thought. An officer with a camera had come into the room. She wanted him to go away but knew he wouldn't, and he didn't. Couldn't they have found a female officer? Damn the police and their thoroughness. She wanted Simon and sleep.

****

Casey and Kelly heard gunshots in the distance. "Go!" Casey commanded.

The wait until Kelly returned seemed interminable. With the car keys already in his hand, he reported, "She's alive! Conscious. In the ambulance on the way to hospital. They've got a head start." He had the car moving almost before he finished speaking.

"Who gave the order to make entry?" Casey enquired.

"Davies. He heard your wife calling for help."

"And the X-ray?"

"Thanks to Davies, he didn't require an ambo." Kelly drove as if he owned the road, blues flashing and twos sounding. Casey just had time to leave voice messages for their parents and Neil Goodwyn that Jenny was out and all right.

"Ring me if you need me," Kelly said, pulling up at the Accident & Emergency entrance at University College Hospital.

Casey was out in a flash, through the waiting room, casting his eyes down the corridors. An officer stood by one of the doors. Casey broke into a run and thrust the door open before the officer could react. Jenny was there, her hair untidy, her face lined with fatigue, dark clouds under her eyes, and smudges of blood on her cheeks. To his eyes, however, she was beautiful. He grasped her hand then leant over to gather her in his arms. After a moment he released her, but her grip on his hand suggested that she wasn't going to let go of him anytime soon.

"I'm ok," she sobbed. "The baby – I think so – but I don't know if – "

"Breathe," he said wanting to calm her. Tears were expected, but he hated to see them.

She frowned and rubbed her ears.

He spoke again, a bit louder. "In, out, slow it down, in, out." He put her hand on his chest to show her and noticed she wasn't wearing her wedding ring. He'd never since their wedding seen her without it.

She saw his glance. "Simon, I had to move it," she stammered. "He would've – "

"I understand," he interrupted. "Well done. Let's just put it where it belongs." He shifted the ring from her right hand to her left then surveyed her condition. They'd put a line into her and taken her clothes. DI Thoms was there, but the officer with the camera was leaving. They'd already taken their snaps of her wounds then. He hated to think of her experiencing that. "Doc? I'm a former medic, so give it to me straight."

"Her eardrums are stressed but not compromised. There are two places I'd have sutured if she'd come in sooner, but she's not unduly harmed. Nevertheless we'll keep her for observation tonight, because of the pregnancy, you understand. No vaginal bleeding at the moment, but your officer has asked that we postpone the ultrasound since at this stage it would involve a vaginal probe. I'll check on her before I go off duty in the morning. At home – plenty of fluids, regular meals, rest. A mild pain reliever is not contraindicated." He left.

DI Thoms spoke. "There's one more examination we need to consider, Mrs. Casey. For rape. It can be done in more sensitive surroundings, however."

She could hear the measured tones of the detective's voice. "No!" she exclaimed, horror suffusing her face. "I won't let you! Go away! He didn't – Simon, he didn't – I don't have to do this, do I? Do I?"

"No, love, you don't," he answered, his relief apparent. He knew only a small part of what had happened to her, and he had disciplined himself not to fill in the blanks.

"It was necessary for me to raise the issue," Thoms said heavily, "to prevent evidence being compromised or lost prior to interview. You may then schedule an ultrasound with your regular physician."

She hadn't asked Jenny any questions so far, Casey noted. Per procedure, she had only supervised the collection of evidence. Now that was done, she would depart, and perhaps then Jenny could rest.

"We'll chat tomorrow then," Thoms continued. "Mrs. Casey, I'm very glad to see that you're all right."

Simon and Jenny were finally alone. With the threat removed and the treatment completed, he hoped for a quiet night, but one interruption followed another. Nurses taking vital signs. Jenny's distress. Jenny's questions. "Did you tell my parents that I'm ok? Is Roy dead? Who saved me?"

He answered what he could, as briefly as he could, wanting to wait for talk later.

Shivering under the blanket the A&E had provided, she grasped his hand like a lifeline. He knew she wasn't very comfortable on the examination table, but she insisted it was better than the bathroom floor where she'd spent the last few nights.

Questions crowded his mind, but he tamed his need to know. He wanted her to sleep. Noises in the hospital startled her, however. Concussion protocols required that they wake her periodically. She couldn't settle. He could change none of it.

At 4:00 a.m. he gave up and summoned the doctor. "I'm taking my wife home," he said. "She's not resting here." When the release papers were processed, he rang Kelly, who brought the bag of clothes Casey had packed for Jenny and a bit later guided them to the car.

CHAPTER FOUR

HOME WAS NOT THE HAVEN for Jenny that Simon had hoped. Bear's unbounded joy didn't affect her the way he'd thought it would. Then he'd anticipated a quick rinse in the shower before rest, but she preferred a bath where she scrubbed all the places not marked by Roy's knife. He'd never seen her use so much soap, and on some parts of her body she scrubbed her skin nearly raw. Only when she washed her hair was she gentle. "He smelled sick," she said. "And his flat was stuffy and stale. I want to wash it all away, but it's sticking to me like barnacles on a ship."

He'd not seen all her injuries at hospital. She'd been treated before he arrived, and she'd dressed herself, and quickly, when she was allowed to leave. Seeing them now brought home to him how hazardous her situation had been. Any one of her wounds could have gone deeper, and – he shook his head to rid himself of the thought. Her arms, shoulders, chest, thighs – only her abdomen had been spared, because she had protected the baby.

After the bath, he rebandaged her and smoothed lotion into the red areas. When finally she curled up in bed, she slept not in the pose of someone relaxed but on her side, her arms and legs positioned like a shield.

"Simon, I want to see you every time I open my eyes."

He lay next to her and held her, listening to her breathe.

"That helps."

"For me as well," he said, but it was not entirely true. He was unsettled, his emotions still percolating. Anger had fueled him during the waiting, when he'd been sidelined and prevented from

participating in her rescue. He was angry even now at the man who
had abducted and hurt her. His death didn't matter, because the
consequences of his actions lived after him. He wished he'd – but
Davies had done for him what he wished.

When she slept, he went into the kitchen, opened a beer, and
took it into the sitting room. When he set the bottle on the table,
he couldn't recall tasting anything. Only the sound of the glass
against the wood told him it was empty. Another would be no
better. If he raged aloud, he'd wake her. What then? Exercise. He
dropped to the floor. Rep after rep of pressups until he could hear
his breathing. He would sweat the anger out then shower it away.
Then and only then could he lie next to his wife and sleep.

****

Jenny was stirring, moaning slightly as she woke. "What day is
it?"

"Still Monday. You've been asleep only a few hours."

"And you even fewer," she observed. He was dressed.

"Good to have you home."

"I thought I never would be. It seemed forever until the
negotiator called, and then it didn't seem to help." She started to sit
up but sank back quickly. "Headache and morning sickness," she
said. "It scared me when I felt it at Roy's. I didn't want him to know
I was pregnant, and I wanted to have the strength to defend myself.
Here I'm glad, because it means the baby's okay."

"Yes," he replied. "It's all done now except for the healing."

"I can do that. I just want to stay home. I don't have to go out,
do I? That detective said she needed to talk with me again."

"Yes, but the coppers will come to you," he reassured. He
brought her some crackers, Sprite, and a mild analgesic.

She nibbled and sipped and then fell asleep again. So did he. A
little later they ate lunch, toast and a bit of cheese.

Neither of them had had sufficient sleep, however, when DI
Thoms and her colourless sergeant arrived. Jenny had woken from
her afternoon nap with a start, as if trying to orient herself to her

surroundings. She swayed a little coming down the stairs from the bedroom into the living room and had to put out a hand to steady herself. She sat on the far end of the sofa with Simon beside her, a barrier between her and the detectives.

After reintroducing herself and her colleague, who'd been with Jenny in the ambulance, the detective inspector asked if she were up to a little chat. "It was our investigation that located you, and with the assistance of the kidnap unit, provided the negotiator and arranged for firearms support." She nodded at Sergeant Riley, who started the tape recorder and gave the standard introduction.

Simon had told her they were coming, but it seemed so soon. And a "little chat" had to be police-speak for something more. Jenny felt a flash of near hysteria. Was she supposed to offer them tea? No, she wanted to get it all over with as soon as possible.

The detective inspector looked very official in a coordinated pants suit with matching scarf and belt, while Jenny had simply pulled a robe over her nightgown. That and her formal speech made Jenny even more nervous. She didn't wait for the first question. "It was overcast, and then it started to rain. I was fumbling with my umbrella when he approached me. At first I thought he intended to help me, but he came too close and spoke to me as if he knew me. I argued with him. When he took my arm, I resisted. Then he must have hit me, because the next thing – the next thing – " She was speaking too fast, and her voice was rising.

"Breathe, princess," Simon said softly. "It'll help calm you."

"Later I realized that I must have walked in the wrong direction, but at the time I was distracted. I had given copies of my book to people at the church, and I was remembering my first husband. I wrote it after he was killed, when I was having trouble adjusting to life without him." She turned to look at Simon. "When it all happened, I just wanted you, only you. I wanted you to come and get me."

The hand that reached out to him was shaking. He took it and massaged her fingers. "Jenny, it wasn't possible. I didn't know where you were. None of us did."

DI Thoms waited, made uncomfortable by the intimate nature of what she was witnessing and surprised at her discomfort.

"When you were located," Simon continued, "I was stood down from my team. They kept a close watch on me. They had to do. I would've broken the door down to get to you."

"Simon, he had a knife. A scary knife." She restrained a sob.

"I could have dealt with that," he said, hoping he sounded reassuring when he was angry, very angry, that she'd had to face a deadly weapon.

"Ma'am," the sergeant said quietly.

Yes, Thoms thought, I'm not in control of this interview. "Mrs. Casey," she said, "we've no desire to make this difficult for you. You must be tired, but it would help if you could answer a few questions. Are you able to continue?"

"Of course, of course," Jenny said quickly. "I can tell you – it was raining, and I went the wrong way. I was looking for the tube station sign, and I couldn't see it. Oh, I already said that, didn't I? I'm so foggy – "

"Mrs. Casey, what do you recall when you first entered Mr. Wilkes' flat?"

"I didn't enter. I mean, I don't know how I got there. I was on the street – and then I was coming to on the floor, hurting all over. My head the most, but I was dizzy and sick to my stomach. I couldn't think. I didn't even know at first that he was the one I'd seen before and that he wasn't going to let me go home. That was stupid, wasn't it?"

It was Simon who responded. "Jenny, you did everything right. You managed to get word out that you were being held. You provided enough information for Thoms' team to identify the bastard and his location. Somehow you made it through."

She gave him a weak smile. "Where was I? Oh – Roy's flat. I had my cell phone in my pocket. I called you because you always know what to do. I coughed to cover the sound of the ringing, but I never knew – I never knew if you'd gotten the message!" An audible sob. "And what took so long?"

"Mrs. Casey, let's back up a bit, shall we?" Thoms suggested.

"Back up? What does that mean? I've told you how it happened! The rest is a blur – I can't – " She broke down.

Riley stopped the recording.

Casey stood, still not releasing Jenny's hand. "We're done here," he said. "It's too soon for a debrief."

"I agree," Thoms said with regret. She would have preferred to accomplish more in the interview. Mrs. Casey's emotions were raw, that was evident. However, since Wilkes was dead, a delay of 24 hours would do no harm. She and Sergeant Riley departed.

"Oh, no," Jenny exclaimed. "News Flash: Met Detectives Fail in Attempt to Interview Distraught Woman. That means they'll have to try again, doesn't it?"

Casey nodded.

****

Jenny had been quiet since the detectives had left and subdued through the dinner that Kelly had brought. It was unlike her; usually he was the reticent one. Thankfully Kelly had provided more than dinner, Simon having acknowledged when he rang that they didn't have much food in. Bread, milk, cheese, eggs, cold cuts, produce, and even Mr. Kipling's Lemon Slices, which Jenny loved. And flowers, a gesture that touched her deeply.

Kelly had also brought a copy of a Monday newspaper. Simon glanced at the headline, and his heart sank. It read, "Gun Cops Take Another Life," not "Gun Cops Rescue Female Hostage." He skimmed the article and swore. Vultures. The story started with a summary of the police shooting of Jean Charles de Menezes on 22 July and then centred on what the writer called the "Islington Siege."

Certain phrases jumped out at him: four-day siege, barrage of gunfire, allegedly only a knife. Where had the reporter got this information? Davies had not fired multiple rounds. And knives were dangerous. Unlike guns, they didn't have to be reloaded, and many stab wounds could occur in seconds. Consequently police officers never considered that a suspect had "only" a knife.

The name of the hostage taker – Roy Wilkes – was given, but not Jenny's. She was described solely as a "thirty-year-old Caucasian woman." Davies was not identified, which was as it should be, but the article concentrated more on the death of the hostage taker and the ensuing and essential investigation of the officer who fired than on the necessity of his action. Now Simon was angry. Armed police weren't rash or undisciplined, as the prose suggested. Didn't the press know how many operations they carried out each year without firing even once? And it would be several weeks at least before investigations cleared Davies of any wrongdoing. More than enough time for this pit bull of a journalist to sink his teeth deeper.

He set the paper aside. Davies would be suffering from perceptual distortion. Studies had shown that memory of actions taken under stress was not reliable if recalled too soon, thus interviewing an officer immediately after a stressful event was counterproductive. Davies would have a couple days before he'd be required to complete a full statement, and both a Police Federation rep and solicitor would be with him when he filled out the forms. However, it would take a long day to be certain details were accurate and his language clear enough to avoid misinterpretation in court, if indeed things went that far.

The procedure was for Davies' protection, of course, but it meant that the Islington detectives wouldn't be the only ones questioning Jenny. Individuals from DPS, the Directorate of Professional Standards, would be interviewing her as well. She and Davies were both bound to events that would unfold beyond their control. Best if she didn't know until she had to do.

He found her asleep on the sofa, Bear at her feet. She cried out and woke. "He's here, Simon," she said, her voice high and tight. "I can't see him, but he's here with his knife, following me like Peter Pan's shadow. I might have to defend myself any minute."

"No," he soothed. "That's my job. I hoped I'd get the chance to look after you again, and now I've got it. Bath? I'll use the scented soap you like and wash round all the hurt places."

He ran the water, and she watched his face, not blank like the detectives' but full of strength. She watched the movements of his hands, which spelled safety. Sometimes his fingers barely touched her, but she still felt cleansed.

Then it was time for bed, but tired as she was, she slept fitfully, and he didn't know how to help. She was sore but not in particular pain. Her headaches had eased somewhat. She'd not been given sleep aids of any kind. He was beside her when she began to talk to him about the images she couldn't erase from her mind. Roy's face, contorted in anger. His knife, puncturing her. Her blood, welling up and staining the blade. His hand on her thigh.

"Jenny, you're home now and safe as houses."

"Not when I close my eyes."

"Sometimes – " he fumbled for the right words – "sometimes when things are difficult, you have to think only on what's closest to you. Not outside the flat, not even in the next room."

"Simon, I thought I'd never see you again. Will you hold me? Will you help me shut everything else out?"

He caressed her cheek, kissed her, and was warmed by her response. He knew it hurt her to move, so he went slowly, hoping she felt the same intensity that he did and trying to avoid all the lacerations and contusions he couldn't see in the dark. Occasionally she cried, and he whispered to her until he thought that she'd turned the corner and lost herself in the world he was trying to create in their bed. When she reached for him, he gently moved her hand away, wanting to be certain of her desire. The next time she touched him, she murmured loving words as well, and they proceeded together. After she clung to him briefly, then like cream into coffee, slipped into sleep.

CHAPTER FIVE

"JENNY, THE SUITS HAVE NEED OF YOU," Simon called
when the detectives arrived after lunch. Strange. She hadn't heard
Bear bark. Had she been sleeping that soundly? He'd been her
shadow, however, since she'd come home, even jumping on the bed
where he knew he was not allowed. She gripped his fur for a minute
before sitting up.

"She'll be with us in a bit," he told them. "She's had a lie-in
today, and it's taken her a while to get going."

Mrs. Casey came downstairs wearing jeans and a long-sleeved
shirt she hadn't tucked in, DI Thoms noted. No makeup, and her
feet were bare. Still a better start than the day before, when she
hadn't been dressed at all, but the detective inspector had no way of
knowing if Mrs. Casey were always this casual or if being shaken by
her experience had led her to be untidy. The flat was still in a state
of minor disarray, pillows out of position on the sofa and
newspapers and post piled on the dining room table. She watched
Mrs. Casey sit next to her husband on the sofa, fold her legs beneath
her, and take his hand. "Mrs. Casey, we hope you're more rested
today. Could you run us through what happened to you, please?"

"Yes, of course. No – wait. Simon, you don't have to go to work
today, do you? Because if you do, I don't want to spend our time
together doing this."

"I'm home today, Jenny. It's all right. Talk to the detectives."

Sergeant Riley started the tape. "Tuesday, 30 August," he
began and then added the time, location, and individuals present.
He set it on the coffee table and took out his notebook.

"Mrs. Casey, what did Mr. Wilkes strike you with? When you encountered him on the street?" Thoms had begun the interview.

"My umbrella, I guess," Jenny answered. "Maybe the handle? I don't remember clearly. But we'd been struggling over it."

"And then?"

Jenny forced herself to think back to her first moments in Roy's flat. "I woke up on the floor. I was too weak and nauseated to do anything. He didn't care about how I felt. His only concern was not letting me leave, and he got really mad when I told him I wasn't Tanya. The first night I slept in the bathroom because I still felt sick. The other nights he shut me in there because he didn't trust me, but I was relieved to be behind a closed door, even though he could open it any time he wanted to."

Thoms asked a question about how much time had passed.

"I don't know. I was muddled, and some of it isn't too clear. Like looking through cobwebs. I must have been in and out of consciousness or just couldn't stay awake because I can't remember everything exactly."

Thoms nodded. "It's a type of amnesia induced by stress. In addition, you had a concussion. You were injured and ill, but your recollections still give us the best picture of what took place. Continue, please."

"The air in the flat – suffocating and stale – made it worse. He didn't change clothes. I don't think he bathed. Sometimes it was hard to take a breath. Sometimes I didn't even want to take a breath."

Simon clenched his fists, angry that she'd had to know any part of this and wishing that he could interrupt the proceedings to bring her something pure and unspoilt: a rose, a piece of fruit. "Breathe now, Jenny," he said.

She gave him a grateful smile.

"Mrs. Casey, what else do you recall?"

"There were pill bottles on the counter, and sometimes he'd hit himself in the head with his fist. He kept calling me Tanya, and I couldn't reason with him. I tried! First I kept saying I was Jenny. Then I pointed out things about him that I would have known if I'd been Tanya. None of it made any difference. He was crazy. And violent – I learned very quickly that he wasn't shy about using his knife."

"When he injured you with the knife, did he show remorse?"

"No. Not once. He was always yelling at me." She felt a wave of love for Simon, who had never raised his voice when he was angry with her. Instead he lowered it, thereby managing to convey how serious he was about an issue without scaring her.

"Could you describe the knife for us?"

"It wasn't a paring knife or any kind of kitchen knife. It was nasty looking, with a large thick handle and a wide blade, serrated on one side and tapered to a sharp point." She shivered. "Could I ask – he's dead, isn't he? Simon said he was."

Thoms nodded. "Every effort was made to save him, but life was pronounced extinct at the scene."

"And Brian was the one who shot him?"

"Constable Davies, yes."

Good, Jenny thought. No testimony. No trial. It's over. She took a deep breath and unwound her fingers from Simon's. "Is he ok? Is Brian ok?"

Simon answered. "Jenny, it's his first lethal. It'll stay with him."

"Mrs. Casey," Thoms added, "we'd like you to know – the Met protects the privacy of its firearms officers. Therefore PC Davies' name will not be released unless and until we are legally bound to do so. You are married to a firearms officer, so your name will be withheld also. Our officers have spoken with the individuals at the church you visited, and they will refer any enquiries to us. Fortunately your book was published under your previous married name." She saw Riley's raised eyebrows. Yes, she was offering more reassurance than she usually did. "Mrs. Casey?" she prompted.

Jenny blinked as if seeing the inspector for the first time. "Oh. Yes. The flat. I wanted so badly to get out! That first morning I tried, but I couldn't unlock the door. I was still weak and unsteady, but I don't know why – why – why couldn't I unlock a stupid door?"

Thoms smiled. "We'd like to be able to answer that, Mrs. Casey, but at the moment the door's not in sufficient shape for our forensics officers to make a judgement."

"No, of course not," Jenny acknowledged. "They destroyed it. It sounded terrible when they came crashing in, loud and very frightening. I heard yells and gunfire and then I couldn't hear anything." She paused. "Who – who helped me?"

"Sergeant Howard took you to the ambulance."

Nick, Jenny thought. Thank you, Nick.

"But before that, Mrs. Casey?"

"I – I threw hot water at him."

"Could you explain?"

"I'd run out of delaying tactics. Negotiations had broken down. You have to understand – I was desperate. I'd given up on getting out by myself. I'd tried suggesting that we go out together – for a meal or just to show the police that I was all right – but nothing worked. He'd begun touching me. I didn't realize until I saw the water heat up that I finally had a weapon. Weapons."

"Water, Mrs. Casey?"

"Yes, I started to boil water for tea. First I thought I could hit him with the saucepan, and then I decided to make the water as hot as I could, to make it worse. When I threw it in his face, I wasn't sure it would stop him, and it didn't slow him down for very long. I ran for the door, but I couldn't get it open. He grabbed the knife and started yelling and pulling me back and I was screaming, and that's when your officers broke in, thank God."

"Steady on," Simon said. "It's done now."

She smiled briefly. "You see, Roy was losing it. It was getting more scary all the time. Everything was a risk because I never knew how he would react."

"Are you referring to the second day?"

"No, not just the second day. All the time. I couldn't predict what was coming or when."

"Mrs. Casey, could you tell us – how was the second day different from the first?"

The sergeant smiled to himself. Thoms was attempting to organise the interview.

Jenny thought for a minute. "It was worse, because I didn't know if anyone knew where I was. The negotiator didn't begin calling until the third day. At last, contact from the police! Roy was distracted. I had time to look around a little, and I started to notice that some of Tanya's things were still in the flat. That was really creepy! I wondered why she'd leave personal items behind. Why did she? Where is she?"

"We haven't located her," the detective inspector answered. She counted silently to ten. She wanted to progress the interview, but Mrs. Casey wasn't as settled as she'd first thought. Perhaps varying her approach would help. She gestured to Riley, who had been taking notes whilst Jenny was speaking. He produced a photograph and showed it to her.

"Is this the flat where you were held?" Thoms asked.

Jenny shook her head. "I don't know. I never saw it from the outside. But it looks forbidding, doesn't it?"

No response, just another question. "Could you describe the interior for us, please?"

Why? Jenny thought. You must have seen it already. However, she described what she could, acknowledging that she never went into Roy's bedroom and wasn't allowed to enter Tanya's sewing room. "It was a lose-lose situation. When I said I wasn't Tanya, he got mad and threatened me with the knife. When I decided to let him think I was Tanya, he wanted affection. When I tried to delay him, to plead for time, he got really angry. Everything was escalating, and I couldn't stop it. If he'd really pushed for sex, I would have fought him, but he was stronger, and I'd have lost. I couldn't let it go that far. And all the time I was worrying about the baby."

"Did he know you were pregnant?"

Jenny shook her head. "I did everything I could to keep him from finding out. I blamed all my symptoms – headaches, nausea – on his initial attack. If he'd known, he would have been so jealous, he would have killed me for sure."

"Did he have a gun?"

"What?" Jenny asked, startled by the change in subject.

Thoms repeated the question.

Jenny frowned and shifted her weight. "I don't know."

"Did you see a firearm?"

"He mentioned a gun. I never saw it, but he would have said anything to make me stay put."

More questions followed, seemingly endless, about Roy's behaviour. What he said. Specific threats. What he did. How she responded. What his reactions had been. Every detail she could recall about how things had evolved. It was hard to concentrate, and she had to ask them to repeat some of the questions. "We've spoken with the negotiator, but it's important that we have as complete a record from you as possible," Thoms explained.

"I know, but – I'm tired. I don't feel right," she said, turning to Simon.

DI Thoms took the hint. "Mrs. Casey, we've a much clearer picture now. May I suggest that we resume tomorrow? Just some follow-on questions, you understand. We'll take our leave now and let you rest."

Riley stopped the tape and pocketed his notebook.

After the detectives left, Jenny sipped her tea. She felt heavy, and the steps leading to the bedroom upstairs looked steeper than she remembered. She leaned on Simon as she climbed them, and even with his help she went at a turtle's pace. He brought her a light dinner which she barely touched. She bathed slowly. In contrast, sleep came quickly.

Simon woke suddenly in the night. Jenny had fallen asleep with her head on his chest, but she was not next to him now. He could hear her soft calls coming from the loo. He found her lying with her hand across her belly and the pool of blood between her legs spreading.

CHAPTER SIX

SLIGHTLY MORE THAN FORTY-EIGHT HOURS since Jenny's rescue, and PC Davies, husband, father, and firearms officer, had accomplished nothing. When his wife Beth went to work on Monday, he told her he'd rest. And cook. He'd done neither. He hadn't watched the telly. He was advised not to do. Or read the newspapers. Beth had collected them before he saw them.

His chief superintendent rang him on Monday. To ask after him and to report that Jenny was all right and being interviewed by detectives. And on Tuesday. To confirm the time on Wednesday when he'd give his formal statement. To inform him that there may be some procedural questions.

He was told not to drink too much alcohol. What was the difference between enough and too much? He consumed what they had on hand. Not enough, but Beth refused to buy more.

She was concerned. He appreciated her attempts at conversation but couldn't follow her trains of thought. He wanted simply to hold her, to hold his children, their wiggly little bodies and chatter affirming life.

He replayed the scene in his mind a hundred times, a thousand times. The X-ray – hostage taker – yelling. Jenny – screaming. His decision to make entry. Each episode ended the same way. He had to fire. He knew he'd have to answer for each round, but he'd had no option.

He hadn't hesitated. He'd seen the knife in the X-ray's hand. Moving. When it was done, he'd wanted only to know that Jenny was all right and being removed from the scene. He hadn't wanted her to see what he saw, what it looked like when two rounds fired at close range struck a man in the chest. He hadn't participated in the mandatory first aid attempts. That was the responsibility of others. He'd turned away.

He'd been taught that when help was needed fast, he was required to provide it fast. He hadn't time to think, only to act. He smiled bitterly. He had time now to think. It was all he'd done since. And question. What could he have done differently? Nothing. The actions of the X-ray had determined his.

He expected to be held accountable. They all did, whether they carried a truncheon or an MP-5. Was his action justified? Was his use of force appropriate? Others would answer those questions.

He was on his way to the Leman Street base. His Federation rep and a lawyer would be waiting for him. Preparing a full statement might be time consuming but wouldn't be difficult. He'd simply put on paper what had been going through his mind since the incident. He was certain of the facts. Nothing would change them.

CHAPTER SEVEN

NOT WANTING TO WAIT for the ambulance, Simon drove Jenny to the hospital himself. At the Royal Free, she was seen quickly, which she found frightening and reassuring at the same time. The pain in her belly and lower back had not dulled, and she was still bleeding.

"I'll just have a look," Dr. Varma said when he came in. He then explained in a soft voice what dilation and curettage involved and why it was necessary. "You'll be prepped for the procedure in a few minutes." He nodded at Simon and left.

"Simon, I want the tsunamis to stop."

He smiled at her metaphor. "As do I," he said.

"And I want your look of concern to go away. I want the reasons for it to be behind us."

"Jenny, in the Special Forces we trained for every eventuality in order to be successful even in the worst case. We do the same on the Job. But there are some challenges it is not possible to prepare for, and this is one of them. Sometimes all we can do is weather the storm." He moved his chair closer to the examination table and stroked her fingers. She had small hands with slender fingers, made elegant by the red polish on each nail. Now, however, the polish was chipped and the nails uneven. Another part of her broken.

"And I want to talk to my mom. I need her."

He nodded. The miles that separated them made Jenny's relationship with her parents more difficult. He'd been the one to report on recent events, but perhaps contact from Jenny would bring a good result.

Then their shared waiting was over.

"Simon, I'm scared."

"I know, love. If I could take your fear away, I would." He held her hand and walked with her as long as he was allowed. "I'll be here when you wake up." He watched until they had pushed her out of sight. Heartsick, he made his way to the relatives' area and waited alone for news.

He found a chair in the corner. There were magazines on the end table, but he did not read. He thought of Jenny, of what she'd been through and where she was now. His chest tightened, and he swallowed hard. He reached out slowly to extinguish the lamp on the table. How would she feel when she woke? With no baby? He sat as still as he could, strangling the armrests with his hands and shutting his eyes, but he was unable to stem the emotions he felt. Calls to relatives would have to wait.

The doctor's voice startled him. "Mr. Casey? Your wife came through the procedure beautifully. You'll be able to see her shortly."

"Is she awake? She's been through a rough patch lately, and I promised her I'd be with her after."

Varma smiled. "The recovery area's not crowded now. I'll speak with the nurse."

"Doctor, did I cause this? I – we – " Casey stopped, uncomfortable with his own question. "I don't know much about women medically."

"Sexual intimacy doesn't increase the risk of miscarriage, if that's what you're asking. Neither, usually, does a blow to the abdomen. The fetus is well cushioned. These things just happen sometimes. But she'll be off limits for a while. She needs time to heal, for her body to right itself."

"Severe stress?"

The doctor knew Casey was still seeking an answer. "Rarely. As difficult as it may be to accept, sometimes there's just no why."

"She'll want to go home as soon as possible."

"I used a general anaesthetic. It's best if she's with us for the next several hours."

"I'll be looking after her. What do I need to know?"

"You'll receive a detailed instruction sheet when she's discharged. Briefly – she'll have some bleeding and discomfort for several days, possibly longer, but most normal activities can resume within a week or two. Nothing more than over-the-counter pain medications will be necessary. Emotional healing is, of course, another matter entirely."

Casey understood. The body always healed faster than the mind. Irrational as it might be, he felt he had failed to protect her, first from being held as a hostage and then from losing the baby. She would be relying on him, and he could not fall short again.

CHAPTER EIGHT

MIDDAY WEDNESDAY Jenny was released from the hospital. Simon rang their parents and collected the newspapers and post.

When the Islington detectives arrived, Simon sent them away with the most trenchant of explanations and opened one of the papers. The police action in Islington was still in the headlines, most of it negative. He hoped Davies hadn't seen the articles.

The stillness of the afternoon was followed by a restrained Wednesday night. Fewer tears than he expected and not much chat. She refused any pain medication. "I'm numb everywhere else," she said. "I want to feel this." She'd already slipped off her shoes and socks to feel the unforgiving wooden floor and the comforting softness of the carpet. He felt a thickness in his throat but managed to get a couple pints past it.

He settled her in bed then climbed in next to her. They'd been apart too much lately, and he missed her physical presence.

"Simon, I want a cocoon," she said.

He could manage that. He embraced her, the bed sheets and blanket tucked tightly about both of them.

When Thursday morning arrived, she wanted to know only if he had to go to work. He did not. He'd rung Leman Street to explain the situation and been given a few days extra leave. Lunch was a quiet affair.

One week ago she had been taken. Did the date register with her as it did with him? He didn't know what was best to do. A river's clear until you step into it. Then the movement muddies it. Should he ask if she wanted to tell him anything or would he simply be stirring up the pain?

He reviewed again the data sheet from the Royal Free. Time seemed to be the most important factor in physical recovery. Mild exercise was permitted once bleeding and cramping had stopped. A follow-up appointment with the doctor should be scheduled in two weeks. At that time she would be told how long she needed to wait before resuming intercourse. Attempts at conception could be delayed for one menstrual period or more because healing had to be complete in all parts of the female anatomy. The list of emotional consequences was longer than the physical. Grief was complicated, involving depression, guilt, anger, and loss of self-esteem. Difficulty concentrating. Disturbed eating and sleeping habits. The duration varied from individual to individual.

He left the bedroom to give Jenny some privacy as she talked with her mum. The relationship was not easy, there being lapses on both sides. Jenny had been preoccupied with settling into life in London and hadn't kept in touch as often as her parents wanted. Jenny's mum had felt uncomfortable dealing with the challenges her daughter faced. The time difference hadn't helped. They had e-mail, but a personal connection was missing.

Her dad didn't address the issues either, preferring to send computer notes with quotes from figures in American history, the subject he taught at university. These emphasised strength and perseverance rather than comfort. Only the most recent, from Martin Luther King, Jr., was encouraging: "We must accept finite disappointment, but we must never lose infinite hope." Jenny still appreciated her dad's efforts, however, and e-mailed an acknowledgement each time because he had thought of her and sent them even if they missed the mark.

"How'd it go?" he asked when she came downstairs. He could tell from the way she moved that she was still hurting. She eased down onto the sofa.

"She was sympathetic," she reported, "but she didn't really know what to say. I know words won't solve everything, but on the phone words are all you have! I wouldn't have cared if she repeated herself. Anything would have been better than the silences. Remember when you told me that I couldn't go home again? That my family wouldn't understand what I'd been through and how it changed me? That has become true in so many ways, but she's still my mom."

"How can I help?"

"Hold my hand. I know it sounds like a small thing, but it has always meant that we had a bond. Even from the beginning, before we loved each other."

He rested one of her hands in one of his and ran his fingers over hers.

"Simon, I think I'm a disappointment to her. She wanted me to go to graduate school, and I didn't. She wanted me to live in Texas, and I don't. She wanted me to marry someone with an advanced degree or an executive position, but I didn't fall in love with any of them. I'll admit that safety is an issue for me, but Dr. Knowles told me once that he didn't consider it an unhealthy dependence because love was the primary emotion. Feeling safe – trusting you – they're the icing on the cake. Of course, she wanted me to have a family, and – " She swallowed hard. "The family part didn't work out."

"Jenny, nothing has defeated you. You've not let anyone down."

"She's proud of my brothers, and she should be – BJ's a corporate lawyer and Matt an IT expert. But now that Matt and his wife have a baby, they've repurposed my room to make space for a crib and baby things. Why my room?"

It was a question he could not answer.

"BJ has a nice apartment, but they've left his bedroom intact. Matt's, too, although he and Emily live in the area. But they're happy, and baby Landon looks adorable. I'm glad for them. It's natural that my mom would feel close to them, but I still miss her."

"We could visit, Jenny. If you want to go. Stay in a hotel. Show you're an independent adult."

She sighed. "I'd rather they come here, but not for a while. Actually I'd planned to ask my mom to come to London before my due date so she could be with me when the baby was born. Now – I don't have a due date, so I'll have to go back to being a tourist guide. At least it occupies the time. And they escape Texas weather. I was going to take her to the British Museum."

"You've already been, love," he commented, curious about her choice.

"Yes, but it's so impressive – what this small island nation has accomplished. Mastery of the seas, excellence in science, literature, and the arts – no matter what subject I studied in school, Britain had always played a major part in it. The museum highlights the birth of greatness for this country. All I wanted to do was experience the birth of one small, precious child, and I couldn't." She paused. "It's just – I wanted so badly to move forward, but I feel like someone's taken away my crutches."

"Lean on me, princess."

She did and felt his arm around her. "Simon, your mom's proud of you, isn't she?"

"She was dead worried about me a good deal of the time, but yes. And of you."

"Of me?"

"Yes, for loving me. Jenny, when my dad left, my mum had to go back to work. I had to be more than a big brother to Martin sometimes. It's not the same, but you may have to be the parent as well. Be patient with your mum. Allow her to get to know you again."

She snuggled closer. "That's hard to imagine. Would – would your mom mind if I called her?"

"She'd like that very much, I think."

"Didn't you tell me that she lost a baby? Martin's twin?"

"Yes, early in the pregnancy."

"She's never said anything about it."

"Not necessary. But she will now. All you need do is ask."

The doorbell rang.

"Who has such poor timing?" Jenny asked.

Simon went to see.

"May we come through?" Detective Inspector Thoms asked. She and Sergeant Riley had returned.

What would happen if I said no, Jenny wondered, or if I slammed the door in their faces?

They moved into the sitting room.

"Mrs. Casey, I'm so very sorry about your loss," Thoms said. She noted Jenny's pale face, bare feet, and loose clothing.

Jenny did not reply. Having Simon near was wonderful, but these two – it would take so much energy to answer their questions. She closed her eyes briefly, wanting to shut them out.

"Mrs. Casey, we've just a few questions."

"I have a few of my own," Jenny countered. "Do you have children?"

Thoms and Riley exchanged glances. "No, I don't," Thoms replied.

Riley was silent and wary. No one ever asked the DI personal questions.

"Did you ever try?"

"Your question is not germane to our investigation," Thoms said, annoyed.

Then she can't understand, Jenny thought. She leaned forward, picking up a section of newspaper from the table. Very deliberately she began to tear it into strips, letting the pieces fall haphazardly into piles on the table and the floor. "Can you put it back together? Can you?" she asked through tears. "I don't know how you can expect – " She rose and climbed the stairs to the bedroom.

Simon saw Thoms frown in confusion. "She's just given you a demonstration of how she feels," he explained.

"We'll need to continue at a later time then," Thoms said, nodding slowly.

"Wait one," Simon responded. "Allow me to confirm that." He headed upstairs.

Jenny was sitting on the edge of the bed, looking dazed. Words, which had always mattered to her – which needed to be chosen accurately and precisely to reflect thoughts and feelings – now had no value. Touch was all that counted. Simon's. His fingers massaging her palm until she felt they would wear a hole all the way through.   However, she was the first to speak. "Simon, it hurts. Where the baby was."

He kissed her hair.

"And other places. The places where he cut me."

"Show me."

She unbuttoned and opened her shirt.

He examined each injury, trying with some success to control his anger at the perpetrator. "Jenny, you're healing. It's phantom pain, a result of your memory, and not surprising. These were inflicted under trying circumstances. But it will pass."

She leaned into him. "I have to go back downstairs, don't I?"

"No. You can choose to delay them."

"But not defeat them."

"No," he said again. "They will finish what they have begun." He waited. He watched her close her eyes and take several shaky breaths. Then another breath and another, shallow but steadier. Finally deep, even breaths.

She opened her eyes. "I feel like I'm boxed in, sort of. But I think you'd tell me the only way out is through." She buttoned her shirt.

He nodded.

"Then I want to get it over with," she said, "with your help." She gripped his hand as she stood and didn't release it until she reached the bottom of the stairs.

Both detectives were standing. "Mrs. Casey," Thoms began. "I may not understand your grief, but I respect it. I'm sorry for your pain. If you're able to continue, we'll be brief." She sat on the edge of her chair.

Simon guided Jenny to the sofa.

"We've been contacted by the Devon police. Tanya Hanson has spoken with them. Evidently she left Roy Wilkes, her partner, when he became violent and uncontrollable. According to her, he wasn't a bad man, but his personality changed. She went to stay with her sister, Ida Hanson Horst. Officers there will be interviewing her further, about the timing of her departure and his state of mind. It's possible that her leaving was a trigger – a catalyst – for his abduction of you. Of course, we cannot demonstrate that conclusively. Fortunately she has no desire to extend or contest any part of our investigation."

Jenny did not respond.

"As you may know, the estate is scheduled for demolition. Ms. Hanson will need to relocate permanently, but she will be able to return soon to collect her belongings."

Who cares about any of this? Jenny thought.

Thoms then moved to the question phase of her visit. Mrs. Casey's reflexes were slow, she noted. The gaps between queries and responses grew, and Thoms was forced to ask some of the questions a second time.

The session did not seem brief, and the fog of exhaustion seeped under her skin. It deadened the voices of her examiners and muted the colors in the detective inspector's clothes. The whole process felt inconsequential.

They were interrupted by the arrival of two uniformed officers from Camden, a pencil-thin pale PC and a colleague with a broad face and bronze skin who looked as if he revelled in second helpings. As way of introduction, they extended their warrant cards.

More police? Jenny thought.

"Why are you insinuating yourselves into my investigation?" Thoms asked heatedly after giving her name and rank.

Confusion was written all over their faces. "We're investigating a report of an alleged domestic involving Actual Bodily Harm," the first officer said.

Simon was white with anger at the charge and Thoms equally incensed about the threat to her authority. "You're out of line," she hissed, the scorn in her voice nearly palpable. "These accusations are baseless."

"She's got marks all over her upper body and defensive marks on her arms," his partner informed them.

"How do you know this?" Thoms demanded.

"Ma'am, we're not at liberty to divulge the source of the complaint," the taller one said.

"She may be using her sleeves to cover the evidence of abuse," the other insisted.

"We've a duty of care to follow through on – " "Her injuries were reported to be – " "Her husband's behaviour could have caused her to abort – "

Sergeant Riley's bass voice simply added to the din: "The DI's seniority means that she can – "

The two PCs didn't modify their position: "We can't ignore a possible incidence of – " "We need to document – "

Thoms joined in: "She's the sole witness to – "

Jenny's scream silenced them all. She'd risen to her feet and thrust her shoulders back. Her muscles were tight and tender, like rubber bands strained almost to their snapping point, and the stretching accentuated her aches. She looked at the two PCs, whose names she didn't care to know. "Go away," she said. "I haven't been abused by my husband."

"Her defence of her husband doesn't mean he's innocent," one of the PCs muttered under his breath.

Jenny shook her head at him and turned to Thoms and Riley. "I've cooperated fully. Roy is dead, and you don't need anything more from me."

She held a pillow to her chest and addressed all of them. "I'm hurting. We're grieving the loss of our baby. I have nothing else to give any of you. I want to be alone with my husband. If you can't find your way out, I'm sure he'll show you." She collapsed on the sofa. Simon went to her. "Make them leave," she begged, loudly enough for them to hear.

He straightened and headed toward the door, his hands directing them and the expression on his face making them hurry.

"Representatives from DPS may wish to speak with her," Thoms said quickly. "You'll tell her?"

"When the time is right," Simon assented. His fierce features had subsided somewhat.

"And the abuse allegation?"

"Someone at Royal Free, perhaps. We didn't mention the abduction during the emergency, but they would have seen the results."

"A logical consequence then. However, I'll make certain the enquiry goes no further," Thoms said.

He closed the door behind them.

"Simon, how do you stand it?" Jenny asked, anger and grief making her voice shaky.

He knew she wasn't referring only to the officers and their procedures. "I still have you," he answered. "When that bastard had hold of you, I feared I'd lose you both. Then you came home, the two of you. Now – there's just one of you. This little one didn't have a fair shot, and I'm sorry for that, but the future's not empty, not in my book. In fact we've a good deal more than we had before. Now we have the knowledge that we can do it. Goodwyn would call that – hope."

"But we never got a chance to know him. Or her. Like when you go to the beach and your feet make depressions in the sand. Then the waves come and wash them away, and it's as if you were never there."

His voice was hoarse when he responded. "But we know because we remember. And because however intangible, we loved what was inside you. And that was real."

"Simon, I wanted to say good-bye to skinny Jenny. I wanted to be fat. Not to be a waterfall wife like I am now."

He saw the tears. She wasn't intending humour, but her comments cheered him. "Come here to me, princess," he whispered. "We've a crisis here, but we'll weather it together. And when you're ready, we'll try again."

CHAPTER NINE

A WEEKEND OF SHORT TALKS and shorter walks. Jenny tired too easily to reach the Heath, Hampstead's natural park. From 220 acres in 1871 to its present almost 800 acres, the original village common of Hampstead had existed as an entity for centuries. Over the years, efforts to develop the Heath for commercial purposes had failed, and Jenny was glad, because during her time in Hampstead, the Heath had become a regular part of her exercise routine. It dared her to reach the top of its rising paths and made it worth her while for the view when she did.

The village of Hampstead, too, had character: the uneven paving stones on the sidewalks, the trees whose roots had broken through the concrete, the slight rises and falls of the streets. Today, however, she was not equal to Hampstead's or the Heath's challenges. The Heath's beauty escaped her. She could see only the trees that had been felled. Their foliage was brown and sparse, but their trunks showed no sign of the hollow within. They had died inside with no external evidence. Her steps were heavy. "I feel like I'm walking under water," she said. She needed Simon's support as they mounted the steps to the flat.

"We'll make it farther next time," he encouraged.

She hoped so. The Heath, home to fields, forests, and ponds, had been first an enjoyment, with walkers, joggers, cyclists, bathers, and artists peopling its expanse. When she needed a distraction, she'd observed individuals on bird-watching tours, insect explorations, and 5-K runs. Summer concerts and circuses were held there. Families picnicked and flew kites on the meadows. When she needed an escape, she'd walked to the zoo in Golders

Hill Park or paid admission to Kenwood House, summer home of the Earl of Mansfield and now the site of a magnificent collection of Old Master paintings. The Heath had embraced her, soothed her, and revived her. It had laughed with her, wept with her, and sighed with her. How many times had she stopped to marvel at the peacefulness of its ponds and the way the wind and sun had rippled and sparkled their surfaces? No matter what her mood, the Heath seemed to reflect it, and like a best friend, it was always there when she needed it.

She read and was disturbed by recent newspaper articles describing the devastation caused by Hurricane Katrina in her country. Hundreds were stranded in their attics or on their roofs when the flooding from Lake Ponchartrain in New Orleans occurred. Others sought refuge in the Superdome only to be caught in a nightmare of epic proportions. Evacuation efforts proved to be too little, too late. How could so much of a city be under water? It was incomprehensible. The pictures of the damage were horrible, from New Orleans across the Gulf Coast through southern Mississippi and into Alabama. Recovery had barely begun and would be slow. Fortunately landfall had been too far east to have affected her family in Houston.

In contrast, most of the injuries she'd suffered at the hands of the hostage taker were healing, though the sorrow of the miscarriage inundated her.

"'When sorrows come, they come not single spies, / But in battalions...'" she told Neil Goodwyn when he came by. She saw strength in his willingness to face tragedy and trauma with others, and his former service with the British Army had caused Simon to respect him as well. He never minimized the seriousness of any situation.

"Shakespeare was eloquent," Goodwyn nodded, "and his words are fitting, because I've come to hear about your sorrows, however you care to express them. As you well know, the initial pain of grief is sharp. Over time it softens but never dissipates entirely. A life has been lost, after all."

Yes, like a wisp of smoke, Jenny thought, relieved that he understood about the baby. She wanted to thank him for not calling her loss a fetus, but her throat was too tight for her to reply. She knew that he – she – had not been sufficiently developed to survive outside the womb, but she still felt that what she had had inside was the beginning of a human being, not a thing.

She went into the kitchen to make tea but felt a moment of inertia. Tea was an everyday staple in most British homes but for her bittersweet. The boiling water had been a desperate move which resulted in her escape from Roy's flat. Now, however, it was a reminder that she had no baby to protect from the caffeine.

"Jenny?" Simon asked, hearing no sounds from the kitchen.

"I'll have it brewing momentarily," she answered, setting the water to boil and placing cups, sugar, and milk on a tray.

"May I pour for you, Jenny?" Goodwyn asked when she returned to the living room.

She nodded and took several sips. Still too hot. Both Simon and Neil added milk to their cups and drank more deeply.

"This is a difficult and complex time. Sometimes our thoughts become rooted in the past, and we are unable to move forward. For example, have you been asking yourselves what you could have done differently? I ask because often grief and guilt come together."

When she was silent, Simon answered. "I would've got her away from that bastard sooner. Alone or with a couple Special Boat Service mates. We'd not have negotiated. Instead I sat in a police vehicle with an officer to mind me and felt useless."

The chaplain made no comment. "Jenny?"

She sighed. "I could have done everything differently. Not written a book about grief. Not delivered it to that church. Or delivered it on another day, when it wasn't raining and there were more people on the street. I could have paid attention and not gotten lost on my way back to the tube station. I could have fought harder. Screamed louder. Something. Anything. I was the one who was rational. Why didn't that give me an edge?"

"No, Jenny," Simon responded. "The hostage negotiator was both rational and trained, and he couldn't convince him to come out."

"And now I'm as unproductive as old yeast. I'm mad at Roy, but I'm mad at myself, too, because I couldn't control my body."

"Jenny, I'd like you to forgive yourself," Goodwyn suggested.

"Do you think I caused this? Any of this?" she asked.

"No, but I believe that you do, illogical and irrational though it may be. Simon, you as well, because you weren't able to protect her. But hear me – you cannot rewrite the past. Trying to do so is accepting blame which does not belong to you. It's contrary to healing. It will make hostages of both of you."

"That's the what-not-to-do advice," Jenny said. "I need to know what I can do."

"You know that already, I think," Goodwyn answered. "You did, after all, write a book about it. The difference this time is that your grief is shared. Talk to each other. Take some time for the two of you together."

"All I have is time," she answered. "But Simon will be going back to work soon."

"Yes, and he'll take his grief with him when he goes. He'll not be escaping it." He paused. "You're sitting close to one another, and I'm glad to see that. It's normal to be rather self-absorbed when tragedy strikes but a bit dangerous as well. A wife, for example, may believe that she's sparing her husband grief by not speaking of hers, yet the opposite is true. The isolation will damage both parties."

"But I don't want to talk about only one thing," Jenny said softly. "I don't want to be one-note Jenny."

"Allow grief to ebb and flow, and that'll not happen," Goodwyn said.

After uttering a short prayer, Goodwyn stood, and she realized that although his brown eyes were the same, his mahogany hair was now flecked with gray, and the lines in his face were deeper. He was no longer slim but slight, and she thought that facing difficult issues with people was wearing him away. He extended his hand first to her and then to Simon. His palm was warm and his grip firm. She hated to see him go.

"Jenny, what are you not telling me?" Simon asked when they were alone.

"I'm adrift. On the water somewhere. After a while I realize that it's much deeper than I thought because it's the ocean. I can swim – and tread water – but I'm getting tired. I know I can't do it indefinitely. The horizon is far away, and I can't see anyone else no matter what direction I look in."

He didn't speak right away, and when he did, the words came slowly. "There was a time – when I was a frogman – when I had to swim out at night to meet the sub. I couldn't see it for the longest time. I had to trust that it would be there, and then it was." He stopped for a moment. "We had to learn to trust each other as a team, to trust that others would do what they said they'd do. Once I did, everything else was easier. We each had to carry our own weight, of course, but the burden seemed lighter when we knew we could rely on others."

She reached out to take his hand.

"You're the other half of my home team. We have to believe in one another."

"But I've let you down," she whispered. "The baby – I couldn't hold onto him."

"Jenny, that's nothing to do with you. The doctor was very clear on that."

"You talked to him?"

"Yes, of course."

"But what if – what if this one's our last?"

He knew her question was born out of fear. "What if it isn't?" he countered. "What if we have so many we can't keep up with them?"

"Oh, Simon," she sighed. Any other time she would have climbed into his arms to further their closeness. Today the motion of his fingers on her palm would have to be enough.

****

Jenny couldn't sleep. She slipped out of bed and sat down at her desk in the corner. Her throat was tight, and she needed to release some of her despair. Not wanting to wake Simon, she angled the lamp away from the bed and began to write. *My Sorrows, Past and Present,* she titled the page.

1. Rob was killed in college. He'd died in a single car accident, on his way to tell his parents that he was serious about her. Had he lived, she would never have come to England.

2. Colin was killed in London. They'd had so little time together, not even enough to start a family.

3. My baby died inside me. Hers and Simon's. So recent, so heartbreaking.

4. My career. After the violence she'd experienced following her arrival in London, further study of English literature seemed irrelevant. To this day, however, she'd found nothing to replace it.

5. My family. When she had lost her innocence through sexual assault, a connection had been cut. Her parents didn't know how to address the issue, so they didn't, making acceptance elusive at best.

Usually doing something more than once made her better at it, but grief didn't seem to fit into that category. It was cumulative, yet there was no familiar ground. She functioned, but without the same faith in the future she'd had before. She'd had virtually no support system after Rob died and had isolated herself when her grief after Colin's death had reached its peak. Nick Howard's intervention had started her on a rocky road to recovery. The baby – it was Simon's loss, too. Something that belonged to both of them. The worst part was not the shock or the pain but the loss of hope.

She heard a rustle next to her. "What's this?" Simon asked. He ran his eyes over her list. "Seems a bit one sided, doesn't it?"

"That's true. I wasn't objective. Melancholy initiated it."

"You loved that young man at uni."

"Yes, and he loved me."

"You and Sinclair had some good years. I wanted you then, but more than that, I wanted you happy. And you were, I believe."

"Yes, we were. But where did it all go? And why? It doesn't make sense."

"Is it meant to? Often reality doesn't respect our plans. Goodwyn would say that that's why we have God."

She was quiet.

"We haven't lost love, Jenny. Come back to bed."

She hesitated.

"There have been times – in witness protection and later when you were married to Sinclair – when all I was able to have was your affection. I was glad of it then, and I'll be glad of it now. And it'll help you to have mine."

"Simon, I've been so focused on how much I need you that I haven't told you how much I love you, but I do." She took his hand, and they went together. Stretching out next to her, he put his arms round her before kissing her cheeks, her ears, her neck. Chaste kisses which she returned in kind. He was warm and alive, and she was not alone.

CHAPTER TEN

ON MONDAY THE DREADED ANSWER to Jenny's question came: "Yes, I've got to go to work today."

How unfair – on a day when the clouds appeared as bruised as she felt, he had to leave. But she should have known. He always shaved on work days because facial hair interfered with the seal of the respirator, which they had to use occasionally. "What if you don't come home?"

She wasn't generally so direct. It wasn't surprising her fear had surfaced, considering her recent experience, but he must defuse it. He put his hands on her shoulders and held her gaze. "I'll be home tonight," he said. "There's no doubt."

The eyes that looked back at her were as blue as ever, but the crow's feet at the corners of them were more pronounced.

"Promise?" she quavered.

"Jenny, I'm more than capable of defending myself, should the need occur, and as team leader, I'm last to make entry on a raid. That means that the premises have already been secured, and any danger is past."

"I'll miss you. Are you okay?"

He kissed her cheeks and responded. "It's a hangover, and I've never had one that lasted this long."

It was as good a description as any.

She waited to cry until he left. Nothing broke the tedium of the day. She stared at her full plate at lunch, but it reminded her of her emptiness inside, an emptiness that seemed to swallow her. It was hard to get down more than a few bites, so she fed most of her sandwich to Bear. She looked out on the weather, the rain coming down so fast she'd have felt submerged if she'd gone out in it. The afternoon wore on, the usual sounds in the flat seeming suspicious and interfering with her rest. When she heard Simon's key in the door near dinner time, she traded in her nightgown for a pair of jeans and a t-shirt.

"No ops for a while," he reported as they ate. "The teams are being reorganised. Davies is stood down. He won't be considered for reinstatement until twenty-eight days after the incident. He's been given office duties. We have two on holiday."

Then it was quiet, neither knowing what to say, the endless evening looming ahead of them. Several times she tried to initiate conversation, but instead of his concise answers amusing her as they usually did, she wished he would elaborate on something. Any topic at all. "Are you sad?" she inquired.

He didn't respond. She asked again.

"More than," he admitted. "On the Job we're briefed so we know who the enemy is, but this time – I've lost to an enemy I can't see."

"Tea?" she asked.

Silence.

"Something else to eat?"

He shook his head.

The evening dragged on, Jenny unable to focus on anything for very long and Simon withdrawn.

She brought him a bottle of Peroni. He looked up but didn't speak, nor did he take the beer. She set it down on the coffee table, but he did not pick it up. She stood in front of him for a minute. He did not acknowledge her.

"Simon, I need you."

Nothing. Had she spoken too softly? She repeated her statement, to no avail. She sighed. We're like prisoners on two separate islands, she thought, marooned by rough seas. Words weren't connecting them; perhaps touch would.

She sat next to him and took his hand, unfurling his tense fingers and thinking about how strong and gentle they could be. In the past he had soothed her by caressing her palm, so she did the same. He didn't break the silence, only responding by covering her hand with his. It was all he could do, but they both knew it wasn't enough. After a few minutes, she released his hand and stood.

She let Bear outside for a few minutes, giving him a treat from the kitchen when he returned. She heard the front door open and close, ending any expectation that Simon would approach her. Finally she went upstairs and lay down on the bed. Their bed, where they had together conceived the baby. She couldn't stay there; despair drove her to the shower. Before stepping into it, she looked at her body, a map with highways and byways like faded ink that traced her history of trauma. There was no sign, however, that she had ever been pregnant, and the rivers of water that cleansed her also erased her tears and covered the silence she could not bear to hear.

The shower door opened. Simon, fully dressed still, stepped inside and put his arms around her.

"Simon, what are you doing?" she asked, her voice shaking slightly. "You'll be drenched."

"Water's no bother," he answered, leaning down to whisper in her ear. "But there's something I shouldn't have done. I stood down. I'm angry at the bastard who caused this, for you, for us, and for Davies, but that shouldn't signify."

She clung to him, unable to respond. She couldn't have said how long they remained together, both soaked but with the water washing away the distance between them. Finally he reached up to turn off the flow. They toweled each other dry, he removing his clothes and she donning a nightgown. She fell asleep in his embrace, wishing that would solve everything.

****

In his absence, Tuesday brought more monotony. When the doorbell rang after lunch, she hurriedly pulled a robe on over her nightclothes before answering. It was Brian! She hugged him before he even stepped inside. "How are you?"

He released her. "On light duty at the moment, which is normal procedure. The only downside is Croxley. He's still not been assigned after his last negligent discharge. No one wants to ride with him."

She closed the door behind him. "That name doesn't ring a bell."

"Clive Croxley, an ARV guy who thought he could do a course and be an instant expert. He failed selection for the teams. We call him 'slightly' for slightly intelligent, slightly qualified."

"What's a negligent discharge?"

"Incompetence, essentially," Brian snorted. "It means your firearm discharged when you didn't intend. This time it was at the armoury, so fortunately no one was harmed."

They stepped into the living room, and she saw his eyes fall on the newspaper resting on the sofa. If she'd known he was coming, she'd have put it away. The latest headline claimed that gun cops were cowboys, quick on the trigger. She knew it was false, but many would read and believe it. "What else?" she asked.

"Not sleeping well," he admitted. "Drinking rather too much. You have any – ?" He gestured toward the refrigerator.

"I can make tea."

"You wouldn't have anything stiffer on offer, would you?"

"Everything, including ale. Help yourself."

He did. "Sorry to come empty handed. I'm not doing much cooking these days." He took a few generous swallows and sat with her in the sitting room. "Meg and Robbie don't know what I did."

"They're too young now, Brian," she answered, "but one day you should tell them, because they'll be proud. You saved someone's life. My life."

"I'm glad for that, but at the same time it haunts me." He finished the bottle of ale and retrieved another. "I'm angry, because he could have stopped. Surrendered. Dropped the knife. JJ, it didn't have to happen."

She liked hearing the nickname. He had given it to her long ago when she'd been a witness waiting to give testimony in a Crown court and he had been one of the officers protecting her. "Brian, he would never have done any of those things. He had peaceful choices presented to him. By the negotiator. Even by me. He rejected all of them. He was irrational. If you hadn't shot him, I'd be dead." She watched while he drained the second ale. "I'm mad, too, because he caused what happened to me afterward." Until she spoke the words, she hadn't known how angry she was. She'd thought she felt only sorrow.

"Are you in pain, JJ?"

"No, I don't hurt anymore. At least not from that." She was silent for a minute. "A long time ago Simon told me that he wanted what you had – a family. And I haven't been able to give it to him. That's what hurts most. And other than wanting me to love him, he's never asked me for anything else. Brian, when we think about the baby we lost, we can't answer the first and most basic part of the description a police officer would ask: male or female."

They heard sharp knocks on her door. Two men in suits, both with official bearing, greeted her. "Mrs. Casey?" the one with the broad ruddy cheeks inquired. "Detective Chief Inspector Bill Woodson, the Directorate of Professional Standards."

His eyes flickered up and down, and although his expression didn't change, she knew he'd noticed that she wasn't dressed. Two layers of fabric covered her, but she still felt exposed.

She heard Brian stand behind her. "PC Davies?" the other said, his thin face darkening. "Detective Sergeant Bob Terrance. Also DPS."

Jenny waited, but they offered no proof of identification.

Instead they exchanged glances. "Mrs. Casey, you are acquainted with Officer Davies?"

"Of course I am!" she retorted, suddenly less than inclined to invite them in. "He was one of my protection officers before Cecil Scott's trial. Didn't DI Thoms tell you?"

"We've read her report, yes. And we have confirmed Officer Davies' record of service," Woodson said, "but we're here to establish certain facts. Your association with Officer Davies – it began before you married a firearms officer and became acquainted with others on the unit?"

"Bloody internal affairs jackals," Brian swore in a tense whisper.

"It isn't an 'association,'" she stated firmly. "It's a friendship. His wife and I are close, too."

Woodson's face remained impassive. He took a step back. "Standard procedure calls for us to question you, but with Officer Davies present, it would be inappropriate of us to conduct an interview at this time."

"Tomorrow then." Terrance stated.

Jenny resisted slamming the door. "Brian, what's going on? If you hadn't been here, would I have had to face them by myself? Feeling the way I do? And I've tainted both of us by not being completely dressed. They'll make assumptions which could hurt you. I'm so sorry."

"I'd guess they're well informed about your condition but didn't let it alter their procedure. Cold-hearted bastards. I hate the process, but I'm not afraid of their conclusions. I'm more afraid of what Beth will do if she finds I've been drinking. Could I have a cup of strong coffee before I go?"

She resolved two things while making it: dress before Simon comes home and ask Neil Goodwyn to be with her when the DPS officers came back. Brian downed the coffee quickly and headed out.

When Simon heard about the day's events, he took both her hands in his. "I've not wanted to worry you," he said. "I hoped this part of the investigation wouldn't reach you this soon."

"Simon, I've already been interviewed. What do these officers want with me?"

"Two separate investigations are being carried out. DI Thoms' brief was to investigate the actions of the bastard who abducted, harmed, and falsely imprisoned you. Her report is likely complete and has been given to the DPS. The DPS is charged with investigating Davies because he fired the rounds whilst your rescue was taking place."

He tried to explain. "Jenny, all police officers receive complaints from the public. Most are rubbish. If we've not responded quickly enough to their concern, for example, or looked at them the wrong way, they complain. We have to acknowledge the complaints, but usually that's as far as it goes. In the case of Davies' action, which was in my view completely lawful, the process goes further, even if no complaint has been made by a specific individual."

"Simon, I need to know what to expect."

He seemed to consider this before responding. "The DPS hate us. Because they deal with officers who are violent or corrupt, they tar all of us with the same brush. Because they investigate fellow officers, we don't trust them." He did not tell her that the mere mention of DPS caused the hairs on the back of his neck to stand up. "I understand the need for the process. The actions of bad coppers reflect on good ones. And good officers don't deserve to be treated like they're not."

"I wish you could be here when they come."

"Goodwyn will be a good advocate. Their questioning may be intense, and he'll have more restraint that I would."

CHAPTER ELEVEN

THE DAY CAME TOO QUICKLY. Fortunately Neil Goodwyn arrived in time to say a prayer before the DPS officers presented themselves. If they were surprised by the priest's presence, they didn't acknowledge it.

Jenny stood aside to allow them to enter, closing the door then leaning against it for a minute to gather her strength before having to deal with the despots, as she thought of them. She'd dressed appropriately today, even tucking in her shirt and belting her slacks.

DCI Woodson, who appeared significantly older than his colleague Sergeant Terrance, began speaking even before they had seated themselves. "We are following procedure which is standard in all police shootings," he declared. "We are seeking information, not looking to lay blame."

Jenny found his statement aggressive, his vocabulary notwithstanding. Others probably call him "Bull" Woodson, she thought. All he needed were flaring nostrils and a hoof pawing the ground to make the picture complete. She was glad she hadn't worn red, convinced it would have inflamed him. Terrance's plump bow tie contrasted with his hard face and sharp features. He looked as lean and hungry as a hound at a hunt, and he was a detective, too.

When the two of them introduced themselves to Goodwyn, Woodson's rank struck her: detective chief inspector. Her first husband, Colin Sinclair, had been a detective chief inspector, too. He had investigated serious crimes, but Brian had never been the subject. He had respected Brian and trusted in his integrity. Did these two think Brian had committed a crime? A sudden apprehension like a wave of seasickness swept over her, and she gripped the armrest of the chair to steady herself.

Dark hair, dark eyes, small. Pale. No obvious injuries, Woodson noted, but her long sleeves and full-length trousers would have hidden them. His time in the DPS had taught him to be suspicious of everyone. Victim? Almost certainly. But that did not guarantee that her account would be honest or accurate. Interviews were his favourite part of the process. He relished what was to come.

Goodwyn filled the silence. "Before you begin to question Mrs. Casey, I'd like to speak on her behalf. She and PC Davies have been friends, and only friends, for some years. He called by yesterday to offer solace and support in the recent loss of her baby, an experience from which she has not yet fully recovered. Mrs. Casey wasn't expecting him, and she has required a good deal of rest, hence her relaxed form of dress."

Yes, Terrance thought. Her clothes covered her well today, but they would find what she was concealing. He was accustomed to looking past the superficial.

"I would like to emphasise: PC Davies did not visit for any professional reason."

Jenny found her voice. "We weren't getting our stories straight," she said with some resentment.

Neither Woodson nor Terrance reacted, the sergeant setting up the recording equipment and starting the tape.

"Be careful, Jenny," Goodwyn advised. "Words only will be recorded, not tone."

"But they're taping it," she said.

"Yes, and the tape will be transcribed. Most will read, not hear, your statement."

"When you came to London in 1998," Woodson began, "were you hoping to meet a police officer?"

She couldn't figure out why he would ask her such a thing. Why was what happened that long ago relevant? "No, I came to visit graduate schools. I wanted to continue my study of English literature."

"You did, however, come to know a number of our officers very well, did you not?"

"Yes, of course. I was brutally attacked by the son of a very wealthy and influential man. They protected me from him from September that year through the following May, until his trial and the trials of his accomplices had concluded. They even saved my life on more than one occasion."

"For the record, what were the names of these officers?"

She decided to give a formal answer. "Sergeant Simon Casey, PC Brian Davies, and PC Danny Sullivan. When PC Sullivan was shot, PC Alan Hunt replaced him. There were others on a short-term basis."

"You resided with these officers?"

"Yes. That type of protection was considered necessary in my case. I assure you, it wasn't my choice."

"Anyone else?" Woodson continued the questioning. Terrance often remained silent early on. On occasion it caused the subject to feel complacent. When he did join in, their combined front was more effective than if they'd begun in that way. Their strategy was rarely planned in advance. Their give and take was seasoned, so discussion ahead of time wasn't necessary.

"DCI Colin Sinclair was in charge of my case. He didn't live with us, but I saw him on a regular basis until my court appearances were over."

Woodson's next words were flat, but she still felt the menace in them. "You did, however, continue your relationship with DCI Sinclair. You were attracted to him?"

She tried to contain her outrage. "For your information, I'd been raped. I wasn't attracted to anyone. I flew home to Texas as soon as I was allowed to go."

"Yet you married him in December of 1999."

"He kept in contact with me and later persuaded me to come back to London. With psychological help I healed from my trauma and fell in love."

"Following his death, you married Simon Casey in January of 2004."

"Why is any of this relevant to your current investigation?" she asked.

"They are looking to establish bias," Goodwyn explained. "There's a term which I personally find detestable – 'badge bunny' – which describes women who prefer to form relationships with police officers. If they are successful in placing you in this category, any statement you give in support of PC Davies can be considered suspect."

"Maybe your officers are unduly attracted to Texas women," she countered with an edge to her voice. She closed her eyes to wish them away, but when she opened them, they were still there. She raised her chin and addressed Woodson. "I would have felt grateful to anyone who got me away from Roy alive, even you. If that's bias, so be it."

A flicker of displeasure crossed Woodson's face. She did not display the deference he felt was his due.

"I can testify that Mrs. Casey's grief after her first husband's death was deep and prolonged," Goodwyn said. "She remained in London because she had close acquaintances here. She had put down roots, not solely in the law enforcement community where her husband was employed, but also in the Hampstead civilian neighbourhood where she still lives. Her friendship with Simon Casey did not become romantic for some time."

Woodson allowed the silence to become oppressive before he nodded to Terrance to stop the tape. "We'll resume tomorrow," he said and stood. Terrance had not spoken one word throughout.

When they had left, Jenny turned to Neil Goodwyn. "Why would they do that?" she asked. "Stop when they'd barely begun?"

"To unsettle you," he answered.

"It's working," she said.

CHAPTER TWELVE

"DO YOU LIKE LIVING IN HAMPSTEAD?" Sergeant Terrance asked when the next interview began, his hair the colour of the milk-infused tea in his cup. Neil Goodwyn had suggested that she make it, if only to help her relax during the interview.

"We understand this has been your only residence since your return to London in 1999," DCI Woodson added. "Why is that?"

Were these questions their attempt at small talk? They seemed to be loaded questions, although the tape recorder wasn't running. She watched them sip their tea and glanced at Neil Goodwyn, who didn't appear concerned. "It's quiet. And I like the open spaces on the Heath. They remind me of home. And it's a good place to walk my dog." She glanced at Bear, who was curled up at her feet.

"Some people find it difficult to master our transit system," Terrance said, "but we're rather proud of it."

His bow tie was askew, which struck her as funny, because she was the one who felt out of balance. Was his friendliness a trap? She decided to respond with a question. "Have you ever been to Texas?"

"No, only to New York and Boston," he replied.

"I recommend the beaches in Florida," Woodson said.

No response from her seemed necessary. Goodwyn gave her a slight shrug. She waited while the two men exchanged travel stories. She didn't believe that they cared about putting her at ease. Had they learned their professional yet pleasant tone in police school? To lure her into complacency? Finally she'd had enough. "I wasn't aware this was a social call," she said.

Woodson leant back in his chair whilst Terrance started the recording and then painstakingly reviewed the contents of her statements to the Islington detectives. "We want very much to be clear on the sequence of events in your time with Mr. Wilkes," he explained.

She heard his sterile narration and shivered. It had happened to her. Scars were visible on her skin. She lost focus and had to ask him to repeat what he wanted her to confirm or clarify.

Woodson's face gave nothing away. "Were you afraid for your life?" he interjected suddenly.

She was shocked into silence for a minute by the question. He was like a snake, striking without warning. Why hadn't she realized his hair was the color of a copperhead? Did his long sleeves hide his scales? "Well, look at me!" she managed to say. "I'm 5'2". He was around 6 feet tall. First he hit me hard enough to knock me out. Then in the flat he used a knife to keep me from leaving. He treated me like a pincushion, and his behavior escalated. He felt pressured by the negotiator and took it out on me. I thought I was done for."

"Yet you chose not to stay in the loo, even when you could."

He was cold blooded. "Are you kidding?" she exclaimed. "I had to eat! And I wanted to find a way out of the flat, and the bathroom wasn't it. And most important, if he'd come in there, I wouldn't have been able to get away from him."

"Where were you when the tactical team made entry?" Woodson asked.

"At the door," she answered, startled by his change in focus and wondering why he was asking her a question he already knew the answer to.

"We need to know exactly," he persisted. "Two feet away? Three feet?"

Jenny stood and walked to her front door. She put her hand out to touch the latch, measuring the distance in her mind. "It was very loud – the door disintegrating, everyone yelling, me screaming – and very close. But he had pulled me back. A couple feet, I guess." She returned to the sofa.

Woodson nodded. "Your injuries suggest that you weren't struck by the door. Forensic did, however, find splinters on your clothing."

Jenny closed her eyes and shuddered, remembering.

"About the knife," Woodson said. "About the knife," he repeated more loudly. "Could you describe it for us?"

"Again?" she asked, glaring at him. "I described it to Detective Inspector Thoms. We've just been through all that."

"Yes, if you please," Terrance droned, drawing her attention away from Woodson.

Courteous words but not a courteous manner. "It had a fat wooden handle and a long blade, maybe seven or eight inches. It was serrated on one side like a steak knife. He wasn't shy about using it. It hurt!"

"Was it the same knife each time?" "Did he ever threaten you without it?" "Did he always have it with him?" "When he put it down, where did he put it?" "Did you see him pick it up?" Terrance had shifted into high gear, the questions forceful and fast. Woodson was poisonous, but Terrance had fangs, too.

"Whoa!" she said. She was tiring and couldn't keep the pace.

"You'll need to give Mrs. Casey sufficient time to answer," Goodwyn declared.

Terrance disregarded his statement, relentlessly repeating the questions and then asking, "When you went to the door, shortly before the firearms team made entry, where was the knife?"

"In his hand. His right hand."

"When he pulled you away from the door, was the knife still in his hand?"

"Yes! And he was yelling that he was going to kill me! And I knew he could, because of the knife!" Bear's bark startled her. She tried to think of a way to feel stronger against these two merciless men with their expressionless faces.

"Jenny, do you need a moment?" Goodwyn asked.

"Yes – no – it won't help," she said. "They're not going to stop." She stroked Bear's head to calm him and hopefully herself.

Indeed the tape recorder was still running.

"Take us through it again, please," Terrance instructed. "When he came after you, did you see him? Did you turn round to look behind you?"

"No," she said desperately. "There wasn't time. I was looking at the door. I was trying to get it open."

"Then how do you know he had the knife?" hissed Woodson.

"Because he was saying he'd kill me! How else would he have done it?"

"According to your statement," Woodson continued, "the last time you saw the knife, it was in the kitchen."

"Listen to me!" she shouted. "I know he had a knife. When he grabbed me, it was with his left arm around my waist. He was right-handed, so if he hadn't had a knife in his right hand, he would have grabbed me either with his right arm or with both arms. And I will swear to that in any court I'm called to." Their unfeeling inquisition unnerved her. She looked around, cataloguing familiar items to ground herself: coffee table with magazines and TV remote, dining room table with centerpiece, Bear's leash on the knob of the coat closet door.

"Our difficulty with your description is the following: When he grabbed you to pull you away from the door, that action would have caused you to look down, not up. The arm which held the knife, if indeed he did hold a knife, would have been above and slightly behind you. Therefore we don't believe that you could have seen a knife at the time of entry by the firearms team nor can you swear to having seen one." Woodson stood.

He uncoiled himself, Jenny thought. Now what?

"Our job is to make certain that Constable Davies' action was lawful and appropriate," Terrance recited tonelessly.

"Mrs. Casey – " Woodson began.

"Why do you do this kind of work? Doubt people? Act like prosecutors?" she interrupted and saw the irritation on their faces.

"All coppers want to ferret out baddies," Woodson responded coldly. "We simply look for the ones who are amongst us."

"Brian's not one of them!" she argued.

He and Terrance had been considered a bit too zealous on occasion, but their gaffer gave them the difficult cases, and he for one had the taste for them. His ingrained distrust of appearances had often led to successful prosecutions. He nodded at Terrance, who stopped the recording. "That'll be all for now."

She did not respond to his stock phrase. Goodwyn showed them out and then promised to stay with her until Simon came home.

"This should have been easy," she said. "I was in danger. Brian rescued me. End of story. Instead I feel like they stomped all over me. What will they do to Brian?"

"They'll press him, hard, but they'll not get the result they're seeking. I didn't like the import of some of their questions, but the crime scene report will confirm that a knife was found and where. I'm sure Brian saw it, as did others on his team. That should be sufficient evidence to satisfy any enquiry."

CHAPTER THIRTEEN

IT COULDN'T BE HAPPENING! The flat had a basement and three floors, ground, first, and second. Jenny was on the second, and there were puddles on the floor. It had been raining for hours, thundering intermittently, the wind whipping the drops against the windows like gunfire. Water was seeping in near the sills.

What to do? Towels she took from the spare bathroom and shaped into rolls were sodden in seconds when she placed them near the panes.

Was it flooding outside? It was too dark to tell, but it must be, because when she checked the ground floor, she could see that the carpet was wet.

London didn't usually have weather like this! The last hurricane had been in October 1987. She couldn't recall any description of damage in Hampstead homes but knew there must have been, since the "great storm," not dignified with a name, had swept through southern England and caused losses of trees at Chartwell, Hyde Park, Kew Gardens, and other landmarks. Signs on the Heath indicated which trees had been planted in the aftermath.

She ran upstairs. Drops were falling from the ceiling. She shivered. The temperature in the flat had fallen. She couldn't huddle in bed until the storm ceased raging – the duvet was damp. Should she put on a raincoat inside her flat? Maybe rain boots, too. Wet clothes would drag her down. Did that matter? Water was coming in from all directions! When would it stop? Would the leaking roof collapse? Were the walls sufficient protection if the downpour continued? Should she try to get out? How, when she didn't know which way led to safety? The lights flickered. Would she be left alone in the dark?

She hoped Simon was not traveling home in this deluge! A clap of thunder made her cry out. She heard a bark and a voice calling, "Princess, wake up!"

"Turn on the light," she begged. "I need to see." And she did see – her husband's blue eyes, her dog's black fur, and the amber glow that illuminated them. The sheets which covered her were light and soft. Long green stems supported crimson roses in a vase on the walnut chest of drawers. She began to sob in relief.

"Jenny, you were tossing like a ship in rough seas. Bad dream?"

"The flat was flooding," she stammered. "You weren't here, and I didn't know what to do."

"Sshh," he soothed. "You've been under attack of late. First you were a hostage, and then we lost something we made together. And the interviews about Davies' action. It's all been a bit overwhelming, I'd guess."

"What can I do? Besides checking the weather forecast every night before bed!"

He couldn't restrain a smile. "I doubt weather's the issue. Dr. Knowles? He's been helpful in the past."

"I don't want to see a psychiatrist again! I just want you."

"This isn't your first nightmare. It's time we did something to deal with them."

She snuggled against him. "You're right. One crisis after another. I've been swamped. Could we go away for a few days? To somewhere arid?"

He chuckled. "I'll see what I can do. And other changes may be warranted. Give me some time to have a think on it."

"Simon," she whispered after a minute. "Remember our wedding when Neil said, 'You may kiss the bride,' and you did and then swung me around? And we laughed because it was so unexpected that the attendants had to jump back out of the way?"

"I surprised myself," he admitted.

"And do you remember Lymington?"

"Our honeymoon? Of course."

"You knew all about it – the history and even the local flora and fauna."

"Poole isn't too far away. I'd heard of it from Special Forces mates who served with me there."

"You drove instead of having us take the train. And I still wasn't used to the car being on the wrong side of the road."

"Wrong only for you Yanks," he teased.

"We stayed in a wonderful old hotel."

"With a shower too small for the both of us."

"The bed was big enough, though."

"It was," he agreed. "A happy time. Even when we left the hotel."

"Huddling together under the umbrella was fun. But driving down the coast on rainy days was even better. Seeing the New Forest National Park. And bundling up against the cold and wind on sunny days and ducking into the little shops to warm up. We couldn't hurry because of the cobbled streets."

"You bought chocolate at the candy shop on the High Street."

"I had to!" she exclaimed. "It came in a Union Jack box. And we found that Italian box with the words, *Da mi basia mille,* and we bought it for each other."

"Give me a thousand kisses," he translated.

"And I found teacups with baby animals so cute they could have been drawn by Beatrix Potter. And flowery stationery which I probably still have, poor correspondent that I am." She paused. "There were some really good restaurants, too. Remember the one with the avocado cheesecake appetizer? And you had roast duck for your entrée because you'd had seafood to start."

He smiled.

"And I was glad there were so many stairs to our room because I needed to work off the calories from the dessert. Sponge cake, ice cream, and sweetened whipped cream, all with the most wonderful lemon flavor."

"*A tavola non si invecchia mai,*" he quoted. "One never ages when at the table."

"I don't remember you buying anything at any of the shops."

"I had everything I needed." He kissed the side of her head.

There had been no worry, no conflict, and no danger. Simon's schedule kept them apart far more than she liked, and the honeymoon had provided a closeness that was tangible, an intimacy she thought could be permanent, and a union that his long hours on the Job could not divide easily. "Will we be that happy again? Will there be sunlight at the end of this?"

"Yes, love." He tightened his embrace.

"Promise?"

"Yes."

CHAPTER FOURTEEN

FINALLY THE WEEKEND ARRIVED, bringing with it slow walks. She gave Bear's leash to Simon so she could hold onto the man and not the dog. As they passed the ponds, she tried to absorb the hope the Heath had always embodied for her – no matter the weather or season, something was always in bloom – but the sounds and colors that should have been familiar and reassuring, weren't. Today she founds its message of growth oppressive. Green canopies beyond her head, green blades beneath her feet – plants seemed impervious, and their fecundity was a subtle cruelty. She was very conscious that she had changed, and everywhere she looked, she saw pregnant women or couples with children. And she had no patience with the Heath's whims, the puddles so few and far between on this day that she forgot to look for them, the wind snappy, tossing the leaves like confetti, and then calm.

Simon spread out the quilt, and Jenny unpacked their picnic lunch, giving Bear a treat so he wouldn't sample their sandwiches. She leaned against Simon and wondered between bites of her ham and cheese whether she could learn anything from what she saw around her.

"Did you ever take biology?" she asked him. "And do experiments about the soil, water, and light that plants need to grow?"

"Long ago, yes," he responded, wondering why she wanted to know.

"My mom liked gardening. My dad would prepare the ground, and she'd let me put the seeds in. Not too close together, she always said."

"What did she plant?" Having devoured his beef and tomato sandwich in record time, he uncorked the wine and filled their plastic cups halfway.

"Mostly vegetables. Carrots and radishes first, then tomatoes, pole beans, cucumbers, and bell peppers. She always protected the beds from harsh elements and fertilized at the appropriate times, but even so, not all the seeds sprouted."

"Do you want a garden, Jenny? I'd do the heavy work for you."

"No, I'm just trying to figure things out and not getting very far." She finished her sandwich and opened the container which held the fruit. "Why do some seeds grow and not others? Why didn't ours?"

He watched the breeze ruffle her hair and followed its caress with his own. "I can't answer that, love."

They were quiet, sipping their wine and watching the passersby smile at Bear. She held out her cup for a second taste of wine, while he downed his and put the empty items in the picnic basket.

They started their walk back, Jenny occasionally stepping off the path in a perverse rebellion against nature just to hear the sound the twigs made when she trod on them.

"I wish it were snowing," she told him as they passed the ponds, Simon holding the leash because Bear pulled so hard in his attempts to get to the water.

"Jenny, it's September," he laughed.

"I know," she admitted, "but I want snow to freckle my face and dapple my sweater. And kiss me gently, the way Lewis Carroll suggested. And make Bear a reverse Dalmatian, a black dog with white spots."

He smiled at the images.

"But most of all I want snow because each flake creates a sense of wonder. And I've lost that since – since – I became just Jenny."

He put an arm around her. "I rather like just Jenny," he said.

In response she slipped her hand in his until they finished their walk, trying to ignore the orderly tidiness of the houses they passed, the walkways swept, the shrubbery trimmed, the gates closed, because she didn't feel she belonged in this well-behaved landscape.

In the past long, slow lovemaking would have been part of their time together, but now she couldn't imagine being ready for sex, and her appointment with the doctor was still more than a week away. She couldn't maintain her focus on anything for very long, setting her book down before completing a chapter and closing the refrigerator door without choosing a snack. She stretched out on top of the bed, not to nap but because she felt sluggish and heavy. Simon lay next to her with an arm across her chest but did not press her.

"I was afraid I'd never get away from Roy," she said, "never see you again. When I did, I was high as a kite but now I've flown into utility wires and been shocked and crushed. It's too much to take in."

He waited.

"Simon, talk to me. About anything. The best movie you ever saw. Or the worst. Your earliest memories. Just nothing violent or sad."

"When I was small," he recalled after a moment, "my mum didn't work full time. She made pasties and biscuits. Cookies, you'd say. Other things, too, but she really liked rolling out the dough. I got to help. My dad played football with me. He was quick and strong. I remember the night he took her to hospital to have my brother. A neighbour stayed with me. I think he and my mum were happy then. Before things happened that he couldn't correct or control. He didn't deal well with pressure, and in the end he left us."

"Yet you still want to be a father," she said.

"A better father, yes, than he turned out to be. Still do."

"Simon, I can't promise – "

"Let's wait to hear what the doctor says, shall we?"

He knew she was apprehensive about her appointment, about possible further interviews, and about the upcoming week with him at work again, and her anxieties disturbed her sleep.

"Simon," she cried in the night, "I dreamed we were marooned on a desert island. There was a lighthouse, although I don't remember anyone taking care of it. Occasionally unwanted guests came and went, but we weren't able to leave the island. I know that doesn't make sense," she confessed, nestling against him.

"Jenny," he whispered. "Sometimes our minds play tricks on us. We lose hope because we think our trials won't end. But they will." He kissed the side of her head.

"How do you know?"

He was silent for so long she thought he might not have heard her question. "In Special Forces selection," he began, "they ran us up and down hills carrying our packs. Sometimes supporting each other. They told us if we made it to the waiting truck, we'd be done. Then they'd move the truck away from us. Out of sight. The parameters, the expectations, were always changing. We didn't have the strength to stand nor the breath to curse them. It was an exercise to test, not only our physical strength and stamina, but our ability to persist without apparent hope." He paused. "Our situation's not unlike that. We thought we'd made it, but now we have further to go."

She understood. "They – life – fate – whatever you want to call it – moved the truck."

"Exactly."

"Will you carry me if you have to?" she asked in a small voice.

"Always."

"Even if I wake you in the middle of the night just to talk?"

"Even then."

She rested her head on his chest. "Simon, when daylight comes, let's do something non-island-like. Take the tube or the car somewhere or visit a shopping center or be someone's guest."

"Let's visit Davies and Beth," he suggested.

"Good idea. I wish we lived closer."

****

Their time with Brian and Beth was like an elaborate charade whilst the children, Meg and Robbie, were still awake. All of them were upbeat, laughing and talking a bit too fast, and happy to let Meg and Robbie be the centre of the attention, their little bodies busy and their little voices loud. Beth knew that it would be a little more difficult to settle them when bedtime came, but she did not restrain them. No one mentioned how strange it was that Brian, who was an accomplished cook, was neither in the kitchen nor at the barbecue. When they served the pizza that was delivered, Robbie ate only the hamburger from each piece and Meg the cheese slice beneath. None of the adults were as selective, and they shared the bottled ale that Jenny and Simon brought.

When Beth had put the young ones to bed, the nature of the conversation changed.

"Neil Goodwyn came by," Beth reported.

"Our two families are keeping him busy," Jenny commented. "I've been desperately sad."

"Because of the baby," Beth acknowledged.

"Yes, and his visit helped."

"The coroner's court has opened and adjourned its inquest into the death of the X-ray," Brian reported. "That's standard procedure whilst criminal investigations are still ongoing. When the hearing is held, it's not adversarial, like a trial would be."

"I attended an inquest after Colin's death," Jenny said slowly. "There didn't seem to be much reason for it because the bomber who killed him was dead. And the coroner asked most of the questions."

"Inquests attempt to get all the facts on record," Brian explained. "They want to make certain that all investigative bodies have done their due diligence. In cases where the cause of death is unknown or a suspect has not been identified, their determinations may seem more relevant. Mine, when it convenes, should be more straightforward."

"Thank goodness for that," Jenny said.

"In other news," Brian continued, "the DPS has begun interviewing the second entry team. I'll be in their sights later this week."

"I didn't know there was a second team," Jenny said.

"They came in through the dining room window," Brian explained. "Your ears having been affected by the rounds I fired, you'd not have heard them. And we got you out of there pretty fast."

"I still owe you for that, mate," Simon declared. "The rounds and all the rest."

Brian shook his head. "Nothing of the sort."

"Are you still off duty?" Jenny asked.

"I will be until the investigations are complete," Brian said. "I admit I'm counting the days until my suspension is over. I'll be glad to be back on ops, if only to get away from Croxley."

"Who's that?" Beth asked. "He's never been at any of our parties."

"An ARV bloke who's soft on Davies," Simon teased, referring to officers who patrolled in armed response vehicles.

"Christ on a bike!" Brian swore. "I hope not. And he'll never be invited. He nearly got Casey and me killed some time back."

"Simon, you never told me!" Jenny exclaimed.

"It happened before we were together," Simon said. "But we've not forgot it. What we do – it's not a matter solely of accuracy. It's also being able to judge when to fire and when not to do. He shouldn't be allowed to carry a firearm in any circumstances. Let him serve on IRVs. Immediate Response Vehicles," he explained. "They don't carry loaded weapons."

"Or NRVs," Brian said, standing to stretch his legs and relieve the muscle cramps in them. "No Response Vehicles. That's what some of our fair citizens accuse us of anyway: not responding."

Jenny was surprised by his bitterness.

CHAPTER FIFTEEN

ON THE COOL, CRISP MORNINGS, Jenny was reminded of how still Hampstead was. A silence seemed to prevail, though not a comfortable silence. It was a lonely silence, a quiet that created disquiet. To her surprise she wished for a siren to rend the air, an ambulance perhaps on its way to the Royal Free, a sign that somewhere out in the ether people lived and moved. She strained to hear a car driving by. In her neighborhood, away from the High Street, the walkways rose and dipped, much as her mood, as she struggled to use her blessings to offset her loss.

The police hadn't returned her mobile phone, although they must have found it in Roy's flat. She'd lost her travel card, too, and Simon had replaced them both. He wanted to be able to reach her. His mates' wives wanted to be able to reach her. She appreciated the calls, although it was more difficult to connect with the disembodied voices than it had been in the past. When the call ended, the comfort receded with it, as if into an abyss.

She had started a list to force herself to look beyond the negatives: *Positives in my Life.* It was depressingly short: *I survived Roy. I'm not alone, because Simon is with me some of the time. And Bear all the time,* she added. She didn't need a list for the bleak features; they were rarely far from her mind.

Nervous being outside without Simon, she looked all around her to see if anyone could be a threat and was glad to have Bear with her, not just her useless umbrella. On her walks she passed rough-barked plane trees that rose high above her, their canopies sometimes not touching until the very top, yet still providing an embrace, a shield of protection from the noises of the outside world. Bear padded beside her, the only sound his tail thumping against the grass when she stopped to rest. There was very little wind, just a breeze that seemed soft when it brushed against her clothes or her hair. When she reached the bench near Whitestone Pond, she recalled Simon telling her once that its thick undergrowth meant it wasn't a safe place to be, but now the seclusion was like a womb.

Wanting to feel something, any kind of sensation, she cupped her hand and scooped up some of the water in the pond. She felt its chill, but a soft, smooth chill, as she spread her fingers and let the water drip through. She thought about the little life that had slipped away. Like the water she released into the pond, there was no way she could recover what she had held.

The daylight hours passed slowly. She tried reading but instead of being able to focus on the words in front of her, others came to mind. Charles Dickens' "It was the best of times, / it was the worst of times," and Emily Dickinson's "I measure every grief I meet." She set the book aside and assembled the ingredients to make bread. Having pounded the dough into submission, it rebelled and didn't rise. She threw it away.

She reorganized the kitchen, rearranged the furniture in the living room. All the flowers she'd received after the miscarriage had faded, destined to die the minute they were cut. Was that why the baby had died? Had he come loose inside? How could that be, when she still felt connected to him?

She hoovered, as she had learned to call running the vacuum cleaner, but its drone couldn't drown out her thoughts. The appliance echoed on the wood floors, none of which had needed vacuuming because the bag was nearly empty when she finished.

At Simon's urging, she visited the psychiatrist Dr. Knowles, whom she'd seen previously when life's challenges had threatened to derail her. Somehow dealing with the struggles of his patients had not aged him significantly. There was a little more gray in his hair, but the lines in his face were no deeper, and they seemed to correspond more with smiles than with frowns.

Most of the first session she spent explaining what had happened to her. He advised exercise and patience, emphasising that healing took time. He inquired about her support system. He suggested that she use a journal to record her thoughts and feelings. She had one, with a soft red leather cover and cream-colored, gilt-edged pages: much too pretty for what she would enter. And writing in it would be like using a teaspoon to empty a flood. Clearly there were no easy answers.

The second session proved more productive, the psychiatrist acknowledging that uphill climbs could be difficult because new traumas often caused previous ones to return, although generally not with the same power they once had. Her recent traumas, however, held power of their own, causing an inertia that seemed pervasive. She recognized that Simon's presence kept her from hitting bottom even when her grief was most intense. Dr. Knowles had responded with a gentle smile and an instruction to nurture her resilience.

When she reported to Simon, he was quiet for a time before responding that people never got completely shed of the things that happened to them. The goal was to keep those things from taking control. When she asked how, he told her that focus was the key. She admitted then that she didn't know what to focus on, and he replied that he couldn't answer that for her, looking like a drowning man when he said it. That made her glad that she'd gone to see the psychiatrist, because Simon wasn't the only one to bear the burden of her grief.

Indeed she found it hard to fill her physical and emotional emptiness. What would brighten her surroundings and thence her spirit? Something serendipitous, like a prism, which makes rainbow colors if held the right way.

She swapped one outfit for another. The pintuck white blouse was too plain. The pale blue with ruffles on the cuffs too subdued. The denim shirt with lace on the shoulders – too much denim, since she was wearing jeans. She finally settled on a red-and-blue striped long-sleeved t-shirt and a navy-blue vest.

On her walks, however, she didn't need a prism. After the rain, colors surrounded her, the green of the plane trees and the beeches now vivid. A woman with red poppies on her raincoat walked by, the leash she held connected to her dog's blue collar. Colors were often used to describe feelings or behavior. Cowards were yellow – but were they lemon, mustard, or gold? Was her grief cornflower, sapphire, or Wedgwood blue? The skies over the Heath were a darker blue at dusk than at dawn, but she would never have thought them downcast. In fact, she resented the glorious blue that stretched above her, because her spirit was still cloudy.

Anger could be white, red, or black. Shock and despair were often called black – indeed, Winston Churchill had called his depression his "black dog." But black velvet was considered elegant, and her black Lab was loving and loyal.

What color was fear? What color was happiness? It was all a muddle. The only thing she knew for sure was that she could always trust what she saw in Simon's eyes and that she wished he were home.

She cooked long, slow meals, beef stew loaded with root vegetables and served with tossed salad and Sainsbury's crusty bread, and roast lamb with her version of Yorkshire pudding, made from a mix. She baked cookies with the aroma of ginger. She didn't eat much of what she prepared but was thankful that the process made the hours pass.

In a further attempt to move from the cold in her spirit to warmth, she accepted the tea Simon made for her, tea with alcohol added to it. She knew he was trying to soothe her, and she let him by finishing the cup.

She served their dinners on the dining room table with candles lit from the friction of Simon's matches. They spoke only of trivial things. During the meals the wax flowed down the sides of the candles like tears. The flames flickered red, then blue. She watched the glimmering flares and wondered what color a smile was, a laugh, a hug.

Her love for Simon had begun with a spark. She liked to think that their shared love had caused a spark inside her to combine and divide, creating the very beginning of a new life. Now that life had been extinguished. Not even an ember remained.

His days were shorter than usual. None of the officers who were directly affected by the hostage taker's actions and death had been placed back on regular operations. She was glad; she hoped the extra time at home would ease the tension she saw in his face and his shoulders. However, he seemed to need space, changing clothes and taking long runs while she finished her cooking. She knew he wanted to comfort her but was unsure as to the correct course. She tried to reassure him, telling him she didn't need his words because his presence was enough. When she talked, he listened, not avoiding her grief. At night he held her until she slept, and when she woke, she wondered if even their limited embrace had met his need as much as hers.

CHAPTER SIXTEEN

THEY WERE ALL THERE when Brian Davies entered the room for his formal interview: his Police Federation representative Roderick James, the solicitor Arthur Wheatley, and the two officers from the Directorate of Professional Standards whom he recognised from Jenny's descriptions, DCI Bill Woodson and DS Bob Terrance.

When they introduced themselves to the group, James felt an undercurrent of concern. They weren't from the Met; he knew most of their officers. Hence they had been drawn from one of the neighbouring forces, a course of action intended to achieve objectivity. In practice the Met's officers had on occasion been mauled by investigators from outside forces, the ones from Surrey being the most obnoxious. Neither Woodson nor Terrance offered any information beyond their name and rank, which was standard procedure. They were present to gather information not to share any. However, Woodson's speech indicated a privileged background, whilst Terrance's did not. Did Woodson expect automatic respect? Did Terrance have a bias with regard to others' behaviour? Had their professional experience given them reasons to seek shortcomings in others?

James, like Terrance, was a police sergeant, a chunky man whose body was rough hewn. Wheatley's large feet supported his frame, and in his professional life he tried to determine whether each case had sufficient foundation. He hoped the current one did not.

Both James and Wheatley had read Davies' personnel file. In addition, they were aware of the suspicions that dogged the actions of firearms officers. James was forthright in his defence of officers at all stages of an investigation. Wheatley would confine himself to matters of law.

They also knew that Davies was a father with a small son and daughter. James in particular, who had two young daughters, understood the impact of stress on a family and wanted Davies' situation resolved as soon as possible. Divorced with one adult child, Wheatley kept his distance when issues of family were discussed.

Coffee and tea had been supplied by Croxley with the addition of several packages of digestives. Neither Woodson nor Terrance accepted any refreshment, although Terrance appeared to be in need of his next meal. James helped himself to one of the semi-sweet biscuits and poured himself a cup of tea, resolving to remain alert for any detail that might give his client an edge.

Woodson regarded Davies. A big man. Comfortable with his size. Did he use it to his advantage? Irrelevant in these proceedings. Nonetheless he was glad they were all seated. It would have upset the balance of power if he'd had to look up at him, although he was confident in his method. Tar everyone with the same brush and see what sticks. In this case he felt more than justified in his approach. It was a paradox of sorts that he was called upon to investigate infractions by individuals who had sworn to uphold law and order, but the contradiction did not bother him. The public must not cease to believe in the integrity of the police.

Woodson began with a review of Davies' service record, when he had first joined the Metropolitan Police, his two years of probation, his qualifying scores on the basic firearms course, his period on armed response vehicles, and his successful completion of advanced firearms training which entitled him to assignment to the specialist firearms officer teams. Everything was phrased as a question to which he was required to reply, and all questions and answers were being taped, by both audio and video devices.

"Service on the firearms unit is voluntary, is it not?" James, the Federation rep, interjected, sipping his tea and sampling a second biscuit. Fortunately his time on the beat was behind him. His Federation job required mental acuity more than physical prowess.

"It is," Davies assented.

"Do you receive additional pay for your service on this unit?" James asked.

"I do not," Davies answered.

"For the record," James added, "neither Officer Terrance nor Officer Woodson have had firearms training and thus are not authorised to carry a firearm under any circumstances."

"That's correct," Terrance confirmed, frowning at James, who hadn't referred to the rank of either man.

"Fishermen who don't like fish," James muttered.

The solicitor Wheatley smiled inwardly. Clearly James was not shy or averse to conflict. He poured himself a cup of tea and sat back to enjoy what promised to be an interesting day.

"When did you first discharge your firearm?" Woodson asked.

"In training after my application to serve on the firearms unit was accepted."

"I'm referring to your first discharge in the line of duty," Woodson clarified with some impatience.

"Outside St. George Crown Court." Davies gave the date in 1999.

"Describe the circumstances, please." Woodson continued.

"I was assigned to protect a Crown witness. Upon arrival at court for her testimony, we were attacked by an individual armed with an automatic weapon. He wounded another protection officer, PC Sullivan, rather severely, and the witness as well, although less so. I returned fire and managed to injure him, after which he was taken into custody."

"You were investigated following this incident?"

"Yes. The investigation was brief and conclusive. I was returned to duty fairly quickly."

"For the record, I'll repeat that: PC Davies was returned to duty quickly," James said.

"The witness you referred to was Mrs. Casey, was it not?" Woodson asked.

"Yes." Davies refused to let the silence that ensued force him to elaborate.

"The Hackney siege," Terrance mentioned after a cold stare. "Please describe your participation."

The longest siege in British police history, it had been bitterly cold. Davies shivered slightly, wondering whether his recollection or the nature of the interrogation had chilled him. "The hostage taker, Eli Hall, had barricaded himself in his bed-sit. He fired at police officers surrounding his location on several occasions. I was one of those who returned fire but without result."

"Were you investigated?"

"We all were. I surrendered my firearms until the enquiry was completed. I was cleared."

"Let me be sure I'm understanding correctly," James said. "In the course of a ten-year career, PC Davies has fired his weapon three times, once in 1999, once in 2003, and most recently, on 28 August 2005. Three, and only three times. And this is a cause for concern?"

"Fatal police shootings may be rare, but shootings by this officer appear not to be," Terrance responded.

"PC Davies, how many operations have you participated in?" James continued. "Five hundred?"

"More," Davies answered.

"My thought exactly," James said. He turned to Woodson. "I can research the number if you like."

"That'll not be necessary," Terrance answered with an edge to his voice.

"Let's focus now on the incident involving Roy Wilkes." Woodson and Terrance alternated the questioning, Woodson opening by requesting that Davies describe where he was when he first heard about the incident. "How long was it before teams were assembled and arrived on the scene? Where were you first stationed? When was your location changed? Why? Were you aware that negotiations with the suspect had broken down? Were you in continuous radio contact with your supervisor?"

Davies answered each question, the process already longer than he had anticipated. He was relieved when James noted that it was nearing the lunch hour. Davies took the stairs to the SFO floor, where he downed a beer from the team refrigerator before tucking into the lunch Beth had given him. He considered a second beverage but resisted the temptation since he expected a slow, tedious afternoon awaited him.

Returning to the interview room, Davies, James, and the solicitor waited for Woodson and Terrance to appear. A subtle message about who was in charge, James thought. He took the opportunity to ring his wife Sheila and enquire about their two girls.

"Everything's in balance," Sheila reported, not an unusual phrase for an accountant, but James knew she was referring to more than entries in columns. It meant both girls had been in school all day with no calls from the school nurse. His older daughter, Lily, was generally healthy, but Bluebell had had multiple heart surgeries whilst still tiny. Stable now but frail, she'd always be small for her age, and her skin didn't have the rosy hue of her sister's. Troubles came even to those who didn't ask for them, and James wondered if that adage also applied to PC Davies. The good news from home meant it would be easier for him to confine his focus to Davies. He consulted his watch. "Slow bastards, aren't they?" he said.

"Speaking of," Davies nodded, as he saw them approaching.

"Give a description of the minutes immediately preceding your entry into Mr. Wilkes' flat," Woodson directed when the interview resumed.

Croxley's delivery of fresh coffee and tea interrupted them. Davies waited to respond until Croxley had departed.

"The team was lined up in the corridor outside." He didn't mention how long they'd been there, how many hours they'd spent being still, quiet, and yet alert. How carefully they'd relieved the stiffness in their muscles, not wanting to create any noise. "We heard a female screaming for help and a male yelling. Multiple screams. I took the decision to make entry."

"How long did it take for the door to give way?" continued Woodson. "Was the victim still screaming and the suspect still threatening her?"

"Less than a minute," Davies answered. "And yes."

"What exactly did you hear?"

"'Help me!' from the female and 'I'll kill you!' from the suspect."

"Did you identify yourself to the suspect?" asked Woodson.

"Yes. Twice. As armed police."

"What was your purpose upon entering the flat?" continued Woodson.

"To save life."

"How did you intend to do that?" Woodson pressed.

"By stopping the bastard!" Davies swore. "Before his hand – the one with the knife – found its target."

If this case comes to trial, the solicitor thought, we'll have to counsel Davies about his composure.

Woodson gestured to Terrance, who produced a schematic of the flat. "Where was the suspect standing exactly? How many feet from the door? Where were you standing? How far were you from the suspect? Did you have a clear view of him?"

The questions seemed as rapid as automatic fire. If he'd been told that he'd be rattled by two suits, he'd never have believed it, although Jenny had said they'd been rough on her. That angered him. What could their purpose have been? She was the injured party. "I told them the truth – exactly what happened – and it didn't matter," she'd reported.

"Intimidation tactics are inappropriate in the circumstances," the solicitor Wheatley declared, speaking for the first time.

"One question at a time," James added.

Davies took a breath and referred to the floor plan as he answered.

"Did you aim?" Terrance asked.

"No. There wasn't time. Delay could have cost the victim her life. I used sense of direction firing."

"How many times did you fire?"

"Twice." He'd have emptied his magazine, but it hadn't been necessary. He didn't voice that thought.

"How do you account for your second shot? When procedure directs that you reassess the threat after the first?"

"Again, there wasn't time. The incident was at a critical point. It was necessary to stop the suspect's action immediately."

"Why didn't you shoot him in the hand? Since he held the knife in his hand?" Terrance was still asking the questions.

"Because I don't work in Hollywood!" Davies retorted.

"We'll strike that response," the solicitor Wheatley directed. "Constable Davies," he cautioned. "You must show care and respect in your responses. Sergeant Terrance, I'll thank you not to provoke my client. He has been more than cooperative."

"I'll rephrase," Davies said with irritation. "Rounds that strike a suspect in the hand, arm, or even leg, will not reliably stop the threat. Bear in mind that we are moving, and the suspect is likely moving. Accuracy in those circumstances is difficult. We have only one chance, not multiple takes, to get it right. Therefore we're trained to fire at the centre mass to render an offender incapable of further harm."

"We'll take a comfort break," James announced, wanting to relieve the tense atmosphere. These two were a pale example of the treatment Davies would receive in court, if it went that far.

When Davies stood, he realised that his size may have been a disadvantage. The others, although average or above average in height, seemed short next to him. He stepped into the corridor to stretch his legs. No one else moved.

"It has come to our attention that Mr. Wilkes was black. Were you aware of his race? Do you have any bias toward individuals of other races?" Woodson asked when he returned.

"Must I dignify that with a response?" Davies asked the solicitor.

"Silence is an option but not one that I recommend," Wheatley said. "Conclusions may be drawn from it, conclusions that you cannot dispel because you did not answer."

"No bias," Davies averred. "None whatsoever. I don't see colour. I see a threat."

"How large was the knife?" Woodson asked.

"The blade was eight or nine inches long," Davies answered, wondering at the relevance of the question. Didn't they know that small knives could kill as well as large ones? And fatal blows took only milliseconds.

"Was the knife in the suspect's right or left hand?"

"His right hand."

"Held high?"

"Yes, his arm was outstretched."

"Did you immediately recognise Mrs. Casey?"

Woodson's expression was blank, but neither Davies nor James missed the implication.

"Does he need to answer that?" James asked the solicitor.

Wheatley nodded. "In this case he cannot choose not to reply."

"Was I thinking about who I was protecting at that moment?" Davies responded. "No, I was focused on the offender. If I'd allowed myself to be affected by what you're suggesting, I'd have gone in sooner, negotiator or no negotiator. My intent was to stop the suspect, to stop the trajectory of the knife. Do you know how little time it takes for a knife to move? Multiple stabs can occur in seconds. If I hadn't stopped him, I hadn't done my job. On the Job it's black and white. It has to be. There's no time for grey. Grey is for all of you who come after."

Correct, James thought. DPS involvement doesn't begin until an incident is over. They then have more than ample time to examine and reexamine everything an officer has done whilst under pressure of both speed and the maintenance of personal and public safety.

"I agree the job is black and white," Woodson stated, his voice correspondingly sharp. "We either cross the line or we don't. And you may have."

"Is it necessary for the process to be adversarial at this point?" Wheatley asked. "My client has completed a full and formal statement. His intention is to give the most accurate and complete accounting of the event that took place."

Undeterred, Woodson continued, leaning forward to narrow the space between himself and Davies. "How can you be certain that you acted appropriately in your use of lethal force?"

"Because I was prepared physically and mentally and because I was given the knowledge and training to perform well in stressful situations."

"What do you mean by mental preparation?" Woodson persisted.

"Mindset. My mindset is that if I have to defend someone, I will act without hesitation."

"Would it surprise you to know that there are differences in the accounts given by some of your fellow officers?"

"Not at all. We're trained to cover the entire plot, so we may be focusing on different areas when entry is made. The second team broke through the dining room window. It took them longer to breach, and the action was over when they arrived. It went down very fast. It always does."

"Constable Davies, do you retract any part of your original statement?" Woodson asked.

"I do not."

"Are you accusing my client of being dishonest?" Wheatley demanded. "That's inflammatory!"

Woodson declined to answer. Only questioners can elect not to reply to questions, Davies thought. In the silence that followed, he saw Woodson give Terrance the signal to stop the recordings.

"May we consider this interview final?" James asked.

"You'll be hearing from us," Woodson said, refusing to give a conclusive answer.

No doubt he would, Davies realised. He felt a sudden foreboding. Several times he'd had to remind himself that Woodson and Terrance were police officers, not legal counsel. He had expected a thorough approach but not their barely concealed aggression. He had not anticipated being treated like a suspect. And one more thing had happened which he hadn't thought possible: They had made him feel small.

CHAPTER SEVENTEEN

THE HIGHLIGHT OF JENNY'S WEEK was a visit from Georgina McGill, wife of Hugh, a specialist firearms officer like Simon. She blew into Jenny's still flat like a whirlwind, bringing with her a free, easy laugh, wide smile, long, uncontainable hair, and bags of baby paraphernalia for her six-month-old son Matthew.

"He's adorable," Jenny said, her voice choking a little. "Those graceful brows – and auburn hair, like yours. What's his name?"

"Matthew. I brought him with me to give you hope," she said, "because Hugh and I lost our first one at fourteen weeks. Of pregnancy. Most people don't understand, don't think you have an attachment. But you do have. And it's a physical loss as well as an emotional one, as you know. Some days I think I was held together only by buttons, a zipper, or the laces on my shoes."

Matthew's eyes were open but heavy. "He'll sleep for a bit," Georgina added. "Whilst we talk. Whilst I talk, actually. I told Hugh I'd do this – address all the things no one does when you've lost a baby. He rolled his eyes but knew there was no way to stop me."

"Something to drink?" Jenny managed to interject.

"No need to be a good hostess," Georgina assured her. "I'm off caffeine and chocolate. It's a sacrifice, isn't it? But it comes through the milk and then Mattie's either wakeful or has cramps and cries. Just sit back, relax, and listen."

Jenny hoped she could get a word in edgewise.

"Jenny, it happened so early that we hadn't even bought anything yet, but the baby was very real to me. People didn't think

I'd lost anything, which made me really angry. What did they think that collection of cells was going to become? Did they really think I didn't already love and have plans for that baby? I grieved the person I'd never know and the future we weren't going to have. It was difficult for Hugh as well because of course he wanted to do something, and there wasn't anything he could do. Except hear me out. And that he did!"

"No crib or car seat or newborn clothes," Jenny said wistfully. "Or *Winnie the Pooh* or *Paddington Bear* or *Cat in the Hat.*"

"Exactly," Georgina nodded. "So here's the thing. Be a broken record. It'll help. Hugh was very patient. He'd come home and pour each of us a drink – I could have alcohol again because I wasn't pregnant although those first sips were bittersweet – and then listen. He never said much – men don't, do they? But I think it suited him. It allowed him to share my feelings without having to say so. He was grieving also, you see. He'd lost a part of himself."

Simon does that for me, Jenny thought.

Georgina paused. "Sometimes I think about the implausibility of pregnancy, the odds that microscopic cells meet and mate all by themselves."

As Jenny listened, she realized that Georgina, for all her pace and intensity, kept her voice smooth and low. That must be what you learn when you have a baby nearby, she thought.

"Ready for more of my unsolicited advice?"

It was a rhetorical question.

"Pamper yourself a bit. New restaurant you've been wanting to try? Do. See a new blouse that appeals to you? Buy it. For me it was shoes, always shoes. Pumps, heels, loafers, sandals, wedges, flats. Even sneakers! Hugh says that I've marked every event in our relationship – and many nonevents as well – with shoes."

Jenny tried not to look at Georgina's feet and failed.

"I know," Georgina smiled. "See what I mean? Lavender! These don't go with anything, do they? That's why I like them. They're so – unlikely. And they make me smile every time I wear them. It doesn't solve anything, you understand, it's just a bit of a distraction and helps the time to pass whilst you heal."

Matthew fussed a little, and Georgina rocked the baby carrier back and forth with her lavender-clad foot. "Find something to do," she advised. "Time will weigh more heavily on you than before. I couldn't handle much at first – or even think clearly! – but making some decisions for myself gave me a sense of power, of control, and that helped, if only a bit."

As Georgina spoke, Jenny made a mental list of things to tell Simon. *Ways to Deal with the Avalanche,* she would call it, because that was how grief felt.

"Reconnect with Simon. Be intimate with him. As soon as it's allowed. You may have to take the lead. It's likely he'll feel selfish if he does it." She saw Jenny's frown.

"But I feel dull, listless. The opposite of sexy," Jenny confessed.

"I felt that way also at first. But it's so important. So much focus on the feminine – blokes feel isolated, excluded. Sex restores the balance. On the Job they're in control. Here they're helpless. And they don't feel connected with you until you've been together. Hugh needed me, and I love him. So I thought about our honeymoon, and then I wanted him! Besides, it's a way of fighting back. But be warned," she laughed, readjusting the barrette that kept her hair from her face, "once that door opens, it never closes!"

The rocking wasn't soothing Matthew any longer. Jenny watched Georgina scoop him out of the carrier, unbutton her blouse, and offer him a breast.

Jenny felt a pang of grief so sharp that her breath caught in her throat. She'd decided to try for a baby after seeing a young mother nurse hers, and watching Georgina now reminded her again of her loss. She unconsciously touched her own breast. Georgina didn't seem to notice, however. She chatted on. "He'll be sitting up any day now," she said.

"We don't know why it happened," Jenny commented.

"That always haunted me as well," Georgina said. "The why. I suppose there are some things we're not meant to know."

Matthew responded after a short session of burping and then was given the other breast.

"So – I cried a good deal – and leant on Hugh – and wondered if I'd ever feel myself again. I just went with the flow. When I had a good day, I reveled in it. When I had a bad one, I just got through it. And then my due date came and went, and it was easier." She readjusted her blouse and placed the baby back in the carrier. "That should hold him until we get home. Sorry to be in such a rush! I've said too much, as usual. One more thing: When people tell you to move on, tell them to! Good luck. I'll be thinking about you."

Although the flat looked the same after Georgina and Matthew left, it didn't feel the same. Nothing was visibly disturbed, yet Jenny's spirit felt fresher and cleaner. She'd been transported by Georgina's energy and optimism. She'd sought solace but hadn't known where to look for it. Attitude, activities, indulgence, discourse – and the other kind of course.

CHAPTER EIGHTEEN

GEORGINA MCGILL, née Georgina Hollister, was the youngest of four children. Her three older brothers were stairsteps. There was then a substantial gap before she was born. Neddie, Haddy – because she couldn't say Harry – and Peter.

Her brothers were delighted with her and eager to teach her. She walked and talked early, but she wasn't precocious; she simply had a surfeit of instructors. Equally enchanted by her brothers as they were with her, Georgina was eager to please but never to her own detriment, because she never believed that anyone would hurt her. With her brothers looking out for her, no one did. So for most of her life she'd have said that she had only happy days.

Other than giving her a head start, they did not coddle her overmuch on the sport fields. She was expected to kick or catch the ball as well as the rest of them. And run. She wore her auburn hair short so they couldn't grasp it, however briefly. Predictably they called her "Red," which annoyed her because from a very early age, she knew her hair was more brown than red.

As she grew, her brothers parented her as much as her mum and dad did. They encouraged her to speak her mind, as they did, and so she did. Her mother despaired at her unladylike behaviour, and indeed, she sometimes went too far. Her brothers teased her about being a plus and a minus, and whilst there was some truth in their laughter, she liked being included their joshing. It made her feel equal.

Two of her brothers studied law, the other mathematics. She read history, fascinated by how individuals had used their forthrightness. Churchill had used his, at first without result, to warn of the Nazi menace and later to galvanise his countrymen to persist until victory was theirs. False frankness with charisma could lead people to war, as Hitler had done. A straightforward approach could also work without words: Mother Teresa had been forthright in service. The character trait Georgina had been praised and criticised for had been used by some for good and others for evil.

When she was a teenager, Peter was seriously injured in a traffic accident. Extended rehabilitation was required following his surgery, and for a time he had to set aside his legal studies. Progress was painful and slow, but after a brief period of shock, Georgina became his greatest cheerleader. She would not allow him to give up; no matter how depressed he became, he could not disabuse her faith in him. She regaled him with stories of famous Peters in history and was never satisfied until he'd taken at least one more step than the physiotherapist had instructed. Over time he developed the ability to stand without assistance, and when she saw him take his first steps – his limp notwithstanding – she felt that her righteous anger at the injustice he had suffered was vindicated. His sedentary period gave him additional time to prepare for his examinations, and multiple offers of employment resulted. She was not surprised when he decided to use his legal training and expertise to defend people whom the system did not serve.

Hugh McGill was well aware of the crisis which had threatened her family and her role in her brother's healing. He had been intrigued by her commitment to his recovery. Some wives were impatient with the amount of time their husbands spent on the Job and the inherent risk that came from carrying a firearm, but he thought that Georgina would give him staunch support should something unanticipated happen to him. He'd disclosed the nature of his employment to her early in their relationship, and she had both encouraged him and understood the necessity of his restraint.

He'd been flattered by her candid compliments of his appearance, but he fell in love with what he called her freshness, which cleared the cobwebs he'd inherited from his staid family. He trusted her because with her openness, he always knew where he stood with her, and he promised honesty and faithfulness in return. To his credit, he never used her nickname. He cautioned her, however, in the exercise of her verbal skills. With maturity came judgement about when and where to speak out. Like the figures in history she'd studied, she could use her frankness to heal or to hurt.

She was passionate. Setbacks did not deter her. He spent his days in activities that protected others. When she confessed that she wanted to be more like him, he married her. Since then she had endeavoured to make her trademark directness her gift.

CHAPTER NINETEEN

SIMON CASEY watched his wife, more animated than she'd been in some time. She was relating the news from Enid Stanley, the librarian who lived with her historian husband in one of the flats in their block, and laughing that she called her stuffy Wilfred, "Freddie."

"I'm not sure which one is more pedantic," she continued, "but maybe that's why they get along. And they're both round in the same places! They probably ran into each other in the stacks and never checked out anyone else!"

Smiling at her humour, he took a second bottle of ale from the refrigerator and poured a glass of wine for her. A little bit relaxed her and brought a slight flush to her cheeks, which he thought was lovely.

"They found a diary," she reported as they ate their beef baguettes. "From a great-great-aunt in Enid's family who served with the VAD – the Voluntary Aid Detachment – in World War One. She was trained in some nursing skills but wasn't fully qualified as a nurse. Enid said they found it in a box in someone's attic and want to have it transcribed. I never felt I connected with her, so I was surprised by her disclosure. It must be a measure of her excitement about it, but she's so reserved it's hard to tell."

Simon was glad for Jenny's enthusiasm, so rare lately, but impatient to hear the issue she'd not addressed yet, her followup visit to the doctor. Should he ask? He'd not known what was best since they lost the baby. Like navigating through uncharted waters, he'd often felt he didn't have the right words or enough of them.

He'd lost mates, though they had been fully formed fit men who'd accepted there was risk in their military service, not a wee one who couldn't survive outside the protection of Jenny's body. The extra pints he'd consumed then hadn't helped this time. And he couldn't lose himself in her, as he would have in the past. They both still struggled on occasion even to express affection when they knew they could not follow through.

However, she'd seemed on a more even keel lately. Goodwyn's visit had given her a lift, as had Davies', and the more recent time spent with McGill's wife had resulted in some positive changes. She'd been more open about her feelings and hadn't pressed him for his nor objected to his frequent runs. Her inner resilience manifesting itself, he hoped. She needed it. After worrying about her parents' safety during Hurricane Rita, she'd called, only to hear complaints about the inconvenience, the record high heat, the traffic jams during evacuation, and the downed limbs and other debris they'd had to clean up later at home. They'd then apologised profusely for their focus and renewed their invitation for her to visit. She hadn't committed herself one way or the other. She had received a sympathy card from her brother Matt and his wife and had tried not to feel disappointed that it had been a purchased sentiment and not a personal note, their new baby notwithstanding. BJ had not communicated with her at all.

In contrast she'd heard from the pastor at the Methodist church on Caledonian Road, where she had visited just prior to Roy accosting her. In his first communication he'd expressed relief that she had been rescued from her ordeal and in his second, condolences for her loss and news that a grief support group in the church would be using her book as a resource. She had been surprised and deeply touched that someone who had met her only once would be so thoughtful and complimented because he had recommended her book to other congregations. It was time for her to resume its distribution.

For his part Casey had wanted to do something. First, he'd rearranged the pictures in the sitting room, hanging some of them upside down. His effort had resulted in a brief moment of levity from Jenny, and she'd hugged him and insisted that she preferred the new perspective, so he considered his time well spent.

In addition, he'd met with Sean MacKenna, a retired ex-copper who had watched Jenny previously, and requested soft surveillance for her. He didn't anticipate a threat, but a bit of protection would do no harm. Daily monitoring wasn't required, just an appearance often enough for her to feel that she wasn't alone.

She'd been reassured when he told her. "I'll feel better about returning to the school in Highgate," she'd said. "They want me to talk to teenagers this time, but I may still introduce them to works by American poets. It'll capture their attention better if the verses are unfamiliar to them. 'O Captain! My Captain!' or 'The Raven.' Could we let Mr. MacKenna know when I'm scheduled? So he could be available?"

He agreed. He'd also taken what was for him a bigger step: asked his ops supervisor about restricted duty. After meeting with the chief super, Denison had reported that he'd been assigned to the OCU Commander's Patrol. "Operational Command Unit," he explained to Jenny. "I'll do whatever I'm asked. Special projects, security consultations, advising visitors from other forces, providing short-term instruction, and the like. Some days I'll be home; on others I'll have shorter hours than the teams. None extended."

"For how long?"

"Two months max."

He was taken aback when her eyes filled with tears.

"Jenny, what's wrong? This is a good thing."

"I know," she managed. "It is for me. But it's a sacrifice for you. And it's necessary only because I've become so dependent, so helpless."

"You've had a setback," he responded. "We both have. Easier to make it through if we're together more. That's all."

For the first time a smile peeked through her tears. She gave him a prolonged hug.

After resettling herself, she continued. "I told Enid I'd like to help with the transcription, if they'll let me. I've been looking for a constructive way to spend my time, and this could be it. They're very protective of it, of course, but since we live in the same building, it would never be far from them. She's going to check with Freddie and let me know."

She needed a routine. Perhaps transcribing the diary would provide that. However, she still hadn't addressed the news he sought. Their dinner now completed, she hadn't mentioned her physical examination. He could hold back no longer. "Jenny," he said, "what did the doctor say? Are you all right?"

She had been about to clear their plates but now set them down on the table. She didn't meet his eyes. "I was nervous, and I was right to be. It's bad news. He gave me birth control. He wants us to wait another cycle or two."

He held his breath.

"To give us the best chance of conception. So I'll be as healthy as possible through and through."

"I want that as well, Jenny. For you to heal completely."

"But then who knows if – if – it seems so long!" She began to cry.

"What did he say about us, Jenny?"

"We're okay. I'm okay," she whispered.

"Then it's good news."

Her tears were still coming.

"Jenny, why wouldn't you tell me this straightaway? We've both had a loss, but I thought we still had each other." He stood and went to her, taking her left hand in his. "When we exchanged rings, we made promises. For better or worse, as I recall." They'd never been apart this long. He wanted to hold her, to comfort her in the way he knew best. Didn't she want the same? He sighed. He had spoken more firmly than he'd intended. "If you need more time, I can give you that, but I need you to talk to me. Not push me away. I thought we were a team."

Her heart broke. Her stoic husband needed comfort, and she had been too focused on herself to see it. She had thought her grief deeper and sharper than his, but was that true? He had simply chosen not to burden her with his. "Simon," she sobbed. "I'm sorry. I'm scared, and I've lost my way."

"Come to me then, princess," he said more gently. "I'll not hurt you. Don't you know that? Come home."

They left the dishes. He ran a bath for her, resolving not to hurry her. There were times in the past when her bath had been a prelude to more significant physical activity. On those occasions she'd responded by stroking his shoulders and chest, leaning forward for a kiss, and smiling at his attempts to restrain himself. Some baths were therefore shorter than others, but their anticipation was enhanced nonetheless. Tonight, however, although she was healed on the outside, she seemed absent as he washed her, and he began to doubt their success.

After settling her in bed, he stripped off for a quick rinse himself. He then resumed his ministrations. He kissed her fingers, her palm, her wrist, the inside of her elbow. He cupped her face in his hands. "Are we stopping?" he asked. "It's your call."

"Simon, I want us to be together. I'm sorry I'm so slow," she murmured. "Please don't give up on me. I love you."

He didn't consider a verbal response necessary, and besides, she had followed her words with kisses. Gradually they joined, and she didn't move away from him after. Eventually he did, but every time he shifted his position during the night, she moved closer until at last they shared one pillow. He liked having her near.

She also liked the nearness. For a time when her bare body had touched his, she'd felt a newness, a hope, a healing – but one so fragile that it dissolved when they separated. Whole together, broken apart.

In the morning she begged him not to go and wept when he did. He soothed her as best he could but left with a heavy heart, wondering why their lovemaking had opened more wounds than it had closed. When he rang during the day, however, she seemed recovered, attributing her upset to undertow, the oceanic current that could pull swimmers out to sea when they thought they were in safe waters.

CHAPTER TWENTY

"PC DAVIES TO SEE YOU, SIR," Croxley announced.

"Thank you, Davies, for answering my summons so quickly," Chief Superintendent Brierly said. "Do come through." He nodded to Croxley. "That'll be all."

Chief Superintendent Morgan Brierly wasn't the only officer in the room, Davies noted. Chief Inspector Carl Denison was present as well. "Sir," he said first to one and then to the other. Seeing Denison was a good sign. This meet must concern his reinstatement to firearms operations.

Brierly indicated the chairs at the conference table. Flanked by windows that overlooked the police car park, it dominated the Chief Super's office. As Davies chose his seat, he could see vehicles below marked with the distinctive yellow dots that identified them as armed police transport. He'd be assigned to one of those soon, he hoped, back to a productive life instead of this treadmill where all he could do was run in place. For some reason his eyes were drawn to the horizon, where the skyscraper St. Mary Axe stood. It had replaced a building bombed by the IRA in the early nineties. A bad omen? Surely not. Since its construction, it had been referred to in a lighthearted way as the Gherkin. A good omen then. He felt his heartrate increase in anticipation.

Davies respected both officers, as did the rank and file. Denison, a lanky man with prematurely thinning hair, had been in charge of operations for several years and still kept his firearms qualifications current. Brierly, his compact frame a bit older, was still fit. After accepting the post of chief superintendent, he had gone through firearms training voluntarily to give himself an understanding of the issues his officers faced. He dressed the way the troops did except for the shoulder boards.

"I have managed to obtain an unofficial copy of the forensic report on the market estate flat of Roy Wilkes," he began. "I asked Carl to join us because this report may give us an early indication as to how far the investigation of the shooting at that location will go. I'd like to review its contents with you, to make you aware of the relevant passages and their import. I'll then leave it for you to examine in its entirety, although I cannot allow it to be removed from this room."

Denison spoke. "As you know, we have two officers whose actions, taken in 1999, are still being questioned. More than questioned, actually. They've been hard done by. Besieged."

He didn't give their names; he didn't have to do. Every firearms officer, Davies included, knew them. Their nightmare had begun six years ago. They'd received information about a man carrying a sawn-off shotgun in a bag. When the two officers arrived at the scene and identified themselves, the suspect raised the bag in a threatening manner. Both officers had fired, one of them killing the suspect.

They'd been through multiple investigations, reviews, and referrals to the Crown Prosecution Service, only to have their situation turn from bad to worse. Reportedly new information from earlier in the year had shown that the suspect had been shot in the back. Consequently the officers had been arrested on suspicion of murder and other charges. Fortunately, Davies thought, his situation was clear. His suspect had possessed a deadly weapon. He had witnesses to his action, and that action had saved the life of a member of the public.

"A more recent fatal shooting, which occurred in the spring of this year, has still not been ruled lawful," Denison continued. "The circumstances being what they were – a gangster reaching for a gun when our officer fired – one of our most experienced officers, I might add – a quick resolution should have resulted and not this unconscionable delay." He realised that he'd raised his voice a bit and took a deep breath to moderate his frustration. "And it's unclear at this time whether the officers who mistakenly shot the young Brazilian de Menezes after the tube bombings this summer will be charged with murder or manslaughter."

More history, Brian thought. Relevant to his circumstance or not?

"We are only as good as our intelligence," Brierly commented.

"My officers – indeed, our officers – " Denison emphasised, "are working under extremely stressful conditions. I'm keen for any information that can resolve this current enquiry."

Both men seated themselves across from Davies, who managed not to let his impatience show.

Brierly nodded. "Yes, we are all deeply concerned," he responded heavily. "We trust in the integrity of our officers, and we regret the turn of events. We must, however, also trust in our legal system." He opened the folder. "Returning to the matter to hand, there is overwhelming evidence of Mr. Wilkes' presence in the flat and of his medical condition. There is also evidence of the previous occupancy of another individual, female, through the presence of clothing and other items, although it does not appear that any violence was done to her there."

He turned several pages.

The Chief Super was thorough, Davies knew, but he wished the issue of his reinstatement would be addressed first. This document should confirm the facts in his formal statement and pave the way for his return to operational duty. His obligatory 28-day suspension period had expired the previous week. The timing, therefore, was right.

"Mrs. Casey's presence has been confirmed. We know that she was injured as well as sick because drops of blood, although most not overlarge in quantity, were found at a number of locations. In addition, face sheets in the lavatory held chemical composition consistent with tears." He paused. "It's difficult for me to say, but we therefore know that she cried."

Davies found it difficult to hear as well. He shifted his weight in his chair. "Will this data be shared with Casey?" he asked.

Brierly and Denison exchanged glances. "It's unnecessary," Denison responded. "His wife has received medical treatment. In addition, she will have related her experiences to him. She has been interviewed by detectives both from the Islington nick and DPS. He will have been present for some if not all of these. I consider him fully informed."

And don't wish him inflamed all over again, Davies thought.

"To continue," Brierly said, "there were no firearms found anywhere in the flat. All kitchen knives and other implements were in their appropriate locations. The knife which both you and Mrs. Casey described as being held by Mr. Wilkes was found, bearing Mr. Wilkes' fingerprints and Mrs. Casey's blood."

They heard a knock at the door. "Tea, sir?" Croxley inquired.

Brierly glared at him and spoke slowly and firmly. "No. We do not wish to be disturbed."

He waited for the door to close and for the sound of Croxley's footsteps to recede.

Brierly dropped his official tone for a moment. "Davies, we in this room are firearms officers. We share a unique responsibility and perspective which sets us apart from most who serve Her Majesty. I would like to emphasise: You are the Job, yet you are more than the Job. Yes, you are a teammate, but you are also a husband, a father, a son, and a friend. During this next phase of your life I recommend that you give extra focus to these other roles."

Why am I hearing this? Davies wondered. He took a deep breath.

Brierly sighed. "It is difficult sometimes for those outside our unit to understand that judgements must be made in fractions of a second and that those judgements can have serious consequences. We'd not be human if we didn't on occasion have regrets for actions we have taken or been forced to take. That said, I'd not like you to question yourself overmuch. Chief Inspector Denison and I will, of course, follow this through with you, as will your Federation rep and solicitor."

Apprehension began to roll across Davies' stomach. He glanced at Chief Inspector Denison, whose face had darkened.

"The difficulty is the location of the knife. It was not found anywhere near the door or in plain view in the sitting room or on any of the articles of furniture. Rather, it was under the sofa in the southwest corner of the sitting room, a considerable distance – " he thumbed through the report – "over ten feet from where Mr. Wilkes was reportedly standing when you made entry and fired. The carpet was in poor condition but not the sort of surface that would have allowed a knife to slide."

Davies' misgivings had now multiplied. Get on with it, he thought.

The chief superintendent closed the file. "It is not the brief of forensic investigators to draw any conclusions from what they discover in the course of their examinations, rather solely to document their findings. However, the DPS will require at the very least a reasonable explanation for the presence of the knife there. Therefore your reinstatement to armed policing is on hold. There will be further interviews to determine if you can establish a sequence of events to account for this. You will be notified when these are scheduled."

Reinstatement on hold? Davies could not say the words aloud. For how long? he wanted to ask, but the Chief Super was still speaking.

"Records of all interviews, forensic data, post-mortem, and so forth, collected by DPS, will be eventually turned over to the IPCC who will in due course make a ruling. At present – your statement and the statements of others notwithstanding – it appears that you may have killed an unarmed man."

PART THREE

The Assessment

"There is only the fight to recover what has been lost
And found and lost again and again..."

T. S. Eliot

CHAPTER ONE

PC BRIAN DAVIES had not shifted since the senior officers had departed. Not left his chair at the conference table. Not opened the folder. Swathed in disbelief, he could not summon the strength to move.

He closed his eyes. The image in his mind was as clear as it had been when he'd entered the X-ray's flat: a large knife with a serrated edge held high in the X-ray's hand, his fingers wrapped round the hilt. How could he describe it so well if it hadn't been there? He was telling the truth. Not the truth as he saw it but the absolute unimpeachable truth. He was careful, deliberate in his approach. The speed with which he'd acted did not negate that. He knew that some of his mates described him as steady. In his line of work, that was a good thing to be. But he didn't feel steady now. Tremors of uncertainty were infecting him.

What would happen to him? The two firearms officers Denison had mentioned – their ordeal had begun six years ago. For six years they'd sworn their action was appropriate. For six years their lives had been threatened with prosecution. There had been multiple police investigations, inquests, referrals to the Crown Prosecution Service, and judicial reviews. New evidence had come to light recently, resulting in charges of murder against them and spawning even more violent media attacks. When their names had become known, it had been difficult for their wives but worse for their children. They'd been taunted at school, their classmates accusing their fathers of being killers.

He'd heard that scientific data, positive to the defence, had been presented not long ago to the CPS, but no one could predict what their determination would be or when.

His children were too young to understand the circumstances of his action but not too young to be hurt by abusive comments. Was that what awaited him? Years of being unable to protect his family? Beth was strong, but she had already commented on the changes in him, his nightmares, his drinking, the temper he'd never had before, his unreliable libido, the times of voluntary isolation. These could worsen. He would not be a whole man.

The officers involved in the July Stockwell shooting – against a suspected terrorist in a tube station – were still awaiting a ruling on their actions. No one knew if criminal charges would be brought. In his view they had simply done what they had been ordered to do, but an innocent individual had died.

His job. The Job. The Met would not fire him whilst investigations were under way, but he'd not be allowed to do the job he'd trained to do. His skills and training wasted, he'd be reduced to escorting visitors and serving tea. Like Croxley. He swore aloud. He could be facing years of suspicion, years of baseless accusations in the court and in the press, years of having to defend himself.

He allowed his mind to wander for a moment. If there'd been no knife in the X-ray's hand, what then? He'd likely have broken Jenny's neck. He was threatening to kill her. Firing even then would have saved her life. But there had been a knife. He had seen it. If he'd held fire, the X-ray would have plunged it into her abdomen. He could not use the term for hostage now. She was Jenny, and she'd been carrying a baby in that abdomen. If he'd held fire, the X-ray would have taken two lives.

Neither Brierly nor Denison had referred to his firing of two rounds, that action being outside the scope of the forensic report. That issue, however, had been raised during his interrogation by the DPS officers, and he felt certain that he'd hear more about it in the future. Were two rounds too many to save two lives? He did not think so. And now Jenny and Casey were grieving the loss of an innocent life.

He could restrain his anguish no longer. He bowed his head. His shoulders shook, for Beth, for his children, for Jenny, for her baby, and for his career, which he no longer controlled. With a few trembling sighs, he recovered himself. He could not recall the last time he'd wept, even briefly. That alone set this day apart from any he'd experienced before.

What to do then? Being angry at the X-ray wasn't productive at this point, but he was anyway. Follow it through, as Denison and Brierly had said they would do. He knew who he was, what he had done, and why. He would not quit. Others might have their hands on the rudder, but for him the way ahead was clear. Integrity demanded that he continue to tell the truth, no matter how it was received. Others' belief that he was lying did not signify.

One more thing. Love demanded that he protect his family. Even if it meant leaving them, he could not permit them to be drowned in the cruel waves that lay ahead.

CHAPTER TWO

ANOTHER LONG DAY FOR JENNY. She thought she'd adjusted to missing Simon until the loss of the baby. Before that grief, she had felt alone but not suffocated with loneliness. Now just dressing was a trial. Bright colors seemed to emphasize her paleness, while dark ones accentuated lines she hadn't noticed before in her face. Nothing in her closet appealed to her, so she put on a shirt of Simon's with her jeans. She considered walking to Waterstone's to find something new to read but discarded the idea when she realized that her concentration wasn't equal even to a crossword puzzle.

Walking on the Heath with Bear would have to suffice to distract her. People often saw his wagging tail and stopped to speak with him. Some even knew his name, although they didn't know hers, a fact which in the past would have caused her to smile. Today, however, their friendliness seemed invasive, and she couldn't enjoy the little exchanges.

Returning to the flat, she resolved to discipline herself by making a list of positive things she wanted. Why, she wondered, when the hand holding the pen shook, did the simplest tasks have to be a trial? She tried clenching and unclenching her fists, pressing her palms firmly against the table, and last, massaging one with the other, but her action was not as effective as when Simon did it. When she began to record her ideas, her wobbly writing notwithstanding, the pen in her fingers seemed to have a mind of its own. For every light or upbeat item, two or more less than optimistic ones appeared on the paper.

When Simon came home, relief was her primary emotion. She'd worried all afternoon that a knock on her door would reveal a police officer, either one with more questions or worse, the news that Simon had been injured.

"Nice shirt," he commented as he joined her on the sofa.

That brought a brief smile. "It suits us both." She paused. "Simon, I've made a list of things I want." Her thoughts had ricocheted while she recorded her entries, from believing that grief was normal to not wanting to be sad in front of him all the time. She resolved to show him only the good things on her list.

"Popcorn with melted butter. A Coke poured over so much ice that there is hardly any liquid in the glass. Pizza with bakery crust and double toppings."

"I can manage that," he said cautiously. "And?"

"To smell brownies when they first come out of the oven. Eclairs, even the vanilla ones. Guacamole with chunks of avocado and tomato and a hint of lime. An egg salad sandwich with slices of bacon. Wearing boots. And a book with a plot so compelling I can't put it down."

"Sounds good to me."

"What's on your list?" she asked.

He thought for a moment. "Seafood stew," he began. "Ale to come in larger bottles. Your Yorkshire pudding."

"I use a mix!"

"I know," he said, "but I still like it. Is there more?"

She hesitated. "There are some negative things on my list."

"Mine as well," he admitted.

"But I want to be the bright spot in your life, not the dark spot. You don't want to come home to this."

"Yes, I do. Tell me."

"I'm rambling. I can't seem to move forward. And I don't want to, because that means leaving him or her behind."

"We're on the same road then."

"And I want a way to remember our baby without it hurting so much." She paused. "I look the same. Nothing hurts physically now. There's no sign of my pregnancy except this – this emptiness.

Simon, I've been marinating in grief, and my life has a different flavor now. This loss has made me remember Colin. He was everything to me. I didn't know how I'd be able to go on after he died. I mourned the life we'd never have, and I was alone."

He moved closer to her on the sofa and took her hand. She didn't speak much of her first husband, and he wasn't certain he wanted to hear what she had to say, but he knew it would be unwise not to listen.

"But he was a separate and mature being. He'd had a career and been successful at it. He'd seen the world. He'd experienced love. With this little one, I lost a part of myself and a part of you. He – or she – was never fully formed. Never breathed apart from me. Never laughed. Never knew us and how much we loved him. The only saving grace, if there is one, is that I'm not alone. You had a loss, too. And things mean more to me now. You mean more to me."

His colleague Hugh McGill had asked after Jenny. "It takes awhile to recover, mate," he'd said. He'd not been wrong. It was true for both of them. Now Simon struggled to speak. "Yes. And – and you to me."

She snuggled closer. "We should eat soon," she said, "but I feel better for being close to you."

He did as well. "When you're ready, we'll order pizza," he said. "And I'll put all my ice cubes in your glass."

****

Jenny opened her eyes. They were in bed, but Simon had stopped caressing her.

"What's this?" he asked.

She had been quiet, but he'd noticed her tears. Making love was hard for her because it reminded her of how they had conceived the baby they had lost. "I miss our baby," she stammered.

"As do I," he replied after a moment. He paused. "Steady on, princess." He climbed out of bed. She could hear his steps on the stairs and sounds in the kitchen. When he returned, he had two bottles of wine and glasses for each of them. "To our little one," he said, sitting on the edge of the bed. His hands didn't falter as he opened the first bottle and poured.

She took a sip, all that would slip past the lump in her throat. He downed a generous swallow. "Your turn," he said.

"To the one I'll never hold," she wept.

They drank.

"And never know," she added.

Again they drank.

"My son or daughter," he managed. He drained his glass, refilled it, and topped off hers.

"With your blue eyes," she choked. "And blond hair."

"Or your brown." He gave each of them another serving then opened the second bottle.

"I wanted to hear our baby talk with an English accent." Her swallows were nearly matching his now. "And laugh."

"See his smile," he added. "I was hoping it would resemble yours."

"He – or she – never knew that we loved him."

They continued, she with tears streaming down her face and he responding as best he could, while the second bottle of wine grew empty. When he'd poured and they'd consumed the last drops, their arms were around each other. She was sobbing aloud. He was quiet but unsteady when he asked, "Should I have brought more?"

"No," she whispered, "the ones we finished served their purpose."

In a gentle voice he continued. "Jenny, what are we going to do about this?"

"Of course I can't know for sure what he – or she – would think, but isn't it possible that he'd want us to love each other?"

In response he tightened his hug.

She felt relaxed in his embrace. When she kissed him, she had a final taste of the wine. She found that this time she could stay in the moment, an oasis from grief. His skin felt warm next to hers. She wanted more of him. "Simon, I'm ready for you," she whispered.

He was ready for her. After he held her closely a long time.

CHAPTER THREE

"THIS SHOULDN'T HAVE HAPPENED! None of this should have happened!" Jenny's exclamations echoed Simon's feelings. Both had erupted with anger when they'd heard the DPS' determination of Davies' action. And the latest headline had intensified it: "Gun Cop Killed Unarmed Man." Simon wondered where the information in the article had come from. The firearms unit wouldn't have released it. Nor did he think it had been sourced from DPS, although if it served their purpose, he'd not have put it past them.

"Don't they know that firing is a last resort?" he demanded. "We're taught that our best weapons are our eyes, our ears, and our voices. Negotiation is a priority. Davies didn't proceed until no other course of action remained."

Neil Goodwyn agreed but recognised at the same time that Jenny's involvement and their inability to affect Brian Davies' circumstances escalated their feelings.

"It's all Roy's fault," Jenny declared. "He was the one who forced Brian to save me and who caused my miscarriage. If Brian hadn't shot him, I'd be dead. Who cares about where the knife ended up as long as it wasn't in me? And then I lost the baby. Because of what I'd been through."

And was still experiencing, Goodwyn thought. There was no colour in her cheeks. Her Oxford shirt seemed large, and she had belted her baggy jeans. She must not be eating sufficiently, and he wished he'd brought digestives or tea cakes.

"That evil bastard ruined two lives."

Jenny was surprised at how cold and hard Simon's voice could become with no increase in volume.

"I'd like to suggest," Goodwyn began, "that he was not evil, only sick. A man to be pitied until he crossed the line. But I understand your anger and grief. And concern for Brian. I've spoken with him. He's taking it hard, but it's early days yet. He has a long road ahead of him, but this may yet be resolved in his favour."

He turned to Jenny. "You know, perhaps more than any of us, how traumatic the legal process can be. It's difficult at times not to see only the dark side. I've suggested that he go home to his family in Norwich for a bit. He's been given some leave, you see. Beth will take a week off from teaching so she and the children can go with him. He needs distraction as well as emotional support."

Jenny had made tea, which none of them had been relaxed enough to finish. She went into the kitchen to make a fresh pot. She could hear Simon and Neil's voices, one still angry and the other unrelentingly calm. They both emptied their cups in anticipation of the fresh brew.

"Jenny, I'd like to recommend the same for the two of you – some time away. Grief can set you apart if you let it, but action on your part can interrupt that process. This loss will always be a part of you. However, your perspective on it will change. When you look at a window, you don't look at the glass. You look through it. The day will come when you won't see only your current circumstance, you'll see beyond it. That's a sort of healing. Not forgetting – not minimising – but healing nonetheless. Trauma doesn't have office hours, but a new setting, even a temporary one, can offset its impact."

She'd brought the tea and realized she'd forgotten the milk. Success, even in the small things, seemed to escape her. She retrieved it and set it on the tray. The sugar bowl was still full. She put a cube in her cup and then added a second.

"I feel so powerless," she admitted. "For Brian as well as for Simon and myself. I don't know how to move forward."

Simon combined a few drops of milk with his tea whilst Neil added tea to his milk, acknowledging the unusual ratio. "Movement in and of itself will help. Sometimes we only know we've moved forward when we look back."

"Jenny, we could visit Portsmouth. Perhaps at the weekend. My mum would welcome us."

She hesitated. Packing sounded exhausting, but she'd never been to Portsmouth in the fall. She'd enjoyed their previous visits. She realized both men were waiting for her response. "Okay, yes."

Neil smiled in approval. "That's a very positive step. Before I go, I've an idea I'd like to introduce to you. Courage precedes forgiveness, and I know the two of you are unusually courageous. So I want you to ask yourselves: What will my life look like without this anger? What will take its place? What will forgiveness cause to bloom in my life?" He saw Jenny cross her legs, an unconscious gesture that revealed what she thought about his suggestion. "Forgiveness is the most difficult spiritual discipline we are called to perform yet perhaps the one with the greatest potential for healing. Forgiving isn't giving in. It's letting go of anger so that healing can take place. You have suffered enough." He gave a short prayer then embraced Jenny and shook hands with Simon.

CHAPTER FOUR

JENNY WISHED THAT SHE HAD THE ENERGY Simon's mother, Celia, had. A surgical nurse at Queen Alexandra's Hospital, she woke early for her morning shift yet still managed to cook Simon's favorites for dinner. After a quick change out of her uniform into worn jeans and sloppy sweaters, she made the most of her small kitchen, producing recipe after recipe involving seafood, followed by apple and gooseberry crumble for dessert.

When Simon's brother Martin joined the Royal Navy, she had moved from Penzance in Cornwall to Portsmouth on the southern coast. Renting a two-bedroom corner flat on an upper floor with no elevator didn't disturb her. Half a foot taller than Jenny, she had sinewy strength from years of walking up and down stairs and steep streets and lifting patients in the hospital.

She confessed that she didn't have either the eye or time for decorating, so she'd used neutrals throughout, the only splashes of colour coming from the profusion of flowers she grew in pots on her balcony. Each window revealed stunning vistas which made the rooms seem larger than they were, and each piece of furniture had been chosen for comfort.

"I'm indoors all day," she told Jenny, "so when I'm home, I want to see what lies beyond my four walls. And I love living near the sea. Somehow it always seems to reflect my mood, yet when its mood changes, I do also."

"Like Hampstead Heath does for me," Jenny responded. "I know it so well that it seems like we're friends."

Simon kept Jenny busy whilst his mum was at work. They passed the place where Rudyard Kipling had lived as a boy and stopped to admire hydrangeas the colour of raspberries and flowing wisteria in pale purple and white. They visited the D-Day Museum, where the Overlord Embroidery used needlework panels to honour the faces of the political leaders, the air and land offensives of the Normandy invasion, and the conflicts that followed. Every stitch had been created by human hands, a five-year labour of love.

Upon her request he took her to the Royal Marines Museum, in spite of his usual desire to maintain a low profile where his military service was concerned. The wind coming off the Solent, the body of water between Portsmouth and the Isle of Wight, made her glad that they had not planned to take the tour boat to visit the Isle. She wanted to hurry inside the museum but was delayed by the sight of a larger-than-life statue of a Royal Marine Commando in the car park outside. Called the Yomper Statue, it was laden with equipment.

"Was that you?" she asked.

"For a time, yes," he answered.

"What's a yomper?"

"Yomp is slang for a long-distance march carrying full kit."

Inside the museum Jenny held an SA80 assault rifle and was shocked at how heavy it was, but Simon confirmed that he and others had carried more than just this weapon on the "30-miler," the distance recruits had to cover across Dartmoor in eight hours. "We had to dig deep," was all he answered when she asked how he had done it. Other exhibits highlighted the formation, history, and training of both the Royal Marines and the Royal Marine Commandos.

In the restaurants where they lunched, they also enjoyed being out of the wind and cool weather, chillier than Hampstead. They warmed up eating chicken with piripiri sauce, leek and potato soup, and the English classic, porridge, seasoned with cinnamon and brown sugar. Jenny ordered still water, having learned that it would come in a chilled bottle, like a Coke. Tap water was served room temperature, and if she requested ice, she was never given more than three cubes.

Thus Simon provided diversions whilst Celia, candid and conversational, addressed personal issues. She was direct in her speech but not hurried, a good method for giving bad news she must have learnt in her medical service, but not her purpose on this occasion.

"I've wanted to console you but haven't known how," she began. "I have two strong, healthy sons, but I've still experienced loss. As you may know, Simon's brother Martin was a twin. I wasn't able to carry his sister full term. When I started bleeding, I went to hospital, of course. The doctor examined me and could still hear a heartbeat. I hadn't known I had twins until then."

Jenny held her breath.

"As a result they let me empty on my own. Expectant management, they called it, and after several days they sent me home. Bed rest for a time. That was all. We were all waiting for the other shoe to drop, so to speak, but Martin flourished, and here we are."

Simon had told Jenny about Martin's twin but had, as usual, been short on details. Now he added, "I remember hearing Martin speaking to someone I couldn't see and asking him who it was. My imaginary friend, he always said."

"Simon's father became angry, not at me, at least not at first, because he'd wanted a daughter. We already had Simon, you see, so he had a son. He always had a temper, but after this – he could start an argument with no one about. He began to drink. He lost his job and didn't take to the next one. When he expressed his anger physically, Simon became my protector. And Martin's."

And later mine, Jenny thought.

"That was the beginning of the end, although I didn't know it at the time. Then one day he'd had enough of Simon defending me, and he left. So I had one sudden loss and another gradual one."

"Did you ever divorce him?"

"I wasn't certain how to do it *in absentia,* and the longer he was gone, the less necessary it seemed, making it legal. When I stopped crying myself to sleep at night, I considered the divorce final. And I've not been unhappy. I have friends when I want to go places and privacy when I don't. My sons are in and out of my life, which is as it should be."

"I'm so sorry about your daughter," Jenny said.

Celia sighed. "They didn't handle infant death very well in those days. No one acknowledged the loss because I still had a baby. And a child at home. However, after that it was difficult for me to serve near the maternity wards. I moved to surgical nursing." She paused. "When you've lost a child during pregnancy or shortly after birth, there's a void. It's more than emptiness. It's a space you can't fill because you have no memories of that little one."

"No memories," Jenny echoed. "It haunts me. And I don't know how to deal with it. It's like being on a train that slows a little when it approaches the station but doesn't stop. So I can't get off."

"If you'll permit me – I'm not meaning to be bossy or insensitive – make memories with what you have. And who. That's what I tried to do, with my boys. And you can as well, with the help of the one you love." The stress lines around her mouth softened as she smiled.

Jenny tried to smile back but couldn't.

"I have something for you. Something with bold colours that I hope will encourage you to face your future with strength." She handed Jenny a small box.

Inside was a cuff bracelet with waves of two-toned turquoise interwoven with dark blue and gold. Southwest colors but more – the colors and motion of the boundless sea, the gold reminding Jenny of the sun's molten rays on the rippling water and the blues redolent of the ocean's swells and depths. Colin's mother had given her a bracelet, too, she recalled. Georgina McGill had bought shoes, but it seemed she was destined to collect bracelets.

CHAPTER FIVE

FOR JENNY, coming home from Portsmouth meant reuniting with Hampstead Heath but de-uniting from Simon. His return to work after days of his presence full time was wrenching. She hadn't been won over to British TV, and her other activities – walking, cooking, reading – occupied her only sporadically, so she was happy to hear that the school in Highgate had invited her back for another poetry presentation. The students in the senior school seemed confident, so she'd had them participate in reading aloud the poem she'd selected.

When the formal part of her program was over, they'd peppered her with questions. What is your favourite poem? Have you ever written one? Have you ever been at a loss for words?

"My favorite changes," she'd said, "according to my mood. If I'm angry, I may seek the WWI poets. If I need to be reminded that there's beauty in the world – one of the British 'Big Six' romantic poets. Shakespeare's sonnets are elegant, concise, and timeless. I encourage you to search for your favorites." She paused. "I love words. Words are powerful, so please use them with care. They can harm or heal." She didn't tell them that sometimes words were inadequate. These young people felt invincible, and it wasn't her place to assassinate their innocence.

Since, however, she was speaking to an older group, she decided to refer them to Rupert Brooke's *The Soldier*. "Your teacher can instruct you in the context and form of this poem. I'd just like to ask you what your next lines would be. It begins, 'If I should die, think only this of me: / That there's some corner of a foreign field / That is for ever England...' How would you like to be remembered? It's not too early to give some thought to this, because your answer could shape your life."

She'd asked Simon once if, when he was facing combat, he thought that he was a piece of England. "Nothing so poetic or personal," he'd responded. "On a mission, team comes first. The needs of the team surpass those of the individual."

Today, with no presentation to make, she donned jeans and an embroidered t-shirt she'd bought in Portsmouth, put the leash on Bear, and set out. The Heath beckoned to her, its paths like outstretched arms. She knew the Heath in all its seasons, naming them by what she saw: yellow green, true green, deep green, and the white of winter covering all green, except for occasional rebellious vegetation which persisted no matter the climate. She felt she could identify the location of any photo taken of the Heath, much the way she thought she could recognize Simon, even from a distance, by his stance and gait.

The Heath never slept completely, and she thought the grief process was similar, sometimes dormant and other times fully awake, sometimes dark and other times with oases of light. She was glad to see Mr. MacKenna, who gave her a little wave but did not approach her. She waved back, grateful for his protection, regardless of how unnecessary it was.

When she and Bear returned from their walk, Enid Stanley was waiting for her with a large rectangular box in her hands. "The diary's inside," she told Jenny. "From my great-great-aunt Elspeth Tillman. Freddie's decided to let you have a look at it."

"Come in," Jenny responded. She refilled Bear's water bowl and then sat down at the dining room table with Enid.

The box held three small volumes. Jenny removed one from its plastic bag and opened it. "This is a book of poetry," she said, puzzled. The cover was worn and the spine of the little book broken, but the words on the title page were still legible.

"The diary pages were hidden," Enid explained. "That's why they weren't discovered for such a long time, and since the pages are loose, we've no way of knowing if any are missing. The box they were in wasn't labelled, so no one had ever examined what was inside." She smiled sheepishly. "Freddie and I cherish these little volumes and their contents. You'll not take them out of the flat, will you?"

"No, of course not," Jenny assured her. "But I'm curious – can you tell me a little about her?"

Enid nodded. "As you may have read, the war began in August 1914, yet everyone thought it would be over by Christmas."

"But it wasn't."

"No," Enid responded, seeming a little irritated that her narrative had been interrupted. "It lasted for four long years, ending at the eleventh hour on the eleventh day of the eleventh month of 1918. But long before that, Aunt Elspeth and other young women had begun to sign up to provide care for the young men who were fighting. History tells us that a young woman volunteering to serve in the VAD had to be twenty-three years of age. Most were given only three months of training here at home before being sent overseas. Aunt Elspeth was a bit headstrong, or so we're told. Not a black sheep, you understand, but perhaps a grey one." She smiled at her own joke. "She had an older sister and a younger one, both of whom married well. It was said that an inappropriate assignation of hers was terminated by the family. Beyond that, we don't know."

"I'm intrigued," Jenny said. "I'll begin on the transcription today. And I'll take very good care of everything."

Jenny saw her out and then sat down again at the dining room table, this time with a pad of paper and a pen, having decided first to record in longhand what she read. The diary pages were better preserved in some places than those of the host books, whose pages were dark on the edges, chipped in places, and with letters that were often missing or blurred. The diary pages were also slightly smaller, but the first few were difficult to decipher, the old-fashioned script being small and challenging to read for the unpracticed eye. It was slow going.

What was clear, however, was how unprepared Elspeth was for what she encountered, her training at the hospital beforehand notwithstanding. There were so many adjustments. The noise, the smell. The hard cot, the thin blanket. She had never heard a man cry, much less scream.

I've been in France for days – somewhere in France I'll call it because we're discouraged about being more specific. So far I've learnt that my stamina is insufficient so I've done naught but what I've been trained to do. My small space is shared with another VAD. I've my own cot, stool, and locker, but there's just one small stove and mirror, which is a blessing and a curse. We wear grey cotton dresses with white pinafores and cuffs. We keep our hair swept under our caps. We've not spoken much. Time is evidently not wasted on the living until it's clear they'll be staying, and my roommate's not certain about me. Neither am I, for I was unprepared. The hospital where I trained was relatively quiet, unlike the wards here where men are often crying out in pain or remembered fear and various personnel are calling for help or equipment. Fortunately the sisters who noticed how pale I was said nothing.

The Matron has such a harsh voice and predatory beak that I hope she'll be busy with administrative duties and have no time to appear on the wards. Her face is gaunt; will mine be similar in a few months' time?

The pecking order: we VADs are at the bottom. The work is so unending and overwhelming that I can lose myself in it. I must learn to control my mind, which runs to shock and horror because conditions are far worse than I expected. I expected the men to be cold and tired. I didn't expect them to be hungry.

There was a space before the next entry.

Sounds travels, particularly at night. Tonight I heard distant thunder and thought how restful and comforting a gentle rain would be. How wrong I was, on both counts. Fortunately I didn't mention my observation to anyone, because when scores of wounded began to arrive, I realised my error. The thunderous sound had not been produced by nature; it was the rumble of guns.

Rain, which nature does produce, makes mud and therefore filthy wounds and unremitting laundry. I remind myself that after the muddy trenches, even one clean item is deeply appreciated, because rain does not wash this world clean. It only creates more mud that splashes on everything and seeps into my boots, my stockings, my pores. Perhaps my possessions are not infected, but they seem so. Pack light, we were told, because you may have to move stations with very little notice, and I am glad that I have obeyed that directive.

There followed a list of what her luggage had contained, meager at best. Jenny was struck with how dirty and how crude Elspeth's conditions were. In response she put her sheets in the washer. The next load would be towels. It wouldn't hurt to dust and run the vacuum cleaner again. She looked around the flat. She was living in the midst of plenty, while Elspeth had served in the midst of privation. She glanced at her watch. More time had passed than she had realized. Simon would be home soon, and she would tell him that one project had engendered others. She had clothes she hadn't worn in a long time and housewares she'd replaced but kept undisturbed. These could be given away. A spring cleaning in the fall was called for. She marked boxes with "Give away" or "Throw away" and set them by the front door when she had filled them.

"Simon, I've just started," she told him when he arrived, "and already the diary is compelling. I want to know about the First World War, more than I learned in world history and from the WWI poets I read."

"The war deteriorated into a stalemate, with trenches I'm sure your diarist will mention. Hundreds of thousands of men fought and died to move the boundary between them only a hundred yards. Almost every family had someone killed or maimed."

"Was the southern shore of England attacked? Is that why the sound of the guns was loud enough to be heard in Hampstead?"

"No, but the east coast was bombarded by German cruisers. Warships. And zeppelins bombed London. The first blitz. The British barrage prior to the Battle of the Somme was what people in Hampstead heard. Another bloody engagement, in both senses of the word."

"Anything else I need to know?"

"The war ushered in a new sort of technology, poison gas, flame throwers, and machine guns being only a few examples. A perverse kind of progress, some would say. And medically we would find it all very primitive."

"Then she was vulnerable, wherever she was," Jenny commented. She had reheated pot roast and served it with mashed potatoes. Now her appetite wasn't equal to what she'd put on her plate. "Some of my favorite poets wrote during that period in history. Siegfried Sassoon commented that 'the rain sluiced down.' So descriptive. And that 'the only safety was in death.' Wilfred Owen recorded that 'many had lost their boots, / but limped on, blood-shod.' Both Owen and Rupert Brooke died before the war ended. Now I know why their lines are so powerful. They must have seen firsthand some of the things you mention."

"No war is pretty, Jenny."

"Yet you served in the military."

"The discipline of the training matured me. When combat came, belief in the purpose helped, as did the camaraderie with those round me. Life is sweeter for having been threatened."

"Given the choice, I'd rather gain that perspective without the loss."

He had cleaned his plate. She put both their dishes in the dishwasher and turned it on.

"Jenny, are you up to this? Clearly it's not easy reading."

"I want to do it, Simon. Expose myself to someone else's experience. It may help me to put my own losses in perspective. And my blessings, of which you are one."

"Keep at it then," he smiled.

CHAPTER SIX

BRIAN DAVIES WAS DONE with duty counselling. All it had accomplished was getting him away from Croxley temporarily. He wished he were done crossing paths with the man, but perhaps that was inevitable, both of them being restricted to Leman Street.

He wished he were done with having an advisory as opposed to an active role on ops, but his legal status had not changed. God, the wheels of justice turned slowly! His Federation rep had assured him that lack of apparent movement did not indicate movement in the wrong direction, but it was worrying nonetheless.

He wished he were done with Beth monitoring his alcohol consumption. His sleep. His demeanour. His patience. Her actions were borne out of love and concern, however, so perhaps he should be more accepting.

Fall was meant to be a peaceful time of year, when the weather turned crisp and cool, the leaves left behind their green, and soup pots bubbled with comfort. In the past he would have happily done the cooking. These days both his energy and his appetite were unreliable.

Notification had just come in that the Crown Prosecution Service had decided not to proceed further with the murder charges laid against the two specialist firearms officers whose incident had occurred almost six years ago.

A scientist from the States had analysed all the forensic data, reviewed the many reports and photos, and even walked through a detailed reconstruction of the event the officers had described. He had been able to demonstrate scientifically what had occurred. The CPS had then concluded that prosecution would not be successful since the degree of force used by the officers had been reasonable and the expert's analysis had shown that the officers had not lied about the circumstances which had led to the suspect's death. They had always maintained that the suspect had been facing them when they fired, although one of their shots had hit him in the back. Fortunately the American scientist had been able to show that the natural response of the suspect, when hit by the first shot, had been to turn away. Hence the next shot, although fired when the suspect was looking toward them, had not struck him in the front.

At Leman Street there was more relief than celebration, which he understood. He was only two months in, and he was tense all the time. He suspected some bitterness remained on the part of the officers concerned – how could it not? – as well as at least a bit of disbelief and doubt. Disbelief because it would take awhile for the determination to sink in and doubt because it was difficult to trust that the process would not be resurrected at some point in the future.

His emotions were mixed. How had the officers endured? They had the support of their mates – which he did also – but their families had been deeply affected by the seemingly unending legal process. Surely his own vindication would come in weeks, not years.

CHAPTER SEVEN

"REMEMBER, REMEMBER, THE FIFTH OF NOVEMBER"
– all British schoolchildren learned the rhyme to help them recall
Guy Fawkes Day, the day in 1605 when Catholic conspirators
planned to blow up Parliament upon its opening. Their intent was
to remove King James I from rule and restore Britain's Catholic
monarchy. The explosives expert Guy Fawkes hoped to watch the
detonations from Parliament Hill, the tallest vantage point in
Hampstead Heath. Fortunately Fawkes had been discovered,
arrested, and then made to reveal the names of his fellow rebels. His
particularly gruesome death did not, however, prevent centuries of
widespread celebrations of the event, including bonfires, fireworks,
and effigies burnt of Fawkes, and in some cases, Pope Paul V.

This year the displays, at least in London, had been scaled back
as a result of the tube bombings in the summer. Exhibitions were
held, but few had the taste for any sort of revelry associated with a
bombing.

Jenny set the newspaper aside, not in the mood for festivity.
She had just begun her second menstrual period, another reminder
that she was no longer pregnant. Without the events ten weeks ago,
she would have been halfway to her due date, her baby about the
size of a banana but with a rapidly growing brain. She and Simon
would have been discussing baby names and refinishing the room
they had designated as the nursery. Now her grief was as bitter as
over-percolated coffee.

When Neil Goodwyn visited and told her that the seed of
healing was already within her, she thought his choice of words

unfortunate. Of course he couldn't have known what the date meant to her. "On my walks with Bear, I watch the wind blow through the trees, the gusts making the larger branches bend and snapping the smaller ones. Bend or break. I have to learn how to bend." She took a sip of her tea. He always joined her in the kitchen while she made it.

"Bending and not breaking is the best definition I've heard of resilience. Those who are strong and hard, break. Those who are strong and soft, bend. As you do, I believe."

"Then why do I feel broken?" she asked, her voice trembling. "I still feel like someone let the air out of my balloon."

"Because you lost hopes and dreams and those losses don't heal as quickly as the body does," he responded. "I'd also like to suggest that strength with flexibility comes from having a deep foundation. The God I serve provides that for me."

"And you provide treats for me," she said, enjoying her second of the mini chocolate croissants he had brought and ignoring the religious reference. "In the meantime I have a project I'd like to tell you about. It began as a distraction, but I think it's going to be more than that." She described the diary of the VAD she was transcribing and its origin. "I've made good progress."

"What have you learnt so far?"

"First, how difficult the living conditions were in France. And the weather. She wrote about the wind – icy cold and so strong that it cut through her and kept her off balance. She dreaded having to leave the ward, even to trudge back to the little stove by her bed. It was too cold to change clothes, and she wrote that soldiers came to them in uniforms they'd worn day and night for weeks on end. And that's not all. They had rain that penetrated like icicles, drenching her no matter what she wore. She hated it but not as much as she hated death and the pain that preceded it. It's chilling to read, in more than one sense. She must not have had much time to record things, so she uses shorthand. CCS refers to a casualty clearing station. The DIL is the dangerously ill list. And TPR means temperature, pulse, and respiration. The nursing sisters considered the VADs second class citizens because they didn't have the same training, but some of the doctors taught them skills. Part of their private war against the army of insufficiency, she says. But she mentioned the chaplains, and I thought of you. I'd like to read those pages to you."

She stood and collected her notes from the dining room table. "I'm in the second volume, but the entries I'm looking for are in the first. I made one page of notes to correspond with each diary page."

At the outset I considered my work, though menial, to be sacred. This ideal is fragile now. I'm glad I have the chaplain to encourage me. I pray not to become callous yet if I do not, how shall my soul survive what I have seen?

I am in awe of our chaplain. At first he seemed the quiet sort, but over time I realised that he has listened and learnt. He knows the names and needs of each individual, whether a member of the medical staff or a patient in one of the wards. There's nothing he can't do – carpentry, cooking, comfort, correspondence, and more. It's all in God's service, he says, so he never refuses a request for help, no matter how far it is from his religious duties. He has brought tea to us more times than I can count. He holds the hands of the living and the dying. He is the only one who can tell the MOs what to do because he has a quiet authority that everyone respects. Sometimes his prayers are whispered and sometimes shouted in order to be heard over the guns. I do not know when he rests.

"Isn't that moving? By the way, 'MOs' stands for medical officers," Jenny clarified.

Neil nodded. "As you read, I was thinking about my time in the Middle East serving men and women in uniform. I wasn't as versatile in my skills as the chaplain you read about was, but the weather was a complicating factor for both of us. It could be as fierce an adversary as the enemy, particularly the sandstorms. And the work was never done."

"Elspeth Tillman, the woman who wrote the diary, would agree with you. Often she had to choose between sleeping and eating; there wasn't time for both. Some nights she was too tired to remove her uniform. And once she was so fatigued, she fell asleep on her feet. She didn't realize it until she began seeing things that weren't there."

"Jenny, her writing was a release for her, but also possibly a remembrance. So perhaps it's time we discussed the function of memory."

"I'd rather forget."

"That's not possible, I'm sorry to say, but your memory of losses can soften and strengthen you at the same time. That's where resilience and perspective come in. You've overcome the events that caused the bad memories. And I'd wager that the loss of your baby has connected you and Simon in a new way. As T. E. Kalem wrote, 'The heart is the only broken instrument that works.' My time serving men in combat gave me greater compassion."

She was silent for a moment. Her tea had gone cold; Neil had finished his. She refilled his cup from the teapot.

"New bracelet?" he asked, noticing the bangle on her wrist.

"Yes, I've started collecting them. Georgina McGill – the wife of one of Simon's fellow officers – suggested that I pamper myself a little bit. I like this one because the bright colors remind me of flowers, and flowers are alive."

"I know Georgina well," he said. "One of her brothers was severely injured at one point, and her unqualified support of him was a factor in his recovery. She was understandably incensed at his circumstances, and that indignation has never burnt out."

"'Tyger, tyger, burning bright / in the forests of the night,'" Jenny quoted.

"Your William Blake verse is apt," Goodwyn commented. "Hers was a fierce grief, but it was always accompanied with a fierce devotion."

"Is she ever depressed?"

"Of course, but she rallies, as you do. There are many types of resilience. I always find myself cheering for her, as I do for you. I must add – you're not going to forget your baby or stop loving him, because love and grief are intertwined. Grief isn't an end; it's a beginning. And at its core, grief's not about death. It's about life."

"That's a concept I don't understand," she admitted.

"I would encourage you to recognise that memory is a gift from God. It can lead us somewhere if we allow it to do. As Lewis Carroll wrote, 'It's a poor sort of memory that only works backwards.' Most people think of memory only as a journey backward, but it can be a journey forward as well. Memory can be a journey to understanding or insight, a journey to forgiveness, to clarity of purpose, or to recommitment. I like to use the metaphor of a journey because in some sense we are always moving in life. We never stay the same."

"Then 'what's past is prologue,' as Shakespeare put it."

Neil smiled. "Exactly so. And there's one more thing. Stubbornness is a part of you. It's the part which refuses to give up. Use it. Apply it. Make your hope stubborn."

"You've certainly given me food for thought," she acknowledged.

"Before I go, I want you to know: I marvel at your strength. If there's one thing I've learnt, it's respect for those I counsel. My best to Simon." He uttered a short prayer and departed.

CHAPTER EIGHT

AN EARLY RUN. Simon Casey didn't have to parade until a bit later this morning, and he was glad of it. He needed time to think on all the questions that were crowding his mind.

He'd met with Sean MacKenna, who'd been keeping a watch over Jenny from time to time, with the intent of releasing him from this responsibility since none of his previous accounts had indicated any potential danger for her. However, a new observation had arisen.

"Call it my old copper's nose," MacKenna had said, "but the other evening when your wife travelled to Hayes, I followed. Someone was lurking about in the shadows, someone who kept himself so well hidden that I didn't spot him until he moved – when PC Davies arrived. Your wife had already knocked and been admitted to the premises. A stocky Caucasian individual of average height with short dark hair. Sorry I've not got more. It could be the reporter who's been writing those appalling stories. Would you like me to find out?"

Neither he nor MacKenna could imagine how that would help Davies, but they had both felt that more information was preferable to less, so Simon had altered his assignment. MacKenna would identify the reporter, survey his actions, and relate anything suspicious.

Davies. It was early days yet as far as the legal system was concerned. No reason to think anything would go wrong in the long run. The intolerable waiting was, however, wearing on Davies. Many days his own duties with the OCU took him away from Leman Street, and when they did not, occupied him away from the teams. Davies, in contrast, was as confined to the base as a day prisoner. He must remind Davies to concentrate on the immediate, both the tangible and the intangible: the tasks to hand at Leman Street, the support from fellow officers and friends, the love of his family, even the food on the table. He suspected Davies was placing a bit too much focus on drink, but that was understandable and would pass.

At times in the past he'd attempted to drown his own sorrows, but generally a concrete incident had been the cause and his lapse of discipline had been temporary. Although Davies' source lay in the past, it had consequences that were as yet undetermined. Davies was a big man with a correspondingly large capacity to absorb drink, but even he could exceed what was wise. If that word got out, it could be used against him.

When he'd been down that road himself, he'd learnt that retracing your steps – accepting what had been jeopardised or lost – was difficult. Sometimes beyond reach. He'd have a word with him, perhaps at the pub where he could monitor what Davies consumed, or on a run with him at the weekend.

He'd also been seeking a way to make a tangible change in Jenny's life, and unwittingly two things she had mentioned had led him to a possible solution. He'd had the seed of an idea when she referred to the moves the diary writer had made. It had grown when she tried to describe the heart of Goodwyn's conversation about journeys. He'd grasped most of what he thought was Goodwyn's intent – to help Jenny focus on what lay ahead, not behind her – but it had led him to thoughts of a real journey, a physical move the two of them could make.

He'd seen her grief over the loss of their baby. Occasionally he'd find her in one of the rooms which would have been the nursery, undecorated still, unfurnished. The Hampstead flat – it had been Sinclair's, then hers, never his. Hence not theirs. The large rooms seemed to make their emptiness more apparent. He'd lived in flats all his life. He wanted a home.

He wanted the woman back who was always eager to try a new recipe and managed to involve every pot and pan in the process.

The woman with a sense of fun who sometimes cast her umbrella aside and dared the drops of rain to dampen her cheeks. The woman who, when he threw the Frisbee, raced Bear to catch it. The woman with a sense of mischief who played spontaneous games with him. Seduce the Soldier had been his favourite, in which she tried to see how long he could resist her attentions. Sometimes her kisses alone were sufficient to ignite him; other times he could resist a bit longer. On his part more control or less didn't signify. She felt complimented when he lost. She'd laugh, he did as well, and they were happy together, having both won.

Until her pregnancy had ended. What she considered a defeat, he deemed a setback, but they were still affected by what might have been, and the carefree nature of their lovemaking was absent. It would take more courage to seek parenthood this time. And not just for her. Would they both be emboldened by new surroundings?

He'd forgot his own adage about never being able to land on the same beach twice – because circumstances always evolved – and the flat was the same beach. They needed a new place, a fresh start. A mission they could undertake together, much as when they had decided to start a family. And perhaps one would lead to the other.

CHAPTER NINE

"JURY STILL OUT ON GUN COP" read one of the headlines. Two months on, Brian Davies had had enough, but the tabloids were just getting started. They smelled a story, another in the continuing line of articles guaranteed to inflame anti-police sentiment, and they thought they could make it a big one. The truth? Less interesting. Their approach amounted to persecution of officers who had been forced to discharge their firearm. When would it stop? Was this how other officers had felt? Helpless, frustrated, their characters under attack to sell newspapers? Mired in a seemingly unending legal system? Unable to move forward? His only good weeks were the ones when he was allowed to train with the teams. The heft of the Glock still felt comfortable in his hand, and the firmness of the stock of the MP-5 was familiar. Some things at least remained the same.

Chief Inspector Denison had called him in and explained that all lines of enquiry were being pursued. "All lines?" What could that possibly refer to? What mattered besides Jenny's account and his?

"On the very few occasions when one of our officers has to fire, there is no presumption of innocence," Denison had said.

Davies had known that. All officers expected to be held accountable for their actions. But to feel declared guilty whilst investigations were still taking place? That did not seem just or fair. Editors and reporters sat behind desks. Police officers were on the streets, facing unknown dangers, not computers and coffee cups.

His interviews with the Directorate of Professional Standards, the internal affairs department within the police, had ended some time ago. Their findings had been sent to the Independent Police Complaints Commission, the external watchdog which would make a recommendation to the Crown Prosecution Service regarding legal action. He'd been required to meet with the IPCC but had heard nothing conclusive from them. More waiting.

Today, however, he finally had something to celebrate. It was 24 November, the first day pubs were allowed to remain open twenty-four hours, instead of mandatory closing times being before midnight. The sun had been bright when he'd set out, illuminating every detail in the landscape, but to him the sights were dreary because the truth of his actions was still obscured. Now, after raising a few pints, his spirit was lifted as well. Twenty-four hours. That meant no deadline sending him home. He smiled bitterly. With no closing time, police would be busier because those who over indulged could be leaving the pubs at any time. He had no plans to leave. He'd spun a story to Beth and told her not to expect him tonight.

His mind wandered. Recently in a dark pub not unlike this one, he and Casey had shared a few. Casey had told him about his plans to move from Hampstead and asked for the name of his estate agent. He'd confessed that he hadn't introduced the idea to Jenny yet, uncertain whether she would be willing to consider such a major life change.

They'd arranged to meet, and he had suggested that Casey meet him on the Commons in Chorleywood, since Rickmansworth, where he lived, didn't have a place where they could run. The Commons wasn't as large a park as the Heath in Hampstead, but it was less crowded. He'd been glad for an excuse to be out of the house, and he knew that Beth had always liked and respected Casey. As they jogged, he'd also been glad for his long legs. He had a good five inches on Casey, and his height had helped him to cover the ground without betraying what poor shape he was in. Fortunately Casey had been more focused on the fortuitous location of the park, next to a nice housing area, and likely didn't notice that his stamina wasn't what it should have been.

CHAPTER TEN

I AM SURROUNDED BY HEROES. Every man who goes over the top. The stretcher bearers who brave extraordinary dangers to bring the wounded back to us. The men who ignore their own serious injuries and gesture for others to be treated first. The medical officers who somehow manage to keep going no matter how many hours they've already worked. They do all they can, and when it is not enough, they grieve the last patient even as they work on the next. And infection is another enemy. It can kill those you thought would live.

Heroes and human beings. For every doctor who is rude, condescending, and ungrateful, there are two who try to teach us and the orderlies such things as how to splint suspected fractures, how to remove relevant clothing gently, and how not to bind wounds too tightly since swelling may occur. Some of them mutter to themselves whilst they work, whilst others curse. Some pray. Some are silent except for issuing instructions to the attending nurses, and occasionally one narrates his procedures, as if lecturing to himself to avoid error.

Even sans bombardments the nights are not quiet. The racking coughs of the men, the mournful cries, the screams of nightmares conspire to keep us all from sleep. I have seen the spirits of men die before their bodies do. I have learnt to smile at them as they died, a skill I never hoped to acquire. I have held the hands of wounded men, some with bloody hands, some with callused ones, most with muddy ones. The human touch – so critical in healing for those who will recover and such a comfort for those who will not. It helps to sustain me as well – holding a man's hand – although I thought I had closed off that part of me.

We do receive the occasional afternoon off, but truly there is no escaping the war and the things we've seen. A walk or flowers in bloom or virgin countryside – none of these can distract us completely. Fear, pain, and death are omnipresent.

Letters from home. I don't receive many, which is a good thing because I have so little time to read them and even less desire to be put in mind of events that happened before the war. When others enquire, I pretend disappointment and credit my many moves as the cause. Best to leave it all behind, far behind. Best to look forward, though that is very difficult to do here. Look forward to more attacks, more wounded? Perhaps best to look only at the present moment, whatever that is. With one exception: the medallion. Cold and dead until I cradle it in my palm and close my fingers over it. Then it warms into life with memories that multiply its size. I shall never let it go.

Jenny paused in her transcription. The writing was heart rending, and now there appeared to be a mystery surrounding a possession that was precious to Elspeth. Perhaps it had belonged to someone who was beloved to her before the war. She had given Enid her notes from the pages hidden inside the first volume of poetry. Now she was well into the second volume, and this was the first mention from Elspeth of her personal life. Had someone she cared about given her these books of poems? Any inscription had faded away long ago. Had her individual sheets been placed between the phrases of poems which had touched her? Although the printed words at the top and bottom of each page had faded, Jenny could recognize some lines in the middle that Shelley had written, others by Keats. If the volumes of poetry were any indication of Elspeth's literary preferences, she had liked the romantic poets. Jenny read on.

Moved again. New location but all else the same. The doctors are frustrated with the time they must spend in paperwork; there are always forms to be filled out. The men are exhausted, their clothes dishevelled. They don't march, they trudge. They are angry, at their limitations, at the pain, at being sent home. I am angry at the heartbreak. Everywhere there are sad stories.

I have been ravenously hungry lately. One of the nurses noticed my increased appetite and commented, "Fear." She is likely correct. She advised taking deep breaths, but they provide no calm, only a light-headedness which is frightening in these environs. When the big guns are fired, the ground shakes, an unwelcome reminder that the future is unknown for all of us. We have a near permanent feeling of apprehension. I see no indication that the war is coming to a close. Instead the convoys of wounded continue to arrive, full of individuals that someone loves.

Jenny stopped. She had reached the end of the pages secreted in the second volume. Fortunately she could close the book on the war, although some of Elspeth's comments reminded her of Simon's recent recommendation. "Moving from here," he'd said. "I'd like you to have a think on it. You'd be moving away from a place with bad memories. Moving to a place where we can create new ones. Possibly moving closer to Davies and Beth. Neither of us chose this flat, but we can both choose our next dwelling." He'd looked right at her when he said it, his way of letting her know how serious he was, and held her hand, too, perhaps because he did not want to let her pull away.

She called for Bear and attached the leash to his collar. The new gold bangles on her wrist showed below the sleeve of her sweater and added a touch of brightness to the gray day. On her walk to the Heath, she noticed what was alive. Above ground were the trees and their leaves, below ground the root structure. Where were her roots? Were they deeply embedded in Hampstead or would she be capable of flowering in other ground? The Heath in particular had been a constant in her life, introduced to her by Colin even before their relationship had truly begun, continuing during their married life, and being more of a home to her after his death than the flat they had shared.

Although large in her history, she was small in its history. The Heath, an epitome of equality, treated all the same, no matter the nationality, age, height, and weight, all the characteristics others found so important. It had absorbed the footsteps of thousands upon thousands, and it would absorb hers. No record of her presence would remain. For all its virtues, the Heath had no memory and no heart. It woke, it slept, it aged and was reborn. Its winds dispersed her laughter, and its ponds diffused her tears. For the first time she thought there might be wisdom in Neil Goodwyn's belief that memory could be healing.

Where had Elspeth found peace with war all around her? The Heath promised peace even in the shadows beneath the trees because she could rest against a gnarled trunk and still see greenery in every direction and feel the soft, cleansing breeze under the branches.

Today, however, the sun was playing hide and seek behind the clouds, and then it retreated altogether, turning the trees black. The gray sky and rumbles overhead warned her to head home, but these sounds came from a natural source, not the artillery of warring armies. Although she and Bear were both soaked before they reached the front door, it was a small price to pay for forgetting her umbrella and all the times she'd watched the clouds dance and felt the sun's caress.

In addition, the Heath had provided endless entertaining images, from the picnickers with more alcoholic spirits than sandwiches to children climbing like monkeys to the top branches of trees to dog walkers with canines of all sizes. She'd heard snippets of conversations in German, Italian, and French, and some in English that had made her smile: "The startup phase is the most time consuming because no one ever knows when they've finished starting!" "Have you got used to their accent yet? They say, 'mi-li-tare-ee' instead of 'mi-li-tree.'" "Nothing she's got has made her happy." Talk of relationships forged, relationships dissolved. Once she'd heard a young man singing along with whatever he was hearing through his headphones. His enthusiasm exceeded his musicianship, and it wasn't possible to recognize the melody.

She had lost so much since coming to London: her innocence, her home in Texas, her husband Colin, her place of renewal.

Did Simon know what he was asking?

CHAPTER ELEVEN

JENNY WOKE WITH A WEIGHT on her chest. She knew the reason but was surprised that it still affected her so deeply. December 8: the date six years ago when she and Colin Sinclair had married. They had barely celebrated their second wedding anniversary when he was killed. Simon must have also remembered the day, because he entered the bedroom with a cup of tea and a chocolate croissant on a tray.

"How are you?" he asked, sitting next to her on the bed.

"A little sad," she confessed. "I'll always love Colin, and I still miss him sometimes, but it's easier now because you have filled my life." She smiled. "And brought me chocolate."

He caressed the hand that didn't hold the pastry. "I don't like to see you like this," he said. He hoped the sweet would soften what he intended to do next.

"It doesn't mean I love you less," she said, finishing the croissant and sipping her tea.

"I'm aware of that," he acknowledged. "Jenny, there are some things we need to do today. Shall I collect your dressing gown?"

She set the tray aside and donned the robe.

"Come with me," he said, taking her hand. He led her into the room adjacent to the master bedroom. "Tell me what you see, Jenny."

She hadn't heard his no-nonsense voice in a long time, and it startled her. "A room."

"What else?" he pressed. "What's in it?"

"Nothing. It's empty."

They walked through it to another room. "What's this?" he asked.

After a minute she answered. "Another empty room."

He led her throughout the flat. Three floors, with more rooms unused and unoccupied than employed. "Weigh it up, Jenny," he said more gently.

"I'm empty, too," she said through tears. "But it's not my fault! Why are you doing this?"

"Jenny, I've had a good think on what Goodwyn said. You're hostage to this flat. We both are. I want us to journey together away from our past. A fresh start will give us the chance to run our own race. I'm asking you to trust me."

"But Simon – I've lived in some part of this building ever since I came to London. And Colin bought it after we were married so we'd have income from the residents of the other flats."

"That won't change, except that you'll be able to let this flat as well." He paused. "Jenny, I remember your early days in witness protection when Davies, Sullivan, and I were assigned to protect you here. Those weren't happy days for any of us. As I recall, you were in too much pain to walk."

"And I was afraid all the time," she added, "but I got better. You helped."

"Later you were stalked on these streets, after Sinclair's death."

"That's true. The Heath was a danger then, not a haven, but I love it now. And Simon – we first made love in this flat."

"Yes, and I'll carry that memory with me wherever we go."

Her fingers found his fingers, and she gripped them. He always encouraged her to face things, and he was always at her side when he did it, but the process still hurt. "It's as if I've been branded, like calves on a ranch. I'll forever be marked by what I've experienced. I can't change that."

"Sometimes we can't get the world to do what we want it to do. Action on our part is required, but if you'll give me our financial data, I'll do the legwork. You don't have to sign on the dotted line until I find a place I believe will suit us and you agree. And you'll have veto power. For now I want you to understand what I'm doing and why. Setting priorities. Working them one at a time. Each solution then helps us deal with the next."

She thought for a minute. Neither of them was a big spender. He had lived simply when he was single, which had enabled him to save money. She had an Audi that she never drove, so Simon had sold his 4x4 after they married, keeping only the motorcycle which was his primary mode of transport to and from work. He didn't need the flat in Ruislip. She thought they'd be approved financially.

"Simon, will moving help you?"

He met her gaze. "Both of us, yes." He paused. "A walk on the Heath is called for, if you're up to it."

He waited whilst she dressed. They took Bear with them, Jenny putting the leash in Simon's hand so she could take his arm.

"What do you see, Jenny?" he asked when they reached the edge of the park.

"English plane trees. A stately procession of them. Slivers of sun piercing their branches. A paved path."

"Describe the trees."

"Thick trunks. Rough bark in a patchwork of beige and gray. Lots of branches and leaves." She thought for a minute. "Places where branches used to be."

"They lost limbs, yes, and they recovered by growing over the scars where the limbs were."

She looked up. "Yet some of them have flourished – look how tall and wide their branches are."

"That's true," he acknowledged. "But if we come this way tomorrow, will they still be here?"

"Yes, of course."

"Because…"

"They can't move."

"Right. They're anchored by their roots. They're stuck in their one environment, subject to whatever comes. But we're not."

She understood. "We can move. I've put down roots only metaphorically, so I can pull them up and plant them somewhere else. But do I have to? Simon, the Heath is healing to me. Something is always green. It gives me hope. Couldn't we just move closer to it? I love the fields and paths and ponds. And I'll miss the benches engraved with the names of lost loved ones."

"I'll build a bench for you," he said. "When the time comes."

CHAPTER TWELVE

STILL SOMEWHAT SHAKEN by Simon's proposal, Jenny wasn't certain she'd be able to concentrate on the third volume of Elspeth's diary. Although he'd assured her that he wouldn't initiate action without her consent, he hadn't taken such a strong stand on any issue they'd faced together so far in their marriage. She remembered his comment that neither of them had chosen the Hampstead flat, and in an indirect way he seemed to be suggesting that they were both living in Colin's shadow. He clearly believed that this idea was one he had taken on her behalf, and he was probably right. Mired in grief, she had lost her ability to take bold steps, but he had not. In the past she'd felt reassured, safe, when he had taken charge. She was still focused on the loss of a dream, and although he was grieving, too, he had found a way for them to move forward, to create a new one. She looked around her. The flat was familiar, but that did not mean that remaining in it was best. All he was asking for was trust. Surely she could manage that much.

She sighed and opened the volume of poetry. When she saw the title that preceded the first entry, she knew that the writing itself would give her whatever attention was required.

The Somme.

It had been an almost five-month campaign, and its tragedy and duration had evidently impacted Elspeth deeply, because it was the first time she had mentioned anything by name. Hundreds of thousands of men had been lost on all sides, including nearly 60,000 casualties in the British Army on the first day alone.

*In future years, if I live, all it will take will be those two words,
and the burden of memory will once again rest on my shoulders. So
many casualties that it sometimes seems that the war is more alive
than those who fight in it, its heartbeat louder and more regular, its
lifespan longer. Waves upon waves of wounded come in.
Sometimes all we can do is sit with them, wipe perspiration away,
listen to halting prayers, and give drinks of water. And they yearn
to be recognised, to be spoken to by name. When I address a man
by name, he feels for a moment a valued individual, someone whose
life matters. It is a kindness, a way to combat the anger and
bitterness many carry with them as constant companions.*

*There is no such thing as a shift when wounded arrive. We all
work past exhaustion. At first I wished for silence enough to sleep,
but I know now that silence means death, not healing or peace.
Selfish of me to want it for myself.*

*No time to think of anything but the work we do, and that is a
good thing. I am never completely at peace. Even when I can't hear
the guns, I can feel them in the unevenness of the wind or the slight
trembling under my feet. And the gas, the insidious, merciless gas.
It comes with very little warning, sometimes during the day and
other times at night. Sudden and always frightening.*

*As I walk from ward to ward, I see bits of clouds scattered across
the sky, as if an explosive has detonated in the atmosphere instead
of on the earth. Some days I miss both the sunrise and the sunset,
so a day when I can see either is a special one. On clear nights there's
the moon and surrounding stars, of course, so majestic and pure
whilst here on earth everything is in a state of ruin.*

*We are all changed, irrevocably changed. I cannot remember
how it felt to be young. Laughter and the ability to see humour in
life are casualties of this war. Gone my energy, for I feel certain that
no matter how long I live, I shall always be fatigued. Gone too my
idealism and my naivety. In their place? Unending grief and
fatalism tempered with determination. I will see this through to the
end.*

Jenny could not hold back tears. Elspeth was serving in horrible circumstances. No matter what she did, she could not escape the war for very long. She, on the other hand, had a wise and loving husband who wanted her to step out of a depressing and disappointing environment into another more satisfying one.

Names were so important. She recalled her time in witness protection, when Simon had required her to address him as Sergeant Casey. He'd wanted to maintain his professionalism during the assignment, but it had also served to keep her at a distance. When he had finally told her his given name, the barrier was erased, and they had developed a friendship that had flourished, and after Colin's death, become far deeper.

Consequently there was something they could do together: give their baby a name. Stop referring to him or her but use a name that could apply equally to a child of either sex. Alex, for example, could be a nickname for Alexander or Alexandra and would give weight to a life that had been so short lived. Ginger was a girl's name in the States but a boy's name in the UK. Leslie? Lesley? None of these seemed quite right.

Jenny turned several pages in the book of poetry before more diary sheets appeared. Needing a break, she walked into the kitchen to make a cup of tea. As she prepared it, she mused about what a luxury even this simple procedure was, because it was safe and unhurried and quiet. When Elspeth made a cup, did she ever have the time to drink it, or could the intensity of war be measured in the number of brews she left behind? Jenny took a sip of the warm liquid, well sugared, as Simon would say, and returned to her work.

The Americans are here. Many believe their involvement will make all the difference. Already I can see an improvement in morale. They are tall and well fed. Their energy and even their clean uniforms give us hope, the medical staff as well as the men, for we have all been downtrodden and demoralised. Yet their participation, even if it leads to an end to this war, cannot replace what has been lost, the countless lives. Instead we have inestimable grief from which many families will never recover. I wonder now if victory, if it ever comes, will be pyrrhic, not a great triumph accompanied by an exultation of spirit but an exhausted, mournful sigh.

The Somme ended in November 1916. America didn't declare war until April 1917, Jenny recalled, so U.S. troops might not have seen action until sometime the following year. However, there had been other major engagements. Surprised by the gap in time in Elspeth's entries, Jenny wondered if she had missed pages but could not find additional ones for that time period. Maybe some pages had been destroyed, or Elspeth had been moved too many times or been too drained by the need to care for the excessive number of casualties to record anything.

Oh Perry, I have looked for your face in the faces of so many wounded and dying men. Each time I am struck anew, and the blade cuts my heart in two. I always hoped our paths would cross. Will I ever know if you are alive and whole?

Will we ever have the perspective to assess whether the war was worthwhile? When the loss was so great, of poets, artists, scientists, engineers, educators, doctors, even those who toiled in simple ways yet kept the wheels of agriculture or commerce in our great country turning?

Rest in peace, we say, because there is no other peace for them but that which is to be found in death. And what of those maimed in body or spirit who will carry the scars of war with them as long as they live? The war will never be over for the man who is blind, the one who struggles to breathe with lungs damaged by poisoned gas, and many others here and in hospitals across the empire. Will they say it was worth it?

Simon had been in combat. An injury had ended his military career, and he had been angry, but he had come home. How had he healed? Had his Special Forces training given him a mindset that had carried him through? If not, they would never have met. What would her life look like without him? Surely it didn't matter where they lived, only that they were together.

She returned to the project, examining the remaining pages of poetry once, twice, a third time, but no additional sheets of Elspeth's script were there. The diary had ended – in anger, not in celebration or even relief — in an anger that reminded her of the words that the poets Siegfried Sassoon and Wilfred Owen had penned. How many deaths had she seen in one day? One week? One year? Men whose lives had ended before their stories were complete? Had Elspeth's anger eased? If so, how?

Who was Perry? The subject of the inappropriate relationship before the war? Had the medallion been his? There was no one alive who could answer that question. Was it among her possessions? Had pages been lost, or had she stopped writing? Had she been killed? Or died in the Spanish flu pandemic? Jenny had always assumed that she'd had a life after the war, but perhaps she, too, had been a fatality. She would ask Enid when she returned the material to her.

Elspeth existed now only on the disembodied pages she'd written, but she seemed real nonetheless to Jenny. She didn't know even the most basic details of her appearance; her intangible traits were what made her come alive. She had backbone. She was intelligent, perceptive, and eloquent. Reserved yet compassionate. Capable of enduring commitment and love. She must have assisted each soldier as if he were Perry.

Jenny looked up. The sun was setting, and her heart felt suddenly heavy. She thought of her baby – hers and Simon's – whose life had ended even before his story had begun. Too sorrowful to walk, she sat on her front stoop, Bear beside her, and regarded the blood-red sky. She wanted Elspeth to have lived, to have felt warm, clean, and rested. She wanted her to have had leisurely strolls through a pristine countryside, where the only sounds were the singing of the birds and the caresses of the breeze through the trees. She wanted her to have dined in restaurants with crisp white tablecloths and someone she loved across the table from her, raising a glass of wine and quoting a beloved passage of verse.

She wanted her to have had the gift of memory, as Neil Goodwyn called it, because over time the pain of remembering tragedy and loss fades.

Even razor-sharp images become less clear. Even a stubborn survival allows hope to be reborn and peace to follow. Would living in a new place on a new street kindle those for her? Was that part of Simon's purpose for both of them?

CHAPTER THIRTEEN

JENNY'S ROLLER-COASTER DAY began when she returned the final transcript to Enid Stanley, who seemed unsettled when Jenny wanted her to come in for a few minutes.

"Won't you sit?" Jenny asked. "I can make tea for us."

"Thank you, no," Enid replied. "I'm just here to collect everything from you."

"Of course, it's right here," Jenny said, wondering why she was in such a hurry, "but Enid – I wanted to tell you – I understand how special this memoir is to your family. I'm not related to Elspeth, but I feel that I know her. I have so much respect for her! It's appropriate that works of poetry surround her recollections because her writing is almost poetic. What a heritage you have!"

Enid did not respond, seeming a bit uncomfortable with Jenny's American enthusiasm.

Jenny continued. "As usual, I provided one page to correspond to each diary page as well as a continuing transcription of each section. My work is complete, but I hate to let it go. It feels unfinished. Her last entries were so angry! She stopped writing long before the armistice, and I would have liked to know how she felt about it. Peace was proclaimed, but was that her experience?" She paused. "So I have to ask – were there other pages found in her belongings? I wanted a conclusion to what she began, but the end is missing. Was she killed? They were all in danger, nearly all the time."

"No, she survived," Enid answered, still standing and seemingly uncertain what to do with her hands. "She became a nursing sister after the war and worked in a mental health hospital, somewhere in Scotland, I believe. She treated men who had shell shock or other mental issues resulting from head injuries. She never married."

She lived but never loved, Jenny thought. She picked up the diary and her transcription but didn't extend them to Enid. If she did, Enid would leave, and she would never know. She asked again. "Could you tell me, was there any other writing found in her possessions?"

"No loose pages, I'm afraid, in her steamer trunk. Some of her clothes, however. A lace collar. Lace gloves, so impractical in the Scottish climate. A coin of some sort, although not official currency of any kind. A number of line drawings, unsigned. Elspeth never showed any sort of artistic talent, so perhaps one of her patients drew them for her after the war. Her Bible."

The medallion, Jenny thought. She waited, but there was no more information coming. She didn't feel she could broach Enid's English reserve to ask about Perry, but she did have one more question she thought wouldn't be invasive. "Enid, what did Elspeth look like?"

Enid seemed startled. "We don't know," she admitted. "The family has no pictures of her. Her sisters were slim, with dark hair and eyes, so we can only assume she was as well."

"Thank you. Enid, the memoir is powerful. Publishing it is a very important project. I'm so happy you and Wilfred are planning to do it."

Enid prepared to leave. "I'm glad you found the work agreeable," she said. She held out her hands for the material then clasped it to her chest, preventing Jenny from embracing her.

Jenny opened the door and wished her well. Then it was time for a quick lunch and walk with Bear before meeting Beth for tea in Rickmansworth.

She took the Metropolitan line north from Finchley Road on her way to Ricky. After she got off the train, she passed a jewelry store with a bracelet in the window that caught her eye. She was wearing one with brightly colored beads, but the one on display was a purple wrap-around style with amethysts on each end. It wouldn't match anything she wore, and she thought of Georgina McGill's lavender shoes and smiled. She made the purchase and tucked it into her purse.

Beth was waiting at the tea shop and remarked on Jenny's bracelet as soon as she sat down.

"Georgina McGill suggested that I find a way to indulge myself," Jenny explained, "by collecting something, and I have." She showed Beth her new purchase.

"I don't know where she finds her energy," Beth commented. "She has come by to see me several times, and Meg and Robbie like seeing little Matt. I gave her some of the clothes that Robbie has outgrown."

"Did she wear her purple shoes?" Jenny asked.

"No, the last time they were orange," Beth laughed, "and they didn't match anything. Even the baby bag was in a subdued colour. It's funny – I feel both energised and exhausted when she leaves."

"She's brave, though, isn't she?" Jenny said. "She visits even when we're struggling and always seems to address the issue – whatever it is – directly."

"That's what I need to do," Beth confessed. "I'm so concerned about Brian. I'm losing him! He goes to work but either stays later than he has to or leaves and doesn't come home straightaway. When he is home, he's too quiet. Sometimes I wake up and find he's not in bed with me. He has trouble sleeping. All he does is worry over what the investigation will conclude and when."

"I think Simon has spent some time with him."

"Yes, but I don't know how much they talk. What does Simon say?"

Jenny smiled ruefully. "You're right. Not much. He just says that Brian's going through a rough patch and that they run together."

"He runs by himself as well, long distances, but at least then he's not drinking. Oh, Jenny, he's ageing before my eyes. There are lines in his face that weren't there before, and some of his hair is even turning grey."

"Tea, madam?"

"Yes, with a slice," Jenny told the waitress, wanting to add lemon instead of cream to her cup. "Is he angry?" she asked Beth.

"No, depressed, I think. I'd take anger any day over depression, because it's causing him to doubt himself. Jenny, he was always big for his age. He protected the smaller ones when they were picked on. He didn't need to be aggressive; his size alone was enough to give most bullies second thoughts. So for him to be accused of impropriety? Impulsive behaviour? I want to scream!"

"Beth, Brian protected me – in the only way he could. I don't understand why the investigation is taking so long. I've told every detective who interviewed me that his action was essential. He had no other course. If he hadn't fired, I would have died. I don't know what else they need to know." Jenny's tea was delivered. "Beth, will you share a dessert with me? A tart? A croissant?"

"A lemon tart, if you have one," Beth said to the waitress. "Two forks, please."

"Has Neil Goodwyn come by?" Jenny asked.

"Yes, and sometimes we're both home, but often he has to speak only with me. He believes that Brian needs emotional support – validation. He needs to be returned to his regular duties so he'll feel useful. And most of all, he needs resolution. For an end to come to this. In the meantime he said both of us need to abide – wait with hope."

I need that, too, Jenny thought.

Beth watched Jenny sip her tea. "Jenny – there's something I'd like to ask you. Neil suggested that I go to church. He said it might bring me a feeling of peace. I'm so desperate I'm considering it. Would – would you go with me? Brian won't. Christmas is coming, and I'm not even certain he'll go with us when we visit our families."

Jenny nodded. "It wouldn't hurt me to go. I've been missing what could have been, and now Simon has decided that the solution is for us to move. He wants to buy a house. Not here in Hampstead – maybe in Hayes, or Ruislip, or Rickmansworth, where you live. He wants us to live closer to you and Brian."

Beth's face reflected her conflict. "I'd love it if you were closer, but I'm so sorry – I've been preoccupied with my own worries and have neglected yours. Are you okay?"

"Losing the baby – it's a little easier than it was at first. And the idea of moving is the same – a little easier to accept now than it was at the beginning. He promised not to bother me, as he says, with the process until there's something attractive to view. I think he's afraid that if I see homes that I don't like, I'll change my mind about it. I don't know how he's going to find the time. His restricted duty is over, so he's working long hours again."

The lemon tart was placed between them on the table. Jenny and Beth just stared at it. Neither had any appetite after all. "Shall I take it home?" Beth finally asked.

"Yes. I'd fight you for it if it were chocolate," Jenny smiled, "but I'll cede this one. And Beth – I'm going to call Brian. Find a time when we can get together. I want him to know how grateful I still feel and that I'll stand with him all the way, no matter how long it takes."

Beth's eyes filled with tears. She busied herself wrapping the tart in a napkin and hugged Jenny before she left.

****

When Simon came home in the evening, he'd already eaten, so he and Jenny sat together in the living room. Jenny first related the news of her day, beginning with her meeting with Enid. "The diary ended so abruptly," she said. "Elspeth was angry, so angry that she stopped writing, I think. It gave me a new perspective, because it occurred to me that neither she nor I had an armistice. Maybe when we move, I won't be on this battlefield anymore."

He smiled. He'd heard the "when." "Jenny, I'm on the battlefield now – at least it feels that way. I have an estate agent and will be selecting a mortgage provider and a conveyancing solicitor. They're inspecting the financial documents we gave them. I've not yet seen a single house, but that should happen soon."

"Simon, Beth is terribly worried about Brian. I'm going to ask him to come by. Maybe some reassurance from me will help."

"Good idea," he agreed. "Speaking of Davies. The other night when you went to Moe and Laurie's party in Hayes, Mac saw someone following him. So I've given Mac a change of assignment. We both feel you're secure, but if Davies is being tailed, it could have something to do with the recent negative articles in the press."

"I wondered why I hadn't seen Mr. MacKenna lately, but I'm glad you asked him to help Brian. Because that reporter must be making it all up. No one's supposed to know it was Brian."

"That's correct. Davies' name won't be officially released unless and until the Crown Prosecution Service decides to lay charges. In the meantime, however, the stories continue."

"One reporter in particular – Hodge? – seems to be the author. And what he writes has gotten worse. The firearms officer is described as boastful, a man who talks about how eager he is to show off his skills. Who has no regrets. A man without a conscience. Even without a name, it's damning. And Brian's not like that at all."

Simon agreed. "Davies rarely speaks of the incident except in very controlled circumstances."

"The last headline I read asked, 'Are Armed Police a Threat to Society?' Where is this negative sentiment coming from?"

He sighed. "The seeds were planted long ago. From the beginning of the police force, few officers carried firearms, and the public was suspicious of any departure from that. However, some recent incidents increased the public's opposition to guns. In 1987 in Hungerford, not too far from London, a former soldier shot sixteen people and wounded fifteen others. Then in Dunblane, Scotland, a worse massacre occurred in 1996. Sixteen children and one teacher were killed at a school. Again fifteen others survived. In both cases the bastards who were responsible had obtained their firearms through legal means. Legislation was then enacted which made ownership of most handguns illegal, but it didn't change the shock and anger of the public. The distrust of firearms which climaxed then remains and now extends even to the police."

"Is that why you don't disclose the nature of your work to people we meet?"

He nodded. "We used to have a travel ticket which we could use on buses or trains, to relieve us from having to show our warrant cards in public. And the number plates on our private vehicles were not listed. When both those programs ended, I purchased the motorcycle. If I'm seen leaving the base, the number plate is smaller and therefore more difficult to record, and I don't have to rely on public transport."

"And you've told me that you always wear civilian clothes to work for security reasons."

"Yes, and the others do as well. What we change into depends on what sort of job we're tasked to carry out."

"I've seen articles which reported how upset people were to see armed officers on duty having a meal in a restaurant. That always puzzled me. I'd feel safe if there were police eating lunch where I was." She paused. "So it's even more important for Mr. MacKenna to do anything which can help Brian, isn't it? Because some people will be prejudiced against him, even though the shots he fired were meant to defend me."

"Yes," Simon agreed. "Mac and I believe the reporter has a contact. He's getting these stories somewhere, false and inflated though they may be. He's located the reporter, but the description didn't match the individual he saw in Hayes. The reporter is in his mid-thirties. Clean shaven. He has light brown hair and recessed eyes, one of which appears frozen into a permanent squint. And glasses. With a soft chin and small ears, close to his head. Medium height and weight. The man in Hayes was larger and stockier with darker hair, although Mac wasn't able to see his features clearly. He'll try to establish the reporter's routine so he'll know if he's meeting someone who could be feeding him information."

She nodded. "I trust Mr. MacKenna."

"I don't think it's likely that you'll have anything to fear from the man he's seeking or the reporter. Any member of the press, even if they were able to discover who you are, would know that your point of view would support the police. But I'll not be mentioning any of this to Davies. And I'd recommend against you doing so as well."

CHAPTER FOURTEEN

HE DIDN'T KNOW WHY they told him their secrets. Perhaps it was because he was quiet, apparently a good, even sympathetic listener with an understanding face. Did they want to be noticed? Valued? Gain revenge? Even the shy ones eventually shared what they knew. It helped when he confessed something first, of course. He was a good liar. Not only did others believe him, he also could always hear the lie when he was told one.

He didn't call them his informants. That was too pejorative a word for people who had contributed to his success.

He'd grown up in Wales, a country of mountains and coastlines. He studied psychology and English, wanting to know what made people tick and how he could best express himself. Welsh weather drove him indoors, so what better way to spend the cloudy, wet, and windy days than to write a novel in which an unassuming Welsh lad became powerful and famous because he knew more than anyone else? In fiction people came to him for guidance and advice, which he dispensed with impartiality if not compassion.

When he failed to find a sponsor for his work, he landed a job with a newspaper, establishing his reputation bit by bit. Newport, then Swansea, then Cardiff. He wasn't popular in newsrooms, but it didn't matter because he spent so little time there. Editors appreciated his willingness to sink his teeth into a story. His macintosh for the rain, his notepad and pen for the role, and his hidden digital recorder for backup. If an individual changed his or her mind about a disclosure, he had evidence, and if he needed to build trust, he could appear to erase it. And he was generally vague about which entity employed him.

Then came the move to London. Neither the *Times* nor the *Telegraph* took him on, his writing samples notwithstanding, so he applied other places. Eventually he found a home where his kind of journalism was accepted. His good fortune made him feel everything he was not: tall, strong, handsome, even sexy. With some sources, being difficult to describe was a sort of protection. If they wished to locate him after, they couldn't delineate his unremarkable features. Having distinguishing characteristics could have worked against him. Even his hair colour was unexceptional, not a warm brown or a copper brown but a dull pasty brown. He did, of course, keep it medium length, not too short, not too long. People didn't tell their deep darks to blokes who looked like centrefolds. They talked to forgettable chaps who made them feel special and safe.

One of his sources, unhappy with the pressure to supply information, had struck him in the face. He had photographed the injury and documented the treatment. Fortunately it hadn't affected his vision, although concealing that fact gave him more power over the offender, and the glasses helped him maintain the deception. A good disguise, not a necessity.

He was never homesick. Neither lamb stew nor leek soup made him miss his humble beginnings, his father a labourer, his mother old before her time, his sister not clever enough to keep the *mhabis,* or babies, from coming. She would never make anything of herself.

Few in London spoke Welsh, a difficult language to learn with more consonants and fewer vowels than English. He'd clothed insults in that lilting language, once calling a woman a *neidr,* a snake, and she had kissed him! On another occasion he'd complimented a lass on her *llyfn croen,* her smooth skin, and been rejected. Usually he was the one who stepped away. When a woman had told him all her secrets, he lost interest in her.

He never felt any guilt for sharing what he was told. Higher animals fed on lower animals. It was the way of the world. Amazing what a physical relationship, or even the prospect of one, could unlock, in women with a weak view of themselves but also in a few men as well. He didn't discriminate.

Rarely had he had such an enthusiastic contact as his recent source. He suspected that what he heard was embellished somewhat, but it didn't bother him, although usually embroidery was his job. To make for better reading. The whole truth was for courtrooms, not print media.

The one maxim he'd lived his life by had served him well: It's not a secret if you tell it.

It was all worth it for the byline: Lionel Hodge.

CHAPTER FIFTEEN

STILL STRUGGLING WITH the unfinished nature of Elspeth's diary, Jenny asked Simon if he'd accompany her to the Imperial War Museum. They took the tube from the Hampstead station, heading south on the Northern line to the Elephant & Castle stop. She'd figured out the route herself, despite the directions and names. It was necessary to go south on a northern train. And she had no idea how the two nouns elephant and castle combined for a significant title. In many ways life in London was still a little odd, if not arcane.

Less than a mile's walk from the station, they entered the grounds of the museum. Whoever had designed the front had a flair for the dramatic: two huge naval guns were outside. In addition the opening gallery held World War I tanks and a German trench periscope that was over eighty feet high.

Part of one floor of the multi-level museum was dedicated to the First World War. Paintings, photos, and dioramas were displayed as well as mannequins wearing the uniforms, complete with helmets, of both German and British soldiers. Trench knives, serrated like Roy's and used for close combat, looked razor sharp. Rifles with seventeen-inch bayonets attached to them caused Jenny to stop and catch her breath. The damage done by these weapons was almost unimaginable, and Elspeth would have seen it.

In the Trench Experience, a special exhibition, they followed a dark, loud, and cluttered route which took them past depictions of the ground seen from the parapet and the barbed wire of no-man's-land in the distance. What an apt phrase, she thought – that land had indeed belonged to no man because opposing armies had fought over it for years, advancing a few yards and then being pushed back. However, her walk was on dry duckboards, not marred by the omnipresent and dreaded mud that Elspeth had chronicled. And there was no wind or bitter cold. But a bell rang, like that which had warned soldiers of toxic gas, and the sounds of war were almost constant, the distant rumble of artillery and staccato bursts of machine-gun fire from both sides.

In other areas she looked through glass at a nurse's uniform and that of a civilian with the Voluntary Aid Detachment. The diary of a former VAD, Vera Brittain, was open. Her writing was a little larger and easier to read than Elspeth's and comprised of notebooks with dated pages, some filled fully and others with only a few lines. When she saw it, she realized that she was feeling something akin to grief for Elspeth, a woman she had never even met, and she had a new understanding of what the war had done to a nation, because its citizens had mourned people they had known and loved. She remembered after Colin's death how much the merest courtesy had meant. Was this war the origin of the sincere British politeness and concern which was extended even to strangers?

Simon accompanied her throughout, adding a comment only now and then, stopping when she stopped and patient with the times she pressed her hand into his.

More than two hours passed, she had moved so slowly through the gallery. When he asked whether she wanted to visit the Holocaust Exhibition, she replied in the negative. She still felt claustrophobic from her simulated trench walk and wanted to stop only in the gift shop briefly before escaping outside.

In the store she purchased a red poppy pin and Vera Brittain's book, *Testament of Youth*. Brittain had begun the diary before the war as a way of chronicling her life, her childhood, and her education, not intending it to become a war diary. Jenny was less interested in the parties she'd attended as a young woman and more concerned with her impressions of her wartime experience. Scanning her bio, she noted that Brittain had lost her brother, close friends, and even her fiancé during the war, yet she had married and had a family in her postwar years. That alone was more information than she possessed about Elspeth.

Jenny thumbed through the pages. Brittain, too, had written about agony, agony seen and agony felt, pain too great to allow speech, and the weather, the beastly weather. By the end of the war her profound sadness for what had been lost had turned to anger, anger at campaigns that made no sense, at loss of life on a scale that made no sense, at pain and fear that made no sense, and lastly, at sacrifice that made no sense. Unlike Elspeth, who never mentioned home visits, Brittain had been impatient with what the civilians called crises: the shortages and loss of help. She was grieved by the realisation that she was less innocent than her parents.

Leaving the museum, Jenny stepped into a day blessed with a bright British sun and skies so clear she thought they could stretch all the way across the English Channel to warm the graves of the British soldiers buried in France and Belgium. She hadn't wanted to express her feelings when they were inside the building, but later over dinner and wine she told Simon how much she appreciated his presence. "When we set out together, I didn't know that I couldn't have made this journey alone. Thank you for being with me. But you were so quiet."

"Jenny, it was your mission, not mine," he responded. "Did you find what you were seeking?"

"I found truth. Elspeth's observation that when you hear bad news, your mind takes in all the irrelevant details of your surroundings, resonated with me. I could still tell you every impression I had of the night I lost the baby, although none were sufficient to distract me from what was taking place. With regard to Elspeth's service and experience, I had hoped for some closure, but I didn't find it there. Foolish of me. I should know better."

CHAPTER SIXTEEN

SEVERAL DAYS PASSED before Jenny reached Brian. "Come by the flat," she pleaded. "I'm cooking, so curiosity should motivate you."

"Or fear will keep me away," he replied, but without humour in his tone. "Smells good," he said when he arrived.

"It should – it's your recipe," Jenny answered. "Pork roast with stuffing. I used apples, shallots, pecans, and herbs, with a little cream cheese to hold it together. Help yourself."

Brian placed asparagus and roasted red potatoes on his plate as well. They sat at the dining room table, too large for just the two of them but easier for Brian, whose long legs made eating on his lap difficult. He'd gained weight. At 6'5", being a heavy man made him even more imposing. He opened the bottle of ale Jenny offered him.

"Are you still cooking as much as you used to?"

"No," he admitted. "I'm consuming more liquid calories."

"Taste familiar?" Jenny asked after he'd had a few bites. "I tried to follow your instructions. Most of the recipes I make are ones you taught me, except for egg salad. That was Danny's, if it can even be called a recipe."

Brian smiled for the first time. "Sullivan's sliced cooked egg on tomato and bread," he said. "I remember. Jenny, Casey tells me you're wanting to move."

"Actually he's the one leading the charge on this, but he's winning me over to his point of view." She turned her head to follow the progress of an ambulance. "I won't miss the sirens on their way to the hospital."

"Don't start packing yet," he advised. "It's not a short process. Beth and I had to wait to be told what we could afford, and then it was a couple months before we found something that suited us. That's when the real waiting begins. We had to rely on others to complete their paperwork. You'll have plenty of time to celebrate lasts – last meal at a local restaurant, last walk on the Heath, last night cooking in this kitchen."

She put down her fork. "Brian, I asked you here to talk about something else."

He did not respond.

She could sense his reluctance. "We'll always be linked by what took place in Roy's flat."

He looked down at his plate. "You've ambushed me. Is that why you went to all this trouble?"

"Yes, because food fortifies you. That's what you always said. Brian, when I was a hostage with Roy, there wasn't much to eat, and most of it I couldn't keep down because of the morning sickness and headaches. I was scared to death all the time, which didn't exactly improve my appetite. He was no longer speaking with the negotiator. I didn't know if there were any police nearby. I tried to get away, but I couldn't. You put an end to all that, and I'll always be grateful."

He tried to clear his throat but had a swallow of the ale instead. "I should have made entry sooner, Jenny. If I had, perhaps you and Casey would still be expecting a baby. Instead, my score's not very good. I saved one life – and I'm glad of it – but lost two."

"Brian, if you hadn't come in when you did, both the baby and I would be dead. I tried to protect him – or her – but I couldn't. The doctor said that Simon and I will have another chance. But this first little one – that was Roy's fault, not yours. I was trying so hard to get along with him, to keep him from getting angry. I thought if I could do that, I'd be safe, but it wasn't working. And the worse he got, the more dangerous it was for me. I told all the detectives that you had to do it."

"Because of the knife?"

"Yes."

"And if there'd been no knife?"

"Even then. But there was. I have marks from it all over."

"Yet police are investigating me," he said in a puzzled voice. "That's the system – I understand – I'm not disputing that I should be held accountable – but officers who have never held a gun are judging what I did with mine."

"I agree, it isn't fair," she said. "But the question is, what do we do now? Besides having second helpings," she commented as she saw his empty plate.

He limited himself to small servings but gestured for another bottle of ale. She handed it to him and topped off her glass of wine.

"Do you remember how much help I needed when I was in witness protection? Danny brought me flowers, and Simon made me exercise. I had to have psychological help. Spiritual help. I read about Winston Churchill, who never gave in to his depression. You mustn't, either. Even Hunt helped by serving me chocolate. And you – a thousand thoughtful things. You sat with me. Listened to me. Cooked for me. The legal system didn't work very fast then either, but you helped me to see it through. You taught me to trust, to be on the team."

"I've not got a team," he said.

"Brian, you have Beth, Simon, me, others. You have a legal team."

He shook his head. "No word from them for a time. Not much to do but wait."

"You can't just run in place – you have to do something. In Texas we used to say, 'Don't squat on your spurs.' We meant, 'Don't do something you'll regret.' The converse is true, too. If you don't fight back, you'll never forgive yourself." She wasn't sure she was getting through. "Brian, as a police officer, you train for every eventuality, so you need to prepare in every way you can – physically and mentally – for what might lie ahead with this. There's bound to be a psychiatrist with the Met. Maybe it's time you considered consulting him."

He gave his head a half shake. "It shouldn't be necessary."

"It may not be, but if it helps you feel better even short term it will be worth it."

"For you and Beth."

"Yes, but for you, too. Don't the newspaper articles make you mad?"

He nodded slowly. "I remember Casey wanting you angry before the trial. It gave you fuel for what you had to face."

"Yes, and I'll be with you all the way. When these glacial investigations finally conclude that your action was lawful, we'll laugh together at their colossal waste of time."

CHAPTER SEVENTEEN

AS CHRISTMAS APPROACHED, Jenny realized how special this year's holiday needed to be for her and Simon. Only their second as a married couple, and they'd experienced significant trauma and loss. Simon bought the tree, and they decorated it together with red ornaments, Santas, candy canes, and red ribbons tied in small bows. She cooked ahead of time – corn pudding instead of cornbread stuffing, green vegetables blanched and chilled with an herb-spice dressing, scalloped potatoes with béchamel sauce and a hint of cheese – so she wouldn't have much to prepare besides the turkey on Christmas Day. She skipped Christmas pudding, which she had disliked from her first taste. Having given up on mastering the culinary distinctions of a crumble, a crisp, or a cobbler, she simply entitled her fruity dessert an apple concoction.

They took their Heath walk early, bundling up against the cold which seemed to invade her every pore, much the way her grief had at first. Their scarves and hats and other forms of insulation became isolation, because holding Simon's gloved hand wasn't intimate, and the climate wasn't conducive to conversation. Sometimes their wordless walks were comfortable, but today she needed more interaction than the whipping wind would allow. The Heath looked as if it had lost the war with the elements, the paths muddy and the colors of the landscape muted. In the process the Heath had aged, its greens now gray, and the leaves beneath her feet evidenced all the little deaths of the season.

She was glad to return to the warmth of the flat and strip off the layers of separateness. With hot coffee brewing for him and hot chocolate for her, she began to talk.

"Simon, I've been wanting to tell you. The night isn't as dark as it was. I still miss our baby, but something in the diary gave me an idea. Elspeth wrote about how important it was to use someone's name. I remember in witness protection how formal you were – I had to call you Sergeant Casey until the end – and when you told me your name was Simon, it made such a difference. So I think our baby should have a name. I've thought about several, but I've settled on Sam, for either Samuel or Samantha. If it's okay with you." She sipped her cocoa and waited for him to respond.

"Sam. Sam Casey. I can manage that," he said after a few moments. "More than."

"Also, I'm finding myself wanting to do normal things. Walking slowly enough to absorb every molecule of air – when it's warmer, of course. Listening until I can hear the difference between the rustling of a bird's wings and the falling of leaves. I want to smell every flower I walk past, to see the ripples in the ponds. Silly, isn't it?"

He waited. He had learnt not to agree when she asked that question.

"I want to see you coming back from your run, and I want to hug you, sweat and all. I want to start the new year with new goals, and moving is one of them."

"Jenny, you'll not have regrets. I promise."

She smiled. "One more thing – I want Brian's ordeal to be over."

"Two of us then."

"Simon, I know we planned to wait to exchange gifts until later in the day, but I've changed my mind. I want to be Father Christmas and give you yours as soon as I've put the turkey in the oven."

"I'll be ready," he smiled. "And in the meantime I'll help you."

He did, setting aside the parts of the bird they'd simmer later to add to the gravy and discarding the rest. They rinsed and greased the turkey and set the oven on a low roasting temperature. She set the table, adding a Christmas cracker at each place, and removed her apron. They unwrapped presents from family members and put them to one side, knowing they'd exchange phone calls later in the day.

He then opened several small gifts from her, books he hoped he'd have time to read, and watched whilst she carried a large and not completely wrapped item into the sitting room. It was a portable Questar telescope, known for its superior optics and velvet controls.

"Do you like it?" she asked anxiously. "It came highly recommended."

He pored over the directions. "Jenny, it's a fine 3-1/2-inch and has a clock drive."

In response to her raised eyebrows, he explained. "A clock drive compensates for the earth's rotation, so when you view the stars, they appear to stand still."

"I wish I could give you the time to use it and clear skies to go with it," she said. "Then you could teach me the constellations and the stories that go with them."

"We'll find those nights," he assured her. "Now it's your turn."

The first present was a matching poinsettia pin and earrings, followed by a Christmas detective mystery by one of her favorite authors, wrapped in red paper.

"I'm sensing a theme here," she teased.

"One of several," he admitted. "Now, something to add to your collection." He handed her a small box.

In it she found a bracelet with deep red glass beads and a certificate confirming its Italian origins.

"*Bene,*" she laughed. She held out her arm, and he slid the bracelet onto her wrist.

Last she opened a gold-colored box with a bracelet of emeralds and rubies. She gasped.

"A remembrance of the holiday," he said.

"That's an understatement!" she exclaimed. "The colors of the season in precious jewels. It's the best." She hugged him. "Simon, do you know why I collect bracelets?"

"Of course. And I want to help you heal." He helped her with the clasp.

"You've outdone yourself. How did you find time to buy these?"

"I had the entire team scouting for me. I told them red was your favourite colour, and I'd make a personal inspection of anything with red."

"Then I owe thanks to all of them," she said. "But I have something more for you. Really it's for both of us. It's something I can't wrap. I thought about putting it in a card, but I couldn't find any that seemed to fit the sentiment." She moved closer to him on the sofa and took one of his hands in hers. "Simon, I want to think about the future and not the past. Since it's Christmas, it's a good time – I want to try – " She stumbled over her words.

"Out with it, Jenny," he said gently. "My curiosity's at an all-time high."

She swallowed hard, surprised by her nervousness. "We're a family of two, but – but I'd like us to be a family of three. A baby, Simon. That's what I want to give you. Give us. It's a good day for all kinds of celebrations, don't you think?"

She looked like a gift, her gold shirt shiny and her black trousers belted with a ribbon. He took her in his arms. "Jenny, it's a great day. All I need for Christmas."

"There's just one thing missing," she said. "The mistletoe."

"An English tradition," he acknowledged, "but we're going to do fine without." He kissed her. "How much longer will the turkey be cooking?"

"More than two hours," she answered.

"Then we'll not have to hurry," he said.

"What about the Queen's speech?"

"We'll make missing it another good English tradition," he chuckled.

CHAPTER EIGHTEEN

A BLOODY WAY TO START the new year, Brian Davies thought. Sitting in a shrink's waiting room. Institutional décor, of course. He should have been used to it by now, but for some reason he had expected a psychiatrist to have more congenial surroundings.

He'd had one benefit even before meeting Dr. West: Beth's attitude. She'd been at him to go and was now relieved that he was. He hadn't told her that he hadn't made a long-term commitment. He intended only to test the waters.

The door to the consulting room opened, and a lanky man with greying curly hair, cut very short, stood for a moment as if surveying him before speaking. No worries. Brian was doing the same. He noted the doctor's relaxed face and alert eyes. Feeling a bit rebellious, he did not stand until the psychiatrist addressed him. He hadn't decided whether he'd allow the doctor to be in charge.

"PC Davies? Gerry West."

His handshake revealed a firm grip.

"Come in, please."

No artificial familiarity. Good. Brian acquiesced. He surveyed the room, noting the desk to one side of the circle of sofas and chairs. Framed certificates covered one wall – his credentials, Brian guessed – and incomprehensible modern art on another. Dr. West sat in one of the chairs and waited for Brian to choose his seat. He opted for the largest and sturdiest, sufficient to contain his large frame. Others generally found his size imposing, but Dr. West didn't seem intimidated by it at all. Suddenly Brian felt a bit uneasy. He was used to police situations in which he was in control. Now the rules of engagement were unclear. He sat and waited for West to begin.

"Tell me why you've requested this meeting," West said.

He means me, Brian thought, and again felt misgivings about agreeing to come.

"Perhaps I should mention that everything we say in here is confidential. I'd not be very good at what I do without. If you're more comfortable beginning with your background, please do so. How many years you've been with the Met, with the firearms unit, and so forth."

West listened to Brian's recitation. "You're a well-trained, responsible, and experienced officer functioning in a very high stress environment then. That's a good context for examining events of a more specific nature."

Brian took a deep breath and described how Jenny's first call had come in and how the scenario had unfolded. As he spoke, he gained confidence. Everything had been by the book: the notification of New Scotland Yard, the involvement of the Islington detectives, waiting for the negotiator to arrive and initiate contact, the positioning of the tactical teams, the resolution of the incident.

West appeared to listen intently. "Let me summarise. You were on the tactical team on site. When you believed the hostage was in danger, you made entry and shot and killed the hostage taker. Am I correct so far?"

Brian nodded.

"Did you expect the negotiations to be successful?"

"No, because they rarely are. That's why we develop a tactical plan and stick to it."

"Did the identity of the hostage direct your actions?"

"No. The actions of the hostage taker did."

"Did you act with malice?"

"What sort of a question is that?" Brian demanded. "I did what I was trained to do."

"Did you experience a dulling of the senses? I'm referring to a slowing down of motion, tunnel vision, or muffling of sounds."

"On the contrary, it happened very fast. I was focused on what I had to do. My rounds, when I released them, did not seem overloud to me, and I had no difficulty hearing the shouts of my mates."

"Are you currently under indictment?"

"No, but my duty is restricted because the investigation is still under way, and my authorisation to carry firearms is being withheld. The DPS has completed their interviews and turned their material over to the IPCC."

"Independent Police Complaints Commission," West nodded. "I'm familiar with the procedure."

"They've not yet issued a ruling. However, a firearms incident that took place at the end of April was found lawful only last month, so that officer waited almost eight months to be returned to full operational duties. I'm relieved for my mate but concerned because the forensics in my case seem to be less clear cut."

"And those forensics are – ?"

Brian shifted uncomfortably in his chair. "Some findings seem to suggest that the X-ray – the hostage taker – was not armed, although I know that he was and the hostage has sworn that he was."

"An unwelcome complication," West commented, "which is likely to have added to the potential trauma you may have experienced with this event."

"You think I'm traumatised? Why would I be? I fired in the line of duty."

"Trauma is more common than most people realise. In police officers, in particular, it often goes undiagnosed. May I continue?"

West took Brian's silence as a form of assent. "Trauma symptoms can be short term and long term. In the circumstances it would be reasonable to expect a lack of concentration, decreased interest in your family and hobbies, even in the Job, as well as a demeanour that reflects how tired and irritable you are. Periods of numbness or withdrawal may occur. You may experience physical symptoms such as headaches and muscle aches or cramping. Your eating, sleeping, and sexual habits may also have been affected. I'd expect that you've been repeatedly reexamining your actions with no productive result."

Brian's face darkened. With his height he was accustomed to dealing with low ceilings, but he now felt as if his mind were being pressed down as well.

"Officer Davies, your time is valuable, although you may not consider it so at the present moment. Hence I prefer a direct approach. The symptoms I have described to you, I'd like to emphasise, are to be expected for an individual in your situation."

Brian let out a slow breath and felt the tightness in his chest ease slightly. West had been respectful. He had not made a judgement about his action, focusing instead on its psychological manifestations.

"You have tangible and intangible issues to face. I've seen a number of newspaper articles which, whilst not citing you by name, are critical of your actions. I recommend that you respond to these in two ways: first, by not reading beyond the headlines, and second, by tearing them up and tossing them into a wastepaper basket. That's the only thing to do with trash."

Too right, Brian thought.

"You're bound to be angry about your Job status, and you have, in my view, every right to be. The question is what to do about it. Are you a runner? Do you have access to a gym? If so, use it. Take up boxing, perhaps. Whatever you do, keep moving, because moving combats depression and may cause physical changes in your body which will impact your emotions."

"One of my mates runs with me," Brian volunteered.

"Excellent. That leads me to the less concrete and consequently more difficult aspects of this circumstance: how to deal with the challenge of waiting in a constructive way. First, accept that waiting is a normal part of the process and not an indicator of worse to come. Accept that you may not feel as productive during this time. Accept that you may need more emotional support than before. You may be feeling powerless. Police officers don't like that. No one does, actually."

"My wife is supportive," Brian said.

"No doubt she'd be more supportive if you let her."

Brian nodded.

"Consider that a recommendation. Anyone else?"

"Others in the firearms unit. The hostage herself."

"Do you have legal assistance available to you?"

"Yes. My Federation rep and solicitor were present during my interviews. They'll continue to provide legal advice if the case progresses. My years of paying Federation dues may prove to be worthwhile."

West was quiet for a moment. "Our time is coming to a close. I advise another meeting, and between that time and this, I'd like you to complete a homework assignment. First, determine what is real, that is, what has actually happened, as opposed to what is imagined, or what you fear could happen. Second, list what steps you have taken or will take to improve your situation. Third, identify what actions you have taken that have caused your situation to worsen."

"The intangibles," Brian commented.

"Yes, and I think you'll find that putting them down on paper puts them in perspective." He stood. "Thank you for coming in."

CHAPTER NINETEEN

THE MIDDLE OF JANUARY, and Simon and Jenny's second wedding anniversary was approaching. Until recently he hadn't given her any ideas about what he wanted or how he wished to celebrate. Finally he told her that he wanted her to say yes to him again if she could.

"Simon, of course I can," she replied, wondering why he needed reassurance. "I love you."

"Don't be hasty," he cautioned. "I'll be asking something of you. You'll see."

"And if I can't?"

"We'll sort it."

Something he wanted but would be okay with if she didn't. It was all very mysterious. When the day came, he provided only a few additional details.

"A day trip," he said. "We'll take the tube and return to Hampstead in time for a special meal at the Gaucho."

He knew she loved that restaurant, usually starting with Argentine turnovers called empanadas. The various cuts of beef they served were measured in grams and cooked to the customer's preference, including choice of sauce, which for Jenny was always béarnaise. An assortment of salads and vegetables was also on the menu, and he could generally predict that she would succumb to the chocolate and praline mousse for dessert. It would be a wonderful evening, but she had to weather what he had planned for the afternoon first. There was a significant difference between agreeing to something in principle and doing it.

She dressed for the cold and clear weather and walked with him to the Finchley Road tube station, where they boarded the Metropolitan line underground train. "Are we going to see Brian and Beth?"

"Not today."

"Are we adopting another dog? Touring a historic home?"

"Not exactly."

She peered at him. His expression gave nothing away. She sighed.

They passed the Rickmansworth stop and exited above ground at Chorleywood.

"Chorleywood?"

"Yes, in the county of Hertfordshire. It was originally part of Rickmansworth."

He directed her onto a steep paved path marked "Private Road" with shrubs and ivy overhanging a tall fence on her left and uncut grass past the handrail on her right. Where the fence ended, the path leveled and widened into a road with houses on either side. Some had bay windows and flower boxes behind wrought-iron fences. Others sported decorative designs in the brick, and one had an empty wooden trellis mounted next to a window. Occasionally a yew tree or privet hedge paralleled the street. Cars were parked either on the sidewalk or on the short driveways that fronted some of the homes.

They stopped in front of a two-story house with a royal blue garage door facing the street. Its front door and window shutters were a corresponding blue on brick the color of clotted cream. An estate agent's sign included the word "villa" and a phone number. Villa sounded Italian, but Jenny knew that in the UK it referred to a middle-class dwelling.

"Simon?" she queried, her voice rising. "You brought me to see a house? On our wedding anniversary?"

"Trust me, Jenny," he said, with as close to a plea in his voice as she'd ever heard.

The estate agent arrived by car a few minutes later, parking in the small, paved area in front of the home. A well-fed woman in her late fifties, Stella Reynolds introduced herself to Jenny, unlocked the front door, and then stepped aside to let them enter.

Jenny noted the brass lion door knocker and wondered which of the lion's characteristics it would foretell. Strength? Courage? She needed both.

"A very attractive and unique property," the agent began. "A bit more contemporary in décor than some would like, but – " She stopped at a sign from Simon but handed Jenny a brochure with a description of the house and photographs of the main rooms and their dimensions.

The foyer had a black-and-white checkerboard-tiled floor and a mirror on one side. All was dim until Mrs. Reynolds opened the draperies in the living room beyond. Light flooded in, making the hardwood floors shine.

Jenny walked through room after room, some upstairs, some down, most with an accent stripe in a bold color. She didn't hurry, but she didn't stop to wait for Simon. He followed behind but didn't disturb her. The house was quiet, the sound of the train they had taken more a purr than a rumble, and she hadn't heard the siren of an ambulance since they arrived.

She catalogued in her mind the spaces she passed through. A formal dining room with a modest kitchen and breakfast area behind it. Pantry with shelves on both sides. Living room with built-in bookshelves and a fireplace that extended to the master bedroom upstairs. The absence of a wall between the living and dining rooms widened the perspective.

Climbing the stairs, Jenny tripped on the last step, falling forward and sprawling on the floor of the bedroom. The suddenness of the fall brought angry and embarrassed tears. "Simon, I feel ridiculous," she said as he helped her to her feet.

The estate agent heard the commotion and called out to them.

"We're all right," Simon answered. "We found the trip step." He explained to Jenny that the last step was made higher on purpose to warn of danger. "A useful feature," he added.

"No kidding," she said, but she was not smiling. She continued her tour, noting that the bedroom had a small stained-glass window on one end. The sun was shining through it, creating an abstract painting on the opposite wall. As the day progressed, Jenny thought, its form and color would alter. She paused to take it in before proceeding to view two additional bedrooms. None of the rooms, as they said in England, were overlarge, but there was an abundance of windows to let the natural light in. Whatever the world held, she would see it coming.

Returning to the main floor, she gazed for the first time through the French doors into the garden. Opening one of them, she stepped out. Some of the shrubs were overgrown, but there were bare spots in the flower beds, perhaps dormant due to the time of year. She glanced to her right and saw a wooden bench a little the worse for wear. She heard Simon's voice behind her.

"I'll sand and paint it for you," he said, his heart having leapt at the sight of it.

She bowed her head briefly.

In relief? In surrender? In acceptance? Simon could not tell. He knew she was peeved with him, but he had resolved to let her make up her own mind. With difficulty he said nothing more.

She took a second tour of the house, stopping in each room to close her eyes and then open them again. She located the two full bathrooms, their colors relatively neutral, and the half bath. She opened closet doors. The garage had room for only one car. Her face was somber.

"Overall it's somewhat stark. I'll have to soften the rooms somehow. And compared to our flat in Hampstead, it's a little small," she said, "but compact."

He couldn't hold back. "We'll do our best to make it crowded." He turned to the agent. "If you'll hold the fort for us, we'll return in a few." He took Jenny's hand and led her back to the road. "There's one more feature you need to see."

They walked to the top of the street. To her left she saw a row of pastel houses and a sign for the Rose and Crown Pub. On the right were a veterans' hall and a golf club. Across the road lay a wide field with natural grasses, and in the distance, groves of trees.

"Is it a heath?" she asked.

"They call it Chorleywood Common," he answered, "but it's like a heath. Only about two hundred acres but closer to the house than the Heath is to our flat in Hampstead. Just modest portions have any public development. Davies and I have our runs here. I've seen benches, people walking their dogs, and some wildlife. There's a church on the far side with a small cemetery. And a restaurant with Sunday roasts that Davies recommends." He took a deep breath and waited.

"Is this all of Chorleywood?"

"No, only a small part. Most of it's on the other side of the train station. Shops, restaurants, and the like, and a much larger residential area. This house has been vacant for a time, and the owners just reduced their asking price."

"Have you seen other houses?"

"Yes, but I could tell from photos that they wouldn't suit."

"Simon, this trip today – I thought I was ready, but seeing a house makes our decision to move real. It was harder than I anticipated. I feel hurried. It seems so soon. I understand why you didn't tell me in advance."

"When a decision's been made, nothing's to be gained from waiting to act."

"I just thought I'd have more time to get used to the idea." They were still holding hands, and she was glad. "A pessimist couldn't live in that house," she said. "There are no dark corners. Did you think it would be the one?"

"I saw pictures. I knew the Common was nearby. I hoped."

"Had you seen the bench?"

"No, interior snaps only. But I liked the openness, the simplicity, the size. And there's virtually no crime here."

"It's farther for you to travel to work."

"No worries."

She leaned into him, putting an arm around his waist and resting her head on his shoulder. Simon, her lion-hearted husband. "Simon, I shouldn't have doubted you. I'm so, so sorry."

"Done and dusted, Jenny."

She felt an unfamiliar feeling rise from her chest, a warmth, an appreciation for him, no, something more. It was happiness, because he had kept his promise to her. "The Common – it's the icing on the cake," she said, her eyes full, "because I can't imagine that we'll find a better house. A fireplace in the bedroom! And the yard – with that bench."

He felt a weight lift from his shoulders. "Is that a yes? Shall I make an offer? If it's accepted, the process will be under way."

She realized he'd been holding his breath. "Yes, and you'll have a hard time finding an anniversary gift next year that will top this one," she smiled. "Will the agent mind if I have one more walk through?"

****

At the Gaucho they were seated at one of the black tables, the crisp white napkins and plates providing stark contrast and the single candle making the glassware gleam. Something in the fabric of Jenny's dress sparkled even in the dim light. They'd already exchanged anniversary gifts, she giving him a heavy duty tripod for his telescope and the three-volume star atlas to guide his explorations of the night sky. He'd presented her with a box of chocolate candy and a bracelet of chocolate diamonds, which she had sworn she wouldn't remove from her wrist until their next anniversary.

A complementary selection of breads was delivered to them, accompanied with butter and chimichuri sauce, a mixture of parsley, garlic, shallots, oregano, and other seasonings. Jenny savored her meal, from the first bite of her appetizer to the last of her entrée. Simon finished his in half the time and spent the rest drinking his wine and watching her.

"It was a stressful day," she confessed to him. "An emotional one, but a good one. The future isn't unknown now. I'm going to a specific place. However, I'm more tired than I expected to be." She smiled. "The wine is relaxing me." Nevertheless she decided to forgo the dessert. "I'm replete."

As they walked home through the Hampstead streets, she linked her arm with his. "Remember what Robert Louis Stevenson said about matrimony? It's a 'sort of friendship recognised by the police.' I think our marriage is far more than that."

He agreed.

"Let's tell the story of us," she asked, leaning into him. "I'll start. When you were put in charge of protecting me for the Scott trial, you didn't like me very much."

He smiled. It was a request he never denied. "You're correct. It wasn't love at first sight. However, I wasn't paid to like you; I was paid to keep you safe. But I began to notice you when you defied me. It showed strength of character, I thought. Then your father came to take you home so you wouldn't have to testify, and you didn't go. Consideration turned to respect."

They were at the bottom of the hill, about to turn from the High Street. "On New Year's Eve, I came back from a brief leave. I'd been on the town with my brother, hitting the clubs, drinking. We found women willing to party with us, but when I came back to the flat, you were wearing a black trouser suit, and I wanted you. Sullivan noted it as well, and Sinclair never took his eyes off you."

"You didn't join in the toasts for the new year," she said.

"I couldn't. It was my turn to stand watch." He paused. "When we escorted you to court and you were shot, I still had the objectivity to treat Sullivan first, but when you became ill – and thought you weren't going to make it – you said goodbye to me, remember? I was gutted, and I knew then I'd gone beyond respect and desire."

"And yet you never intervened when Colin's and my relationship began to develop. I wish I'd known. I was clueless, and I'm sorry."

"He had more to offer you."

"We'll never know if that's true, but the things you've given me have made me very happy."

"You were worth waiting for, love." He slowed his pace. "Your turn now."

She smiled. "You were in charge of my witness protection team, and I was afraid of you. You were so stern, so serious about my medical care, my rehab, even what I ate. When I tried to talk to you about how I felt, you never participated very much, but every time I needed help, you responded. I trusted you, and you made me feel safe."

"Not a bad foundation for love," he commented.

"Even for an unlikely pair like the two of us," she laughed. "Much, much later, after Colin died, I looked back and realized that you'd always been there for me. And then came the night when you needed me instead of the other way around, and everything changed."

"I like your version better than mine," he said, "but you'll need to finish your account before we get home."

"Being with you was like skating on a frozen pond and knowing I didn't ever have to be afraid of thin ice. And here we are."

"You left out the punch line," he teased. "Here we are – husband and wife."

"Our stories end the same way. That's what counts."

CHAPTER TWENTY

JENNY'S CELL PHONE RANG. It was Enid Stanley, asking if she could call by.

"I'm walking my dog," Jenny said. "Give me about thirty minutes to get home." Too cold a day to tarry, she had still wanted to walk in a place that was familiar to her, particularly now that she knew she would be leaving it. She loved that the Heath was always open. No office hours.

"Would you be willing to take on a bit more work?" Enid asked when she arrived. "We've found some of Aunt Elspeth's pages in her Bible. I'm not certain why we didn't think to look there before, but we've left them where we found them, in case there's any significance in their location."

"I always hoped there would be more," Jenny said. She held out her hands for the holy book.

Enid started to speak but seemed to change her mind.

"I'll be careful," Jenny assured her.

Enid nodded her thanks and departed.

Jenny thumbed slowly through the slim Bible. Its pages were thinner and more fragile than the pages in the volumes of poetry. Should she be using tweezers to separate them? Elspeth's entries were written on pieces of paper nearly half the size of her previous ones, and therefore better hidden.

No one was more surprised than I when one of the doctors showed an interest in me. I am so thin I no longer have any curves to speak of, and my only voice is my professional one. His voice was soft and quiet, and I leant toward him to hear it, a mistake because he pulled me close and tried to kiss me. As I wriggled away, he stepped back, an apology in his words but not on his face. Ah, we are all lonely.

An endless procession of white faces, some white from loss of blood but almost all white still from fear. Sometimes the men ask the nurses direct questions about their care, and in each case the nurse has to decide which would be easier for the patient to hear: the truth, a lie, or a briskness that is no answer at all. Bad news from home may elicit everything from a rapid blinking to hold back tears to a sharp intake of breath and closed eyes to weeping in total collapse. Rumours of an enemy offensive can terrify the best of them. No one speaks of it, but we all know that the better job the doctors do restoring the wounded to health, the more complicit they are in sending them back to the front, where they will again be in harm's way. The nurses are a part of it all and must be affected as well as the men.

There is still so much blood in my dreams. I smell it, see it, and can't stop the flow. Can we not be kind to one another? Surely we must endeavour above all to be kind.

When they cannot save a man, his uniform and kit are sent home. I wonder sometimes at the practice. Does the receipt bring comfort or prolong anguish? I do not know. For those who return home alive, how long do they continue to believe themselves in the trenches?

An armistice has been declared. People are calling it victory and are celebrating because the war is over, but is it victory? What have we won? When so many have died and others are forever dead inside? When our wards are still full? Will the families who have lost a father, husband, brother, or son be celebrating? I find it cruel.

Then followed Elspeth's frustration with the political terms. An armistice meant an agreement to stop fighting, but did the cessation of hostilities mean surrender for one party and victory for the others? She did not offer a conclusion, simply positing that perhaps in the circumstances survival was a victory, albeit for both sides. And silence – no sounds of guns or pain. No orders, no calls for help, no weeping. Sun and silence.

Jenny thought for a minute. There were all kinds of victories. Sometimes winning seemed more like losing, particularly with the casualties of war. However, could something good come from a loss? Maybe it took time for that to happen, as well as believing that it could. Maybe how one reacted made the difference.

She found the next of Elspeth's pages in the Book of Joshua.

Alive! You are alive! Tonight one of the nurses said, "The head injury in the last bed seems agitated. Would you speak with him? The doctors have done their best, but they don't know if his sight or reason will return." I carried out the assignment, and then I was the agitated one, for it was you, Perry. I would have known you even without your identity disk, the severity of your injury notwithstanding. You did not react to my voice, so I did not identify myself. Many wounded have temporary hearing loss. Instead I held your hand, and that seemed to calm you. You will be sent to hospital in England when your vital statistics have become stable, but I will locate you.

What an irony! The war has given back to me what was taken away in peacetime. If you never know me, my heart will still be whole, for I have enough love for both of us. And I now know what I will do when the wards are empty and I am returned to England: I will become a nursing sister and will work to restore you to health. If that is not possible, I will be your eyes and your memory. Joshua 1:9.

Jenny checked the exact words of Scripture, and several seemed particularly important to her. "Be strong and of good courage; be not afraid, neither be thou dismayed." That sentiment could be hers, she thought. Her challenges were far less than Elspeth's had been, but she could also use an affirmation to strengthen her as she and Simon waited for symptoms of pregnancy. She thought about Beth, who was considering attending church because she knew that she needed courage to support Brian in the days ahead. And she thought about Brian, his future unknown, his career in the hands of others.

She gingerly turned the rest of the pages in the Bible, but Elspeth had written her last words. Had she prayed that verse for Perry?

She had never married. Had she found Perry? Had he recovered enough to recognize her? If not, had Elspeth's brave words, words of hope and resolution, been sufficient to sustain her? They called upon a higher power, a cry that Neil Goodwyn would consider to be worthwhile and wise.

CHAPTER TWENTY-ONE

WHEN BRIAN DAVIES ENTERED the chief super's office, they were all there: Chief Superintendent Morgan Brierly, Chief Inspector Carl Denison, his Federation representative Roderick James, and his solicitor Arthur Wheatley. None were smiling.

"Close the door, Croxley," Brierly said to the officer who had escorted him.

Brierly gestured for Brian to sit, but Brian declined. Something in the atmosphere told him that he needed, not to relax, but to have his wits about him. One by one the others stood. Brierly moved from behind his desk. To his credit, he never looked away from Brian when he spoke, and he addressed him formally, which Brian appreciated. It helped him to maintain his composure. When Brierly finished, he heard other voices, snippets of sentences, isolated words: "here to advise you," "counsel available," "guidance," and "support." Finally Brierly said, "An officer will see you home," and Brian knew that he was dismissed. The meeting was over, but the ordeal had just begun.

The tabloid the following morning covered it all and more:

CPS TO LAY MURDER CHARGES AGAINST GUN COP
By Lionel Hodge

LONDON — One can only commend the Crown Prosecution Service for its courage in bringing charges against a member of a fraternity with which they, as a general rule, work in concert. Investigations of the incident which prompted this action were prolonged and extensive, the incident itself occurring near the end of August of the preceding year.

To recap, a female hostage, whose name has not as yet been released for reasons unknown to this reporter – was taken on Thursday, 25 August, in the vicinity of a market estate near Caledonian Road. Police were notified, both officers from New Scotland Yard and detectives from the Borough of Islington, who took charge of the investigation. Two days passed before the alleged hostage taker was identified and contacted, at which time a police negotiator entered into talks with him.

The female hostage was rescued when armed officers made entry to the hostage taker's flat on Sunday, 28 August, in response to cries of distress, they claimed. Members of the firearms team also maintained that the hostage taker was warned that they were armed police and given every opportunity to surrender himself before shots were fired. In spite of attempts to sustain his life, the two rounds which entered his chest proved fatal.

The hostage taker, Roy Alden Wilkes, was a confused and terminally ill 52-year-old male of Scottish/Jamaican descent. Why, this reporter asks, was the negotiation process so minimal in duration? Was race a factor in the police's decision to respond so rapidly and with lethal force? Why was an officer who had discharged his weapon on two previous occasions allowed to carry a firearm on this one? Why, in fact, does this officer need a weapon at all? Standing at 6 feet, 5 inches in height, he should have been more than a match, even without a gun, for any individual. The hostage taker was reported to have threatened the hostage with only a knife. His medical condition could have rendered him weaker than a healthy individual of the same age.

Does the equation Gun Cop = Cowboy Cop apply here? If not, why not? The shooter, Police Constable Brian Davies, is an experienced veteran of the Metropolitan Police Service and their specialist firearms unit. How much training and how many years on the job, this reporter asks, does it take for the killer instinct to be muzzled in a man? What are his colleagues like, those who defended him in interviews with the Directorate of Professional Standards and the Independent Police Complaints Commission? These bodies were established to provide consequences for officers who acted outside the law. Clearly the need for them is essential, particularly in this instance.

Trial date to be determined.

Part Four

Before the Trial

"And we are here as on a darkling plain
Swept with confused alarms of struggle and flight,
Where ignorant armies clash by night."

Matthew Arnold

CHAPTER ONE

HAD IT BEEN A DREAM? Brian knew the findings of the Directorate of Professional Standards were complete and had been forwarded to the Crown Prosecution Service. He had waited for the CPS to report that they would not be charging him with any offence. Instead, he had been told by Chief Superintendent Brierly that they would be laying charges against him. He had been given the name and address of the magistrates' court where he was to appear. He had gone at the prescribed time, accompanied by his Federation rep, who reported that a second representative would be assigned to him. Whether that was a sign of progress or the lack of it, he did not know.

Meeting him at the magistrates' court were his Federation solicitor and the barrister he had recommended. Whilst it was true that barristers could be hired either to prosecute or to defend, his heart sank. Fiona Courtland was renowned for her success in prosecuting criminal cases. Could she adequately argue on the other side of the aisle? Despite the shock he was feeling, his brain guided his body to the dock.

He heard the words, "Brian Allen Davies, you are charged that on the twenty-eighth of August, two thousand and five, you did murder Roy Alden Wilkes, contrary to common law."

Handcuffs had then been applied. He would never forget how they'd felt on his wrists: like a hangman's noose. The judge didn't say, "Take him down!" as they did when a criminal's guilty verdict was read, but the guards, both of whom seemed wary of him – perhaps because they sensed how angry he was – took him into the custody area below anyway and put him in a cell until the van taking him to the Old Bailey Crown Court arrived.

At the Old Bailey he again stood, guarded, in the dock whilst his barrister made the petition for bail. Her petition for his anonymity was now a useless exercise. The press hounds, who haunted the historic court, had been alerted and knew that something noteworthy was taking place. Leeches, every damn one of them. He was required to provide a bail address, and he used his residence in Rickmansworth.

He heard the judge grant the application for bail, which granted him temporary freedom, but evidently he was still considered a danger, because for the time it took to process the paperwork, he was led below and again locked in a cell. He looked down. According to his watch, only two minutes had elapsed. That couldn't be true; what a time for it to stop working! He tapped it. The second hand was moving, but clearly nothing in the legal process was. He tried without success to avoid looking at it again. Previously he'd thought that time stood still only in science fiction movies. Now he knew better. And walls which he'd thought were fixed in place seemed mobile, making the cell feel smaller than when he had first stepped into it. Was this what his future would look like?

When the cell door opened an hour later, he still felt confined. How it felt to be a criminal had been brought home to him and what lay ahead could be worse, much worse. He must be certain that his will was current and that Bethie had power of attorney to make decisions in the event of his absence. She would have to return to teaching full time soon. If he were convicted, she'd need income he couldn't provide.

Fortunately his mates were waiting, Casey amongst them, and he was whisked away, but not to his house. Since attention could be drawn to their residence in Rickmansworth, Casey and Jenny had arranged for all of them to stay with them in their Hampstead flat. What an irony – Casey and Jenny were buying a house in Chorleywood to be closer to him and his family, and he had been advised not to go home. At least if anyone left threatening material at his house, Beth and the children wouldn't see it.

No, the events of that day had been no dream. On the first morning after, he had woken in Casey and Jenny's flat. They had thought of everything – beds for Meg and Robbie, toys, children's movies. His children loved Bear; they took him for walks on the Heath, where they counted the ducks, threw sticks at tree trunks, and collected leaves. Too young to read, they were blissfully unaware of the reason for their change of scenery. Hence they did not see the article which included his name. How had that information been discovered? Anonymity should have been respected.

He, on the other hand, could read and remember. It had all been far too real, the stink of the transport van absorbed by the pores in his skin and the words of the charges striking his eardrums like iron anvils. His wrists had felt tender and his limbs stiff, as if his bulk were suddenly too heavy for his bones to carry. Bethie was with him now, but he did not know what to say to her. He wanted to yell at the system which had brought him to this point but had been rendered almost mute. His Job was to join with others to fight criminals and the evil they caused. Now this mission had been taken away, and nothing could replace it.

CHAPTER TWO

THE PARISH CHURCH of St. Mary the Virgin, Rickmansworth, belonged both to the Church of England and the Methodist Church. Like many places of worship in England, it had a long and illustrious history, the first recorded vicar having served in the twelfth century. Although originally designed as an elaborate setting for a smaller congregation, during the twentieth century the altar décor was simplified, with the intent of bringing the priests and the larger numbers of worshippers closer to each other.

The old and the new had been beautifully combined, the stained glass windows a reflection of the old and the wooden, ledged pews a symbol of the simplicity of the new. Bouquets of fresh flowers rested on each window sill, and light flooded in from the high arches above. As Jenny and Beth waited for the Sunday service to begin, they could hear the bells in the tower calling the community to worship. The church bulletin highlighted the special features in the sanctuary, including a roll of honour and book of remembrance for those killed in wartime action. Jenny was reminded of the reception area at New Scotland Yard, where glass cases housed an eternal flame and roll of honour book that recorded the circumstances in which each police officer and civilian staff member had died.

In addition she read that St. Mary's was part of the Diocese of St. Albans, and her throat constricted. St. Albans had been the first British Christian martyr and the name of the church in Kent where she and Colin had worshiped when they visited his mother. Four years ago this month his memorial service had been held there. One grief must beget another, she thought. Colin's death; her miscarriage; Brian's legal situation – all losses with impact beyond the individual and the present moment.

Jenny felt no particular attraction to churches other than their history and architecture. Like courtrooms, if they heard the cries of those who came to them in crisis, they didn't show it. However, she noted an unusual warmth on the part of the congregants, who left their seats to welcome visitors and to proclaim God's peace to all. Beth seemed to appreciate their good wishes, although she did not give her last name or indicate that she was married to a police officer. Jenny had learned not to refer to Simon's profession outside the police community and certainly not to his service with the firearms unit. Neither would Beth. She would do her best to keep the details of Brian's current circumstance private. The priest's homily emphasized that God's people were not anonymous to Him, but at this point in Brian's life it was best if he remained anonymous to everyone but God.

Provisions had been made to include children in the service, and Jenny wondered whether in the future Beth would bring Meg and Robbie with her.

After the service, when Beth did not want to stay for coffee and refreshments, Jenny felt a little disappointed. The brick and stone structure, although built by men, had, according to the priest, been consecrated by God and by His grace and remained so today. She was reminded of Neil Goodwyn, who had told her once that Christian rituals celebrated something that had already taken place. A building dedicated to God had received His blessings even before the first stone was laid. In the case of marriage, love had been born before the engaged couple exchanged vows. He would have argued that if the music and prayers had soothed her, it was God's spirit which was the cause and not just the change of venue.

"I've been away from Brian long enough," Beth whispered to Jenny. "He's been too quiet lately. I hope they'll all be watching the Olympics when we return, but I feel uneasy not being with him."

Germany was leading in the medals count, with the United States not far behind. Great Britain, however, had sent only forty-one athletes to Italy and had so far won only one medal, a silver in the women's skeleton. Jenny had never heard of that event and was told that the competitor had to lie face down and head first on a small sled, with speeds approaching eighty miles per hour. An event for those who considered extreme physical risk to be fun, she thought, and a distressing description of what the competitors would look like if their participation led to their demise.

"He's been preoccupied, of course," Beth continued. "He must still be in shock. Perhaps if I make a roast with mashed potatoes, he'll help me with a bit of the cooking. And the kids can make mountains out of their potatoes and pretend their forks are sledding down. I have ice cream snowballs in the freezer for dessert. All to go with the Olympics theme."

They walked back to the train station, and Jenny marveled that the British systems of transport could be trusted, even if their legal system could not. She understood Beth's anxiety. Justice was intended to protect the innocent and guarantee fair and reasonable treatment for all. Justice, as well as the Queen, was Brian's mistress, and even blindfolded, she should have been able to see that his actions had been warranted.

CHAPTER THREE

SEAN MACKENNA was glad for the assignment from Simon Casey. He understood the intent: help PC Davies, which he was eager to do. The articles in the newspaper had angered him, and he wanted to do all he could to clear Davies' name. Law enforcement was a brotherhood. Attacking one was attacking all. Although he had retired from the Metropolitan Police Service some years ago, he had never ceased to regard himself part of the organisation at large. In the past he'd twice been called upon to assist Mrs. Casey when she was thought to be in danger and recently when his presence would provide reassurance. On this occasion Davies faced a very different sort of threat.

As was true in every operation, specific questions needed to be answered. Trace, identify, and eliminate was the order he would follow. He had begun by ruling out the involvement of Davies' neighbours. Next, he focussed on Lionel Hodge, the reporter. Did Hodge have a source, or was the prejudice entirely his own? Who was the man he'd seen observing Davies in Hayes and was he related to this investigation? He'd only been able to determine that that individual was not the reporter.

MacKenna located the reporter's place of residence, a small flat in Queen's Park, an area of London which sounded royal although Hodge's accommodation wasn't. When he followed him to work in the morning, he learnt that although his departure times varied, his general practice was to take the tube after the morning rush had subsided. His work colleagues had been named and dropped as sources for information about Davies, and MacKenna hadn't seen Hodge meet with non-newspaper individuals during the day.

Hodge spent most of the day at the *Ledger,* a periodical noted for its exposés of famous and not so famous figures. *The Ledger* had all the usual departments – city, society, finance, entertainment, sport – but reserved its headlines for articles about bias and wrongdoing, criminal and otherwise.

Consequently MacKenna varied his approach and made himself available to observe Hodge's movements at day's end. Since he had not been engaged for full time surveillance, he stationed himself outside the Ledger's offices on odd days, then on even days. However, no pattern existed that he could see in either Hodge's timing or activities following the workday.

The stories about Davies weren't the only ones Hodge wrote, but if he communicated by phone or internet, MacKenna would have no way of gaining access to that data. However, the nature of the information in the columns about Davies implied an inside source, someone who understood the importance of not creating a trail of evidence. Hodge, therefore, would be forced to receive material in another way.

How would he have done it, MacKenna asked himself, if he were the informant? Arrange a chance encounter then pass a note with a meeting place, a time, and instructions to bring the note. At that first meeting – held where neither of them was known – he'd destroy the note when presented to him, leaving nothing tangible to connect them. The first meet would serve as an initial transfer of information, an agreement of the working relationship, and the settlement of details for future meets. A regular schedule would not be allowed. Nothing, then, would exist anywhere that could implicate either of them. The only flaw in MacKenna's reasoning was that it did not allow for meets on short notice.

Tonight Hodge did not seem to be meeting anyone. MacKenna followed him from the newspaper office to a pub, where he ate quickly and alone. Now he was waiting with several other individuals for a bus, his usual transport home. Hodge did not speak to any of them and boarded the appropriate bus when it arrived. The only man who got on at the same time was tall and lanky, not the same body type as the man MacKenna had seen lurking outside the house in Hayes.

So far MacKenna's surveillance of Hodge had resulted only in dead ends, a form of progress but one which frustrated his copper's curiosity. Someone was feeding information about Davies to Hodge, some of it inaccurate, most of it confidential, all of it bigoted. An insider could be a law enforcement officer or civilian within the law enforcement community. If so, MacKenna would need to up his game because Hodge's source would take extra care in the location of his meets with him. That would give him an advantage, but MacKenna had always been a patient and thorough man. During his active service, he'd often been described as a dog with a bone, and because he kept his beard and moustache neatly trimmed, he imagined himself a trim, medium-size shorthaired hound, his fur showing some signs of age but his energy level only slightly diminished.

At home MacKenna spread out all of Hodge's articles on his desk. The initial one, "Gun Cops Take Another Life," was slanted against the police but general in nature. Specific details hadn't begun to appear until the next: "Gun Cop Killed Unarmed Man." How had this information been discovered? Davies would have been advised confidentially of the DPS' conclusion but would not have spoken of it outside police circles, nor would senior officers have addressed it. The DPS was unlikely to be the source; they did not publicise their work, although they did not dedicate themselves to clearing officers of suspected wrongdoing.

An article which mentioned Davies' drinking – a supposition at best – had appeared after the party in Hayes, where MacKenna had first seen the shadowy figure. The gathering had not occurred at Davies' home but at the residence of another member of the firearms unit. That information would also have been unavailable to the public.

Further columns covered details which should have remained private, including a physical description of Davies accompanied by the observation that Davies' body was in essence a weapon. Worse, in spite of the tradition of officers being granted anonymity by the court, Hodge had published his name. How had he known it? No one on Davies' legal team would have given it.

Perhaps Hodge had found his informant after the early article was published. Another possibility was that his informant had found him, that someone had read his words and believed that he would be sympathetic to further intelligence. If so, this someone was very careful to guard his identity. Hence, someone close to the investigation or with access to the DPS interviews could be the source. Again MacKenna was forced to consider that someone on or close to the Job was his target.

The most recent article was particularly damning. "Does the Met Have a Serial Shooter?" it asked. In it Hodge reported that Davies had discharged his firearm before with no disciplinary consequences. Only a brief mention was made that neither incident had resulted in death and that Davies had been cleared of any negligence in both cases. Hodge's emphasis rested on three questions: Is this gun cop a cowboy, someone quick on the trigger? Will his lack of restraint injure another member of the public? And, is the Met harboring an officer with poor firearms skills? In his conclusion, he stated that on this occasion Davies had fired twice, contrary to established procedure.

MacKenna sighed. He made himself another cup of tea, which had tasted better when his wife had made it. Married forty-two years, she had contracted cancer shortly after he retired from the police and was gone in mere months. All the plans they'd made for travel had come to naught, all the time he now had to spend made meaningless. He still missed her. Their house was too quiet. His children, one of whom lived in southern England, the other across the Channel, wanted him to move, but he wanted to stay where he was. Where she had been. He used her tea cup.

Now, sipping the warm brew, he studied the timing, not the content, of the articles. Most had appeared in the weekend editions, the time of the week with the highest readership. Hodge must have received intelligence at least a day or two prior to publication. Thus instead of changing the days he watched Hodge, he would focus on Tuesdays and Wednesdays only. Relevant headlines did not, however, appear every week or every other week. With no publication pattern apparent, MacKenna would have to commit himself to a prolonged operation.

Had he made assumptions that had cost him success? He thought of a possible one, that Hodge did not ride the bus all the way home but left somewhere along the route. If his contact did not appear at that stop on any given night, he could simply take the next bus the rest of the way. No advance notice would be needed. MacKenna could do the same.

However, if he were to debark from the bus on regular basis, he'd need to take steps to avoid suspicion. Hodge might not be wary, but MacKenna wagered that his informant would. He would alter his appearance then, an easy task. If necessary, he could enter one of the establishments on the street. He could seem to be walking with someone. He could continue down the road until he was out of their sight then double back.

He would plus up his travel card to be ready for multiple bus rides. Perhaps he had not followed Hodge far enough.

CHAPTER FOUR

FEBRUARY 23, and Jenny hadn't thought the date would affect her. She couldn't forget Colin's death day and knew Simon didn't expect her to, but the intensity of her grief surprised her. She felt in a fog when she put on her makeup, and the colors of the clothes in her closet seemed pale. Maybe her loss of the baby, and thus of a part of her future with Simon, had made this year more difficult than she anticipated. Determined to push the thoughts away, she took several deep breaths to ease the tightness in her chest. She was not going to let the insidious calendar control her. She was going to focus on what lay ahead for them. Their offer on the Chorleywood house had been accepted, and they were going to see it again and tour the rest of the city.

Fortunately it was a cumulus kind of day, with dollops of whipped cream in the blueberry sky, and she felt her spirits lift in spite of the chilly winds.

Simon drove, admitting that he had recced the site so their time would be well spent. The estate agent, Mrs. Reynolds, met them at the house, and Jenny was relieved that she felt just as drawn to it as she had when they'd first seen it. They'd made a big decision based on only one viewing; now she smiled as she walked through the rooms and tried to picture which pieces of furniture would fit in the smaller spaces. She recalled their tension on their previous visit. Today her feet were light on the steps, and the interior seemed to sparkle, as if the sky itself were taking up residence, telling her that the future was limitless.

In the master bedroom, she again appreciated the stained-glass window. When the sunlight flickered, it came alive, a reminder that a sign of life could be found even in the most unlikely of places.

In the back yard she was at a loss, able to identify only the flowing wisteria and a hydrangea as large as a tree. "Daffodils there," Mrs. Reynolds noted. "They'll bloom soon in a sunny yellow. The vines which cover the fence near the bench are winter jasmine. They'll be white. I'm glad to see there's a good balance of bulbs and perennials."

Jenny agreed. The life of a flower was so short. She wanted flowers that lasted and pregnancies that did, too.

"But everything needs a trim, doesn't it?"

"Even the weeds," Jenny commented. She had a marked preference for anything that was resilient enough to come back year after year, but although weeds seemed to triumph in that category, she couldn't welcome them.

Next Simon parked at Christchurch. Posts with arrows marked the way through the oak and birch trees of Chorleywood Common which bordered it. Jenny noted the polka dots of light between the branches. They walked past ponds with sparkles on the water and memorial benches with worn inscriptions. A golf course occupied part of the grassland. Completing the circuit, they couldn't ignore the cemetery on the church grounds.

One marker in particular touched her, an angel with a broken wing and a missing hand, an angel who was hostage to the earth. Was a child buried there? With no headstone or legible engraving, it wasn't possible to know. Had someone erected this stone to memorialize a loss that went so deep that it could only be represented with scarred stone? She felt a wave of dizziness and leaned against Simon to regain her balance. "I need to sit down. Could we go inside the church?"

He went with her, watching as she glanced at the fresh flowers at the rear entrance and the bookstore in the back. Some of the alcoves on the sides had stained-glass windows. Passing a large plaque between two of the windows, she paused, gripping his arm. *In memory of the brave men of Chorley Wood who fought for freedom & justice in the Great War,* it read, with names and ranks listed. "Elspeth might have crossed paths with some of them," she said.

She sat in one of the pews, and he joined her, taking her hand when he heard her sigh. Neither of them spoke, the breeze outside providing the only sound. Few others were in the church, but strangely it didn't feel empty. Words of Scripture, proclaiming God's promises to His people, arched over the altar. Even the ceiling was decorated. Gradually her equilibrium returned, but her eyes were still wet when she stood.

"Wait one, Jenny," he said quietly. "It's peaceful here."

She stopped, surprised but relieved. The service at St. Mary's she'd attended with Beth had been soothing. Had Simon felt some of that here today? Their hands were still connected, but now she felt that she was holding his instead of the other way around.

"May I help you?" a man with a clerical collar asked as they prepared to leave. "We have a healing ministry here."

Jenny accepted the pamphlet he offered and tried to smile but did not reply.

Across the street they saw the Gate, the restaurant Brian had mentioned. The posted menu had items which appealed to both of them, but it was midafternoon, too early for dining. She gestured to the listings and asked, "Promise?"

"I promise," he laughed.

Next he drove to the High Street, parking at one end and guiding her down one side and then up the other. They passed a deli, an Italian restaurant, a restaurant with Oriental cuisine, a family butcher's, and a fish market. The tea room showcased chocolate eclairs, napoleons, and croissants, and Jenny resolved to try every flavor. Other establishments reminded her of Hampstead but on a smaller scale.

In the open grocery, however, her heart nearly stopped. A rack with newspapers held a broadsheet with the headline, "Gun Cop Still Drawing Salary." The first few lines read, "PC Brian Davies, the gun cop legally responsible for the death of Roy Wilkes, has been removed from active operations but is still drawing his salary.

Is this just? There is no question that he fired the shots which caused..."

Despite feeling rooted to the spot, Jenny couldn't read any further. "Simon, what are we going to do?" she asked. "Brian's in quicksand. Nothing I've done or said – in all those appalling interviews – has helped him find solid ground."

Without a word he paid the grocer for all the copies of the paper. As they returned to the car, he told her he'd planned for them to drive through some of the housing areas and then have dinner in Chorleywood, but with her approval, he wanted to make a change. They drove to Rickmansworth, and at each newsstand on the High Street, she exited the car and bought all the copies of print media with Brian's name. From there he drove down Brian and Beth's street to confirm that their home was quiet, as MacKenna had reported, but it seemed to Jenny that clouds loomed over it like a bad dream.

"Is it safe for Brian and Beth to go home?" she asked.

"I'll have Mac check. If there's no one loitering for the next day or so, they'll be able to go."

"I love having them as houseguests, but I'm glad they're with Brian's family for a few days. I wouldn't want them to see this article."

Back in Hampstead they threw away all the newspapers they'd bought, and Simon rang the other team members to ask them to purchase the ones in their neighbourhoods. Over a pizza meal, Jenny confessed that she had been shaken by the day's events.

"Neil Goodwyn says that memory brings healing, but it didn't today. I thought I could stay on top of things, be free of the feelings that go with the past, but I couldn't. This Hampstead flat is larger than the house in Chorleywood, but it seems smaller. Confining. Almost claustrophobic. I wanted to be thinking only about us and our future, and instead I was distracted. Colin – the baby – Brian. I can't imagine what Beth must be feeling."

He watched her twist her napkin. "Jenny, the game's not over for Davies. And he has an entire team working on his behalf."

"You serve with him. I worry so much about you getting shot, but that's only half the picture. I should be afraid that you'll shoot someone. You could do the right thing, like he did, and still be facing inquisitions and judgments and loss of – everything. I should be honoring you above everyone." Her voice shook, and he rose with her, not certain how he should respond.

She cleared their plates, rinsing them before placing them in the dishwasher.

"Jenny, I'll admit it's been worrying," he said after a pause, joining her in the kitchen and hoping his even tone would calm her. "This isn't the first time that we in the firearms unit have thought an appropriate action on our part resulted in inappropriate action on the part of others. We volunteered for this duty. Some are considering turning in their authorisation to carry firearms and returning to unarmed police work. I'd not like to do that myself. I believe the city needs my training, experience, and willingness to protect and defend it. But it's an option I can't totally discard."

"Simon, what can we do?"

"Stand together. Control what we can. Let go what we can't."

"Appreciate what each day brings," she added. "Maybe tomorrow won't be a see-saw kind of day. I want the ups without the downs."

He opened his arms, and she walked into them.

CHAPTER FIVE

BRIAN DAVIES arrived at the psychiatrist's office at the appointed time. He walked past the seating arrangement and peered out the window whilst Dr. West closed the door.

Dr. West could see his white knuckles and the tense, careful way he breathed. It was the first time he had seen Officer Davies angry, yet it was evident that he was controlling his temper. He moved to his chair, crossed his legs, and picked up a cup. "I've made some tea. Care to join me?"

No answer. West waited. "Officer Davies," he said firmly, "name five items you can see in this room."

Brian turned. "What?"

"Five items," the psychiatrist said again.

Brian frowned but complied. "Sofa, chair, table, desk, filing cabinet."

"Now, four things you can touch."

"My coat, my keys, my mobile, my wallet."

"What can you hear? Three examples, please."

"Your voice. The furnace. Traffic outside."

"What do you smell?"

"The perfume of your previous patient."

"Name one emotion you feel."

"Frustration," Brian replied and sat down.

West nodded. The exercise had had its intended result. "I'd like to remind you that this is a safe place. Nothing you say here will be recorded or repeated."

Brian regarded him with a steady gaze. "You'll make notes when I leave."

"Yes, something to the effect that you're an emotionally healthy man stressed by events. On occasion my files have been subpoenaed. I've learnt to be very circumspect in what I write." West saw him relax his fists. "What causes the most frustration?" he asked.

"I can't protect my family. They're suffering because I'm under legal and media attack, and I can't respond to the newspaper articles. I wish I could sue for slander or libel. Something."

"Slander refers to something said which damages your reputation, libel to something published."

"So is the press reporter liable for libel?"

West smiled at the choice of words. "I'm afraid not."

"Because there's going to be a trial on the charges he highlights and inflates?"

"Yes." When Brian did not continue, West asked, "Other frustrations?"

"Not being allowed to serve fully as a specialist officer. My skills are being wasted. Firearms officers are required to achieve and maintain peak performance. We train and retrain, with a variety of firearms. Superior attention to detail is a matter of course. We could be called upon to act at a moment's notice. The public – the public doesn't understand the degree of focus that is needed, the risks we take on a regular basis, the upset many of us experience because of what we've seen. Our families sacrifice as well."

The psychiatrist watched him make a conscious effort to control the flow of his words.

"Please continue."

"In the past I've been able to leave all that behind when I'm with my family. My children are young, and their issues aren't complex. I'm relaxed when I'm with them. Now, however, I'm on edge. Have they heard something about me, even if they don't understand it? Have they realised that strangers are sometimes hanging about? Do they sense the tension at home?"

"You were angry when you came today."

"Of course! I'm still angry. I'm a well-trained responsible officer being treated like a criminal in the courts. The incident has become a case, and it's going to trial. Doesn't the CPS have anything better to do than prosecute law-abiding citizens? Particularly those who enforce the law?"

West understood his reference to the Crown Prosecution Service.

"I'm good at the Job. No one disputes my aim. They're disputing my judgement, which is worse. It feeds the anti-police sentiment. We firearms officers are there to stem the tide of crime. The more critical the media are about us, the more emboldened the criminals become. And the facts seem irrelevant, both to the CPS and the press. That bloody reporter."

"What steps have you taken to improve your situation?"

"I have legal counsel." After a moment Brian added, "And psychological counsel."

"Have you done anything to cause your situation to worsen?"

"Nothing. I've. Done. Nothing. This thing has a life of its own."

"Are there any positives?"

"I rescued Jenny, the hostage. We don't often get the chance to save a life. I'd do the same even now, when I know what my action could cost me." He thought for a moment. "My mates have stood with me. My sergeant and his wife, Jenny – yes, the same Jenny – have taken us in, my entire family, until the press loses interest in my residence. I live in Rickmansworth, and Casey and Jenny will be moving sometime this spring to Chorleywood. That's the next stop on the Metropolitan line. They'll be closer if – if Beth needs them. If I'm not home." He now knew how constricting a prison cell would be. He pushed the thought away.

"Anything else?"

Brian laughed shortly. "It's minor, but Croxley is back on ARV duty and not confined to the base with me."

"And that is – ?"

"An irresponsible firearms officer, but no one's writing him up in the newspapers."

West heard the bitterness. "I won't understate the seriousness of the charge against you," he said. "And you'll have to trust your legal team to affect the proceedings if they can. However, there are some steps you can take to minimise its impact at this stage. First, acknowledge the apprehension – in this office I call it anxiety – that you're feeling. That alone may ease it. If not, ground yourself by using the five questions I voiced when you arrived. Next, look for distractions that will give you a psychological rest. Exercise, social activities. Last, I'd like to recommend that you visit with your family places that tourists frequent, where you're less likely to be recognised. The London Zoo, for example."

"Beth's been attending a church."

"You could consider accompanying her. The serenity could calm you, give you the opportunity to centre yourself. That's all for today."

CHAPTER SIX

MID-MARCH, and Jenny was proud of herself. She'd been apprehensive about her due date, but it was now behind her, as well as an irrational expectation for pregnancy she hadn't known was there. A victory of sorts, although followed by a defeat, because the end of the month brought Mothering Day, as they called Mother's Day in the United Kingdom. She didn't want to get out of bed, dress, or in any other way pretend that she felt normal on a holiday she couldn't celebrate. Simon, who had been up and about already, came back to bed and said that for them Mothering Day could be the day she became a mother. When he promised to be ready and willing to do whatever was required of him, she had laughed and loved him for it.

Her next big hurdle came when she began to prepare for their move to Chorleywood. She had decided to identify items she didn't want to keep and had assumed that it would be a time-consuming and somewhat boring process but not one that would upset her. Then, in the back of her closet, she came across the plastic bag which held the clothes she'd been wearing when she saw Colin for the last time.

It had been a normal day until the young policeman had knocked on her door with the news that Colin had been injured in a terrorist attack. When she arrived at the hospital, no one knew what to say to her because he was already gone. She had climbed into the hospital bed beside him and tried to tell him how much she loved him, hoping that somewhere, somehow, a part of him could still hear her. When she embraced him, the blood from his injuries had stained her clothes. And then Brian and Simon had taken her home.

She had never been able to bring herself to throw the clothes away. Now she held the bag gently. Would it be disloyal to Simon to keep it? Or could it be considered a reminder of what she had overcome? Either way she didn't want the movers to touch it. She put it in the bottom of the suitcase she'd use to transport her personal items and changes of clothes, surprised that the memory was so intense.

Colin's and her relationship, which had ended in a hospital, had also begun in a hospital, when he had come to interview her after her brutal attack. Hospital to hospital – she had refused to say good-bye to him there, but she could not escape the farewell when she buried him in his family's cemetery in Kent. She had thought that was their last good-bye, but leaving Hampstead was yet another. It had been his flat, not hers. Nor hers and Simon's. Truly it was time to go.

She returned to her packing. Since Simon's clothes didn't fill Colin's side of the closet and his other possessions were also minimal, Simon had finished his. There'd been one surprise, however: a small blue box with the words, *United States of America* printed in gold letters on the top, and a Bronze Star, an American service medal, inside. When she asked, he explained that there had been times when the SBS and the Navy SEALs worked together.

"I gave a bit of assistance to them," he acknowledged. "They thought I was helpful."

"A hero who lived," she breathed, running her fingers over the medal and embarrassing him, but he did not mind her kisses.

So both she and Simon had held onto something from the past, although his spelled victory while hers embodied loss.

Needing a distraction, she called Beth to see if she'd like to tour Chenie's Manor House and its gardens with her. Located in Buckinghamshire, not far from Chorleywood, the Tudor house, with its steeply pitched roofs and plethora of chimneys, had existed in some form since 1180. John Russell, who had owned it in the

1500s, was a member of Henry VIII's court and had modified the house to be suitable for royal visits.

When Beth rang back with the news that Brian wanted to go also and bring the children, Jenny chose a day when Simon would be available, too. The bright sunshine and mild temperatures ensured a large number of visitors, but the gardens were vast, covering five acres, and Jenny felt sure that no one would feel crowded.

They started in the manor house, but when Simon and Brian saw the staid rooms and areas roped off to keep even the adults in check, doubt crept over their faces, and they suggested that they explore outside with five-year-old Meg and two-year-old Robbie whilst Jenny and Beth walked through the interior.

"Who would have been the most disinterested in the inside?" Jenny asked Beth. "Robbie?"

"No," Beth laughed. "He's a little sponge, taking in everything, although his energy is a bit unrestrained at times. No, I think it's a tie between Brian and Simon."

As would be expected in a house that was essentially a museum, every room was perfectly coordinated, and everything had a place.

"Fit for royalty," Beth commented. "They say that Henry VIII and Anne Boleyn stayed here."

"It's certainly neat and orderly," Jenny said, "in contrast to the current state of my flat, where everything is out of place. Boxes and some furniture items are waiting for charity pickups, and we've set aside boxes and luggage with articles we want to move ourselves. We've rolled up rugs, taken down paintings, and stripped beds that aren't in use, to make the moving process go faster. But it's a total mess."

Beth agreed. "With two children, nothing in our house stays where it belongs for very long," she laughed. "Let's go outside."

On their way, they stopped to peer into the priest's hole, a relic of a shameful period in British history when Catholic clergy were considered traitors to the Protestant royal rule and had to hide or be killed.

"How's Brian?" Jenny asked. Although not as frequently, articles were still appearing in the newspaper, malevolence screaming between the printed lines.

"Restless," Beth answered. "Not sleeping well. If I wake in the night, he's often not beside me. He drinks whatever alcohol I have in the house, so I buy less. He's settled somewhat, however, since consulting the psychiatrist. And Neil Goodwyn calls by regularly, always with something encouraging or comforting to say. He says God is reaching out to us even when we're not reaching out to Him. It's hard to believe, but I do feel more calm when he's with us. How are you?"

"Eager to be pregnant again and frustrated because I'm not," Jenny said. "Our parts are connecting, but our microscopic parts haven't yet. But Simon doesn't seem to be discouraged by our lack of success so far." She lowered her voice slightly. "Beth, sometimes he reminds me of a pirate, the glint in the eye and all that. The other night he came into the bedroom with only a pillow – to put under my hips to promote conception, as the doctor recommended – and a smile."

"No clothes?"

"No, nothing," Jenny laughed. "And I've told him that since I couldn't conceive with Colin and did with him, he must have a magic wand. I appreciate what Simon does, but it isn't all fun and games. I want to be through with the trying to have a baby and reach the phase where we actually have the baby. I want what you have. Every time I see Meg or Robbie climb into your lap, something tugs at my heart. I read books to my younger brothers and played ball with them. I want to do the same and more with my own child."

They'd reached the garden. The glorious colors and scope of the manicured grounds silenced them both for a few minutes.

"What do you feel looking at all this?" Jenny asked.

"Respect," Beth replied. "And despair! It's clear I have a back yard, not a garden, and if I weed away all the brown, I won't have anything left."

"You need to name your house," Jenny suggested.

"Davies' Domicile?"

"No, that's not nearly grand enough," Jenny smiled. "Beth's Bower has a ring to it but that implies shade. And you need a maze, at least one."

"Where I could lose the children," Beth smiled. "Or hide the toys."

They proceeded through arbored walkways and past sculptured shrubs. The maze had bushes with small soft leaves that caressed them as they passed.

"Look, here's Creeping Jenny," Beth exclaimed.

"That sounds like a disease." Jenny read the caption on the accompanying post. "A vine," she noted. "And like me it can be guided but not contained!"

Several of the Lenten Rose bushes were flowering, their cup-shaped blossoms drooping. "It doesn't look like a true rose," Beth commented. "And it's poisonous! How can anything associated with Lent be toxic?"

"Maybe you're supposed to give it up for Lent," Jenny suggested with a grin. "Look at its botanical name: hellebore. But the colors – pink, burgundy, purple, deep blue – are heavenly."

"And here's Chocolate Cosmos," Beth said. "It's not flowering yet, but its leaves are pretty, and the sign says that they smell like chocolate."

"If it doesn't require much cultivating, I'll plant it in my yard," Jenny declared.

They saw the men and the two little ones in the distance and waved.

"Jenny, I should tell you," Beth said before they approached. "I've been thinking for some time about having another baby. Robbie is growing up so fast! But then this thing with Brian made me feel I should wait. Now I can't think of a better way to show him how much I believe in him. Believe in our future. And if he's sent away – I'll have more of him with me. I just don't know if he'll agree."

In reply Jenny hugged her. "Good luck," she whispered. "To both of you."

"Mummy, Uncle Simon was silly," Meg reported as they came closer. "He hid behind a tree and played peek-a-boo."

That was a concept she'd have to get accustomed to, Jenny thought: silly Simon.

"We sat on every bench. Daddy said we could. And there was a biscuit thief," Meg continued, showing Beth and Jenny what was missing from her snack bag. "It was Uncle Simon! Daddy caught him."

"I promised never to do it again," Simon smiled, "and to bring my own biscuits next time."

Robbie was asleep in his pushchair. Everyone else was awake but just as relaxed, Jenny thought. She felt strengthened for her next challenge: moving.

CHAPTER SEVEN

JENNY HAD THOUGHT that moving day would never come, but it had. The whirlwind of activity had begun early in the morning, when the removal van arrived. Simon was there to direct operations, and several of his mates were assisting. She put Bear on the leash to keep him from escaping through the perpetually open doors and mused about her first visit to the Heath's Parliament Hill and her last; the many times she'd kept Bear out of the ponds; and the unique wooden bench with the articulated arms. Bluebells, white wisteria, and forget-me-nots were blooming on the Heath. She'd had a final steak baguette at Café Rouge and shared a ham and cheese crepe with Simon after watching the cook in the food truck on the High Street prepare it. She would not forget, but the familiar was not as satisfying as it had once been and she knew they would find new favorites in Chorleywood.

The day before had been Easter Sunday, and Beth had invited them to go to St. Mary's for one of the holiday services. White lilies were displayed throughout, symbols of humanity's new state in the risen Christ. Meg and Robbie seemed subdued by the music and spirited cheerfulness of those around them, although the bow on Meg's Easter dress came loose as she wiggled and the laces on Robbie's dress shoes refused to stay tied.

Jenny thought of Neil Goodwyn and how his faith had helped her and then of her husband, whose religious beliefs were neither specific nor definite but who had engineered their new start. He had seen the need and then handled all the details which were making it real for them. This morning he had willingly donned his suit for the occasion and taken her hand during the priest's homily about hope, but whether the gesture was meant to help him or her, she didn't know.

Brian had barbecued for their Easter lunch, and Beth had done everything else, including making a potato casserole from a recipe of Brian's and an Easter cake which she had frosted to resemble an Easter bonnet. Today's lunch would be simpler – sandwiches for all of them, the professional workers and the volunteers. They wouldn't eat tonight until the van was loaded and had departed. Then sleeping bags on the floor in the Chorleywood house. Tomorrow their belongings would be delivered.

****

Morning came early, the sun shining into the bedroom before Jenny wanted to open her eyes. A metaphor for what lay ahead? Happiness before she was ready for it? Was that even possible? In her experience sorrow was what she had been unprepared to meet; happiness had crept up on her. She reached out for Simon, but he was not there. His sleeping bag was rolled up against the wall.

Now taking in her surroundings, she vowed never to shade the stained-glass window. Its colors radiated, changing when the light changed. She stretched slowly, listening for activity downstairs, but all was quiet. Our baby will be conceived here, she thought, in this peaceful space. He or she will never know the chapters of my life that were written in Hampstead, but I will teach him the colors of the rainbow in the glass and laugh with him when he tries to catch them.

They'd been trying to get pregnant for four months. Only four months, she told herself. The tasks associated with moving notwithstanding, she and Simon had found time for each other because becoming parents was a priority for both of them. They'd begun to have conversations about things they would do differently with their child, things they'd change from what they had experienced as children.

In the meantime she had her work cut out for her. Arrange the furniture, add new rugs, take a stab at trimming the enthusiastic shrubbery in the back yard. And flowers – she'd decided that she wanted some indoors, too. Maybe orchids or another variety whose blossoms would not fade in one day.

She was happy they were downsizing; the Hampstead flat had rooms she didn't even need to enter, and every square inch of the Chorleywood house – no, home – would be used. They would have new experiences here, and her hope that this move would be a new start, and not just a starting over, was as intense as a prayer.

She'd be taking Bear for walks on the Common, its partly settled expanses a better representation of her life now than the wild, unmanicured Heath. She'd learn where the benches were and where a baby stroller could be easily pushed. She heard voices downstairs. Perhaps Brian was there. He had offered to help. The trip step would not be a problem for him; it was just his size. She hurriedly pulled on a pair of jeans and a work shirt and danced down the steps to wait for the movers to arrive.

CHAPTER EIGHT

A MORNING RUN was in order for Simon Casey. He wasn't on early turn today, and he needed to clear his mind. The newspaper articles by the man they all referred to as "that bloody reporter" had continued. One had accused Davies of overreacting during the incident and asked whether his actions were that of a calm, reasoned man. Others were general in nature, asking what sort of man should be allowed to carry a gun, questioning if the training armed officers received prepared them sufficiently for what they would encounter, and wondering whether these officers were examined psychologically to prevent potential murderers from being accepted.

At any rate, the headlines had appeared less frequently, making MacKenna's job more difficult. He'd not seen Hodge meet with anyone on the days he observed him. MacKenna would see it through, but they were frustrated by his inability to move the investigation forward.

In the meantime headlines reporting England's success in the World Cup – or lack of it, according to your point of view – filled the top columns in Hodge's broadsheet and other papers as well. Jenny and Simon needed the distraction, but even the suspense of the events involving athletes from their respective countries could not dispel their dread completely. And Casey's attempts at humour – he enjoyed needling Jenny a bit about calling the sport soccer when everyone outside the States knew it was football – had likewise been short lived. In addition, her country's performance was cause for teasing: the powerful United States had not made it to the round of sixteen. European football had dominated, with Italy the final victor on July 9, followed by France, Germany, and Portugal.

For both of them and many others, the excitement of the World Cup was overshadowed by the first anniversary of the London tube bombings. Public memorials, held in Regent's Park and some of the bomb sites, were observed as well as private memorials and a nationwide two-minute silence at noon. Casey was reminded of the vigilance he and other officers needed to maintain as well as the risks they took doing the Job they were called to do.

He and Davies had continued to run together, but the sound made when Davies' feet hit the pavement was one of desperation, not release. He'd reminded Davies that each bloke runs his own race. Some are better going uphill, some down. "You're no sprinter, Davies," he'd said. "You're built for long distances. Let this thing play itself out." The preliminary hearing was approaching. He'd promised Davies that he'd be in attendance.

The preliminary hearing notwithstanding, meets had already begun for Davies with his legal team. He'd kept his two Police Federation reps apprised of their content and disposition as requested. He appreciated the apparent thoroughness of his defence team, but neither individual would indicate whether they thought the hearing would be the end of the process.

Jenny had settled significantly. Having unpacked the boxes in record time, her focus was on making the Chorleywood house a home, and she spent time arranging and rearranging furniture, adding accent items, and looking for antique china plates which she wanted to hang in the kitchen. She didn't seem overly upset that she hadn't yet fallen pregnant, although he had made it his mission to remain optimistic with her whenever the subject arose.

There'd been one exception. The day of her birthday he'd had to depart early. When he returned late in the afternoon, she'd reported a wave of despair because she was thirty-one years old and not a mother until the surprises he'd arranged had begun to arrive. First, a bouquet of fresh flowers followed by an assortment of chocolate treats – better than birthday cake – from the bakery on the High Street. A copy of the newest release from her favourite mystery author had been next. Then, after lunch, the gift of lingerie he hoped would fit her with a bottle of wine shortly thereafter. Intending to encourage her further when he came home, he mentioned that they'd just been a bit off the mark when it came to conception. He volunteered to work on his aim but warned that it would take practice. She had laughed and stripped off his clothes, making them late for their reserved table at the Gate. It was no bother for him, of course.

For himself, he liked the house. It was snug. Cosy. Safe, now that he'd made some changes to increase its security. She had, however, reported seeing a man looking at it. It could have been a neighbour they'd not yet met or someone using their lane as a shortcut to the train station or the High Street. She had given him a civilian's – and therefore less than useful – description: medium height at best, hair so short she wasn't certain what the colour was, and wiry build.

He also liked the work they did together, even working in the garden with her, although most of his tasks so far had been uprooting undesirable plants. Replacing them with new ones would come, though, and that thought alone lent an air of permanency to their residence that the flat in Hampstead had never held.

CHAPTER NINE

"SO MANY WINDOWS, so many angles of light," Neil Goodwyn commented, after Jenny had welcomed him with a tour of her new home. "It's a gem."

"Even with the trip step and empty walls?" she teased. "You can see I don't have any paintings up yet. The views through the windows will have to be my landscapes for now." Bear had waited for them at the bottom of the stairs. "He hasn't quite adjusted yet," she said. "The house is like an obstacle course. He's waiting for things to settle down, and so am I."

Goodwyn nodded, encouraging her to continue.

"I had such high hopes that this home would be a new start for Simon and me, but some days I feel like we've just traded one set of walls for another. We want to have a family here, but – " she shrugged her shoulders.

"Waiting is difficult, but it always has a purpose in God's kingdom," he said. "Perhaps this is a good time to introduce you to a Biblical concept: waiting with anticipation. It doesn't mean that you're inactive. In means that you do whatever you can whilst you wait for God to do what He, and only He, can. We call it, abiding. It means waiting for what you trust will come."

"Looking beyond the present – I like that," she said. They were standing in the living room, and she realized she hadn't been hospitable. "We could have some tea."

He followed her into the kitchen and turned on the heat under the water.

"I'll get the sugar. And milk," she said with a smile, remembering his additive of choice.

"Yes, I do like tea with my milk," he confirmed, "rather than milk with my tea. What do you like, Jenny?"

"Lemon in my tea; brownies warm from the oven; walks with Bear when the sun is out and there's a light breeze; hearing Simon's key in the lock and knowing he's home. And safe. Because I worry about him."

"I do as well. And for Brian and all those who put themselves in harm's way."

She put their cups on the tray with the teapot and carried it into the living room, setting it next to the gifts Neil had brought, a bottle of single malt for Simon and Ghirardelli chocolates for her.

"I've been to church with Beth," she said. "And we all went on Easter Sunday. It was peaceful yet happy at the same time. There's an Anglican church here in Chorleywood, but Simon and I haven't attended a service."

"Yet," he ventured.

She laughed. "Yet." She took a tentative sip of her hot beverage then unwrapped one of the chocolates, offering one to him.

He shook his head.

"I like the house. Simon does, too. I don't mind the challenges of being in a new place, but I'm not starting at square one. I haven't been able to make or even eat one spoonful of soup since I was a hostage, because Roy made it. Just thinking about soup makes my stomach turn over."

"Some things can't be hurried," he remarked. "However, I'm confident that you can have a very fulfilling life even if a serving of soup never crosses your lips." He set his empty cup on the tray and accepted a second serving.

She laughed. "Is there a theological term for this?"

"No, I just call it history. It's what makes us complex people. If you're able to share your experiences with another person, the way you have with Simon, you will both be strengthened by them. There is a Scripture which supports this point of view, noting that two are better than one. But there's more: 'a cord of three strands is not easily broken.' That's what happens when we invite God into our understanding of life."

"You seem so comfortable talking about Him."

"I've known Him for many years." He smiled. "He also brings us the grace to forgive. Perhaps you're coming closer to forgiving the man who took you hostage. It was the disease, after all, and not the man, who harmed you. You'll be stronger for it when you do, not weaker."

Her tea was cool enough for more than a sip. His cup was again empty. "I'm not sure I can do that," she said. "His actions didn't just hurt me; they had terrible consequences for other people. Simon and I lost the baby, and Brian is under legal attack."

"There are always obstacles on the road we walk, but I believe that God puts people in our path to help us overcome them. I believe He helped you to recover from your grief, and I believe that He's working to help Brian."

She thought for a minute. "That's a lot to take in. You make it sound so easy, but we live in a violent world, a flawed world. It's hard to see God in it."

"We have to look," he said gently. "Because whatever we look for – the good or the bad – we will find. It's our choice."

He stood and returned the tea tray to the kitchen. "By the way," he said as he walked with her toward the door, "did you have a visitor today before me?"

"No, I was alone," she said. "Why?"

"I saw a man who appeared to be leaving as I approached. He was of average height, casually dressed, a bit older than I am."

"That reminds me – I saw someone looking at the house recently."

"Perhaps a curious neighbour," he suggested.

"Or a disappointed buyer," she said.

He kissed her on both cheeks. "I see God's light in this house," he said. "May you encounter His saving grace here."

"Amen," she whispered, because his words had sounded like a prayer. She watched as he turned toward the train station. No one else was in sight.

CHAPTER TEN

SIMON CASEY'S FISTS were clenched. He couldn't tell from where he was sitting in the courthouse whether Davies' were as well but they must have been. He was in the dock at his preliminary hearing and must be raging inside, feeling a prisoner already, regardless of the early stage of the proceedings. In addition, someone in the press had snapped Davies' photo as he entered, hence stealing the last vestige of his privacy.

He felt Jenny stir beside him, placing her hand over his. He unfurled his fingers to intertwine with hers. He hadn't wanted her to come today, but now he was glad she was with him.

The CPS presented their case, led by the barrister Joel Hilliard, a physical contrast to the solicitor whose name he didn't catch. The solicitor, who had jowls like a bulldog, appeared to be straining at an invisible leash, and it was amazing that the papers he held didn't automatically crush in his mastiff's paws. Of course, he would never address the court.

The barrister was tall and slim, with wavy grey hair and a rich voice, like the kindly uncle you always wanted. He was personable and courteous, concealing his alertness in a broad smile, and Casey felt an undercurrent of concern. However, he was not a Queen's Counsel or QC, which puzzled Casey, unless the CPS didn't feel that a barrister with confirmed excellence in advocacy was warranted in this case. An indication of their confidence in the outcome? His apprehension deepened.

"They have a paucity of evidence," Jenny whispered to him.

He liked her vocabulary, always spot on, and he appreciated her encouragement.

Davies' barrister, Fiona Courtland, the only female, as well as his solicitor, Arthur Wheatley, were present for the defence. Seated apart from them but not too far away were his two Police Federation reps. Roderick James was the shorter, thicker man who had not, according to Davies, been shy or averse to conflict during his interviews with the officers from the Directorate of Professional Standards. Henry Lloyd, the other, had been assigned recently to support him, a man with a rotund face unexpected in someone otherwise slim. Casey wasn't certain why the Federation had felt two reps for Davies were warranted. Were they concerned that the process could be prolonged?

Courtland rose and addressed the court. Although it was difficult to be certain from his vantage point and with her high heels, she appeared taller than Jenny. Everything about her seemed understated, from the small diamond studs in her ears to the neutral polish on her nails. Her hair, under the wig, must be short, because only a few curls escaped its confinement. Davies had some reservations about her, since her experience, although extensive, lay in prosecution and not defence, and she was not a QC. However, she spoke clearly and persuasively, and Casey hoped that she would be able to anticipate all the tactics the prosecution would utilise.

"This entire case," Courtland declared, "is based on forensic findings. They alone suggest that our officer was untruthful and may have acted in an unlawful manner. Since we do not believe that our officer took any action other than what was necessary to rescue a vulnerable hostage, we request that a full audit of this department be conducted with the express purpose of preventing any miscarriages of justice. If any irregularity exists in their procedures or evidence, it is our duty to expose it. Mishandling of forensic data will render it impossible to guarantee fairness in the criminal justice process, in this case as well as in others."

"I like her," Jenny said quietly. "She's attacking the heart of their case."

Casey approved of Courtland's adversarial approach as well as her use of the word, "rescue," whilst the CPS had referred to "the incident."

The judge responded immediately. "It is not the province of this court to rule on the credibility of the evidence, only the sufficiency required to justify a trial. Is your client entering a plea at this time?"

"No, your honour," Courtland replied, remaining on her feet.

"I therefore find for sufficiency and bind this case over for trial," the judge said. "I will expect a plea to be entered at the Plea and Case Management Hearing, to take place in a few weeks' time." He nodded at the CPS lawyers. "The defence will expect to receive full information from you." He sat back in his chair. "A trial date will be set at the PCMH. Court is adjourned."

Casey was stunned. The swiftness of the judge's ruling and the unequivocal nature of his language sucked the air out of the room. Had the defence expected this?

"It's – it's a travesty," Jenny stammered.

He couldn't have worded it better himself.

CHAPTER ELEVEN

ALTHOUGH NOT WITHOUT LOVE, Fiona Courtland's childhood was one of conflict, a series of skirmishes with first her mother and then her father. An only child born to parents older than her classmates' parents, she was given every chance to excel – but as a girl. She suffered through ballet lessons, tap dancing, and gymnastics, wishing she had a chance to engage in something substantive. In addition, she was small for her age. She hated being chosen last for every team regardless of level of skill, but more than that, she hated the bullies. She would never forget their smug looks and gleeful laughter when they knocked down her books and stepped on her shoes. Fighting back only made her situation worse; her feeble flounderings seemed to empower them for further ridicule. She was not the only one they preyed upon, and she often saw that bullies who should have been put in their place either weren't disciplined or escaped notice entirely. She wanted very badly to level the playing field for those who suffered.

She'd have been better off with brothers. Less indulged, perhaps, but certainly more protected. Bullies stole the dignity, peace of mind, and feeling of safety from others. She'd needed martial arts training, not ballet and the more ladylike endeavours.

At university, she began to challenge others with her mind, by excelling in her classes and then, upon graduation, choosing law school to give her the necessary tools to guarantee further success. No special privileges were given to her, not in school or in court, nor did she expect any. She relished fighting for each grade, each decision, each point of law. She wanted more than a fair hearing; she wanted to win. Sometimes she had to prosecute individuals for whom many advantages were not enough or people who'd never had many and thought that taking something from someone else was a reasonable act, a way to correct an imbalance they had not invited or deserved. And there were those at neither extreme who put forth meagre excuses for breaking the law. All deserved the judgements that were handed down, and she was glad to be a significant part of ensuring that their actions resulted in consequences which could deter them from repeating their offences.

In court nothing must detract from the image she was trying to create regarding her client. Nothing about her could be allowed to make a witness or jury member feel inferior including her intelligence, which she revealed as gradually as the climax in a complex novel. Correspondingly she concealed her curly brown hair, streaked with grey, under her wig. She applied her makeup carefully. She did not wear ostentatious jewellery. Her only vanity was her choice of high heels, because she was determined not to look slight or weak. Only then did she realise that she had learnt balance, grace, and control from her childhood activities.

Energy and enthusiasm were warranted but without the aggressiveness that often accompanied them. Aggressiveness on her part could be implied on her client's part. In much the same way, the opposition would modify their attack on her client, lest any harshness result in the jury being angry on his behalf.

In a murder case, competition always existed between the victim, spotlighted by the prosecution, and the alleged killer, represented by the defence. Details about the victim were shaded in just the right way to cause others to identify or at least sympathise with him or her. Similarly she would be shading the details about her client, working to make him steady and sensible, an individual you would want for your neighbour.

She identified with Mrs. Casey, who had been kidnapped, injured, and terrorised by the bully, Roy Wilkes. He had committed the original crimes. How could she not represent the officer who had stopped him? Her task, however, was to make PC Davies, an oversized man who had been armed at the time of the alleged offence, nonthreatening. She would overprepare; she had been backfooted once and had never forgot it. It was essential to be on the front foot but without sounding hurried or shrill. Haste would convey lack of confidence.

It was a delicate dance, not a ballet in the classical sense, but a symphony of movement, orchestrated yet appearing spontaneous. High heels, not toe shoes. A tailored suit, not a leotard. Power without dominance. Music only she could hear.

Was there a bully gene? She had wondered often enough when men interrupted her or kept talking in loud voices to overrule her when they couldn't prove their point with reason and logic. Davies, however, was calm and courteous, even whilst under stress. Perhaps his gene was recessive.

Stress from the court, which she experienced as a matter of course, must not be allowed to follow her home. Consequently she had begun the practice of making collages with odd lots of fabric. She snipped them into small pieces, not uniform in shape or pleasing in the combination of their colours, and glued them at random to predrawn shapes. Sometimes the swatches didn't stay in the lines, creating frightening looking displays, like unrestrained beasts or new plant forms whose growth could not be contained and seemed likely to jump off the paper and attach themselves to her.

Participant in no more than an occasional liaison, she lived alone, hence no one else would be exposed to her psychological expressions. She had never considered having a pet. Dogs took more time and affection than she had to give, and cats were often as aloof as judges. Not a good basis for a relationship.

When the trials concluded, she threw the collages away, secure in her victories and certain that her anxieties were temporal. Criminal beasts taken down and her personal demons as well.

CHAPTER TWELVE

WHO WAS FUELING the libelous press campaign against PC Davies? That was the question that Sean MacKenna was still trying to answer by following the reporter Lionel Hodge, who was writing the stories. Contrary to Mac's previous assumption, Hodge did not vary his bus rides home. Although the times he departed from work differed, he took the same route to one of the northern stops in Queen's Park. Having deboarded there, he passed the Queen's Park tube station on the way to his flat. The only deviation in his behaviour came on Wednesdays, when he paused to pick up a copy of the *Evening Standard* from its rack just outside the station. He remained briefly, perusing several sections of the paper before folding it under his arm and heading toward the neighbourhood where he lived.

On Wednesday next another individual also lingered after collecting a copy of the *Evening Standard.* He was above average in height, a broad, stocky man with dark hair, not unlike the shadowy figure MacKenna had initially seen in Hayes. To avoid arousing suspicion, Mac declined to move close enough to hear the words the two men exchanged, if any. And a single encounter could, of course, be both innocent and irrelevant to his mission. He did, however, capture a photo of them with his covert camera.

After the thickset man again appeared outside the tube station coincident with the reporter, MacKenna resolved to intensify his watch. Knowing approximately when Hodge would arrive, Mac stationed himself ahead of time at the newsstand just inside the tube station. Fortunately the proprietor also sold magazines, snacks, and sweets, so Mac could occupy himself without attracting attention.

When Hodge approached, the unknown figure with the heavy build stepped to one side with the newspaper partially shielding his face. This meet was a bit longer, and Mac felt his heartbeat increase. It could be the beginning of a pattern. Again he photographed the event.

Three days on, an article critical of Davies appeared in the *Ledger* with Hodge's byline. I've got him! MacKenna thought. The timing is right! I've solved it! Now I need to develop the evidence that will prove it: more snaps of the two men with dates and times linked to inflammatory columns written by Hodge.

As he made his way home, MacKenna reflected that more crimes would be solved if the police were able to devote sufficient manhours to their investigations, enough manhours to trace every possibility to its logical conclusion. However, an active-duty police officer would have access to CCTV, whilst he'd have to track the informant in the old-fashioned way. He welcomed the challenge. He'd continue to choose unremarkable and varied attire with accessories to disguise his features. The right choice caused others to see the garment or accessory and not the person.

After a third meet, MacKenna followed the mystery man into the Queen's Park tube station. With multiple trains and platforms, this task was a more delicate endeavour than trailing the reporter had been. He was one man, not a team. Indeed he lost sight of him when he changed trains after taking the Bakerloo line to Oxford Circus. And since the man used public transport instead of a private vehicle, Mac could not use the plate recognition system to identify him.

Succeeding weeks yielded further success. From Oxford Circus the dark-haired man rode the Victoria Line to Victoria Station. He even took the time to buy a pasty there, an indication, MacKenna thought, that the man was confident in his anonymity.

More rendezvous, more photos. From Victoria Station the man traveled for forty-two minutes to Epsom, Surrey. Who was he? Where did his information come from? Still MacKenna did not know. The block of flats where the suspect lived had numbers but no names. Mac decided to vary his surveillance times to cover the hours when the suspect might leave for work.

Several mornings later MacKenna followed his target back from Surrey through Victoria Station and all the way to London's Liverpool Street tube station. Leman Street, one of the two firearms officer bases in London, was not far. With difficulty Mac controlled his rage as he saw him enter. Was he a police officer or a civilian employee? Since he was not in uniform, Mac could not say. Either way, however, one of their own had betrayed Davies.

CHAPTER THIRTEEN

THE PRELIMINARY HEARING had come and gone, and
Henry Lloyd and Rod James, both Police Federation
representatives assisting Brian Davies, were no closer to getting the
Crown Prosecution Service to see sense. The forensic report, which
had been detailed in full in court, was objective evidence.
Consequently the CPS considered that Davies' and Mrs. Casey's
statements were biased.

He and James, however, believed Officer Davies, so there must
be an explanation for what appeared to be damning evidence. The
knife that Davies claimed was in the hostage taker's hand when he
made entry and fired had been found in the southwest corner of the
sitting room under a sofa over ten feet away. How had it got there?

Meeting in one of their cramped offices in the Federation
headquarters, both men were silent for a time, James reflecting that
they were a strange pair, he with a greater than medium waistline
but exaggerating when he claimed to be of medium height and
Lloyd nearly as tall as Davies but with a slim build he credited to
his mum. James could have used some of Lloyd's quick wit, which
had sharpened after his wife left him. Lloyd never referred to his
brief marriage, although it was said that her family had never
approved of him. Still young enough to remarry and have a family,
Lloyd had done neither. Although he often tried to inject humour
where appropriate to lighten the atmosphere, he had made no
comments that caused smiles today.

Finally Lloyd spoke.

"We've been seeing this back to front. The DPS and the IPCC
conducted interviews and reviewed evidence. They knew where the

knife was found, and that was their starting point. So they determined that Davies is either mistaken or lying. We can concede that it was unlikely that it slid across the floor, its surface having been described as uneven, but let's consider that Davies is telling the truth and see if we can account for where the knife ended up."

They had reviewed Davies' statements and the statements of others countless times but began again.

"None of the officers who entered with Davies reported seeing the knife in the hostage taker's hand, but they're trained not to look in the same direction. No one on the second assault team saw a knife at all. By then the action was over." James looked up from the file. "However, we'll have to speak with all of them. Perhaps one of them saw the knife knocked out of its original position, during attempts to revive the hostage taker, for example."

"Nevertheless the facts as Davies stated them are clear and consistent with what Mrs. Casey reported."

"And I recall no hesitation or doubt in his answers during the interviews," James mentioned. "He is a man of integrity. It's wrong to conclude that his acquaintance with Mrs. Casey led him to kill a man unnecessarily."

"His previous record does not indicate a buildup to this incident," Lloyd observed. "Firing at an attacker approaching outside a courthouse – which he did in 1999 – or returning fire from a hostage taker in Hackney – which occurred in late 2001 and early 2002 – these are dissimilar scenarios." He consulted one of the statements a second time. "Mrs. Casey is screaming. They make entry. Where is Davies' focus? On the threat, not on her. On the knife. Where is the knife? In the hostage taker's hand, but more than that – where is his hand? Raised above his head. What word does Davies use? Trajectory. He wanted to stop the trajectory of the knife."

James picked up his train of thought. "What is the trajectory? What is the natural motion someone makes?" He stretched his arm above his head then brought his hand down. "Was his arm still extended when Davies' rounds hit him? Would that matter? It must do, but how can we demonstrate it?"

"We need more than positive speculation," Lloyd said. "We need a way to provide objective information that will support Davies' testimony. We need data unconnected to Davies."

Both were silent for a moment.

"I can contact the research organisation in America whose help was so pivotal in clearing two other armed officers of ours," James suggested. He rang the Federation chair's personal assistant and was given the relevant information. "It's an appropriate time for a transatlantic call." After speaking with several staff members, he was connected with someone who could answer his questions.

Lloyd waited for the conversation to end.

"No data exists that matches our scenario," James reported. "In addition, this research institute has been in existence only a year, and they have addressed most of their work toward assailants with firearms, not knives. Scientific principles exist, however, which govern how individuals react when under stress. I've been given some suggestions for how to create our own experiments. First, have no fewer than twenty subjects. Next, film each separately. Have each participant hold an implement the same size and weight as the knife. Last, use civilians, not police officers."

"We'll place an advertisement guaranteeing a payment of ten pounds for the first twenty male applicants for a police experiment. We'll stress that no danger will be involved. Perhaps we can use one of the spaces at Gravesend."

****

Several weeks later thirty-six individuals of varying ages and sizes responded to the advert and arrived at the Gravesend Police Specialist Training Centre at the appointed time. James accepted twenty-five, giving each a chest protector and asking them to sign a medical release, explaining that they'd be given a bit of a shove. The observers simply wanted to record how they reacted with the object they were told to hold high, a piece of rubber smaller at one end than the other. In practice the shove was moderate but sudden.

Some did not release the "knife" at all. Of those who did, the implement landed less than three feet from the test subject.

James and Lloyd conferred. The hostage taker had been in his early fifties and nearly six feet in height. The two reps arranged for a second trial two weeks hence, limiting the subjects to males approximately six feet tall and between the ages of forty and fifty. The results were similar. Both reps were frustrated, acknowledging that although they were police officers, not scientists, they needed to be both, and wondering if they could actually collect data that would be persuasive, data that would reflect an objective analysis, not a biased interpretation.

What parameters had they missed? Could they do more to duplicate the circumstances that had occurred? The shove was intended to copy the effect of Davies' rounds hitting the hostage taker's chest, but they could not hit the subjects hard enough. Straining to recall his introductory physics course, Lloyd acknowledged that they could not set up an experiment which would mimic the transfer of energy that Davies' rounds had created. "It's mass times velocity," he said. "A bullet will deform the object it hits and cause the object to move. The body is not a single static unit, however. A strike on one part of the body will cause another part to move. However, any predictable and significant deviation from the forensic report should give us something to work with."

After a brief delay, they set up a third experiment. They reread the forensic details, in which the size and state of the sitting room had been measured and described. The carpet was threadbare, worn through in some places. They gave each participant a pillow and a rubber knife to plunge into it when the door opened. They then had an officer burst through the door and push the subject hard in the chest, attempting to recreate surprise and speed. Armed encounters tended to unfold very rapidly. The hostage taker had heard the team make entry but would not have known what the result of that breach would be. Still the results were not helpful. Even their review of the film in slow motion gave them no new information.

James reported his findings – failures, actually – to the organisation in America and asked for further guidance. These situations are dynamic, he was told. Be as specific in your instructions as you can. Was your subject moving? If so, can you establish how? Can that movement be duplicated in your experiments? Also, if you're intending for any positive results to be presented in court, it would be wise to have a civilian supervising.

"As far as we know, our suspect didn't step toward the police when they entered," Lloyd stated, "unless that movement wasn't documented. Nor did he attempt to run away. His focus was on keeping the hostage from escaping."

"We've more work to do then," James sighed. "There's a school of law and criminology at the University of West London. Their students would not be the appropriate age for our tests, but it's possible that we could ask one of the professors to be our unbiased witness. When and if we have another analysis. We cannot create the exhaustion and mental instability of the hostage taker Davies shot – "

"Nor the villain's murderous intent," Lloyd interrupted bitterly.

"Since, however, we believe that the incident happened the way Davies described," James continued, "we're still missing something."

"Perhaps we should meet with Davies and Mrs. Casey. We have some specific questions to ask that weren't covered in previous interviews."

"Then let's arrange for that in the near future. Setting up and carrying out these tests has occupied more time than I anticipated and been less productive. It's now the end of July. The trial will begin in less than two months, and we've found nothing that will help the case."

CHAPTER FOURTEEN

ANOTHER BEAUTIFUL DAY in Chorleywood, and Jenny put the leash on Bear to take him for a long walk. On one of her recent strolls on the Common, she'd seen a wild bunny whose black fur made him stand out against the green foliage. They'd all been surprised and immobile for a minute, she not taking another step, Bear not pulling at his leash, and the rabbit not moving a muscle. The rabbit must have felt threatened, but he'd held his pose and didn't retreat until a light breeze ruffled the leaves around him. Maybe today, if she and Bear sauntered instead of striding, they'd see other wildlife.

Stepping just outside her front door, she noticed a man just across the road looking at her. She was glad she hadn't locked the door behind her yet, because he appeared to be the same one who had been watching the house not long ago. If he came toward her, could she get inside and close the door before he reached her? Her street was too isolated for help to be available nearby.

"Who are you? What do you want?" she asked, trying to make her voice sound commanding.

"I'm Sebastian Casey, your Simon's da. I've been hoping to speak with you."

"You're Irish?"

"A remnant. Several generations ago someone decided we'd do better to drop the O. It was O'Casey," he explained. "And here we are."

He hadn't come any closer, and he'd kept his hands at his sides, she noted. Hands that had abused Simon's mother. Simon had had to defend her and himself against this man. She was wary. "Why exactly are you here?"

"I've been in contact with Simon's mum. We're trying to make peace with each other. Amends, they call it. I want the same with Simon." Celia had warned him; if he frightened Jenny, Simon would never forgive him. He kept his tone calm.

A wiry man with close cropped slate gray hair, thus the right age to be Simon's father, he had the same lined forehead and furrowed brow. Deep lines around his mouth suggested that he was not a man who smiled much. Her unease grew. "You shouldn't be approaching me," she said firmly, gripping Bear's collar.

"I'll not do that," he said in his raspy voice. "I just wanted a word with you." He reached into his pocket, his sudden movement startling her. "I'm staying in the area." He held out a card to her. "I can be reached at this number."

She did not walk toward him or extend her hand. "Put it through the letter box," she instructed. "And then go away." Still facing him, she found the doorknob with her hand and opened the door behind her. She stepped back inside, pulling Bear with her, then shut the door and locked and leaned against it. A wave of nausea came over her, and she headed for the closest bathroom.

Afterward she rested on the bathroom floor for a time, still registering the shock of their encounter. Simon would be furious at his father but also with his mother for giving him their address. His father had been a violent man. Did she believe he had changed? How confident was she? Why hadn't she warned them that he might be coming?

When her stomach had settled and her breathing had returned to normal, she propped herself up against the wall. When she felt it was safe to stand, she let Bear out for a few minutes in the back yard. She then collected the card from inside the front door and peeked through the peephole. No one was in view, but he could be anywhere. No walk today.

Heading toward the kitchen to make herself a cup of tea, she heard a knock at the door. If it were Simon's father, she was going to call the police. No need – the police were here. The two

Federation representatives assigned to help Brian stood on the front step with their warrant cards open. In her distress she'd forgotten they were coming.

Her heart sank. She knew she should admit them, but she wasn't sure she could give them coherent answers to their questions. As it turned out, they were gentle and patient with her, acknowledging that they were asking her to recall a very stressful time. Rod James liked Bear. Henry Lloyd saw how shaky she was and made tea for all of them. They encouraged her to address them by their first names.

After complimenting her on what Henry called her "water assault" of Mr. Wilkes, the questioning began. She could not understand the import of some of their queries. Did it matter that Roy had been steady on his feet or lost his balance a little? Why did they need to know if he'd moved forward or back after restraining her? Did she stumble? Did she strike at him with her elbows? Was she holding anything in either hand?

Rod reassured her that their purpose was simply not to overlook anything that could assist in Brian's defence. She confessed then that the DPS had made her afraid her testimony wouldn't be good enough to help him. That elicited a comment from Henry, which he'd delivered with a bitter smile: they have that effect on many of the persons they question. He advised taking a moment to collect herself. Rod suggested a bit more sugar in her tea.

She added another spoonful to her cup, although her tea was no longer hot enough to dissolve it or the tightness in her stomach.

They asked other questions she thought they should have known the answers to. How far from the door was she when Roy reached her? Had he held the knife in his right hand? At least they did not seem to doubt that Roy had had a knife.

At their request she described her final encounter with Roy. "It happened so fast! I was desperate. I thought it was my last chance, and it looked like I wasn't going to make it. I was screaming and struggling against him, and he was yelling that he was going to kill me, and then the police broke the door down. When the bullets hit him, he fell backward, taking me with him, so when he fell, I fell."

"Did you hear the knife hit the floor?" Rod asked. "Did you see its location after Wilkes fell and released you?"

"No. When Brian fired – although I didn't know at the time it was Brian – I couldn't hear anything. And the only thing I saw was freedom."

They were all silent. "Mrs. Casey?" Henry enquired when he saw her frown.

"I just realized something. He had to bend over a little to grab me around the waist. Then he straightened, but he didn't stab me right away. For a second – or maybe less – his body didn't move. Why was there a delay? Why didn't he stab me immediately?" She began to cry. "How am I even here?"

"Mrs. Casey – Mrs. Casey – sshh," Rod comforted. "Perhaps he needed to have a firmer grip on the knife. If he picked it up in a hurry when he took after you, he might have held it too loosely. We'll never know, but we appreciate very much this new information." He glanced at Henry.

"A glass of water perhaps?" Henry suggested.

She declined, preferring to sip a Coke instead. Henry provided it, both officers made further comforting noises, ended the interview, and departed.

When Simon came home, she did her best to describe their visit. "They're trying to find an explanation for why the knife fell so far away from where Roy did."

"I've been interviewed as well. All the members of both assault teams have. At the trial we'll be called for the prosecution."

"Simon, no!"

"I expected it. It's necessary for them to establish the sequence of events, and nothing I say will harm Davies."

"Of course not. It's just that for Brian, so much depends on me." She tried without success to keep her voice from shaking. "And it doesn't look like it will be enough."

"Did they make the interview difficult for you? You're not yourself. Did something else take place today?"

In response she gave him the card his father had left.

His face darkened. "What is the meaning of this?" He noted the name of the charitable organisation on the front and handwritten phone number on the back.

"He was here, Simon. Outside when I started to take Bear for a walk. When he told me who he was, I couldn't even move at first."

She had been paralysed momentarily. Not surprising. In combat he'd been trained to counterattack immediately when ambushed, but that action would not have been appropriate in this circumstance.

"And later?"

Her face was flooded with embarrassment. "My tummy reacted. He shocked my entire system."

"Mine as well," he agreed, his voice dangerously quiet and his jaw tight. He stood and began to pace, allowing his anger to show. "I wanted this home to be a haven!" he erupted.

"Simon, if we had carpet in this room, you'd be wearing a path in it. Please stop and tell me what you're going to do."

"Ring my mum," he said.

She waited. The call was long, and Celia did most of the talking. Jenny heard Simon insist that his father couldn't be trusted, no matter what program he'd allegedly completed, and demand to know why she'd given him their address. "One drink, and you know what he'll do." When he put the phone down, he didn't speak right away. She put her arms around him and kissed his tense cheek.

"She said my father was in the States for some years. He'd been dry for a time but started the twelve-step program there. She said he talks about God now, and she wanted me to know how persistent he had to be for her to believe that he's changed."

"Simon, your mom may still love him."

After a quick shake of the head, he took a deep breath. "One more task, and then we'll walk together."

She watched him refer to the number on the card and make a second call.

"Stay. Away. From. My. Wife." He paused. "And don't call me son." He ended the call.

She tried to massage the muscles in his back but couldn't affect their tightness. She rested her head against him.

"I could ask MacKenna…" he said, thinking aloud.

"No. Brian needs him more than I do," she said. "And your father hasn't done anything."

"He will."

CHAPTER FIFTEEN

ARTHUR WHEATLEY, solicitor for Brian Davies, unwound his gangly frame from his chair and stretched. It was past time to call it a day, but this current case continued to develop in complexity. He'd passed on high tea some hours ago and now wished his commitment to his profession had not outstripped his commitment to his wife. Ex-wife, he reminded himself. When he returned to his flat, the only meal he would enjoy would have to be of his own making. He rubbed his cheeks. Had his face always been this thin? When had all the hair on his head accumulated in his eyebrows?

He reviewed his actions. He had observed whilst Davies prepared his full statement following the incident in which the hostage taker Roy Wilkes was shot and killed. Monitored the proceedings when Davies was interviewed by officers from the Directorate of Professional Standards. Obtained a barrister to represent Davies at the preliminary hearing. Instructed the barrister as to details of the incident which had precipitated the legal action. Participated in interviews Davies had with the barrister preceding the preliminary hearing. Was present when Davies entered his plea of not guilty at the Plea and Case Management Hearing.

The two Police Federation representatives had contacted him to report on their attempts to confirm Davies' statement of the incident with objective experiments. Unfortunately none of their tests had substantiated Davies' claim that the hostage taker had indeed been holding a knife when he discharged his firearm. They had even reinterviewed the hostage, Mrs. Casey, seeking any additional data that would help. Wheatley had not known what the next investigative step should be. "Keep at it," he'd advised weakly, "and report further results to me." When they left, he'd wadded up the sheets of paper which held his notes on their useless research and allowed his frustration to affect his aim at the wastebasket.

Davies was definite about what he'd seen and his reaction to it, as was the young woman he had rescued. The forensic report was equally definite about its facts, although forensic investigators never drew conclusions from what they discovered. That role was left to legal eagles like himself.

He sighed. Although having a free press was considered to be an asset to the societies in which it flourished, Davies was experiencing its drawbacks, at times invasive and in some cases vitriolic. A particular reporter was releasing information he couldn't have known or verified, feeding the thirst of the public for blood. Recent articles were making Wheatley's job more difficult, because Davies would not be going to trial with a clean slate. Legally he was, of course, but not in the court of public opinion.

Individual developments were coming together like the confluence of small rivers combining to create a torrent. He removed his glasses and ran his fingers across the bridge of his nose, as if the papers he'd read with his spectacles weighed on him.

He was confident in his choice of defence barrister Fiona Courtland, but there was a limit to what she could accomplish if they could not find a way to explain or dispel the evidence in the forensic report. She was as perplexed as he was by the apparent paradox. Evidence was not usually so contradictory. The hostage considered Davies a hero. Was she biased? The press called Davies a murderer. With no verdict declaring him guilty, that was prejudice. The only untainted evidence, the forensic, made a powerful case for unlawful killing at the least. Find something I can use, Courtland had said. Instructing him, when he was an instructing solicitor! An unwelcome command but one he understood. It was mid-August. The trial would begin in one short month.

He stood and made himself yet another cup of tea. If they could not account for the discrepancy between forensic evidence and witness testimony, their case would be lost before it had well and truly begun. It would be a long night.

CHAPTER SIXTEEN

SEVERAL DAYS PASSED before Jenny reported seeing Simon's father again.

"He kept his distance, Simon," she said. "I told him that he needed to make amends to you, not to me, and that by continuing to approach me, he was going behind your back. He'd have to find another way. He seemed frustrated. At least, I saw him clench and unclench his fists, so I sent him away and postponed my shopping again."

The doorbell rang.

"That'll be Neil Goodwyn," she explained. "I asked him to stop by."

Simon admitted the priest, and Jenny related the attempts by Simon's father to contact them. "He's an alcoholic but claims he has stopped drinking as a result of a twelve-step program. How effective are those programs?" she asked. "We don't know if we can trust him when he says he's changed."

"His participation is commendable," Goodwyn began. "And the step which suggests making amends is one of the later ones, which would seem to indicate that he has taken the program seriously, but there are no guarantees. Because of the confidentiality promised to those who attend, no real data are available to demonstrate its success, only estimates, and these tend to be low. Perhaps only five percent maintain sobriety, although some would place the number as high as ten or twelve percent."

"He's persistent, but he's going about this in the wrong way," Jenny commented.

Simon had listened but had not contributed to the conversation.

Goodwyn smiled. "Abstention doesn't necessarily result in good judgement," he pointed out. "Overindulgence in alcohol usually arises from poor judgement in coping with problems. Some individuals mature in their ability to make good choices, but some do not."

"He made me nervous, but I'm probably more easily frightened than most people. Still, I didn't know if it would be safe for me to go out – my walk to the High Street passes through some areas with few people around. I'd hate to have to call a cab just to go grocery shopping. By the way, I can bring you a soft drink if you'd like one. I'm low on tea and snacks for obvious reasons."

Goodwyn accepted the offer of refreshment then turned to Simon. "There are other methods of communication available to him," he noted. "Perhaps you could suggest that he begin with one of those."

When Simon did not reply, Jenny spoke from the kitchen. "Simon called him and shut him down, but clearly it didn't have any effect. I've felt a little upset physically since he came, but I don't know whether anxiety about him or Brian's approaching trial is causing it. It's essential that I testify on Brian's behalf. However, I'm not looking forward to appearing in a courtroom."

Again Goodwyn addressed Simon. "You have more than one reason then to resolve this. Would you like me to have a word with him? I could suggest that initiating contact with a less threatening means and giving you some time to accept his overtures could be more productive. If he abides by your boundaries, that would be a positive sign."

"I want to know he's out of Chorleywood," Simon answered finally. "Away from my wife. He knows where we live, and I can't protect her whilst I'm on the Job."

"If he writes to you, will you read his message?"

"I'll not destroy it, but he shouldn't expect a rapid response."

"Thank you," Goodwyn said, to Jenny for the soda and Simon for his answer. "And his number?"

Simon provided it.

"I'll keep you informed of his intentions." Goodwyn turned to Jenny. "We all have some normal anxiety about Brian's legal predicament. I personally never thought the process would go this far. I do, however, have confidence in you and in his legal representation."

"I've had a call from his solicitor," Jenny reported. "I'll be meeting with him and with the barrister next week. I don't think they'll come here, though, so…"

Goodwyn set his glass down. "I'd like to reassure you. I'll try to reach Mr. Casey later tonight or tomorrow and will let you know what his plans are." He stood and uttered a short prayer before taking his leave.

Simon closed the door after him and then returned to embrace Jenny. "You're pale," he observed.

"I'm okay," she said. "The nausea is fleeting – nothing like it was when I first saw your father. But it's already the third week in August, and less than two weeks from now will be the anniversary of the day Roy took me. Losing the baby came shortly after that. I don't know how I'm going to get through it. Could we go away somewhere?"

"Let me have a think on it. In the meantime Sean MacKenna has requested a meet. Will you be all right for a bit?"

"Only if you return with pizza," she laughed. "When I told Neil I was short on groceries, I wasn't kidding."

****

Jenny heard the door slam and Simon stomping into the kitchen. She hurried downstairs. By the time she got there, he had already downed one bottle of ale and was opening another, releasing a string of expletives he usually quashed when he saw her.

"Simon, what is it?" she asked. She rarely heard language like that from him.

He took a long drink.

"Throttle back," she advised. "Breathe! Like you've told me to do when I was upset."

"It was Croxley!" he burst out. "Bastard! Bloody traitor!"

"That police officer you've talked about? What did he do?"

"Sold out Davies!" He set the second empty bottle on the counter next to a large envelope.

"Simon, what does that mean?"

He took a deep breath, then another. "He was the one in contact with the reporter. Mac can prove it. The evidence is there."

"Thank God. You've caught the bad guy, and the stories will stop."

"Jenny, it's too little, too late. Legally it doesn't help Davies – it's irrelevant to the forensic data – and actually it may harm him. The stories have tainted the jury pool. Everyone will have decided that Davies is guilty before the trial begins."

"Simon, you have to call Brian."

He released her. "I forgot the pizza," he confessed.

"That's okay," she answered. "I'll find something we can eat while you let Brian know." As she rummaged through the fridge and pantry, she heard Simon on his phone explaining to Brian that he had hired Sean MacKenna and why.

She served bread, cheese, and a few pieces of fruit and didn't object when he opened a third bottle to drink with his meal. She poured a Coke over the ice in her glass. "I don't understand. Why would Croxley do this?"

Simon, having emptied both his bottle and his plate, leant back in his chair. "You are aware that the firearms unit is a specialised unit. We volunteer and then undergo a sort of selection process. Sometimes a bloke will meet the qualifications for an armed officer but not a specialist officer. To become a member of a team requires further and more advanced training. Some pass the first but not the second. Croxley is one of those, and he's bitter. Evidently he's been looking for ways to sabotage us ever since. Mac's report will initiate further investigations which will result in his suspension and then his dismissal. He'll not weasel out of this. In the end the IPCC will nail him. It's past time."

"Wasn't he the one who was confined to the base like Brian?"

"Yes, and MacKenna believes that's how he got his information initially. When Croxley's suspension for negligent discharge ended, he resumed ARV duty. So for a time he had less information to feed the reporter. But he's deserved this for a long time. He was the one who was providing containment on an op which involved Davies and me. He rushed a suspect instead of waiting for us."

"What's wrong with that? Aren't you supposed to catch them?"

"His job was containment, not apprehension. We would have begun negotiations and gathered intelligence. Our goal's not rapid resolution but safe resolution. This suspect had a firearm, and one of his rounds barely missed us. Croxley should have been dismissed after that incident, but he was only removed from ops for a time. But the dressing-down he received then and his later failure to qualify for the teams gave him a reason for revenge."

Jenny shook her head at the magnitude of it all. "Croxley's the one who should be on trial."

"He'll face consequences. He committed a continuing breach of the Met's standards of behaviour, which include honesty and integrity. He shared sensitive material which he was unauthorised to possess. In addition, it will be shown that he provided false information. I'll request a meet in the morning with Denison and will give him all the evidence that Mac collected. Croxley will be suspended, and I'm certain both the DPS and the IPCC will consider it dishonest and gross misconduct, a ruling of theirs I can finally support."

She knew he was referring to Carl Denison, the chief inspector of the firearms unit. She threw the paper plates away and accompanied Simon upstairs. "Simon, I'm worn out, but I think we need each other. I'll find you when I'm out of the shower."

"I'll find you in the shower," he promised. "And Jenny – I've not forgot your request to have a few days away. I'll see what I can do."

In the morning she found a small package on the counter in the bathroom. It contained a home pregnancy test and a note from Simon. *Don't be afraid to hope,* he had written. *If it's not positive, we'll redouble our efforts. Ring me with the results.*

She smiled. In her view they'd already redoubled their efforts.

CHAPTER SEVENTEEN

CHIEF INSPECTOR CARL DENISON tried to make himself available to his officers, so when Simon Casey, one of the specialist firearms team leaders, requested a meet, he did not object. "What's on your mind, Sergeant?" he asked, curious when he saw that Casey had closed the door behind him.

In response Casey removed photographs from the envelope he held and placed them on Denison's desk. The variance of clothing worn by the two individuals in the snaps told the story: not one event shot multiple times but multiple events recorded.

"I recognise Croxley," Denison commented. "And the other individual?"

"Lionel Hodge, the reporter for *The Ledger,*" Casey replied. He saw Denison's jaw tighten. He then showed the pages which detailed the dates, places, and times the photos had been taken.

Denison's focus moved from the damning photos to the extensive lists. "How did you come to have these, Sergeant?"

"I wanted to find a way to help Davies, sir," Casey explained. "These were compiled by Sean MacKenna, an ex-copper – ex-Met detective, actually – whom I engaged to discover who was feeding false information to the press."

"And his method?"

"Mac began by identifying and eliminating work colleagues. He then followed Hodge home in case he met his contact whilst commuting. He took public transport to and from work, and it took some time to ascertain that nothing untoward occurred on any of the busses he rode." Casey took a breath. "Mac studied the timing of the articles that appeared with Hodge's byline. He varied the days and times he followed him. His persistence finally paid off when he observed a brief encounter with an unknown individual. He was able to determine that the unfamiliar face belonged to Croxley. Croxley was very careful. They never met on a regular basis."

"Was money involved?"

"Mac was never able to confirm it. Croxley may have acted entirely out of spite. In addition, Mac never saw Hodge taking notes. He believes that he may have carried a recording device with him."

"How were the meets arranged?"

"Nothing changed hands. Perhaps the next meet was agreed upon verbally before the current one ended, because Mac was unable to find a paper trail."

Denison became very quiet. He looked again at each photo and the caption beneath it. He reviewed the pages which itemised the meets. Casey did not interrupt the silence. "Unfortunately this doesn't clear Davies of the charges laid against him," Denison finally said.

"No, sir," Casey agreed. "The forensic data remains unchallenged."

"The case will proceed to trial, and Hodge has effectively contributed to the prejudice of the public, from which the jury will be drawn." Denison pressed his fingers against his temples and then replied, in as venomous a tone as Casey had ever heard him use, "Due to the malicious misrepresentations of one of our own. Damn!"

Casey waited.

"That bastard has dogged my footsteps whilst restricted to this base. He has tried to ingratiate himself with me and other senior officers. He has betrayed every decent officer in this unit with his slander." With each statement, Denison's intensity grew. He took a deep breath in an attempt to collect himself.

"Sergeant, I am indebted to you. Chief Superintendent Brierly and I will contact the DPS and the IPCC. Further investigation will be necessary, and those bodies have broader investigative powers than your MacKenna. If Croxley sold out Davies for money, they'll find evidence of it. Both you and MacKenna will be called to acknowledge your roles in this. In the meantime Croxley will be suspended with immediate effect." He stood. "We'll take it from here."

Casey rose with him. "Thank you, sir."

CHAPTER EIGHTEEN

HIS NAME WAS the first unforgivable thing his parents had done to him. When he heard his father bellow in his stentorian bass, "Clive Dalton Croxley! Come here!" he never wanted to hear anyone else say the words, no matter how gently. There was no affection in his overloud expression and what followed was never good.

His father was a distribution manager for a city newspaper in the south of England, responsible for packaging, shipping, and delivery. Stable employment, but unfortunately reporting to work early in the morning meant that his father finished by early or mid-afternoon, stealing any respite he might have had when he got home from school. His parents rarely socialised with friends, but on his father's one day off each week he'd spend more than a few hours down the pub.

His parents already had a son when he was born. Anthony Denham Croxley, a noble name. They had a daughter, Amelia Davis Croxley until she wed. What did they need with him? Another target to take the place of those whose growth and activities away from home eventually protected them?

School should have been a haven, but in every class there was someone taller, faster, more accomplished. Two groups existed, the preferred students and then the rest of them. On occasion he'd come to blows with one of the revered ones, wanting to strike before they struck him. That behaviour stopped when he learnt that he'd be punished twice for a single infraction, demerits at school and thrashings at home. He began to keep a low profile, to keep his thoughts to himself, and to choose his battles with care.

He wasn't stupid, although his father said he was. He wasn't a slacker either, although his father said he was. No, he was intelligent enough to do well, but it was never good enough. Try hard – don't – the judgement was the same. So he decided to hold something back, never to do his best. In that way he could protect a small part of himself instead of having his entire system subject to his father's disdain. He learnt not to seek approval because it would never be given. His mum did nothing. She couldn't prevent the name calling, and she knew as well as he where the power lay.

In secondary school he was assigned to a team project for the first time. The members of the team were graded as a group, not individually, and his efforts, or lack of them, could be surpassed by the contributions of the others. He found it was easy to shift blame and easier yet to hide behind a shared result.

He could not conceal his physical appearance. Teased for his preteen chubbiness, he never forgot the insulting remarks even when he grew slimmer. His cursed his parents for saddling him with the sort of body that made it easy for fat to accumulate. As the years passed, his frame broadened, and his voice grew darker and stronger. It was not difficult to sound commanding without raising it or to express a hearty enthusiasm when appropriate.

Following school he held a variety of jobs, and he realised that he didn't have to be the best. He could function very well by reaching a lower standard that did not require as much from him. Trying harder took courage because failure was always possible, and his father had been right about one thing: he didn't have courage.

He was, however, capable of learning social skills from his teachers and employers. They became his role models for behaviour, and over time he knew what to say, what not to say, and how to create the image he wanted to project. He resolved that the chip on his shoulder must never show. So he played it safe. Stayed under the radar. Any attention would be negative attention, so he avoided it at all costs. And he would never let anyone know they'd angered or frightened him. Jealousy, a beast who could never eat enough, was difficult to conceal, so he took pains to eradicate as much of it as he could. Resentment, on the other hand, needed little sustenance to grow deeper and more difficult to detect. The more evident expression of envy could be channeled into an internal strength.

When others were promoted ahead of him, he begrudged their success, regardless of their merit. He'd thought with age he'd become accustomed to having his achievements go unrecognised, but he continued to rail inwardly at the unfairness. By now he opted to be addressed by his initials only, and most employers permitted this, but he still lacked a stable career.

If he joined the police, he'd have a rank attached to his name, a significant plus. He didn't have to be at the top of the class; he had only to pass. On every civilian job there had been someone judging him. At the police academy it was the same, but the rules were more clear. His father came to his passing out ceremony but had little to say, although that was in itself positive. His mum was effusive, which meant naught. He had not invited his siblings.

He survived his first two years on the Job, learning that lighting a cigarette on purpose to needle a nonsmoker was not considered humourous, although others who had a cynical or sarcastic attitude never seemed to suffer for it. Why was he alone reported for letting off a bit of steam? Every acceptance was conditional, so he worked harder to perfect what he permitted others to see. He was certain his father's abuse had made him tough. He would prevail.

Yes, the uniform alone conferred status, but there were elite groups within the police service who received even more respect. The firearms officers, for example – the power they could wield! He volunteered for the training and managed to qualify, in stages. First he became an authorised firearms officer. Later he was assigned to patrol in an armed response vehicle. He had good eyes and good reflexes. Qualifying hadn't been a walk in the park exactly, but at the end of the day he'd done well enough to pass.

He liked the challenges that firearms officers faced, and from time to time he'd taken the initiative, although with mixed results. No one was perfect, even if they thought so. Anyone could make a petty mistake, even with a gun. Guns were often fired accidentally, and no one had been injured when his discharged, even if it had happened on more than one occasion. Again he was at the mercy of others without cause. Why should he allow himself to be disciplined and belittled?

His final goal was to become a member of a specialist firearms team. On that last step he faltered. The club he thought he'd joined rejected him. His flaws had been minor. He'd never shot anyone! Davies had, and now he'd be brought down to size. He smiled at his choice of words: the big man brought down to size. Let him see how it felt, how he liked it.

Yet no one on the Job judged Davies. Support for him and his action seemed to be universal. How could that be? Didn't others see what a sham it was? Judged when you'd made only small errors, accepted when you'd killed someone? That was injustice within the walls of those who had sworn to uphold justice.

He applauded the system which had taken Davies away from his firearms mates. Hearing his legal difficulties had been a balm for his red-hot resentment, reducing it to an ember. Finding a sympathetic ear from a member of the press for the information he provided had further relieved pressure that otherwise might have caught fire. Davies and others had treated him unfairly. His firearms skills would have improved over time.

Of course, Davies was only one man, but what happened to him could be a start. It could affect others. Make them less cocky on the Job, less exclusive in their evaluation of sincere applicants, even cause them to question the nature of their service. The unit wanted to maintain a minimum number. Second chance for him to join, perhaps.

CHAPTER NINETEEN

JENNY'S HOME PREGNANCY TEST was negative, but the nausea had continued, so she made an appointment with her doctor. Although Neil Goodwyn had persuaded Simon's father to return to Portsmouth for a while, she was still nervous about going out, and Simon knew it. In response he asked Sean MacKenna to escort her.

Feeling embarrassed and reassured at the same time, she thanked the reserved man for his persistence in investigating Clive Croxley and then teased him a little by saying that his wealth of bus experience should not be wasted, and she had therefore selected that mode of transportation for them. He took it all in stride, although she was sure she detected a relieved smile when she led him to the train station. As they traveled, she appreciated his gentle care, offering his hand of support when she boarded the train, ensuring that she was seated immediately, and taking her elbow when they stepped on escalators and stairs.

On the train she asked him about himself, since none of his surveillance had allowed them to converse. "I never intended to be rude," he explained in his soft voice. "It was my job to be aware of what was round you, so I could never speak to you or maintain eye contact for any length of time."

"You were very good at what you did. I don't know what I would have done without you."

"I was a detective for most of my career, a product of my curiosity, I think. I discovered that if I listened, people usually filled in the silences, and I learnt then what I needed to know."

"And on the personal side, if I may ask?"

"I was married happily for many years," he said quietly. "I have two children who are independent because we raised them to be. One lives on the southern coast of England and the other in France."

"Are you and your wife still together?"

He paused. "In a way," he answered. "She – Rose – endured all the sacrifices that wives of men on the Job do, only to pass away not long after I retired. One of the many injustices of life. You know a bit about that, I believe."

She nodded, not wanting to say anything that would interrupt his narrative.

"I still live in the house we shared, and the memories it holds make it seem occupied. They say, however, that when policing is in your blood, you're never entirely free of it. So I've been glad for your husband's assignments."

They arrived at the doctor's office, and she left him in the waiting room while she went to the lab, her anxiety and anticipation competing for dominance. In the end, neither prevailed. The doctor's news didn't register at first. She had to ask him to repeat himself. The pregnancy test was positive, but her happiness was overshadowed by his recommendation of extreme caution. He gave her a pamphlet, in which certain words hit her hard. She couldn't think what to ask or what to say. She was scared to hope. When she rejoined Mr. MacKenna in the waiting room, she didn't know whether to laugh or cry.

He hadn't expected reticence on her part and asked gently, "Have you spoken with Sergeant Casey?"

"No. The news is good and bad. I didn't want to tell him over the phone."

"Very right, Mrs. C. And whatever your news is, he should hear it first. I'll just get you home."

When they arrived in Chorleywood, MacKenna asked, "Will you be all right on your own for a bit? If not, I'll wait with you."

Still nearly mute, she shook her head and let him go, grateful that he had curbed his curiosity. Then the day stood still. She let

Bear in from the back yard and hugged him. Not the one she wanted to embrace, but he would have to do.

How to pass the time? The doctor's news had been sobering, and she found that she couldn't concentrate on the novel she'd previously thought captivating or the crossword puzzle that had challenged her. She knew better than to try for something compelling on daytime TV.

Simon's key in the door startled her into tears, and his face was heavy with concern. "Jenny, are these happy tears or sad? You didn't ring me."

"Both," she said, clinging to him.

"You'll have to explain that to me."

"We're going to have a baby! On April 15, if all goes well."

"And the rest of the story?"

She handed him the leaflet the doctor had given her. *High Risk Pregnancies, the Dos and the Don'ts.*

The crease between his brows deepened when he saw the title, but the expression on his face didn't change as he read through all the usual advice about rest, healthy diet, hydration, and moderate exercise nor when the page highlighted the usual admonitions about eliminating stress, alcohol, smoking, and caffeine. Physical intimacy was prohibited for the first trimester.

"High risk," she said. "Simon, I was so upset after the doctor mentioned it that I didn't tell Mr. MacKenna anything."

That brought a brief smile. "I'll ring him later," he said.

"What are we going to do?"

He eased her down on the sofa but kept an arm round her. "Jenny, your doctor made a risk assessment. It's serious, and I respect that. We'll abide by everything he recommends."

"I'll miss you. I love you so much."

"It's just for a time, princess." He set the material aside and turned to face her. "There are two things only which signify. One, you're expecting, and that's good news. It's what we wanted – a second chance. Next, what you're carrying is fragile. Davies' trial is coming soon, and your health is a priority now."

"In three weeks," she nodded. "Brian's solicitor and barrister want to meet with me, to go over my testimony. And the doctor said that if I'm having morning sickness this early, the symptoms could intensify."

"I'll ring one of the Federation reps to see if a petition can be made to the judge for a postponement. You're the principal defence witness, and you may be indisposed."

"Simon, what if the judge won't agree? What if it's too much for me? I'm scared to be happy."

"Jenny, look round you. What do you see?"

"You. Bear. Our new home."

"Are you afraid of anything here?"

"No, of course not."

"Then you don't need to be frightened. At the moment there's no court, no judge, no prosecutor. You're safe. The baby's safe. We're on our way again, and I'm over the moon!"

She smiled and embraced him.

CHAPTER TWENTY

WHEN BRIAN DAVIES stepped into Dr. West's office, he began speaking almost without preamble. He hadn't wanted to come, but Beth had insisted, citing his unusual bad temper and restlessness. "You're either too quiet or too loud," she said. "And don't argue!" So here he was, hoping to get it over with post haste.

"The trial begins with jury selection one week from today. If the prosecution takes the rest of the first week to present their case, then my principal defence witness, who just had medical confirmation that she's expecting, will be required to testify when she's only eight weeks along. My barrister sought a postponement of two months to allow her to be well into the second trimester of her pregnancy."

Dr. West closed the door and gestured for Brian to take a seat. "Why is that a particular concern?"

Brian snorted at the slender man whose hair was cut even shorter than he remembered. Who had time for such things? "You sound like the judge!" He tried to temper his impatience and his tone. "Because she was pregnant when the hostage taker took her, and she lost her baby – her first – shortly after we rescued her from him. At about ten weeks. Her health is more important to me that having my legal predicament resolved quickly. In addition, she's having rather severe morning sickness."

"How did the judge rule?"

"He denied the petition, stating that pregnancy is not a disease. He did, however, recognise her high-risk condition, and as a result will allow for her to be called to testify only in afternoon sessions."

"Other concerns?"

"How much time do you have?" Brian asked with some bitterness. "My wife, my children. Who will look after them? My mates will do their best, but they work long hours, and most have their own families. If I'm sent to prison, Beth and the children won't be able to stay in the house in Rickmansworth. Her income alone won't be sufficient."

"I'd guess the media coverage has made life more difficult for all of you," Dr. West observed.

"Like wolves with a lamb," Brian declared. "Character assassination. Loss of privacy. On occasion we've not been able to remain in our home. The instability is wearing on us. And that's not all. An officer – a bloke I know – is the one who leaked information about me – most of it false – to the press."

"A fellow firearms officer?"

"Yes, the bastard! I was outraged when I first heard, shocked, but at this point nothing should take me unawares."

"Has your training helped you?"

Brian paused. "We're trained to address the worst case, which makes it difficult not to be pessimistic about the outcome of my legal situation. And we're taught to expect the unexpected, but taking fire from someone who should have been my ally is well and truly unanticipated."

"You're referring to the CPS?"

"The Crown Persecution Service, I now call them. On an operation we may have only seconds to determine if a threat exists and then to take action to resolve it. They take unlimited amounts of time to second guess the actions of officers they should be supporting."

"You're disillusioned then. It's not surprising."

Brian shook his head in frustration. "Why do you restate the obvious? My Job, amongst other things, is to restore justice and safety to those who have lost it to society's villains. I don't deserve to experience injustice."

"Officer Davies, I want you to know that I've heard what you're expressing, the emotions and the internal commitment from which they originate. I also want to encourage you to speak further."

"What else is there to say?"

The psychiatrist permitted himself a small smile. "I consider it extraordinary that all the concerns you've mentioned thus far are for the impact your prosecution will have on others. I'd like you to tell me about the potential losses you face."

Brian shifted in his chair and looked away.

Dr. West waited.

"My last thoughts before I sleep? My first when I wake? That sort of thing?"

"The things which haunt you, yes. That's why I'm here."

Brian cleared his throat. "Beth. She's the balance in my life. She's capable and resourceful, but she'll be alone. I could be imprisoned for years. Will she wait for me? And yet – " He stopped. "She wants us to have another baby. I couldn't agree, of course. If I'm taken down, she'll have three to support instead of two."

"And your children?" West prompted.

"I'll miss all the important milestones in their lives. Children need two parents. And eventually they'll know where their father is. Will they be able to withstand the cruelty of other children? Don't you see? I won't be able to protect them, any of them."

"You are the Job, aren't you?" the psychiatrist asked rhetorically. "The officers I consider the best are those whose public and private identities are most congruous. In your heart you protect and serve 24/7, not just whilst on duty."

Brian nodded.

On occasion West had recommended that others focus on a single stressor and then calculate the probability of its occurrence. Somehow he did not think Officer Davies would relinquish his concern for others.

"There are some situations," he said, "in which we must accept our own helplessness. When your wife was in labour, for example, you had to trust others to do what was best for her. On your firearms team there must be regular occasions when you have to have faith that the other officers will have your back. One of the most difficult issues we face as human beings is to cede control. In the best of circumstances, there does, however, exist the possibility that our belief in others will be rewarded and that fate – or however you choose to categorise the future – will be kind."

Brian could not eliminate his defensive tone when asking, "Are you telling me that it will all work out? I've heard that simple-minded sentiment far too often."

"No," West responded. "That would be dishonest, because there are no easy answers here. Although I hope that in the near future, your legal problem will be resolved in your favour, I'm suggesting something else. There are times when we have to take the long view. The young woman you rescued, for example, whose pregnancy ended too soon – she has conceived again. It's possible that the nightmare you've experienced in this last year will also end in a positive way, although I cannot say when or how that will occur. I would like to caution you – trauma lasts. Even if you are cleared of wrongdoing within the month, symptoms may persist for a time. Having your freedom guaranteed will not automatically bring peace."

"At the moment I'll settle for freedom," Brian commented.

"I would as well," the psychiatrist agreed. "And in the meantime – "

"See it through," Brian concluded.

"Exactly so," West replied. He stood and extended his hand, and Brian shook it.

CHAPTER TWENTY-ONE

SEPTEMBER 10, 2006: the day before Brian's trial was to begin. Was it a good sign or a bad that it would start on September 11? Only five years had passed since the terrorist attack on Jenny's country. She did, however, recognize that she would have welcomed the remembrance of any cataclysmic event if it would relieve the dread she felt about appearing in court. Apprehension, Simon would call it, but minimizing the name didn't seem to lessen the impact. She'd given testimony in a trial once before, and she hadn't forgotten how upsetting being a witness had been and how brutal the cross-examination. In her previous experience, her role and Brian's had been reversed. She had been testifying for the prosecution in the case of the man who had attacked her, and he had been in the courtroom to protect her. Now they would both be testifying for the defense, and she hoped that what she said under oath would protect him.

Brian and Beth were again living in Jenny and Simon's flat in Hampstead, having rented furniture and brought clothes, linens, and housewares from their home in Rickmansworth. Attempting to safeguard their privacy, Jenny and Simon had invited them to stay for the duration of the trial. Several of Brian's mates would escort him to court. Beth would wait until her parents arrived to watch the children then be driven separately.

Brian wanted the camaraderie of his mates, a gathering together of those with whom he served, so they had congregated in the Hampstead flat. No one, however, considered the event a party. For a group of physically confident and often vocally raucous men, the atmosphere was unusually subdued. Neil Goodwyn was there to bless the food that everyone had brought, and both Brian's Police Federation reps, Rod James and Henry Lloyd, were present, as were most of the specialist firearms officers not on duty. Every available surface was covered with casseroles and trays, but no one seemed particularly hungry.

Jenny and Simon arrived late, coming directly from their time in Royal Tunbridge Wells, where they'd spent several days in an attempt to distract themselves from what lay ahead. Sometimes they had been successful, eating in the hotel when her stomach had settled and then ambling through the streets, going wherever curiosity led them. Often they hadn't been able to forget what lay ahead. Sometimes she placed his hand on her belly, and he needed no words to know what she was thinking, because he found it worrying as well. She didn't sleep well at night. Once she asked if her body could tell the difference between positive and negative stress, and he had to confess that he did not know.

"Two of us here," he stated more than once. "We'll support each other." He didn't mind her naps. The morning bouts of nausea exhausted her, and he wished that her periods of rest could accumulate, like provisions stored up for the winter which you could draw upon when needed. She could not sustain herself on food, taking careful, restrained bites because most did not stay down for very long. Their concern about her testimony and what Brian faced hung over them as well.

They had been dilatory about listing the flat for lease, the transition to life in Chorleywood being more of a focus for them than the one they'd left behind, and now they were glad. Arranging for a final cleaning, selecting an estate agent, and allowing for photographs to be taken – all these could wait until Brian and his family could return home.

Some conversations were upbeat, and Jenny could hear an occasional laugh, but the upcoming trial cast a pall over everyone in the group. For once Beth didn't track how much alcohol Brian consumed, and she let Meg and Robbie eat cookies first, as if she didn't have the strength to deny anything to any of them.

As Jenny watched each individual speak with Brian, she thought about the community that they represented and worried for him. If convicted, he would lose this comradeship in addition to everything else. In a way, he already had, because he had usually hosted the get-togethers. Now they had difficulty finding a location. Once or twice they'd met in a restaurant's private dining room, but the ambience was not the same. That made today's assembly surprising. Was he in essence saying good-bye?

She chatted with some of the other wives while waiting for an opportunity to speak with Brian. She and Beth were close, but Beth had her hands full now, with two children, a teaching job, and Brian's impending court appearance. Georgina McGill wafted by, her outgoing personality drawing everyone in and her frankness expressing the concern they all felt. When Jenny noted Georgina's turquoise shoes and Georgina saw Jenny's bracelet in the same color, they shared a much-needed moment of levity.

When her turn came to encourage him, however, Brian spoke first, and his words were about her.

"I wish it weren't necessary for you to participate in court or that we'd been able to convince the judge to put off the proceedings."

"Me, too." She paused, hoping an extra minute or two would help her control the tears that were welling up in her eyes. "I'm a little more emotional than usual," she admitted. "Simon and I – we didn't want to tell anyone, unless they had a need to know, about the pregnancy. But when I met with your barrister and your solicitor, I signed a medical release so they could contact my doctor." She took a deep breath. "This should all have been over long ago. But Brian – I want you to know I'll do whatever it takes. Wild horses couldn't keep me from testifying on your behalf, no matter how I feel." She hugged him.

Next she spoke with Beth. "How can I help?" she asked.

"Jenny, I don't know what to do," she said quietly. "I want him to be reassured that I'll stick by him no matter what. I can get a teaching job anywhere, and our families will help us if need be. But if I tell him that we'll move near wherever he's sent, he'll think I have doubts about the outcome, and I don't have. I know he's worried about us even though he doesn't say so. The hugs I give him – he doesn't want to let go."

"Beth, I'll do everything I can to make them see the truth."

"But Jenny – I think Neil Goodwyn's faith and support are having an impact on me, because in the midst of all this chaos and uncertainty, I feel I'm in an oasis where it's calm and peaceful."

"Maybe that's what hope is," Jenny said.

Simon joined them and signaled to Brian. "You're at a crossroads," he said. "A place you didn't ask to be. What's your mindset?"

Brian raised his chin. "Unyielding," he stated. "In the morning we crack on, ready or not."

"Too right," Simon agreed. "We stay the course."

"Simon, I wish I could paint," Jenny said when Brian and Beth had moved on to talk with other guests.

"Where would you like to start?" he asked. "In our sitting room or our bedroom?"

That made her smile. "I don't want to paint places; I want to paint people. I'd like to freeze moments in time, like Brian with Robbie on his knee, his arm around Meg, and Beth's hand on his shoulder. With their home in Rickmansworth as the background."

"Perhaps that won't be necessary. In court you'll paint pictures with words. You're good at describing things."

"It will be important to use the right words, that's true. But if I painted the prosecution solicitor, I'd show him baring his teeth, and I'd put a glaze over the depiction of the prosecution barrister so everyone could see how slick he is."

"And when the trial ends?"

She thought for a minute. "Things that grow and bloom, maybe with buds as the focal point because people feel hope when they look at them. Buds are the beginning of something that will become beautiful. A cacophony of color." She sighed.

"Tired? If so, it's time for us to depart."

She nodded. She didn't know whether the effort of remaining positive had exhausted her or if she were experiencing another symptom of pregnancy. Either way, going home sounded very appealing. They said their farewells.

On their way back to Chorleywood, she leaned against Simon's shoulder as he drove and thought about the upheaval in all their lives. Was the way something began a good indicator of its conclusion? Recent experience would say no.

However, Clive Croxley had been held to account. The DPS investigations had confirmed Sean MacKenna's findings and discovered more. He had indeed accepted money from the reporter. All material had been turned over to the IPCC, which had upheld Croxley's suspension and dismissed him from the Met. Dismissal and loss of pension rights didn't seem like sufficient punishment, but it was possible that he would be indicted for misconduct, an offense which could carry a custodial sentence.

An ignominious end for Croxley, but Lionel Hodge had been masterful in his execution of the information Croxley had supplied. The seeds planted in his newspaper had spread like a disease. Now every periodical carried headlines referring to the impending trial. Surely there were more important items of news than what had been proclaimed today in jet-black ink: "Prosecution Confident of Victory in Murder Trial of Gun Cop."

Hodge's byline was absent, and the brief retractions printed in *The Ledger* were not located on the front pages nor were they recorded in bold type. The headlines she wanted to see – "Bias of Rogue Reporter Revealed" or "Reporter's Claims Discredited" – would not appear. In addition, his pernicious prose couldn't be removed from the minds of those who had read it. He had received unlawfully obtained information, and law enforcement agencies were looking for him. No one knew where he had gone, but he had left a trail of destruction in his wake, and Brian could be destroyed by it.

Part Five

The Trial

"To no man will we sell, or deny, or delay, right or justice."

The Magna Carta

CHAPTER ONE

ON MONDAY MORNING, September 11, Police Constable Brian Allen Davies found himself in the dock at the Central Criminal Court of England and Wales, also known as the Old Bailey for the street on which it was located. He couldn't wear his full uniform because the identification numbers on the shoulders would compromise him, a bitter irony which seemed senseless since his identity was already known. In addition, regulations stated that at this stage in the legal process he was being tried as a private person, not a police officer. His legal team had advised him to wear a solid colour navy suit with a white shirt and understated tie. No waistcoat. On the Job he occasionally wore a clip-on style tie, intended to prevent an offender from choking him, but here the selection of tie emphasised his vulnerability.

He had entered through the Great Hall, his footsteps echoing on the marble floor as he passed under the central dome. Surrounded by smaller domes, busts, and statues, it lent an air of grandeur to the décor. All had ornate painting and carving, but he was only able to read one of the inscribed phrases: "The law of the wise is a fountain of life." Was the law always wise, however, in its application?

Unlike other courts in England, here the statue of Lady Justice atop the dome outside was not blindfolded. With a sword in her right hand and the scales of justice in her left, perhaps she did not need any impediment to seeing the truth. Brian hoped not.

In existence since medieval times, the Old Bailey had been destroyed in the Great Fire of London in 1666, then rebuilt and expanded over the centuries. Severely damaged during the Blitz of World War II and slightly damaged following a bomb explosion by the Provisional IRA in 1973, the court had again been reconstructed, its grandeur undimmed and its presence a stubborn testament to the British people's respect for tradition and determination to survive all assaults. Each iteration had retained the presence of cells underneath, which now numbered seventy-four.

Brian's trial was taking place in one of the eighteen current courtrooms, the nineteenth being used for various press and juror functions. He let his eyes move about the room. To his left were two rows of seats which the jury would occupy when they were impaneled, behind ledges where drinks or papers could be placed. The witness box faced the members of the jury to allow them to see and hear the testimony and thus draw a conclusion as to its truthfulness.

The press bench sat to his right, with an unimpeded view of the entire room, and the public gallery above and to his immediate right, slightly segregated from the action which would transpire. Legal counsel on both sides were in front of and slightly below him with a podium and microphone provided for each lead barrister. The clerk and court stenographer occupied tables in front of the judge.

The judge's bench was located directly across from him, as if they were the adversaries and not the barristers. Elevated and set apart from the rest of the room by wood columns, it underscored his importance to the proceedings. Above and behind the judge, the Royal Coat of Arms was carved into the wood. Lawyers and officers of the court bowed to it to show respect, not to any individual but for the institution of the Queen's justice. Although the details of the shield were not visible from where Brian sat, he could discern the crowned lion on its left and the chained unicorn on its right. He knew the motto, *Dieu et mon Droit,* or God and my Right, was inscribed beneath but could not at the moment recall why it was in French. Whose right? he wondered. His or the Crown's?

Like the judge, he was also set apart, the dock being a waist-high wooden enclosure with glass panels above, giving an impression of openness when in fact he could leave only when escorted by the custody officers who sat with him and had searched him before he entered. His chair was not appropriate for his large frame, and he knew he would feel stiff when he stood. Here he was "the accused," an epithet which gave him even greater discomfort. He felt that everything about him was exposed, even the place where he had nicked himself shaving, although he'd thought his hand was steady.

Listening to the prosecution barrister questioning potential jurors about police officers in their family or circle of friends, he brooded. Amongst his family, friends, and supporters on the Job, tourists sat in the gallery, hoping, no doubt, to see something historic, not the mundane sort of enquiries currently being conducted. When the prosecution completed their examination of an individual, Fiona Courtland, his defence barrister, simply enquired about experiences with the police which might have biased them in a negative way, circumstances with family members whose mental condition might have caused them to be overly sympathetic with the deceased, or habits regarding their subscription to or regular reading of print media. Hardly an auspicious beginning for a process which would result in the selection of twelve strangers who would judge him, who would hold his future in their hands.

CHAPTER TWO

BY MIDDAY WEDNESDAY Brian Davies had learnt the value of exercise. After Monday's sedentary marathon, he'd resolved to find ways to remain alert. Both mornings since, he'd begun with a run long enough to loosen his limbs and increase his heartbeat. Once in the dock, his only movements were standing when the judge stood to enter or depart and isometric exercises he conducted periodically, pressing his palms together then relaxing and pressing his feet against the floor in the same manner. On the Job he often experienced periods of inaction, of course, whilst waiting for the "Go, go, go!" which signalled that an operation was under way. In court, however, his inactivity was prolonged. In contrast, the barristers rose and sat for each examination and hefted voluminous notebooks to their podia as well, notebooks with transcripts of all the interviews, medical and forensic reports, and previous testimonies.

Six men and six women had been chosen for his jury, diverse in age and race. Had jury selection truly been able to remove individuals with anti-police bias? It was not possible to know. Twelve against one, although only ten needed to agree. Still bad odds for him, and he knew the prosecutor would try to mould those twelve individuals into a single declaration.

Once they had seated themselves, High Court Judge Ernest Bradbury nodded for the prosecution to begin its opening statement. The preponderance of red in Bradbury's robe indicated that the hearing concerned a criminal case. Hence Brian had asked Beth not to wear red when she attended.

Due to an unseasonably warm spell, the courtroom was stuffy, with dead air in the dock, although none of the officers of the court appeared as uncomfortable as he felt. Perhaps instead of being dressed informally under their robes, they weren't in fact dressed at all.

His barrister had informed him that the prosecution believed that presenting the facts of the case was synonymous with winning, because the results of the forensic examination of the hostage taker's flat had been unequivocal. They argued that he had deliberately lied to cover his great lapse in judgement in discharging his firearm.

And thus his trial began, like a high stakes poker game but one in which all would hold their cards until the end.

The defence responded by accusing the prosecution of relying solely on superficial and therefore less than convincing evidence. They promised to show that he had judged correctly the nature of the threat to the hostage and that every action he had taken displayed his integrity. He had neither overreacted nor committed any falsehood.

Brian had a direct line of sight to the jury, but that meant that they had the same to him. Did the absence of a uniform help or harm him? In a sense he represented all firearms officers. However, civilian dress was less threatening than his working attire, with weapons and other devices strapped to his stab vest and other parts of his body.

Following the opening statements, the prosecution called its first witness, his fellow SFO mate Simon Casey, although he was introduced as the husband of Yankee 1, the police term for hostage, and not his given name. Gone were the days when every witness had to swear on the Bible or other holy book to tell the truth. Now one could choose to "affirm," or promise truthfulness without a divine guarantee. He was surprised to hear Casey repeat the oath with his hand on the Bible, although he was not surprised to see Casey called to testify. The incident had, after all, begun with Jenny's phone call to him.

The prosecution moved very quickly to establish the initial facts of the case, including Casey's presence in the SFO room when the call had come in. Casey was not given time to offer either a positive character reference for him or his conclusions regarding Jenny's condition. The defence emphasised that he was only one of a large number of officers present since a briefing on an upcoming raid was due to begin momentarily. In addition, all of them knew and felt concerned about the hostage's predicament. When Casey left the witness box, he found a seat in the gallery. He would remain until the judge adjourned for the day. Each day one of Brian's mates would be present, and either his Chief Superintendent, Morgan Brierly, or his Chief Inspector, Carl Denison. Both of his Police Federation representatives, Henry Lloyd and Roderick James, were seated nearby.

Brian's parents were in attendance for the first time today. Even his mum was tall; consequently she and his dad sat in the back row instead of in the front with Beth. He hated that they had to see any part of this.

The next several witnesses had nothing unexpected to present, the line of police procedure evidently guiding the direction of the prosecution's case. The Detective Chief Inspector from New Scotland Yard, Evan Cunningham, testified as to his preliminary interview of Yankee 1's husband and his assignment of the case to Detective Inspector Thoms from the Islington police station.

DI Thoms had got the investigation under way with an in-depth interview of Yankee 1's husband. Her use of uniformed officers on the ground had resulted in the identification both of Roy Alden Wilkes as the hostage taker and of the location where the hostage was being held. She confirmed that she had secured the services of a hostage negotiator to move the process forward. None of these facts were under dispute, so the defence remained quiet, although Courtland reserved the right to recall her.

When the parade of Wilkes' coworkers began, the defence frequently objected to the conclusions drawn by the prosecution, establishing during cross-examination that none of the individuals had had regular contact with Wilkes following his medical retirement, hence they were in no way able to verify either his medical condition or state of mind at the time of the offence. Why had they been called to testify, Brian wondered, when they had so little to offer? Was their involvement intended to cause complacency on his part? He found the process tedious, and he wished he'd been able to stand as often as the defence barrister; he'd only been able to stretch his legs during the lunch break and when the judge had left and then reentered the courtroom.

When the day ended, his custody officers escorted him out of the dock, and he was reunited with Beth and his parents. Just outside the courtroom, he saw Fiona Courtland, the defence barrister, without her wig, her hair still wet from the horsehair accessory. He would have to wait until he was past the press before unbuttoning his suit coat and loosening his tie. He and Beth were being driven separately to Simon and Jenny's Hampstead flat to make certain that no one was able to follow them. He hadn't got anonymity in court, but his mates were determined that he would have it away from the proceedings.

CHAPTER THREE

"COURT RISE!" intoned the usher as Judge Bradbury entered the courtroom. A man with a thin inscrutable face and a nose like a bird of prey's beak, he did not move like a frail man, and his voice, when he called on the prosecution to present their first witness, was surprisingly strong. Thus, like a match lighting a fuse, the fourth day of Brian's trial began.

Joel Hilliard rose gracefully and paused briefly before calling, with a welcoming smile, his first witness of the day. "Please introduce yourself to the Court," he instructed, when the uniformed witness had been sworn in.

"Morgan Brierly, Chief Superintendent, attached to the Metropolitan Police Firearms Unit," Brierly responded.

In response to the barrister's questions, the C/S explained the roles and levels of expertise of his officers, from the authorised firearms officers or AFOs, who provided a reserve strength, to the armed response officers who patrolled in ARVs, to the most highly trained officers, the specialist firearms officers or SFOs. He characterised their training as comprehensive and their actions as exemplary.

Why, Brian thought, was the prosecution eliciting testimony which highlighted the skills of firearms officers? That would seem to work in his favour, not against him, unless they wished to imply that they were not judging all police officers, only him.

"And you are proud of these officers?"

"I am, yes," Brierly answered. "They train as if their lives depend on it, because they do. Their work is dangerous, but it is necessary, and there is no one else who can do it."

"Justifiably so," Hilliard agreed smoothly. "Yet we are all human, are we not?"

The C/S had no choice but to answer in the affirmative.

"Therefore if one of them committed any sort of offence, would he or she be disciplined?"

"Yes, as appropriate."

Brian's heart skipped a beat. He'd never been disciplined; to whom was the barrister referring? Was he planting a seed of suspicion? The jury appeared very attentive. The answer was not forthcoming, however, because Hilliard changed his line of questioning.

"Chief Superintendent Brierly, were you, on the day of Friday, 26 August 2005, heading a planning operation to assist a female hostage?"

"Yes, I was Strategic Firearms Commander for that incident."

"Explain, please, what that responsibility entails."

"It was my job to assist the Gold Commander by outlining the strategy for the firearms operation. We develop a response, should our intervention become necessary."

"And in this case?"

"We began work as soon as we had sufficient intelligence from the investigators. Since the initial call was received by one of our officers, we were all aware that a hostage had been taken and that our assistance might be needed."

"Thank you, Chief Superintendent Brierly. I appreciate your testimony."

Fiona Courtland began her cross-examination. "Your officers undergo a rigorous selection process, is that correct?"

"Yes, and their training is repeated on a regular and frequent basis."

"Does the selection process make performance violations more unlikely?"

"Yes. On occasion an officer will violate the Met's standards of professional conduct, but those instances are rare."

"Has Officer Davies ever been disciplined in any way?"

"No, he has not."

"Let me be certain that I understand your testimony. Are you stating that Officer Davies has never been disciplined?"

"I am."

Brian watched the jury. Make a note of that, he directed silently to the ones with their pens in their hands. I'm one of the good guys.

"No further questions at this time," Courtland informed the judge.

Brierly seemed surprised to be released after such a short session. He stepped down from the witness box and was replaced with Chief Inspector Denison. The proceedings paused momentarily whilst Denison took the oath. He then confirmed that he was a chief inspector attached to the Metropolitan Police Firearms Unit.

"What was your role in the operation which was planned on 26 August 2005?" Hilliard asked.

"I was the Tactical Firearms Commander, responsible for determining the specific details of the firearms operation. In hostage situations we know a negotiator will be called in, but we must be prepared for every eventuality. For that reason my officers recced the site and provided details critical to our operation."

"Is it also your job to be well acquainted with the officers you command?"

"Yes."

"Are you ever required to counsel an officer, perhaps because problems at home are affecting his performance on the job?"

"Yes."

Denison was not usually so succinct, Brian noted. He must have resolved not to give any more information than absolutely required to the prosecutor.

"My lord," the defence barrister remonstrated. "The implication is that the defendant is unstable."

He's not unstable, Beth argued silently. My husband is solid, steady, and dependable no matter what.

Anticipating the objection, Hilliard replied with an even tone. "We are simply examining the scope of responsibility of this officer."

Judge Bradbury nodded. "I'll allow it."

"Officer Davies is one of your more experienced officers, is that correct?"

Again Denison gave an affirmative reply.

"He has served how long with the Met?" Hilliard persisted.

"Seventeen years to date."

"And for how many of those years has he been a member of the firearms unit?"

"He volunteered for and completed firearms training in 1995."

Brian remembered the date and his quiet satisfaction that he'd passed. There'd been no time to celebrate, nor would it have been considered good form to engage in public festivities of any sort. He was assigned to a team, and his increased responsibility had begun immediately.

Hilliard seemed satisfied with the answer, nodding and smiling as he rephrased. "Ten years then, at the time of the incident in question."

"Yes, he is a highly skilled and responsible officer."

Hilliard took a moment before resuming his questioning. "I like apples," he said, almost as an aside before turning to face the witness. "Do you, Chief Inspector?"

Denison frowned, not certain whether he should reply, but acknowledged aloud that he did.

"Yet there's usually at least one bad apple in each barrel, is there not?" Hilliard pressed.

"Objection, my lord, he's not a farmer nor a grocer!" Courtland said.

Judge Bradbury smiled slightly and nodded.

Denison didn't miss the implication and decided to respond despite the judge's ruling. "Not in this case," he replied firmly. "Officer Davies is well respected by me and by his colleagues."

Hilliard allowed the last statement to stand, choosing to ask another question instead of objecting. "In spite of the frequent discharges of his weapon?" he asked.

Brian felt the temperature in the courtroom rise suddenly. His barrister, Fiona Courtland, was on her feet in an instant. Beth restrained a gasp. She had known an attack would come, but not so soon.

"My lord, I submit that this is not relevant to the case at hand and must be excluded!"

"Jury out!" Judge Bradbury ordered.

As soon as the twelve had departed, Courtland continued. "Previous conduct can prejudice a jury and must not be allowed," she argued.

"My lord," Hilliard responded in an unhurried, relaxed tone. "The prosecution acknowledges that Officer Davies has not been disciplined in the past for his actions. We simply wish to include in the record his behaviour on several occasions as part of his employment history. We intend no bias."

"Miss Courtland?" Judge Bradbury asked.

"A jury can never unhear anything they have heard," Courtland emphasised. "My learned colleague is attempting to establish a pattern where there is none, when it is generally accepted that past action alone cannot be used to predict future action."

Judge Bradbury ruled quickly. "I find that the prejudicial effect of entering the defendant's job history into the record will be negligible. However, I warn you, Mr. Hilliard, if you attempt to address the issue of character based on these incidents, I will stop you. Nor can the information you wish to reveal be used to show motive. I will allow facts only." He paused. "Perhaps it will be possible for our tempers to cool during the luncheon period. I will recall the jury following that break. Court is adjourned."

He rose, and the court rose with him.

CHAPTER FOUR

FOLLOWING THE LUNCH BREAK, the jury returned to their seats, Chief Inspector Denison to the witness box, and Brian to the dock, his meal resting heavily on his stomach because he knew what lay ahead.

"Chief Inspector," Hilliard began without preamble, "was Officer Davies one of the officers escorting a witness to St. George Crown Court during the 1999 trial of William Cecil Scott?"

"Yes."

"And did he discharge his firearm during that operation?"

Denison spoke slowly. "When Carlos Moraga, the attacker, fired upon the witness, Officer Davies returned fire, wounding him and sparing the witness from further assault."

"And that witness was – ?"

Courtland and Denison objected almost simultaneously.

"My lord, I am prevented from revealing her name," Denison said.

"Her identity is not relevant," Courtland insisted.

"My lord, she is the same woman who was a hostage in the case we are currently trying," Hilliard explained.

"A coincidence at best," Courtland continued. "That case occurred seven years ago and is dissimilar in every respect to the one currently being heard. And she is not on trial."

"Let's not fight amongst ourselves," Judge Bradbury responded testily. "Mr. Hilliard, you have made your point. Move on."

Hilliard turned a page in his notebook. "When the Hackney Siege began on 26 December 2002, against the Jamaican suspect Eli

Hall, was Officer Davies one of the armed officers assigned to the scene?"

"He was on standby," Denison stated.

"Do you mean to say that he was *initially* on standby?" Hilliard pursued.

"Yes," Denison admitted with some reluctance.

"Did Officer Davies discharge his firearm during this siege?"

"Yes, he returned fire."

"On more than one occasion?"

"Yes."

Denison could not answer otherwise, Brian knew, but he was wary of the prosecutor's approach. With his success in securing agreement from Denison, Hilliard appeared benign.

There was a moment of silence in the court whilst all waited for Hilliard's next question.

"As did several others," Denison added.

A gaffe on Hilliard's part, Courtland thought. His pause had allowed the witness to elaborate, and objecting would reveal his displeasure and distract the jury. He had been trying to show Davies' guilt by association but had failed. Courtland knew, however, that winning her case would take more than capitalising on her opponent's errors.

"Did that incident end with the death of the suspect?"

Denison deliberated. The question required a yes or no response, but the round which had killed the suspect had not come from a police firearm. He knew he would not be allowed to add anything. "Yes," he said heavily, glancing briefly at the defence barrister, who was taking notes of his testimony.

"Turning now to the incident which occurred in August of last year," Hilliard said. "Did the deceased, Roy Alden Wilkes, detain a young woman on the 25th of that month?"

Courtland winced inwardly when she heard Wilkes described as deceased. She could not dispute the fact of his death, but the reference underlined the way the incident had ended.

"Yes, her distress call was received on the afternoon of that day."

"After the identification of Mr. Wilkes, did you put in place a release plan?"

"I cannot comment on details of our operations," Denison stated, "but its intent was rescue."

"I understand," Hilliard responded evenly. "However, may we conclude that you had firearms officers in the area?"

"Yes."

"Was Officer Davies one of those?"

"Yes."

"Did Officer Davies return fire on this occasion?"

"No."

"He did not 'return fire' because the suspect did not fire on your officers. In fact, he did not even possess a firearm, isn't that correct?"

"That's correct," Denison ceded.

"Did you authorise entry into Mr. Wilkes' flat?"

"Not in so many words, however – "

"Excuse me, Chief Inspector," Hilliard interrupted. "I'd like to rephrase my question. Did you – on the night of Sunday, 28 August 2005, *personally* authorise entry into Mr. Wilkes' flat?"

Denison could only reply in the negative.

It was evident to Courtland that Hilliard intended to humanise the hostage taker by the repeated use of his name. He would also make as little reference as possible to his crime.

"Yet this incident ended with Officer Davies firing two shots into the chest of Mr. Wilkes?"

"Objection, my lord," Courtland said quickly. "The question is intended to mislead the jury."

"I merely wish to put the facts of the case on record," Hilliard offered smoothly.

"Overruled," Judge Bradbury said.

Brian was stunned. When was he going to mention the knife? The prosecution counsel's questions implied that Wilkes had had no weapon at all. He had expected a robust examination, but Hilliard was not revealing the full picture, only pieces, like edited film.

Denison knew he was required to answer. Perhaps a short reply would be the least impactful. Perhaps the defence barrister would further examine the circumstances in her cross-examination. "Yes."

"I'm confused," the Judge Bradbury said, frowning at Hilliard but directing his question to the witness. "Did he or did he not have a weapon? Without one, why would the hostage have remained? And why would Officer Davies have fired?"

Ha! Brian thought. He has upset the apple cart.

Members of the jury were glancing from the witness to the judge and back again.

"That will become clear as the case unfolds," Hilliard replied before Denison could answer.

"Ah. Proceed," the Judge Bradbury directed.

Hilliard stood quietly for a moment. The judge's interjection had diluted the impact of Denison's final affirmative answer. "My lord, I have no more questions for this witness at this time."

Courtland hadn't faced Hilliard in court before, because previously she'd been engaged to prosecute, as he was. He had juniors, but she suspected that he would present the majority of the case himself, as would she. At any rate she now understood the prosecution's strategy: present the bare bones or skeleton of the case and omit any language which referred to Wilkes' crimes. Mention nothing with which the jury could disagree. Be courteous, reasonable, and believable so that his infrequent attacks would be more memorable. If she pushed too hard, the jury would deem her unreasonable. Prosecution counsel's later attacks would then be considered appropriate, or even mild, in comparison to hers. She had no choice, however. She must ensure that additional relevant facts were heard. She rose slowly with what she hoped was an understanding smile and did not hurry to place her notebook on the podium.

"Chief Inspector Denison, this is all very difficult, is it not?"

"Yes, ma'am."

"I imagine seeing a fellow officer in the dock makes you very uncomfortable, would you agree?"

"Yes," Denison responded with relief.

"Let's review briefly then the incidents highlighted by the prosecution. Officer Davies first discharged his weapon to protect a Crown Court witness who was scheduled to appear in the trial of serial rapist and killer William Cecil Scott, is that correct?"

"Yes."

"As I understand it, the attacker fired first, seriously wounding the witness and one of her protection officers. Officer Davies returned fire. Yes?"

"Yes."

"What was the result of Officer Davies' action?"

"If Davies hadn't shot him, he'd have evaded arrest. Instead he was apprehended. He later pleaded guilty to a number of charges, sparing the public the cost of a trial. With Davies' rounds in his thigh and the number of police witnesses to his action, the attacker had no defence."

"Was Officer Davies disciplined for his actions in this incident?"

"No. He was investigated, which is standard procedure following the discharge of a firearm. He was then cleared of any wrongdoing."

"Thank you. Moving now to the Hackney Siege and Officer Davies' participation – or lack of participation – in it."

"My lord," Hilliard objected.

"I will make my point clear," Courtland answered.

"Continue."

"Eli Hall was the suspect in the Hackney Siege, was he not?" Courtland asked.

"Yes."

"Who was he?"

"A man wanted by police who had barricaded himself in his building to prevent being taken into custody."

"Why did your officers fire on Mr. Hall?"

"Because he fired on them on several occasions, endangering their lives as well as the lives of members of the public."

"Were any officers disciplined as a result of their actions during this siege?"

"No. Returning fire is permitted under our rules of engagement. No disciplinary action was warranted."

"Were other sorts of resolution attempted?"

"Yes, experienced negotiators spoke at length with Mr. Hall. Water and electricity were discontinued to his building in the hope that the discomfort would cause him to surrender. Our goal was – and is – always to secure a peaceful resolution."

"Was the suspect Eli Hall injured by any of the Met's officers?"

"Yes, a bullet struck him in the cheek."

"Did that bullet come from Officer Davies' weapon?"

"No," Denison replied with a hint of emphasis.

"In fact Mr. Hall was not killed by any of the Met's officers, was he?" Courtland pressed.

"No, the coroner returned a verdict of suicide."

"Just to be certain that I understand Officer Davies' history: the first time he fired his weapon – in defence of a witness – it did not result in the death of the offender, and the second time he fired his weapon, not even injury resulted. Is my understanding correct?"

"It is, yes."

"Do these two incidents – three years apart, I must emphasise – establish a pattern of behaviour on Officer Davies' part?"

"My lord," Hilliard objected, "defence is asking this witness to draw a conclusion."

"It is a conclusion he is qualified to make," Courtland argued, "because it is based on his rational perception of the events."

"Allowed."

Courtland repeated the question.

"No pattern of behaviour was established," Denison stated.

Courtland had effectively countered the misleading questioning conducted by the prosecution, Brian thought. He hoped the jury appreciated the significance of her approach.

"Thank you. Referring now to the hostage situation which began on 25 August 2005. Did the hostage, whom we will refer to as Yankee 1, indicate in her distress call that she was injured?"

"Yes, Mr. Wilkes had struck her in the head, causing her to lose consciousness for a time."

"Did he hold her against her will?"

"Yes."

"Let me phrase that another way. Was he amenable to releasing her?"

"No, any suggestion that he do so was met with resistance and anger. Consequently a plan was developed to secure her rescue."

"Were the skills of a hostage negotiator used?"

"They were, yes."

"Yet you still prepared an armed response?"

"If negotiations are not successful, we must be ready to act."

"Are you kept informed of the progress of negotiations?"

"Yes, of course."

"You would be aware then that Mr. Wilkes had repeatedly threatened the hostage Yankee 1 with a knife?"

Hilliard recognised the subtle way Courtland had phrased her question, but he could not let it pass. "Hearsay, my lord! Counsel is indirectly asking the witness to testify to what the negotiator told him, and the witness cannot testify to information heard by the negotiator. Only the negotiator can do this."

"On the contrary," Courtland replied quickly. "Chief Inspector Denison will be testifying not for the truth of the matter asserted but as a way of explaining why he wanted his officers to be prepared to respond."

Hilliard would not let it go. "With respect, my lord, this is clearly within the definition of hearsay – a statement, made by someone other than the witness, offered as proof to prove the matter asserted, i.e., that Mr. Wilkes repeatedly threated the hostage with a knife."

"My lord, even if you consider Chief Inspector Denison's statement as hearsay, let me point out that it fits within an exception, and indeed, Section 114 of Chapter 2, Part 11, of the UK Public General Acts supports this."

Clear as mud, Brian thought. Would the success of his defence rest on rulings such as this?

"Miss Courtland, I'm well acquainted with British law," Judge Bradbury replied drily. He nodded at the prosecutor. "Mr. Hilliard, I'll allow it."

After a brief pause, Courtland asked the question again and received an affirmative reply from the chief inspector. Hilliard remained silent.

"Chief Inspector, did armed officers enter the hostage taker's flat to rescue Yankee 1?" she continued.

"Yes."

"Was Officer Davies one of those armed officers?"

"Yes."

"Was he authorised to make entry?"

"Yes, indirectly." Denison glanced at the judge to see if he would be permitted to explain. "In addition to Strategic and Tactical Commanders, every operation has a number of operational commanders, the ones on the ground who make the plan happen. Our plans allow for the judgement of these officers, who are closest to the scene of an incident, to prevail."

"My lord, I reserve the right to recall this witness," Courtland said. She gathered her robe round her and sat down. The presence of a knife was now on the record as well as Officer Davies' authorisation to enter.

"We are adjourned," declared Judge Bradbury, his resonant voice confirming his authority. "I've had enough of discord for today."

Beth breathed a sigh of relief. The day was over, and the defending barrister had responded to, and she felt, neutralised each point raised by the prosecution. She would ring Jenny and report that the day hadn't been as difficult as she'd expected.

CHAPTER FIVE

"ALL RISE!" the usher commanded as Judge Bradbury entered on Friday morning, and everyone in the courtroom obeyed.

The prosecution barrister, Joel Hilliard, called his next witness. "Please give your name and title," he directed after the witness had been sworn in.

"Marcus Coulter, Inspector, attached to the Metropolitan Police Crime Operations Group."

"And I understand, Inspector, that you are a trained police negotiator, and that it was in this role that you became involved in this case. Is that correct?"

"Yes, I was called in to negotiate with the alleged hostage taker, Mr. Roy Wilkes."

Finally, Courtland thought, an acknowledgement of the crime.

"Are you employed as a negotiator on a full-time basis?" Hilliard asked.

"No, I have what we call a 'day job' with the police. However, because I have made myself available for crisis negotiations, I have a good deal of experience in this area."

Courtland approved of the term "crisis." She hoped it would come to define the incident for the jury. She listened whilst Hilliard elicited the details of Coulter's extensive qualifications and training. Get on with it, she thought. I need to hear something I can object to.

"What is your primary goal?" Hilliard asked.

"To save lives," Coulter answered. "To end the crisis, whatever it is, peacefully."

"In your experience does each negotiation boil down to a single issue that needs to be resolved?"

"No, that's a far too simplified view of what negotiators do. In many cases, particularly politically motivated ones, there are multiple, complex issues. And we work with an incomplete set of circumstances. We are provided with some background material on the offender, but most of what we know is what we are told by him."

A hostage negotiator primer for the jury, Brian thought.

"In the case of Mr. Wilkes, was there more than one issue to be agreed upon?"

"Mr. Wilkes held a single irrational belief, but he had many needs. It was my hope that resolving the real needs could lead to progress on the other."

"And those needs were – ?"

"Respect, affection, an end to loneliness, to name only a few. He was sick, and he'd been deserted. In addition, he needed some tangible support."

"Did you feel that progress was being made in these areas?"

"Yes. I am trained to provide the active and responsive listening which often soothes the feelings of a distressed person. Also, we sent food to him and indicated that we would be willing to rehouse him and to arrange for additional medical care for his condition. An inoperable tumour was the cause of his delusion and the source of his pain."

"You did not then believe that negotiations had come to an end?" Hilliard continued.

"I did not," Coulter answered. "It's necessary to remember that Mr. Wilkes was not irrational to himself, only to us. Sometimes an individual, particularly one who is not rational, needs a period of rest. I believed it was possible to reestablish meaningful contact that could lead to a peaceful conclusion. Of course, it's not possible to know at this time whether that would have occurred. I can only say that in my career I've had more successes than failures."

"Thank you," Hilliard said.

Courtland waited for Hilliard to seat himself before rising to her microphone. Hilliard had not allowed one reference to Mrs.

Casey and her plight. He had guided the examination away from Wilkes' crime, his possession of a knife, and the fear that his behaviour must have created for his hostage. He had centred his questions solely on Wilkes' needs and taken advantage of Coulter's optimism, much the way she had controlled the flow of information when she had prosecuted cases. Now, however, she felt a frustration that was new to her. As defence counsel she could not cross-examine on material not introduced into evidence by the prosecution. She could only emphasise the critical nature of Coulter's work and hope that the jury understood.

"You have described yourself as a crisis negotiator," she began. "Is that because your skills are required to resolve crises?"

"Yes."

"And was the hostage taker Mr. Wilkes the primary focus of your work during this incident?"

"Yes."

"You conversed with him, then, not because you had so much in common and wished to become friends, but because he had taken a young woman hostage?"

Hilliard raised his hand in objection.

"Yes," Judge Bradbury agreed. "Miss Courtland, I'll thank you to leave sarcasm out of your cross-examination."

Courtland nodded in acquiescence and waited for the witness to respond.

"Of course, yes."

"And he was therefore the cause and centre of a crisis situation?"

"Yes," Coulter admitted.

"Was his single irrational belief a case of mistaken identity?"

"Yes, Mr. Wilkes believed the young woman to be his partner, Tanya Hanson."

"Did the young woman – the hostage we call Yankee 1 – resemble Miss Hanson?" Courtland asked.

"No, it was puzzling, as most delusions are, because she did not."

"Did you consider that to be an indication that his delusion was severe?"

"Yes."

"Would you describe this negotiation as difficult?"

"Yes, because Mr. Wilkes' only demand was to be left alone with his hostage, which of course I could not agree to do."

"Did you tell him you could not meet his demand?"

"No. I rarely give an unequivocal response to a hostage taker. I prefer to answer with 'not now' or 'not yet' to imply that all options are still open for negotiation."

"Thank you," Courtland said. "Then am I correct in understanding that your desired result was to secure the release of the hostage?"

"Yes, although during negotiations I could not allow Mr. Wilkes to suspect that I cared more about the hostage's well-being than his. That would have undermined my influence with him."

"With what result?"

"He could have become angry and taken his anger out on the hostage."

Courtland paused for a moment, anticipating an objection on the part of the prosecution. It would, however, have called attention to her line of questioning, so she understood when Hilliard refrained.

"Anger," Courtland repeated. "Were you concerned that he could 'become' angry because he had already shown indications of that emotion?"

"Yes, because he feared abandonment."

"Did you find his anger to be a complicating factor in these negotiations?"

"Yes."

"And his anger would have created fear on the part of the hostage?"

"Yes."

"When," Courtland continued, "did negotiations break down?"

"In my view, they didn't."

"Was the hostage taker still answering your calls?"

"No, but I had not given up."

"Let me be clear. Your first contact with the hostage taker was on the morning of 26 August, when Yankee 1 had already been captive for two days?"

"Yes."

"And negotiations stalled on the afternoon of Sunday, 28 August?"

"Yes."

"Would it be your considered opinion that this incident escalated quickly?"

Coulter paused, reluctant to answer in the affirmative.

"Allow me to rephrase," Courtland said. "Does a hostage taker's mental instability lessen the chances of success in negotiations?"

Coulter paused. "Not all situations are negotiable," he conceded. "This one was tragic. It has weighed heavily on me."

A victory, Courtland thought, albeit a small one. "I have no more questions for this witness," she announced.

"2 pm. Prompt," Judge Bradbury directed. Court was adjourned for lunch.

****

When the luncheon break ended, Brian found that only his physical hunger had left him. He still yearned to be out of the dock, to hear the judge say he was free to go, to hug his wife and children, and to resume his life. Instead he would witness the legal manoeuvres between the prosecution and the defence and hope that in this elaborate dance Hilliard would make a misstep.

The prosecution barrister Joel Hilliard called Bravo 3 to the witness box, managing to conceal his distaste for his identification code. He would have preferred a more neutral code, but he was well aware that every firearms officer who testified would be given an epithet to protect his identity. And none would wear his uniform for the same reason, but that did not concern him.

Brian watched Nick Howard being sworn in. He'd been the one to remove Jenny from the clamour and gore in the flat.

"You are attached to the firearms unit of the Metropolitan Police?" Hilliard asked.

"Yes."

"And on Sunday, 28 August 2005, you were the leader of the team that entered Mr. Wilkes' flat?"

"Two teams were on site. I was team leader for the primary team, who were lined up in the corridor just outside the flat."

"Did the Tactical Commander authorise your team to make entry?"

"No."

"As team leader, did you authorise entry?"

"I heard the threats of the hostage taker and the screams of the hostage. We all did."

"Bravo 3, you must answer the question that is put to you," Judge Bradbury admonished.

"I did not, but I would have," the officer replied stubbornly. "We don't make entry without cause. And we identify ourselves as armed police when we do."

"My lord," Hilliard objected.

"Bravo 3, you are required to abide by the rules of this court," the judge said firmly, "which means that you cannot speak for others."

"Did you see a knife in the hand of Mr. Wilkes?"

A change in strategy, the defence barrister noted. The prosecution was exchanging his kid gloves for boxing gloves. It was a way of dealing with the less-than-enthusiastic cooperation he expected to receive from Brian's fellow officers.

"As team leader, I was one of the last to enter," the witness stated.

"Did you or did you not see a knife in the hand of Mr. Wilkes?" Hilliard repeated.

The officer paused.

"Bravo 3, you are required to answer," Judge Bradbury exhorted.

The officer's jaw tensed. "No."

Beth had known what his testimony would have to be, but hearing it expressed so baldly was difficult.

"You were one of the last to enter," Hilliard mused aloud. "Was Mr. Wilkes deceased?"

"He was down. I cannot testify to more than that. Medical personnel are required to pronounce that life is extinct."

"Did you see a knife at the time?"

"The hostage taker's weapon was no longer a concern to me. My concern was to remove the hostage from the scene as soon as possible and secure medical care for her."

"Are you acquainted with the hostage?"

"That did not alter my procedure. In a hostage rescue scenario, we try to spare the hostage, particularly a wounded female civilian, from prolonged exposure to bloodshed."

"Bravo 3, it was a yes-or-no question," the judge said, anticipating the objection of the prosecutor.

Courtland stood quickly, also wanting to prevent an objection. "My lord, this officer is part of a team. I'm certain no disrespect is intended."

Brian wanted to cheer. It was now part of sworn testimony that Jenny was wounded. That pointed to the presence of a knife in the flat and further to its use as an offensive weapon. He saw defence counsel make a note. Several jury members did as well.

"As a matter of curiosity, did the hostage recognise you?"

"Our operations are sudden, shocking, and very fast. I'm not certain that much registered with her until she reached the ambulance. And even then, she would have known me only as a police officer. Our headgear conceals our facial features."

Hilliard glanced at Courtland, who indicated with a nod that she had questions for the witness.

"When you say that you removed the hostage from the scene, did you guide or escort her to the ambulance?" she asked after making her way to the podium.

"No, I carried her."

"And that was because – ?"

"She was injured and in shock."

"Injured?"

"Multiple knife wounds were evident."

"Drawing a conclusion, my lord?" Hilliard asked the judge.

"Please rephrase your answer," Judge Bradbury directed.

"Lacerations. The blood that had resulted from them. Her skin had been cut with a sharp object in many places. That's what I saw."

"Thank you," Courtland said quickly, wanting the officer's observation to stand.

Hilliard called a police constable next, whom he referred to as Bravo 8. "What was your role in the incident we are currently examining?" he enquired after Bravo 8 had taken the oath.

Moe – whose given name was Miles Watkins – looked surprisingly defenceless in the witness box, Brian thought. His clothes covered his well-developed muscles, and his bald head gave him an air of vulnerability.

"I was responsible for breaching the premises," he said.

"Could you simplify your statement for the jury, please?"

"I broke the door down," the witness clarified, "and then stepped aside to allow my mates to enter."

"Did you see a knife in the hand of the deceased?"

"I couldn't see the bastard from where I was standing. My device is bulky, and I backed away so I wouldn't interfere with rapid entry."

"Who authorised you to take this action?"

"Backing up?"

"I apologise," Hilliard said with some rancour. "I was referring to destroying the door."

"Davies did." He nodded in the direction of the dock. "But I was ready. The yelling and screaming we heard had us all champing at the bit."

"My lord!" Hilliard exclaimed. "This has gone far enough! I strongly object!"

"Sustained," Judge Bradbury declared.

In spite of this skirmish, Courtland smiled to herself. Prosecuting counsel would not question this witness further. She watched him sit. "No questions," she reported to the judge.

Bravo, Moe, Beth thought.

Hilliard turned a page in his notebook. "Bravo 6," he called.

Aidan Traylor, one of the newer and younger members of the team. Brian gave him a slight nod when their eyes met after he took the oath. He knew Traylor was concerned that he couldn't give unconditional support for him.

"You are attached to the firearms unit," Hilliard stated, "and you entered Mr. Wilkes' flat immediately after the defendant, is that correct?"

"Yes."

"Did you see Mr. Wilkes threatening the hostage with a knife?"

"Davies is a big man, and he was in front of me."

"In other words, no. You did not see a knife. Is that your testimony?"

Bravo 6 hesitated briefly before responding in the affirmative.

I must find a way to counteract this, Courtland thought. She waited for Hilliard to seat himself and then stood, resting her notebook on the podium with her microphone and taking a moment to smooth a page.

"Is it my understanding then," she started, "that variations in what officers see – officers on the same operation – are normal?"

"Yes," the officer seemed relieved to answer. "We have no way of knowing exactly where the offender is standing when we go in, and we are expected to cover the entire space. And regardless of the speed of an operation, we each enter at a different time, which mitigates against all of us seeing the same thing."

Hilliard threw up his hands. "Can the court not strike these improper 'we' phrases?"

Courtland countered the objection. "I asked about officers, plural, therefore the witness' answer was appropriate. However, I will be more careful in the future about the wording of my questions."

Both Judge Bradbury and Hilliard seemed satisfied.

"To continue. With regard to what you see when you make entry, your testimony may differ from that of other officers on the scene because operations are fast, because you do not enter at the same time, and because you are responsible for covering different areas within the premises?"

"Yes."

"Thus several people, even well-trained observers such as yourself and your colleagues, may witness the same event yet report entirely different views of it?"

"My lord," Hilliard interrupted. "The defence is testifying."

"Summarising, my lord," Courtland replied. "Is it also true that an individual's recall of details may also vary according to when his statement is taken?"

"Yes, that's why officers make notes – and only notes – immediately following an incident. A full statement is discouraged within the first twenty-four hours."

"And why is that?"

"Because memory can be distorted."

"Bravo 6, you have testified that your field of view was blocked by the defendant, who entered the hostage taker's premises ahead of you. Then let me put this to you: If you cannot swear that the hostage taker was holding a knife, then you cannot swear to its opposite. You cannot swear that he was not holding a knife, isn't that correct?"

"That's correct," the officer agreed, his voice more firm. "I can't swear that he wasn't."

She could gain no more from this witness, Courtland knew, so she ended her cross-examination. Hilliard next called, one by one, the rest of the officers on the primary assault team. It was overkill, Courtland thought, although she wouldn't have used that term aloud. However, each time an officer indicated that he had seen something in the hand of the hostage taker, she managed in cross to elicit the possibility that it could have been a knife. When Hilliard called the team leader and members of the second assault team, she had nothing to examine, since they had had to scale ladders and then break the dining room window to enter and had thus been too late even to see the hostage before she was removed to safety.

"I do not like to ask a jury to sit late unless absolutely necessary," Judge Bradbury commented, "particularly when we're at the weekend. Consequently this is an appropriate time for me to rise. I hope you will use the time to relax but not to discuss any of the testimony you have heard. I remind you that you are prohibited from communicating about this case in any way, directly or indirectly, verbally or nonverbally. We will resume on the Monday at 10:00 am."

That restriction didn't apply to her and to Brian, Beth hoped. She'd been able to see his tension even through the folds of his suit. They would spend the weekend reviewing the proceedings thus far and encouraging each other for the remainder.

CHAPTER SIX

TWO DISTRESSED SOULS in two dissimilar bodies. Neil Goodwyn had spent the Saturday visiting first with Brian Davies and then with Jennifer Casey.

Brian had invited him for lunch at the Hampstead flat, where he was served pork tenderloin he was able to cut with a fork. Beth made buttered noodles with peas and added a dash of cinnamon and nutmeg to the top of the applesauce. Was Brian cooking more now because he felt better psychologically or because he feared he'd not be able to in the future? Goodwyn did not ask.

When the meal ended, Beth took the children for a walk on the Heath, but not before begging Brian, "Tell him," in an agonised voice.

"Sometimes the things which are the most difficult to say are the ones which are the most important to relate," he'd prompted Brian.

The dreams that Brian then outlined were disturbing, revealing the degree to which he felt helpless and under attack. His reluctance still showing, he haltingly described the first, in which he'd been a new employee at an advertising agency who was asked to deliver something to the printer. The specs are all here, he'd been told, and the printer's just down the hall. But the hall was long and dark, and he couldn't read the companies' names in the dim light. When he went into a place with unfinished furniture in their lobby to ask for directions and glanced at the material he held, the specs were unreadable. The printer had laughed. We already have everything we need, he'd said. It's a trick your boss plays on all new workers.

Brian had been humiliated and confused; should he report for work on Monday or not?

In his second dream he'd been in a flat somewhere with Beth and the children. Rounds of gunfire were striking the outside walls. He'd sent one of his mates to take Beth, Meg, and Robbie to the upstairs loo, an interior room where they'd be safe. The rest of them – mates, but none he recognised – covered all windows and doors and then barricaded themselves where they could, but none of them were armed and thus had no way of defending against the threat. They agreed to allow only one point of entry and to use kitchen knives or their bare hands to subdue the intruders when they breached. Until then they could do nothing but wait.

Goodwyn had regarded the man in front of him, a big man with impressive skills. Yet in his current legal situation his bulk and training did not enhance his strength nor conceal his current frailty of spirit because he knew he was vulnerable.

"You do not feel you're a participant in your own trial," he had observed gently. "I recall during my days as a British Army chaplain feeling at the mercy of what was taking place round me. Sometimes the volume of the enemy's barrages drowned out the prayers I said aloud. I was unarmed, although those with weapons had no more guarantee of survival than I."

Remembering, he had resisted the impulse to speak more loudly, lest Brian misinterpret his increased sound as shared fear.

"Later I realised that our unit had been on the defensive. When the tide turned and we were able to mount an offensive, our spirits changed as well. So I'd like to suggest that because this past week you've been subjected to a withering attack on the part of the prosecution, your feelings are normal. This week, when your barrister presents your case, you'll be encouraged."

But the truth should be evident, not elusive, Brian had argued.

Goodwyn had been forced to agree. If the prosecution were successful in obscuring the truth, the consequences for Brian would be grave. "Nevertheless I trust that what appears to be only a flicker of light will become a blaze," he had said.

Brian had been quiet, not agreeing with nor disputing his words, but his shoulders had relaxed, and the lines of tension in his face had eased.

From previous conversations Goodwyn knew that Brian had a general but undefined faith. Although the contradictions of life confounded him, he was not averse to the certainty of a higher power. "When the events are bigger than we are, we need an ally who is greater than they. The ally whom I sought and found has guided, enriched, and redeemed my life. I will pray that you come to know Him more fully, regardless of the outcome of the proceedings that awaits you."

He'd taken what was for him a rare step and placed his hand on Brian's shoulder when he prayed, on the shoulder of a big, strong man who was afraid. Brian had nodded his thanks.

Afterward they'd spoken of lighter things until Beth and the children returned.

His next stop was Chorleywood, where Jenny, Simon, and Bear were waiting for him. She was concerned about appearing in court, and Simon was apprehensive as well. Bear was at her side.

"I have a new name," she said, her tone not quite matching the levity she was intending. "In court I'll be called Yankee 1, and most people won't even know how appropriate that is – until I answer a question!"

He smiled with her and accepted only her offer of tea, explaining that Brian and Beth had served him quite a generous meal. He accompanied her to the kitchen and offered to brew for all of them.

"Feeling fatigued?" he asked, whilst waiting for the water to boil.

"Bad dreams," she admitted. "Dreams that don't make any sense. In one of them, I'm tossing and turning, but when seven people holding candles approach me, I'm able to sleep. That's backward – why did I sleep better in the light than in the dark? In another, each person looks at me through a camera, and I fall asleep, even though I don't like having my picture taken."

"Who is holding the candles?" Neil asked. "And the cameras? Anyone you know?"

"Men and women I've never seen before." She took cream from the refrigerator and set it on the tray with the bowl of sugar.

"Candles illuminate but don't record," the priest mused. "Cameras record things, thus allowing others to see them. Perhaps the dreams refer to a role you're called to play, something that has been private but will soon be public." He paused. "On the other hand, sometimes dreams are predictions. Truth is often equated with light, as represented by the candles. And cameras need light to freeze a point in time. A camera can record truth, or what in court would be called evidence. Which reminds me – when are you scheduled to testify?" he asked when they were all seated with their beverages in front of them.

"We don't know exactly," she answered. "The prosecution has several more witnesses to examine. Perhaps Wednesday or Thursday. I'll be questioned during the afternoon sessions only, because of the baby." She then seemed unable to focus on anything for very long, starting sentences she didn't complete and taking only short sips of her caffeine-free tea before stopping altogether and moving closer to Simon on the sofa. Bear rested his head on her knee.

Simon explained that a petition from Brian's defence barrister had documented the seriousness of her morning sickness. The court, in an unusually compassionate move, was permitting her testimony to be restricted to the time of day when she felt most stable.

"You will be only eight weeks along then in your pregnancy?" he asked and was given affirmative replies. "You must feel that you're taking a risk, adding stress at this time."

"I worry about the baby, but – but I have to do this," she stammered. "When the chips were down, he was there for me."

"I agree. Hence I'd like to reassure you. Do you know where the strongest trees are? Not where they are protected by their environment but where they are subjected to the extremes of weather and have had to adapt. And do you know why? Because in order to survive, they've had to develop deep roots. I've no doubt that you have these, because you've overcome previous challenges and grown stronger. And that's what peace is: not absence of conflict but calm in the midst of conflict. The peace you seek is already inside you, put there by the God who loves you and who hears every prayer, whether shouted, whispered, or simply thought."

"I wish I could feel that."

"You can. It's a matter of concentrating on the truth at hand and realising that doubt and unbelief are not the same. Doubt means that there are times when you're not certain that God is real. But the corollary is also true: there are times when you are."

She thought for a minute. "When Brian and Beth's baby Robbie was born, I was sure. He was perfect, and I didn't think that could have come from anyone except God. But because of my experience with Roy – and then losing the baby – and Brian's situation – I've questioned."

"As most would do," Neil commented. "But don't give up hope. I don't believe He's through with you. More than that – when you step into that witness box, you'll not be alone. It will be a holy moment because you will be doing what you have been called to do. You may appear to be a single individual, but you have a new life inside you, as well as God's spirit with you, and Simon's and that of many others."

"A team," Simon said, speaking for the first time.

"I'll be the one on point," she said, adopting his terminology.

"Yes, and I'd put money on your internal strength to be victorious in any situation, even this one. Jenny," Goodwyn added, "you are no longer a hostage."

"Will you pray for me?" she asked. "And for the baby? Not just today but until we know that we've made it through this and that he's ok?"

"Yes, and I'll do even more. If you'll let me know which days you'll be testifying, I'll be in court to support you."

Her eyes welled up, and Simon took her hand. Goodwyn wished, as he sometimes did, that so much was not required of God's people, but he kept his prayer positive.

When Simon showed him to the door, he mentioned corresponding with his father. "I've suggested that we meet at a neutral site," he said. "Part of the ground rules I'm requiring. I want my mum to be present as well, so I can observe how he treats her. And Jenny won't be involved until I'm certain there's no possibility of his destructive behaviour. And until she's reached her second trimester. My father now knows she's expecting and is impatient, but I'll have a chance to see how he deals with that."

"I like your parameters. I have just one word of warning," Goodwyn responded. "Do not let the past control you. We all deserve to start with a clean slate."

CHAPTER SEVEN

MONDAY WAS A LONG DAY of testimony. The gallery was crowded, the public enthralled like drivers who gawked when they passed vehicle accidents. Brian knew Beth resented their presence, because they were curious about the identity of the woman whose eyes always rested on him, and they whispered in tones too soft for the judge to hear but too loud for her to concentrate on her own thoughts.

First, the medical examiner Gareth Bortles presented the evidence of the post-mortem. A more than overfed man, he needed the roominess of the witness box to encompass his girth as he testified. His rather long unruly hair clung to his scalp, and he wheezed a bit as he spoke. He had examined the slightly undernourished body of a non-Caucasian male in his mid-fifties approximately five feet eleven inches tall and with a cancerous tumour in his brain. He then provided details of Wilkes' condition that were difficult to hear. Brian wondered if the jury would be able to forget the bloody aftermath of his entry. He hadn't. He saw again the X-ray's blood, the only bold colour in the otherwise drab surroundings. He felt again deep frustration with what he had been required to do. Why couldn't the X-ray have chosen a peaceful resolution? However lawful his action had been, he was again haunted by the fact that he had taken a life.

There was very little for his barrister to challenge. She could not dispute the factual findings, and nothing unexpected in the post-mortem evidence was heard. Hence Courtland's approach was to focus on the less disturbing aspects of the testimony and thus attempt to relieve the impact. "According to your evidence, was Mr. Wilkes a tall man?" she asked.

"Above average, yes. Average height here is considered to be five feet, nine inches."

"Was his disease in an advanced stage?"

"Yes."

"May we enquire as to the types of symptoms it would be reasonable to expect in someone with Mr. Wilkes' diagnosis?"

"My lord," began the prosecutor.

"The witness has a medical degree," Courtland countered. At Judge Bradbury's nod, she repeated the question.

"Fatigue and irritability. He would be increasingly incapable of rational thought. He would be volatile, his emotions labile."

"By labile, do you mean unstable?"

"Yes."

"Thus bursts of anger would not be unexpected?"

"They would not, no."

"Are there other symptoms you would like to include?"

"Difficulty with memory, balance, and concentration."

Hers was not an extended cross, but enough, Brian hoped, to weaken the graphic images of the case before the luncheon break. The knots in his stomach would again affect his appetite, and his trousers felt a bit looser than when the trial had begun.

After lunch Prosecutor Hilliard called Nigel Cooper, the forensic officer. A man who evidently loved detail, he presented, painstakingly, Brian thought, the results of the multiple-day investigation his department had conducted of Wilkes' flat. His words, however, carried no less weight because they came from a trim man, precise in his dress and speech. His physical description included the dimensions of each room, the contents, the bed and bath sheets, fingerprints, and blood stains which came from both Wilkes and another occupant. He mentioned multiple containers of tablets, some to influence the symptoms of the disease and others to ease pain. Could the jury retain the salient facts when there were so many?

The weapon he had used was produced, and Brian saw some members of the jury recoil. Could Courtland cause them to view him as a protector and not as a threat? She objected when his MP-5 was referred to as a formidable and frightening weapon, but Judge Bradbury found those adjectives to be appropriate.

Hilliard proceeded. "Imagine this weapon in the hands of the defendant!"

"My lord!" Courtland objected. "Officer Davies and others like him provide a valuable service to our city, which sometimes requires them to use firearms of this nature."

"Your drama is distasteful," the judge agreed, nodding at Hilliard. "Move on."

The prosecuting barrister then asked, "Did you find a knife in Mr. Wilkes' flat?"

"We found five kitchen knives – " Cooper gave descriptions of each – "and one assault knife." He provided a photo which showed the size and jagged blade. "Nasty," he added.

It was always difficult to control witnesses, Courtland thought. The comment was uncalled for, but the judgement undeniable, and it benefited her client. Hilliard would not object, however, lest it extend the jury's focus on Wilkes' weapon.

"And where exactly was this knife found?" he asked.

"Under the sofa in the sitting room, ten-and-one-half feet from the front door."

Courtland heard a muted gasp and then a sudden hush in the courtroom. No one shifted position or papers. She had caused the same reaction herself on occasion when she'd been prosecuting and had led a witness to deliver the critical blow. Now she was frustrated. How could she deal with this? She had virtually no case. She'd asked the solicitor, Arthur Wheatley, to contact both the Federation reps, who had not been in court recently, hoping that even at this late hour they would find something she could use to defend effectively – no, vindicate – her client. She reminded herself that the prosecution had to prove their case, not offer or suggest, but even a slim margin of victory was beyond what she could see.

Brian was similarly stunned. He forced himself not to look in Beth's direction, nor toward his parents, not wanting to draw attention to their connection with him. It was the *coup de grâce,* the decisive piece of evidence on which the prosecution case rested. He had known it was coming, but hearing it spoken aloud – in a normal tone – still felt like a punch in the gut, so much so that he looked down, but the drape of his coat was undisturbed.

Beth was angry. You can posture all you want to do, Mr. Prosecutor, she thought. Jenny will testify before too long, and she will set things straight.

"Let me be certain that I understand you," Hilliard said gravely. "You did not find that knife near the body of the deceased?"

"We did not."

"Nor under the body of the deceased?"

"No."

"Can you account for its location, over – " Hilliard appeared to consult his notes, when Brian knew that the gesture wasn't necessary – "ten-and-a-half feet from the front door, or close to ten feet from the spot where the deceased fell?"

"Objection!" Courtland exclaimed. "The witness is not allowed to draw a conclusion."

Both Hilliard and Cooper were aware of the restriction, Hilliard having questioned many witnesses and Cooper having testified in numerous other cases. A charade for the benefit of the jury, Brian thought. Courtland reseated herself, but Brian could see one of her feet twitching occasionally, fortunately out of the sight of the jury.

"I'll move on," Hilliard replied, knowing that Judge Bradbury's remonstrance would be coming. "How would you describe the floor covering in the sitting room in this flat? A smooth surface?"

"The opposite," Cooper stated. "The carpet was old and uneven."

"So the knife would have remained where it fell?"

"My lord!"

"Mr. Hilliard, that is a question you may not ask," Judge Bradbury said, his voice a bit shrill, "and one you may not answer,

Mr. Cooper. The jury will disregard that exchange. Mr. Hilliard, unless you have more questions for this witness which are relevant in nature, I suggest that you yield to Miss Courtland for her cross-examination at this time."

Hilliard hesitated before complying with the judge's direction.

"Would you describe Mr. Wilkes' flat as well maintained?" Courtland asked after she had risen and positioned herself near the microphone.

"In a word, no."

"Not clean and cosy then. Of the knives you found in the flat, how many had blood on the blade?"

"One."

"The one which you described as an assault weapon?"

"Yes."

"The sets of fingerprints you found in the flat – to whom did they belong?"

"To Mr. Wilkes, to a woman who has been identified as Tanya Hanson, and to the hostage – I'm not certain of her security title – the woman who was held there."

"Yankee 1," Courtland clarified. "Did the knife – which you referred to as an assault knife – contain her fingerprints?"

Brian approved of Courtland's frequent reference to the knife as an item of assault.

"No."

"Whose then?"

"Those belonging to Mr. Wilkes."

"His and only his?"

"Yes."

"Did you find bloodstains belonging to Yankee 1?"

"Yes, in multiple locations."

"Did you also test the bath sheets found in the lavatory near the front door?"

"We tested all the bath sheets," Cooper replied somewhat defensively.

"Yes, but I'm enquiring about the ones in the front lavatory. What were your findings?"

"They were soiled. They also contained substances secreted by the lacrimal gland."

"And those substances were – ?"

"Human tears," Cooper explained.

"So is it your testimony, based on the factual evidence you uncovered, that Yankee 1 both cried and bled in that flat?"

Hilliard squirmed in his chair but did not object.

"Yes," Cooper replied.

"Cried and bled," Courtland said. "My lord, I have no more questions for this witness at this time."

Hilliard called his next witness and waited whilst he completed the oath.

"Herbert Driscoll, Chief Superintendent, attached to the Surrey County Police Directorate of Professional Standards," he replied in answer to the prosecutor's first question. A man with dark brows and close-cropped hair in varying shades of grey, he removed his glasses, and Courtland felt the full force of his gaze. It was his duty to act on his suspicion of officers, and he must have extended his suspicion of PC Davies to her. She shivered.

"Could you define for the court the nature of your work?" Hilliard asked.

"When a complaint is made against an officer, it is our job to investigate and resolve it. In the case of an officer-involved shooting, no formal complaint from the public has to be registered. Our participation is part of standard procedure when an officer has discharged his firearm, independent of whether death or injury has resulted. As a safeguard against bias, a case of this magnitude requires investigation by another county."

"You will be testifying from material contained in an official report prepared by two of your investigators?"

"Yes. These investigations are very sensitive, and as a result, must be well documented."

Courtland realised that Hilliard had chosen to call the polished head of DPS instead of the investigators, whose rough edges might have affected the jury's opinion of them.

"Your officers interviewed Yankee 1, did they not?"

"They did. They wanted to have as complete a picture as possible of the incident before speaking with the officer under suspicion."

"Did the process go smoothly?"

"It did not. My officers were frustrated in their initial attempt to speak with her. When they arrived at her flat, Officer Davies was there. They were evidently very well acquainted. It was considered inappropriate to interview her in his presence."

Courtland was unsettled both by his implication and detached tone, which made her feel more, rather than less, tense. "Objection, my lord," she said. "The witness is drawing a conclusion."

Judge Bradbury raised his eyebrows.

"Officer Davies' presence in Yankee 1's flat indicates acquaintance, nothing more," Courtland declared.

"Noted," the judge responded, nodding to the jury.

"Please continue," Hilliard said, "regarding the interviews which took place."

"Yankee 1 – " Driscoll paused for a moment – "was questioned fully on two occasions."

Interrogated, Brian thought. Jenny had told him how critical and uncompromising they had been.

"They then interviewed the firearms officer currently in the dock, is that correct?" Hilliard asked.

"Yes, with his legal representatives present."

"The other firearms officers who were part of this response team were also interviewed?"

"Yes, of course."

"And what were your findings in this case?"

"Officer Davies swore that Mr. Wilkes was threatening Yankee 1 with a knife when he made entry and fired. My investigators, however, discerned that Yankee 1 could not substantiate this claim, nor could the other officers involved in the incident."

"Let me be certain that I comprehend clearly your testimony: Officer Davies is the only individual who saw the knife."

"Yes."

"You are able to make that statement categorically? With no doubt or reservation?"

"Asked and answered," Courtland objected quickly. She did not want to prolong the testimony of this witness, nor she could allow Hilliard to succeed in his attempt to emphasise this point of evidence.

"Exactly," ruled Judge Bradbury. "Move on, Mr. Hilliard."

"And the result of these conclusions – reached by experienced officers – was – ?"

"Officer Davies killed an unarmed man. Our report was given to the Crown Prosecution Service, who subsequently charged the defendant with murder."

Brian felt the light in the dock darken, the windows notwithstanding. With every line of testimony, his freedom seemed more improbable. It was always intangible, but in times past he had experienced its manifestations. Now it seemed as ethereal as a wisp of smoke from a dying ember.

His entire life had gone pear shaped, his days spent in court instead of on the Job; his evenings spent with Beth's parents, who watched Meg and Robbie during the day; and his evenings and weekends at Casey and Jenny's flat instead of his own home. Others' lives had been affected as well. Robbie was too young, but Meg was in school and had heard taunts from some of the older children. As a result she had been allowed to complete her assignments at home. What would happen to them now?

Courtland rose then sat down, shaking her head. Nothing she could say would change the testimony of this witness. He would defend his officers and their work. Their conclusions would remain unchanged. But why had Hilliard not elicited the details from Driscoll's statement that Yankee 1 could not confirm the presence of the knife? In a flash she knew. It would avail nothing to ask the DPS officer to detail the reasoning of his investigators. Hilliard was saving his attack for Yankee 1 because she was the strongest threat to his case. She was scheduled to testify for the defence, and he would attempt to annihilate her. Bastard.

"And here we are," Hilliard said quietly. "Officer Davies had the means and the motive to murder Roy Alden Wilkes when the opportunity presented itself. He might have conducted himself differently if a female hostage that was unknown to him had been involved. Bias, however, was present. That concludes the case for the Crown, my lord."

Judge Bradbury indicated his adjournment by rising to his feet and nodding to the usher. The trial was in recess, but the newspapers were just getting started: "Jury Stunned by Photos of Bloody Scene," "Graphic Snaps Presented to Jury," "Gun Cop Caused Bloodbath," and "No Knife When Gunned Down."

CHAPTER EIGHT

"THE DEFENCE RECALLS Chief Inspector Carl Denison," Fiona Courtland announced. When she had prosecuted, she'd often presented her case in sequential order. Now, however, as she began her defence, she considered it more effective to add one piece at a time to the incomplete display, as in a puzzle, until the picture became undeniably clear for all.

Denison was reminded that because of his previous appearance as a witness, his oath was still in effect.

"Chief Inspector, we have heard from various members of your firearms teams about their different views, that is to say, what they saw when they made entry into Mr. Wilkes' flat on Sunday, 28 August. The reasons for this have been explained. However, is there not another factor in play? That each individual's perspective varies over time?"

"Absolutely, yes. That's why we discourage our officers from making a full statement within the first twenty-four hours after an incident."

"Is there a technical term for this?"

"It's called perceptual distortion," Denison replied.

"Can you describe for us in layman's language what that means?"

"During an incident, one's peripheral vision may falter. An officer may also struggle with hearing. As a result, it can be difficult for an officer to remember details, to describe adequately what he or she saw. Officers have even been known to have taken actions they cannot remember taking. In some cases, they cannot accurately describe distances or colours. Because perception and memory are not the same, perfect recall is almost never possible."

Denison had reserved his extended explanations for the defence, Brian noted. He felt an undercurrent of support from the senior officer.

"Are these statements your opinion, based upon your experience?"

"Not solely, no. Numerous studies have been conducted which verify the information I have given you. We know that in emergency situations officers do not have the luxury of calm and analytical reasoning. An officer may be required to react with immediacy, and indeed, we train our officers to make that rapid response nearly automatic."

"Then may I conclude that it is not only reasonable but expected that the other officers on Officer Davies' assault team would remember the incident differently?"

"Exactly so. Distortions are normal."

"Are officers whose statements vary guilty of lying?"

"Absolutely not!" Denison exclaimed. "Memory is not static. It is simply more mobile than most would expect."

"Have you ever known Officer Davies to falsify a report or any portion of a report?"

"Never. No," Denison replied with emphasis. "If he had, he would no longer be a member of my unit."

"Chief Inspector, we have heard some of your officers respond to questions regarding a knife the hostage taker was holding over the hostage when they entered the premises. Does the fact that they cannot confirm seeing a knife mean that it was not there?"

"No. It's entirely possible – likely even – that only the first officer through the door would have seen it."

A brief disturbance occurred near the back of the courtroom, involving a suppressed exclamation when two individuals collided, a dropped coffee cup, and scattered papers.

Courtland waited a moment and then asked, "Chief Inspector, can you describe what just took place in court?"

Denison shook his head briefly as if to dispel any confusion. "Spilt coffee," he said. "Papers fell as well."

"Can you describe to us the individuals involved?" Courtland persisted.

"One was wearing a robe and one wasn't," Denison replied slowly. "I'm not certain which was which. Nor can I give details of their personal appearance."

"You were relatively calm when this event happened," Courtland pointed out. "Is there a reason for your lack of accuracy?"

"I'd credit inattentional blindness," Denison responded. "I was so intently concentrating on your questions that my mind did not register the details of something that was outside my primary focus. I cannot recall something that my brain did not record."

Good answer, Beth thought. She hadn't been paying attention to that section of the courtroom and could not have effectively described the collision either.

"Could that also have been a factor in the variance of witness statements given by the other officers on Officer Davies' team?"

"It could, yes."

"Miss Courtland," Judge Bradbury interjected, "are you guilty of arranging this event?"

"No, my lord," Courtland answered. "Simply taking whatever advantage presents itself in the defence of my client. Thank you for your testimony, Chief Inspector Denison." Leaving her notebook at the podium, she sat down.

Hilliard stepped to his microphone without his notebook. "Perceptual distortion. Inattentional blindness," he repeated. "Chief Inspector, can you also define for us psychobabble?"

"I cannot, no," Denison replied stolidly.

"I submit that babble refers to what an infant or infantile individual might utter," Hilliard said.

"I wouldn't know," Denison commented. "Am I to understand that that is how you are characterising my testimony?"

"My lord," Hilliard appealed.

"It's a rocky road you're on," Judge Bradbury stated. "And one of your own choosing. Do you intend to continue?"

Hilliard shook his head.

"Then we'll all seek firmer ground after the luncheon break," the judge said. "Court is adjourned until 2:00 pm."

****

Fiona Courtland's notebook was open in front of her, but she did not consult it. Instead she pondered the strange combination in this case: Officer Davies, a first responder, who needed a barrister, a last responder

She reflected. She had never borne a child. The years when she had wondered what motherhood would be like were behind her, but she did not have to be a parent to understand the importance of coming to the aid of the innocent, as first responders did. They risked their lives on a regular basis for individuals they did not know, and they trusted that their training would bring them through. They wore protective gear to shield them when they were in harm's way, and she had often hoped that that gave them an extra measure of courage. The bullet would not pierce, the flames would not sear. They would be able to walk away when the incident was over. She had only a wig and a gown, and she was not personally in danger, but she was where they turned when the consequences of an incident did not resolve. Officer Davies had gone from saving victims to becoming one

Yet there were multiple victims in this court's drama. The prosecution had chosen to highlight the hostage taker Roy Wilkes because he was deceased, but legally he was not a victim, his medical condition notwithstanding, because he had broken the law. Mrs. Casey, however, who was referred to as Yankee 1, was the initial victim, and her rescue had created the next, Officer Davies.

She must cause the jury to determine that no other action, save that which Officer Davies had taken, would have been sufficient in the circumstances. She must make them ready to shout, "I'd want him to do the same for me," to agree that he had not overreacted when he'd heard the threats of the hostage taker and the pleas of the hostage and had discharged his weapon. He had not murdered the hostage taker. He had effected a rescue and in so doing had saved a life – two lives, if one considered Mrs. Casey's pregnancy. Her miscarriage following the incident only made the entire situation more heartrending, more poignant.

She would begin with the potential victim, Tanya Hanson, who had seen danger coming and had escaped it. Miss Hanson could establish the mental instability of her partner, but she could also generate sympathy for him. Judge Bradbury would advise the jurors to decide the case based on the facts presented in court, but sympathy was a powerful influence on how a jury weighed those facts. It was a delicate balance, and indeed, when Judge Bradbury returned and the proceedings resumed, she was careful in her questions, spending very little time on Hanson's relationship with Wilkes prior to his diagnosis, instead focusing on his behaviour after.

"When Roy first received his diagnosis," Hanson testified, "he was bitter and angry. He was only 51. I was then 46. It was a blow for both of us. We expected we'd have more time."

"Did his feelings change over time?"

"They intensified. His mental condition was harder to deal with than his physical symptoms."

"Would you please describe how his mental instability manifested itself?"

"He became paranoid. When I needed to leave for work, he accused me of playing away. On several occasions he gripped me so hard that he left bruises. He raised his hand to me, and I had to restrain him. I was continually reassuring him. He even tried to keep me from leaving to purchase groceries."

"Did you fear for your life?" Courtland asked.

"Yes. I tried to remind myself that it was the disease and not Roy, but at some point, I couldn't tell the difference between the two because one had consumed the other. I reminded myself that he hadn't asked for this, but his anger episodes became so severe that I was afraid. I couldn't reason with him. I knew I wasn't safe."

"How exactly were you able to leave?"

"I waited until he was asleep. I had put a robe over my street clothes so he wouldn't suspect what I had in mind. He never rested for very long, so I had to be quick and quiet. I couldn't pack a bag or take anything with me. I locked the door behind me, but I could hear him yelling and struggling with it before I'd come to the stairs at the end of the walkway. I wondered if I'd done the right thing."

"Miss Hanson, why did you agree to testify for the defence?"

"Because I may have contributed to what happened. What he did to that young woman, I mean. I loved him, but I had to leave or risk losing my life."

Courtland hoped the jury would recall this statement when the hostage testified. Unlike Yankee 1, Hanson was in good health and above average in height and weight, yet she had still been afraid. She nodded to Hilliard, who wasted no time on preamble.

"Miss Hanson, did you or did you not have a long-term relationship with the deceased?"

"I did."

"And you have testified that you were in love with him?"

She paused. She'd thought she had got over him, but now she wasn't certain. "I can't defend the things he did, but I think I never stopped loving him."

Hilliard was frustrated. He wanted more concise answers. "He was a good provider?"

"We both had jobs, but yes, together we were able to maintain a decent lifestyle."

"And personally?"

"We clicked. I'd lost my father early on, he'd lost his mum, and we seemed to understand each other."

"Yet you allowed the flat to sink into disrepair? And you chose not to provide companionship and solace for him in his last days?"

Hanson fidgeted in the witness box, swallowing hard and struggling to answer.

Before she could respond, the prosecution asked another question. "Would you please tell the court why you do not appear to be grieving his death?"

"Because – because the disease took the man I knew, long before the police action. I'm still sad, however. It's painful to remember."

"You do not then subscribe to the commitment 'for better, for worse'?"

"My lord," Courtland objected. "The witness has testified that she feared for her life. Surely that is a reasonable exclusion to the marital commitment, and indeed, she and Mr. Wilkes were not married."

"You are not required to answer the last question," Judge Bradbury instructed Hanson.

"May I step down then?" Hanson asked, uncertain about who would release her.

After a pause, Hilliard moved away from his podium, and Hanson took that as permission to exit the witness box. The prosecutor's accusations echoed in her ears as she did so. Instead of leaving the court, she entered the gallery and stood in the back. No one spoke to her, so she was alone with her thoughts. I'll see how this plays out, she thought. It is the last thing I can do for Roy.

Detective Inspector Thoms was the next witness called by the defence. "You are still under oath," Courtland said. "And I'd like to thank you for the testimony you have already given, in which you detailed for us the beginning of the incident we are examining today. However, there are aspects of your enquiry which have not been covered. To be specific, following the armed rescue of the hostage, how did your investigation proceed?"

"The hostage was taken by ambulance to hospital, where I supervised the collection of evidence from her."

"You are referring to physical evidence?"

"Yes, a physician documented her injuries, and photographs were taken of them. Her clothes were also collected."

"My lord, I submit the following evidence," Courtland stated, handing the doctor's report and visual record to the usher. Although the prosecution had received copies of the material during the discovery process, their barrister had neglected to reference them as he presented his case, lest sympathy for the hostage outweigh the sympathy he wanted to create for the hostage taker. Now, however, the jury would see what the hostage had experienced.

"Did you question the hostage, Yankee 1, following her release from hospital?"

"Yes, we spoke with her on three occasions."

"How did she fare?"

"The first two interviews, on 29 August and 30 August, were difficult for her. We were essentially asking her to recall a very traumatic experience. She miscarried late on 30 August, so our third session was postponed for forty-eight hours. She was in pain and grieving the loss of her baby. At one point I thought we'd have to suspend the process, but she rallied."

"And the purpose of these interviews was – ?"

"To gather as much detail as possible, beginning with her abduction and ending with her rescue. She had good recall, considering that she was still suffering from the effects of a concussion, the emotional trauma of her imprisonment, and upon the third occasion, pain as a result of the necessary medical intervention after the loss of her baby."

Courtland paused. She did not want the detective inspector to delineate the events for the jury, lest her recounting of them reduce what she expected to be compelling testimony from the hostage herself. "Were your meetings the end of your investigation?"

"Yes, I had amassed all the evidence Yankee 1 could give related to Mr. Wilkes' criminal actions toward her."

Tanya Hanson winced. It was hard to hear the term "criminal" applied to Roy. Although she had become afraid, she had considered him to be disturbed.

"And those actions would be – ?"

"Abduction, false imprisonment, possession of an offensive weapon, actual bodily harm, and – "

"My lord, these charges have not been brought against Mr. Wilkes," Hilliard objected, "and cannot be litigated because he is deceased! And evidence has been presented which indicates diminished responsibility on his part."

"Quite," Judge Bradbury agreed. "Please rephrase, Miss Courtland."

"My apologies, my lord. The findings you mention, DI Thoms, must be considered 'alleged' until proved. Is that correct?"

"Yes."

A good place to stop, Courtland thought. No matter how the crimes were categorised, the jury had heard the terms, which were now part of the official record. They now knew what Mrs. Casey had faced and why what Officer Davies had done had indeed been a rescue.

Hilliard stood. "Could Yankee 1's concussion have affected her memory?"

"We did not find that to be the case. She was justifiably upset when we questioned her, but she was very clear about what had happened to her. Her memories were vivid."

Hilliard shook his head in frustration. Witnesses who should have known better were expanding on their answers. Managing to control any other gestures of annoyance, he tapped his fingers on his notebook before deciding to sit down.

"Redirect, my lord?" Courtland asked quickly. Upon the judge's assent, she asked, "Detective Inspector Thoms, did you believe Yankee 1?"

"Yes, she was sincere and passionate in her statements."

"My lord, I have no further questions for this witness. Tomorrow I would like to call Yankee 1, however, which will require the court to convene later in the day."

Judge Bradbury nodded. "Jury will report at 2:00 pm, at which time proceedings will begin." He addressed defence counsel. "Miss Courtland, since your witness is vulnerable, I will meet with her in my chambers. Please ask her to report ten minutes before the hour. Until then." He stood and left the bench.

I will return, Tanya Hanson thought. Her curiosity about the young woman they called Yankee 1 needed to be quenched. It was likely an unhealthy thirst, but she would satisfy it anyway.

CHAPTER NINE

THE OLD BAILEY: the most well-known court in the world, but Jenny would rather have toured it than testified in it. When she arrived, escorted by Simon, she noted the armed officers at the security entrance. Her belongings were passed through an x-ray machine, and she submitted to the security procedures. She then had to force herself to walk in, already feeling the pressure of her participation. So much was riding on her testimony. Every word she said mattered. For Brian's sake, she had to get it right.

"Breathe," Simon whispered when she hesitated. She hadn't had much breakfast, her stomach being upset, but now she wished she had. She felt an emptiness in her belly that seemed to spread. Although it was mid-September, the temperatures were still above average, and the rain during the night had resulted in an extra measure of humidity, even with the morning sun. She'd worn a navy-blue dress, with white ruffles at the neck and cuffs, and the bracelet Simon had given her, pearls of varying sizes on a wire which wrapped around her wrist. Already she wanted to unbutton the sleeves and roll them up, but the ruffles, although feminine, made the sleeves too bulky to stay above her elbows. The hall seemed to sway for a minute, so she took a deep breath as instructed to regain her balance. Fortunately she had worn flat shoes, as the defense barrister had suggested, although the barrister's intent was for her to look small in the witness box and hence more vulnerable, not steady on her feet.

Fiona Courtland was waiting for them just past the security station. She escorted them to Judge Bradbury's chambers. The judge's eyes were grayer than his hair, which Jenny realized no one else would see once his wig was in place. Here, moreover, he had not yet placed his robe over his dress shirt and slacks.

Using their security titles, Courtland introduced Jenny and Simon to the judge.

"An American in name and nationality," Judge Bradbury observed. "Welcome to British jurisprudence. And in this regard, I must advise you. I've asked for this little meeting to give you an opportunity to settle yourself. I've been made aware of your medical condition, and I've arranged for a chair to be placed in the witness box. It will remain there for the duration of your testimony. I am required to be objective during the proceedings, but I am not immune to the needs of witnesses. If you need assistance at any time, you need only ask. May I enquire – what is in that bag you are clutching so tightly?"

"It's my survival kit, your honor." She gripped the soft canvas.

"Yankee 1, although 'your honour' is an appropriate form of address in other Crown courts, it's customary in this court – due to its historic nature – to address the presiding judge as my lord or my lady."

"Oh – I didn't know – I didn't mean any disrespect, my lord, sir."

"I don't doubt it," the judge answered crisply.

"It passed through security."

"I'm certain it did. And?"

"Please don't take it away! My doctor suggested it in case I felt sick. It has crackers, breath mints, and a sachet with a lavender scent. A handkerchief. A small fan."

"Very wise," Judge Bradbury agreed. He nodded at Simon. "I will be close enough to your wife to monitor how she is feeling. If at any point I deem it necessary for her well-being, I will halt the proceedings."

He turned to Jenny. "In conclusion I'd like to remind you of two things. First, most discover that the apprehension of a court appearance is worse than the actual event. Second, the prosecution is here only to do the job they have been called to do." He reached for his wig and robe. "Procedure requires that I precede you into the courtroom," he declared with a slight smile.

Jenny watched the judge depart, noticing that he had an unusually long stride for a short man.

"I'll be in the gallery," Simon said, squeezing her hand.

Courtland guided her down the corridor. "They sometimes refer to Judge Bradbury as the 'Old Badger,'" she said, "because his hair used to be black, and one portion remained for a time when it began to turn. Also, he intervened – some would say interrupted – the proceedings with frequent questions or clarifications. I think it helps to know that there's a human being inside the robe." She paused. "You'll be called momentarily. During testimony, try to focus on the immediate, and remember that you're required only to answer what is framed as a question. Good luck."

Jenny leaned against the wall, closing her eyes and surprising herself by uttering a short prayer, for Brian, the baby, and herself. In spite of the judge's words, she was nervous, and there was a mild, nagging nausea in the pit of her stomach which her deep breaths did not allay. The door next to her opened, and she heard her security name, Yankee 1. In the hush of the courtroom, her shoes resounded as she approached the witness box.

When she held the rail at the witness box and hesitated before stepping up into it, she heard the judge's command: "Usher! Some assistance please for the witness!"

The usher moved forward to support her and then held the card for her. She read the words of the oath, trying not to stumble over them. She saw Simon sitting next to Neil Goodwyn. Beth was there, too. She saw Georgina with a lime green ribbon in her hair and wondered what color her shoes were.

The courtroom looked very orderly with everyone in his place, barristers, solicitors, press, and members of the public, but that was a delusion, a thought as deceptive and almost as dangerous as Roy's delusion. She was shocked by the sight of Brian in the dock, as imprisoned as if there had been bars surrounding him, confined there because of what he had done for her. They were both in boxes of a kind, both hostages, but he had to remain silent, trusting others to speak, and speak she would. Words were the currency in court. They mattered – they were being recorded, and the jury would hear, review, and evaluate them.

She tried to coax a rebellious strand of hair behind her ear and waited for the first question. Despite multiple pretrial interviews, she still felt unprepared. Her hands were cold, and she tucked one under her bag, wishing she held Bear's leash instead and felt the peace that came from viewing the picturesque English countryside.

Tanya Hanson was shocked. The young woman in the witness box didn't look or sound anything like her. What had Roy been thinking?

Fiona Courtland started with a statement which the judge cut short.

"Miss Courtland! Do not test the indulgence of this court! You are well aware of the impropriety of using declarative instead of interrogative sentences!"

No one would accuse this judge of bias, Jenny thought.

"My lord, I was just trying to give my witness a moment to feel calm. I'll proceed." She paused. "Will you allow me a word of explanation for the jury?"

"Keep it brief."

Courtland nodded. "I'd like to eliminate any confusion regarding the security title of this witness. You have heard her referred to as 'Yankee 1.' This term is neither pejorative nor descriptive and would be used for a hostage of any nationality. In this case, the fact that Yankee 1 is an American citizen is simply a coincidence."

She turned to Jenny. "Yankee 1, I apologise for the necessity of being so direct. However, are you currently expecting a baby?"

"Yes," Jenny answered. "And I'm only in my eighth week."

"And your pregnancy has been diagnosed as high risk?"

"Yes."

"And your morning sickness, as documented by your physician, is severe?"

"Yes, it is." She automatically noted the stability of her stomach.

"So much so that your testimony is restricted to afternoon hours only?"

"Yes, and I've been allowed to sit down."

"My lord, the defence is engaged in a blatant attempt to generate sympathy for this witness," Hilliard objected.

"I disagree," responded Judge Bradbury. "Carry on, Miss Courtland."

"Yankee 1, why were you in the part of the city where Mr. Wilkes resided?"

"I was visiting a Methodist church in the area. After my first husband died, I wrote a book about grief which I've given to a number of support groups in churches and other organizations."

"Had your meeting at the church concluded when you were attacked?"

"Yes, I intended to return home."

The defence barrister then led Jenny to establish through a series of questions and answers that Roy Wilkes, the hostage taker, had assaulted her as a means of getting her into his flat, that he continued to do so after she was there, and that he had held her against her will.

"My lord, Mr. Wilkes is not on trial here," Hilliard pointed out.

"No, but his actions initiated the entire unfortunate set of circumstances that have brought us here today," Courtland replied quickly.

"Indeed," Judge Bradbury commented.

That must be as good as a ruling, Jenny thought.

"Can anyone else testify about Mr. Wilkes' behaviour?" Courtland persisted.

"No one else was there," Jenny answered.

"Did you ask Mr. Wilkes to release you?"

"Yes, I asked him to take me to a doctor. He'd hit me on the head so hard that I passed out. I said I wanted to go home. He wouldn't let me. I tried to call my husband for help, but the battery on my phone was low, and I didn't know if my call had been received."

"And you told him who you were? Your real name?"

"Yes, because he insisted on calling me Tanya."

Tanya Hanson was startled to hear her name. Uncomfortable, she shifted her weight slightly, but no one took notice of her. All eyes were riveted on the witness.

Courtland paused briefly. "When did you first see the knife?" she asked.

"Right after I regained consciousness," Jenny replied. "It was a horrible-looking thing. He threatened me with it, thrusting it in my direction and breaking my skin." She saw the prosecuting barrister write something down. Her stomach turned over, and she gripped her bag, but her unrest eased.

"Where did you spend your first night, Yankee 1?"

"In the bathroom. My head hurt, I was nauseated, and my body ached all over."

"Did you try to escape?"

"Yes, I tapped SOS on the bathroom wall but nobody answered. And on the first morning I tried to get out, but he caught me and held me back before I could unlock the door."

"And after that?" Courtland continued.

"He didn't let me out of his sight. At night he locked me in the bathroom so I couldn't get away. And he tied my hands together during the day. Even if he hadn't had a knife, I couldn't have fought him."

"How long were you held by Mr. Wilkes?"

"Four days and three nights," Jenny responded.

"Did you stay willingly? Of your own accord?"

"No!"

"Did you continue to ask Mr. Wilkes to release you?"

"Yes, but he wouldn't."

"Did you have freedom of movement within the flat?"

"No. During the day I had to stay in the living room or dining room. The flat had a room that looked like a sewing room, but he yelled at me when I started to go in."

Tanya recalled taking up the craft shortly after Roy's diagnosis. She'd wanted an activity she could pursue in the flat, in case Roy needed her.

"How did he respond when you requested your release?"

"He became increasingly angry, often cutting me with the knife."

"The participation of the hostage negotiator contributed to your safety, did it not?"

"At the start I was encouraged. It was the first contact that had been made by the police, and I finally knew that they were aware of my circumstance. The phone conversations occupied Roy, at least for a little while, so there were periods when I didn't have to be so vigilant."

"And later? Did the negotiations continue to make you feel safe?"

"No. When the negotiator questioned my identity, Roy's anger skyrocketed. And my safety plummeted. He kept a closer watch on me than before, and he was more dangerous."

"More dangerous – why, Yankee 1?"

"Because he wanted affection from me. He stopped answering calls from the negotiator, and I was getting desperate."

"How then did you get away?"

"I pretended to make tea. When the water boiled, I threw it at him and ran for the door. He got there before I could unlock it."

"Was he angry?"

"More than angry," Jenny answered, her voice thick with remembrance. "He was enraged. He said he would kill me, and I screamed for help. And that's when the police broke in. Roy fell backward and dragged me down with him."

"Did you recognise any of the officers who came in?"

"No, their faces were covered. But it didn't matter. Whoever they were, they saved me."

"Did any of them speak to you?"

"I don't know. I couldn't hear anything afterward. I had no idea that gunshots were that loud."

"Yankee 1, please consider this question very carefully. Where was the knife when he was threatening and restraining you?"

"In his hand! His left arm was around my waist to pull me away from the door. The knife was in his right hand."

"Can you be certain of this?"

"Yes!" She glanced at the prosecutor, who was smoothing his hair although none of it was out of place.

"Because you saw it?"

"Because he always had it! I didn't have to see it to know it was there!" During the quiet in the courtroom, Jenny's voice resounded. "He was a violent person. He always carried it."

"Yankee 1," Courtland said somewhat gently, "you are aware that some feel that this part of your testimony is unsubstantiated. How can you account for differences in the interpretation of these events?"

Jenny hesitated, appalled. "My lord, do I have to do that?"

"You must answer the question that is put to you, yes," Judge Bradbury responded.

She thought for a minute. "It was his routine. If you always put two spoons of sugar in your tea, I don't have to see you do it every time to know that you do. I'd know what your pattern of behavior was, and after four days with him, I knew his. My scars are proof."

"My lord, psychologists call this habitual behaviour."

"Defence is testifying," Hilliard pointed out.

Courtland nodded in acquiescence, but Jenny saw a small smile. "Is it your belief that Mr. Wilkes intended to kill you with that knife?"

"My belief?" Jenny repeated. "More than that. I know he intended to kill me with that knife. He said he'd kill me! How else would he have done it? If the police hadn't come in when they did, he would have. And then – " she broke down – "and then I lost the baby, and – "

"Yankee 1," Judge Bradbury interjected. "I cannot allow that last part of your statement to stand. Miss Courtland, in light of the obvious distress of the witness, shall we adjourn for today?"

No one could object, including Tanya Hanson. She realised that defence counsel had guided Yankee 1's testimony, but it had still shaken her. The things Roy had done to Yankee 1 – if she had stayed, he would have done them to her. Followup medical appointments had been available to him after his diagnosis, but he had stopped keeping them, claiming that they gave him no hope. Why had she submitted to his point of view? She could have notified the health authorities that he needed help, but she had been concerned only with her own safety.

CHAPTER TEN

NAP, DINNER, BATH, BED – Simon's prescription for Jenny, following her first day of testimony. "Well done," he told her repeatedly. "You were clear and convincing. For tomorrow – you needn't be afraid of the prosecutor. Nothing he says can change the fact that you were there." He held her until she slept, not disclosing his apprehension. Her fatigue following the day in court had concerned him.

Her morning round of nausea seemed unusually severe, and she wondered if the stress of her court appearances were intensifying the symptoms. Feeling weak and shaky, she dressed, this time wearing black slacks with a short-sleeved white blouse, in recognition of the warm, stale air in the courtroom and with the hope that her attire and sworn statements would demonstrate what she considered the black-and-white issues of the case. Once again Simon accompanied her as far as he could.

She was reminded that her oath to tell the whole truth was still in effect.

"Yankee 1, are you quite composed?" Fiona Courtland started. Upon receiving Jenny's affirmative reply, she then touched briefly on the material covered during the prior afternoon before releasing her for cross-examination by the prosecution.

Hilliard rose and strode to the podium. He stared at Jenny, saying nothing, before turning away from her and resting his gaze on Brian. Still he was silent.

The calm before the storm, Jenny thought.

"We're waiting, Mr. Hilliard," Judge Bradbury prompted.

"May I assume that you have healed fully from your ordeal, Yankee 1?" Hilliard asked, managing to infuse his first question with an overtone of disfavour.

Jenny wasn't sure how to answer. Her hostage experience had ended over a year ago. He couldn't be referring to that. Was he being cruel or misleading? His phrasing seemed to indicate both. Already he had unnerved her. Her eyes found Simon in the gallery where she watched him take a deep breath. She did the same and then wondered whether she should answer the prosecutor's question with a question. However, if she asked if he were being obtuse, she might be cited for contempt. And any behavior that was less than respectful could affect how the rest of her testimony was regarded.

Brian had dreaded this day. He'd seen the way the prosecuting barrister had treated other witnesses, and he knew Jenny was in for a rough patch. Jenny seemed pale already, more than on the previous day.

"Yesterday's testimony was difficult, but I rested well last night," she finally answered.

His high cheekbones and slanted eyebrows gave him a predatory look, and her antennae were out. She did not expect another nonaggressive question. She gripped the bag which held her anti-nausea items and rested her fingers on the zipper opening in case she needed the items inside quickly.

"May I enquire as to the contents of the bundle on your lap?"

Jenny considered her reply. It could hurt Brian if she made an enemy of this man, but in an adversarial system, he already regarded her as one. "No, you may not," she stated. She felt more defiant than she dared to show.

Hilliard raised his eyebrows. "My lord, may I declare this witness to be hostile?"

Jenny felt a wave of apprehension. Not fear, she told herself. Not fear.

Courtland recognised the strategy. Hilliard had no expectation that his petition would be granted; he simply intended his question to upset the witness.

"Request denied," Judge Bradbury ruled.

"Your first husband is deceased," Hilliard stated. "Is it possible that you were feeling lonesome when you encountered Mr. Wilkes?"

"No, it isn't possible."

"Of course. Forgive my lapse of memory," the prosecutor replied smoothly. "You have a second husband. Then give me some guidance here. Why you? What did you do to cause Mr. Wilkes to notice you?"

"My lord, the witness cannot speak to the motivation of the hostage taker," Courtland said quickly.

"Indeed not," Judge Bradbury agreed.

"Perhaps you went with him willingly but changed your mind later, as women sometimes do."

"I object!" Courtland exclaimed.

"As do I," the judge ruled.

"We know that you gained access to Mr. Wilkes' flat," the prosecutor continued. "We do not, however, have an independent witness to support your version of entry, do we?"

"My lord, the prosecutor is harassing the witness!" Courtland declared.

"Gently, gently," Judge Bradbury advised Hilliard.

"He knocked me out. He abducted me. When I regained consciousness, I called for help."

"From your second husband, an armed police officer," Hilliard stated.

Jenny didn't know what to say. Simon's identity had been protected when he testified. Fortunately Hilliard had not phrased his comment as a question.

"If you needed help, why didn't you call 999?" he asked.

"Because I knew he'd do everything in his power to help me," she said.

"Procedure suggests that they might have sent unarmed police officers to resolve the situation, isn't that true? But you wanted someone to help you who had a gun, didn't you? Is that why you attempted to manipulate our emergency services system?"

Jenny felt a moment of confusion. Which question should she answer? Before Hilliard could press her further, however, Courtland came to her aid.

"My lord, may I question the relevance of my colleague's enquiries?"

"Of course," Judge Bradbury replied.

"My lord, the prosecution's case rests on two issues," Hilliard explained. "First, the forensic evidence, which has already been presented to this court by previous witnesses. Second, the character – or lack of it – of this witness, which I am working to establish."

Judge Bradbury nodded.

"Yankee 1, you have testified that you were taken in the afternoon of 25 August 2005. Are we to believe that you could not evade capture by a middle-aged man weakened by a terminal disease?"

She paled. "His attack was sudden."

"He was critically ill. Indeed, it is not an exaggeration to say that he was dying. And you could not defend yourself against him?"

"I resisted, but he knocked me out. Could you defend yourself if you were unconscious?"

Simon smiled. Be careful, Mr. Prosecutor, he thought. You've unleashed her rebellious side.

The prosecutor, however, did not seem affected by Jenny's assertiveness.

"'On the first morning, I tried to get out.' Those are your words, Yankee 1. My question is: If you were afraid for your safety, why did you wait until morning to try to exit the flat?"

"Because I was nauseated and in pain. I didn't have the strength."

"Yet you, in your infinite wisdom, thought you'd have more strength after a night of poor sleep on the floor of the loo?"

"My lord – " Courtland began.

"Sarcasm will not help your case," Judge Bradbury noted to Hilliard.

"What did you accomplish the first day?" Hilliard asked.

Jenny felt a wave of exhaustion, which made it hard for her to concentrate and parry the prosecutor's questions.

"Do you need the question repeated?' he asked. "Or would you prefer another? What did you accomplish on the second day?"

"I stayed alive. I kept my baby alive."

Courtland knew that any mention of the baby would cause the jury to view Jenny in a sympathetic light. Hilliard would move on quickly from that response.

"How many knife wounds did you sustain during your confinement?"

"Isn't there a medical report that answers that question?" she countered. "Photos were taken of my injuries at the hospital."

"My lord," Hilliard appealed.

"Yankee 1, you are obliged to answer."

"There were too many to count."

"Are you telling this court that you couldn't get out of his way?"

"Yes. It was a small flat. I was nauseated and unsteady. He watched me all the time, and I had nowhere to run."

"We've heard testimony from his partner, Tanya Hanson, that he did not prevent her from walking out. Do you mean for us to accept that you could not do the same?"

"Yes, he must have learned from her action. Over and over he told me he'd not let me – Tanya, that is – abandon him again. He locked me in."

Once again it jarred Tanya Hanson to hear her name. Prior to Roy's diagnosis, he had accepted disappointments without losing his innate optimism. After, he had looked at this young woman and been unable to let her go.

"And you were unable to reason with him?" Hilliard continued. "The police negotiator reported a number of civil discussions."

"None of which resulted in my release," Jenny pointed out. "No, I couldn't reason with him, and in the end, the negotiator couldn't either. Roy thought I was Tanya, and nothing I said or did could change his mind. He was crazy."

Hilliard's voice rose. "My lord, I request that the witness' last statement be stricken. She is not professionally qualified to make that judgement."

"Jury will disregard," Judge Bradbury agreed.

"You accuse him of violent and frightening acts, yet you refer to him by his given name. That is evidence of a relationship, is it not?"

She watched him turn a page in his notebook with the tips of his fingers, an unusually delicate gesture for someone with large hands like Roy's.

"We're waiting, Yankee 1," he said, his hostility poorly veiled. "I'm speaking to you."

Jenny restrained a gasp. Roy had used those same words. She'd had to think about him so much lately.

"Did you or did you not have a relationship with the deceased?"

"I didn't! I used his first name and tried to get him to use mine to make him see me as a human being. I wasn't successful."

Courtland was angry. The witness had survived, yes, but she was still a victim, and Hilliard had not moderated his attack.

"Did he ever set the knife down?"

Jenny had gathered her hair in a loose ponytail, hoping she would feel cooler, but now the temperature in the court seemed suddenly higher, making the room feel stuffy. She took the small fan from her bag and began to use it. She felt as if the prosecuting barrister were crowding her, invading her space, although in reality, the barristers were not allowed to approach the witness box. She was glad that Hilliard had a short leash. "When he did set the knife down, it was always well within his reach," she responded, a little breathless. "And anyway, how could I have attacked him effectively with my wrists bound? It was dangerous in that flat. I haven't overdramatized it."

"You have testified that you assaulted him."

"I didn't use those words!" she protested, before he could frame his question.

He continued, seemingly oblivious to her interruption. "Then it's possible, is it not, that he did not have the knife in his hand when you ran toward the door?"

How could she answer? It was possible but untrue. Yet the entire case depended on where the knife was when Brian fired. How could she make the jury believe her? At the moment the prosecutor was winning. She realized that she had held her bag so tightly that she had crushed the crackers that were inside. She clutched the fan instead of waving it. She began to take rapid, shallow breaths. "I – I – " she faltered, distracted by the ripple of voices in the gallery. She began to tremble, so she leaned forward and rested her elbows on her knees to counter the wave of dizziness.

"And isn't it possible that this entire case is built upon a lie?" the prosecutor demanded.

She felt as if she'd been struck.

"We are all awaiting your answer, Yankee 1!"

She's in trouble, Simon thought. Even in the commotion, his low whistle carried, and Jenny understood that he was sending her his support in the only way he could, but she could not respond.

"Will you or will you not end this deception?"

Brian turned and saw Goodwyn's hand on Simon's arm, restraining him. He too wished he could stride across the court to free her. He had freed her once. Now Hilliard had made her a prisoner in the witness box. He rose to his feet, startling the two officers who were there to guard him. Their pressure on his elbows forced him down to his seat.

"I challenge you! Isn't it time at last for the truth?"

"Silence in court!" Judge Bradbury commanded, and she flinched at the abruptness of his pronouncement. "Yankee 1, you are quite pale," he observed. "Are you well enough to proceed?" He paused. "You must answer me, you know," he said with a smile.

She opened her mouth, but no words came. Panic had gripped her throat, and she gasped for air. Her eyes were wide, and her shoulders sagged. She folded one arm across her belly.

"Counsellors!" Judge Bradbury announced. "Court will recess for twenty minutes. Usher, please escort Yankee 1 to the conference room."

"My lord, I object!" Hilliard called out.

"You cannot object to me," Judge Bradbury declared. "I am doing my job – ensuring the safety of the participants here today whilst maintaining the sanctity of the legal process. I assure you – no one will have access to the witness during this time."

"If you'll come with me," the usher prompted when Jenny hesitated. She pushed herself up from the chair. She swayed when she stood and had to lean heavily on the usher's arm. The conference room had a sofa, and she lay down.

"No one will disturb you," the usher said. "I'll be just outside if you need anything."

She closed her eyes, but her heart was beating too fast for her to rest. She took several deep breaths. It was difficult to get the air past the tightness in her chest. She thought about the baby, and she was afraid. She couldn't swallow back the tears. Please, she prayed, let him be strong. Let him be a fighter. Let him be insulated against what is happening in my world. He is innocent. Please don't let him pay the price for this.

A thought then occurred to her. It's not his job to defend himself – it's mine. I'm pregnant. That means I'm going to be a mother. Actually – because I love him – I'm already a mother. And protecting their young is what mothers do.

She wiped the tears away and sat up on the sofa. She realized she had forgotten her bag, but its contents couldn't help her now. Simon would say that she had to get her mind straight. The judge had given her an unexpected reprieve, and she needed to use it, but how? She was tired, so tired.

How? She could make a list. She didn't need paper or pen; she could make the list in her mind. The title: *Last Year Versus This Year*. She was testifying about events that had ended over a year ago. Only one element was the same: pregnancy.

Last year she'd fought nausea to eat the stale, meager food that Roy prepared. Yesterday, in comparison, she'd eaten well. This morning's sickness was a sign that her body was changing, that the little one inside was asserting himself.

Last night she'd slept in her own bed, Simon beside her, not on a bathroom floor in a dingy flat with a dangerous, unstable man not far away.

Last year she'd been a prisoner. This year she was in court, and she could leave when her testimony was complete.

Last year she'd had physical injuries from Roy's attacks. This year the prosecutor's words – no matter what tone he used when he uttered them – could not hurt her. Roy's violence had been escalating, and she hadn't been able to predict his behavior. This year the prosecutor would intensify his questioning, but she knew what to expect from him. The DPS officers had already raised the issues he would address.

Last year there'd been no safety in Roy's flat. Even the negotiator couldn't protect her. This year she was alone only in the witness box. The court was filled with people who supported her: Simon, Brian, Beth, Neil Goodwyn, so many familiar faces.

Last year Brian had saved her life. This year it was her turn to save him if she could.

When the usher opened the door and said, "It's time," he held a glass of water. She smiled her thanks and took it but didn't drink any. She wasn't sure how her stomach would react, so instead she dabbed a little on her cheeks and her neck. She then walked beside him back to the courtroom and into the witness box. Her survival kit was beside the chair, but she did not retrieve it.

Courtland had stayed at her post, as had the judge. She'd watched the prosecutor drum his fingers on his notebook.

"Please respect the witness with your silence and attention," Judge Bradbury instructed the gallery.

Simon's heart skipped a beat. It had been a long twenty minutes, not knowing how she was and being unable to assist. During that time Goodwyn had spoken with him, voicing his staunch and unwavering faith in Jenny and emphasising her determination and resilience. Now Simon saw her ashen face, but her gait was steady. When she faced the prosecutor, her gaze was direct.

Brian, too, had been concerned. If her defence of him caused her to suffer, he would never forgive himself. Fortunately during the recess period he'd been allowed to stand, and he'd shifted his weight from one foot to the other in an attempt to defuse his anxiety.

"Yankee 1, are you quite recovered?" Judge Bradbury asked. "If so, I'll allow Mr. Hilliard to resume."

She took a deep breath and nodded, hoping her voice would be strong enough to reflect her conviction.

The prosecutor was angry. The momentum of his interrogation had been interrupted, but he could not show his frustration. Instead he reminded himself of other difficult challenges in his career and how he had overcome them: by recapturing the attention of the jury. "My lord, if you'll give me a moment, I'd like to remind the jury of the last lines of Yankee 1's testimony. Her upset occurred – conveniently, I might add – when I confronted her about the fact that Mr. Wilkes could not have held a knife when she moved toward the door."

He turned toward Jenny. "Four days in Mr. Wilkes' flat, four days of danger, four days in which you would have us believe that you were in fear for your life, yet your attempts to escape were unsuccessful?"

His words cut into her, but he could do her no physical harm. "I did everything I could," she said, trying to speak clearly and firmly.

"Yes or no, Yankee 1!" the prosecutor demanded, wanting to disrupt her poise. "You could not get away from a pitiable creature like Mr. Wilkes?"

"No."

"Because he had a knife?"

"Yes."

"You threw boiling water in his face and ran toward the door. Did you see the knife in his hand at that exact moment?"

"No, but I know it was there. I'll always be sure! You can't discredit me because I was there, and you weren't."

"Thank you for making my next point for me – you were there, but no objective observer can confirm this part of your testimony!"

"Brian can. He saw it, and he fired. He saved my life."

"Mrs. Hostage," Hilliard said, his mocking tone making the appellation demeaning. "Let me spell it out for you. You were facing the door until he reached you. When he came up behind you, his arm round your waist caused you to bend over. You were then facing the *floor*. It's just not physically possible for you to have seen his hand, with or without a knife. *Is it?*"

"Objection!" Courtland exclaimed. "Prosecution is testifying."

"These facts are necessary to set up my question," Hilliard insisted.

"Only once," Judge Bradbury ruled.

You hyena, Jenny thought. You scavenger. But you cannot sink your teeth into me, because I'm still alive. She wanted to stand, to make her response stronger, but had to settle for strengthening her voice. "He was yelling that he was going to kill me! He didn't make empty threats! If Brian hadn't intervened, I'd be dead!"

"She – did – not – see – the – knife," Hilliard stated, addressing the jury and pausing between each word for emphasis. "No independent third party did. We have a vengeful, untruthful witness – an armed officer guilty of haste and poor judgement – and an injustice which only you can make right. I have no more questions for this witness."

Tanya Hanson was stunned. The prosecutor's treatment of Yankee 1 had been harsh, compounding what Roy had done. If she'd stayed in the flat, would she have ended up in the witness box defending her actions?

Courtland stood. "Redirect, my lord?"

"Indeed."

"Yankee 1, when you can, please tell me: Have you uttered any falsehood in this court?"

Jenny took one breath, then two to steady herself. "No."

"Did Roy Wilkes assault you?"

"Yes."

"Did he abduct you?"

"Yes."

The questions continued, but the answers were easy. "Did he allow you to leave? Did he agree to call for medical help? Did he accept that you were not his partner, Tanya?"

No, no, no.

"Did he bind your hands? Wound you repeatedly with the knife? Did he exhibit controlling and coercive behaviour?"

Yes, yes, yes.

"Did you fear sexual assault? Did he threaten to kill you? Were you so afraid that you risked your life in an attempt to escape?"

Yes, and yes, and yes.

"The days of stress, poor rest, inadequate diet – were you also concerned for your unborn child?"

"Yes," she managed to say. "Even more than for myself."

"Did you in fact miscarry less than forty-eight hours after your rescue?"

Hilliard stirred. "Cause and effect have not been established, my lord."

"They have in my mind," Jenny answered before the judge could rule. "Roy Wilkes took a life, knife or no knife."

Judge Bradbury paused. "Jury will disregard," he said quietly.

Courtland returned to her seat.

The judge regarded the prosecutor. "Redirect, Mr. Hilliard?"

"No, my lord."

Judge Bradbury then turned to Jenny. "Yankee 1, you are excused from further testimony. You may stand down."

It was over, for her but not for Brian. Jenny could not restrain her tears. Brian, she thought, I have done my best. I pray God it will be enough.

"Miss Courtland, please see to your witness," Judge Bradbury instructed before leaving the courtroom.

Courtland approached the witness box and thanked Jenny for her testimony. "If you'll permit me – " she ventured – "what happened in the conference room?"

"I found a new perspective," Jenny answered, exhaustion making her whisper.

Courtland then waited with Jenny until Simon arrived to escort her away.

The seats in the gallery near Tanya Hanson were now empty, and the courtroom was quiet. Her throat was tight as she remembered Roy. They hadn't been youngsters when they met and hadn't made having a family a priority. They'd liked their spontaneous lifestyle, the weekend jaunts. He'd been good to her, cooking special meals and making her laugh. He'd liked the outdoors, and they'd visited all the major parks in the London area and beyond. But if she'd fallen pregnant, she thought they'd both have welcomed the child.

Would anything have changed if they'd had children? His diagnosis would have been the same, his personality would have deteriorated, and she would have had to worry about a child's safety as well as her own.

She looked about. Even the court officials had completed their tasks and left. She would not encounter anyone involved in the case as she departed, and depart she would. Contrary to her earlier promise, she would not return to observe more sessions. She would abandon him again.

CHAPTER ELEVEN

BRIAN DAVIES knew his size was likely a disadvantage in court, but if he slumped as he approached the witness box, he'd look guilty before his part in this circus had even begun. So he squared his shoulders as he entered, although wishing the space weren't elevated, thus adding to his height. He swore his oath with his hand on the Bible. Would that make the jury more likely to believe him? And why were witnesses the only ones who were required to swear to be truthful? With the approach of some prosecutors, as he'd already seen in these proceedings, truth could be a victim and not a victor. Leave your resentment at home, he told himself, but it was difficult.

Whilst in the dock, he'd faced the judge, jury, and witnesses. Now a witness himself, he faced Beth. She was in front of his family and next to Casey in the gallery, her face pale. He was angry that she was being put through this. Neither of them had slept the night before. Would he lose everything? Home, family, friends? The Job – the challenges, the camaraderie with his mates? Who would check the doneness of the Sunday roast?

Others were present, too – all the members of his team, his senior officers, and the chaplain, Goodwyn. His mates had done their best during their testimony, but they were concerned for the outcome, both for him and for themselves. Some were considering turning in their authorisation-to-carry-firearms cards if the verdict went against him.

Jenny's support of him had been powerful and unwavering, but she'd been so fatigued after her second court appearance that Casey had not trusted her fragile stamina to public transport. He'd taken her home in a taxi.

Now it was his turn to argue his case, and he was glad, if for no other reason than in the witness box he was allowed to stand.

Beth watched him enter the witness box, and the sight of him caused her to fall in love with him all over again. Not since their wedding and the christening of their children had he dressed with such care. Three happy occasions and now this, but one thing had not changed: He was still the large gentle man she'd promised her life to.

Fiona Courtland rose and asked him to give his name and rank to the court.

"Brian Davies, Police Constable, attached to the Metropolitan Police Firearms Unit."

"Officer Davies, your family is present in court today, are they not?"

"Yes, my parents have been here every day."

"Is everyone tall in your family?"

"Yes, even my sister. And my two older brothers are taller than I am."

"Lots of experience in team sport then?"

Brian smiled. "Yes, the coaches were always very happy when they saw us coming."

"And what positions did you and your brothers play?"

"Defence, regardless of the game. Always defence."

"Thank you." Courtland referred to a particular page in her notebook. "You took an oath when you became a police officer, did you not?"

"I did, yes."

"You swore to serve the Queen, to prevent all offences against people and property, and to discharge all duties according to the law. What did you understand this to mean?"

"Duty above all. It means defending and protecting."

"What is your primary goal in what you do?"

"Safety. The safety of members of the public, my fellow officers, and individuals we may encounter on an operation. We call it a duty of care."

"You were a regular bobby when you first joined the police, were you not?"

"Yes."

"And then later volunteered for specialist service?"

"Yes, I have additional training pertaining to the use of firearms. That enables me to deal with the more serious incidents that occur, such as armed robbery, drug interdiction, and terrorism, to mention only a few."

"You are also qualified to handle hostage rescue scenarios, such as the one which has brought us here today?"

"Yes."

"Are you required to attend refresher training?"

"Yes, our training is ongoing."

"Could you tell us," Courtland asked in a sincere tone, "what is involved in these training sessions? Without revealing anything that may be confidential, of course."

Brian paused. Explaining the Job to civilians, not to mention the risks involved, was difficult at best. "Because we rarely have complete intelligence prior to an operation, chaos is always possible. We train to reduce its impact, with so much repetition in multiple training scenarios that we can anticipate the actions of each man on the team during a real incident. We have to consider the what ifs because we may be faced with them. On an op, things happen very quickly. There's no time to think, much less to think things through. Decisions must be taken in seconds. And we must win, because when we do, everyone benefits."

Courtland waited a moment to let his statements sink in. "Do you work regular hours?" she enquired.

"No, our duty hours rotate. Early run is 6:00 am until 2:00 pm. Next we have 2:00 to 10:00 pm. Late run is from 10:00 pm until 6:00 am."

"Eight-hour shifts then."

"Our shifts, as you call them, are rarely only eight hours. We need to be suited and booted by start time, and if we're participating in a planned operation, we need to be present for briefings as well, which may take place several hours prior to that."

"Officer Davies, let's take the issue before this court in stages, shall we? When did you first know that Yankee 1 had been taken hostage?"

"She – " Brian stopped, remembering not to use Jenny's real name. "I was present in the briefing room at the base on Leman Street when she rang her husband. We recorded as much of her message as we could before notifying the chain of command that a hostage incident, involving the wife of one of our officers, was under way."

"What happened next?"

"We waited. An officer from New Scotland Yard arrived, who began the initial interview with my colleague. When a general location was determined, a detective from the appropriate borough was assigned to head the investigation."

"When the hostage taker and his location were identified, did you immediately proceed to the site?"

"Yes, two teams were designated."

"Did you – let me see if I can use your terminology – make entry as soon as you arrived at the area?"

Brian appreciated Courtland's step-by-step approach. She was perhaps attempting to counter the way he had been portrayed in the press. "No, a hostage negotiator was called. His function was to contact the hostage taker to achieve a peaceful solution. Sometimes this is done by defusing the emotions of the hostage taker, by wearing him down, by accepting certain demands, or by agreeing on a surrender scenario. We are ready to intervene, but we always hope that reason will prevail. When it does, we go back to base with the same amount of rounds we had when we left."

"But that did not occur in the incident we're examining today, did it? I'm referring to the one that began on 25 August last and ended on 28 August last."

"No, the conversations the negotiator held with the hostage taker did not convince him either to release the hostage or to turn himself in. We were made aware that conditions in the flat were deteriorating, both in terms of the violence and the irrational behaviour of the hostage taker."

"Who decides when you make entry?"

"We have a chain of command."

"You are referring to the various commanders whose roles have been explained to us. Am I correct then in stating that if circumstances on the ground change, an officer closest to the scene may take the decision to act even without prior approval from a more senior officer? Because the best information is available to him?"

"Yes."

"And that was what took place on 28 August?"

"The danger to the hostage had escalated, and speed upon entry is always an issue, so both teams had been moved closer to the flat. We were therefore able to hear the threats of the hostage taker and the screams of the hostage. I knew we had to act immediately. I told the team to go. If I had to do it again, I'd do exactly the same."

"Were you the first officer to enter the flat?"

"Yes."

"What did you see when you made entry?"

"The hostage taker, with his left arm restraining the hostage and his right hand holding an assault knife above his head."

"What did you do when you first made entry?"

"We identified ourselves as armed police and commanded the hostage taker to drop his knife."

"Did he obey your instruction?"

"He did not."

"What was your state of mind?"

"Stop him."

"If you'll permit me –" Courtland spoke very slowly – "stop what exactly?"

"Stop him from bringing his hand down and stabbing the hostage."

"And did your bullet stop him?"

"Bullets." He paused. The medical examiner had already testified to Wilkes' injuries, so he could not avoid correcting the barrister. "We are trained to fire one round and then to reassess the threat before firing again. This incident, however, had turned critical. There was no time to reassess before the second shot. I knew I had to make the offender incapable of further action."

"Did you see the knife fall?"

"No. I saw the hostage taker fall and the hostage fall with him."

"Did your rounds kill the hostage taker?"

"They stopped him. Only medical personnel can certify death."

"Was the hostage injured?"

"Not during our entry."

"One of your team members removed her from the scene?"

"Yes, she was taken to an ambulance for transport to hospital."

"Did you see the knife on the floor at any time?"

"I didn't look for it. My role was finished."

"Officer Davies, I apologise for this question, but it is necessary for me to ask. Were you aware that the hostage taker was of mixed race?"

Brian frowned. "No, colour doesn't signify. I'm not looking for colour. I see a suspect. I see a weapon. I see a threat."

"Is there anything else you would like the jury to hear?"

"Yes." He gathered his thoughts. "I didn't create the situation. I responded to the crisis created by the hostage taker. He was given other options and didn't choose to take them." He felt the necessity of speaking for his entire team. "We rarely have to shoot. Most incidents are resolved without gunfire, but when the most dangerous circumstances occur, someone must handle them. On that particular day it was my job. Three lives were at stake, the hostage taker's, the hostage's, and her baby's. My only regret is that I couldn't save them all."

Courtland returned to her seat without speaking into the silence of the courtroom. She realised that Hilliard had not raised even one objection, but if his cross of Yankee 1 were any indication, his questioning of Officer Davies would be brutal.

"Adjourned until 2:00 pm," Judge Bradbury said.

CHAPTER TWELVE

LUNCH WAS A SOLEMN AFFAIR. On occasion his mates had distracted him from the day's events, regaling him and Beth with colourful stories. Today, however, they gave them privacy, escorting them to a local pub and then stepping away, seating themselves several tables away but close enough to respond if needed.

Neither he nor Beth had much appetite. Instead of reaching for her fork, she reached for his hand. They both needed the physical contact.

When court resumed following the luncheon period, the prosecuting barrister Joel Hilliard began his cross-examination. He'd been rough on Jenny; Brian fully expected even more ruthless treatment to ensue.

Beth had always looked up to her husband in every sense of the word, but now, standing tall in the witness box, he dwarfed everyone in the courtroom except for the judge. A big calm man could reassure – a big angry man could frighten. Brian was more patient than she was and rarely showed a temper, but these circumstances would try any man's discipline.

"Finally we get to meet the gun cop," Hilliard opened.

"My lord," Courtland objected.

"I'll not allow characterisations of that sort in my court," Judge Bradbury stated. "Mind your manners and confine yourself to the evidence."

"Why do you carry a gun?" Hilliard enquired.

"Because I encounter situations in which it is necessary to protect myself, my fellow officers, and the public."

"How many times have you fired your weapons?"

"Many times, in training."

"Don't try to obfuscate the intent of the question! How many times have you fired a weapon on operations?" Hilliard demanded.

"Objection! The prosecution is attempting with his vocabulary to confuse the witness," Courtland declared.

More than that, Brian thought. If he can portray me as unintelligent, it will not be difficult to suggest that I have poor judgement. Unfortunately his barrister's defence of him inadvertently implied the same. He sighed. Court proceedings were a minefield.

"The jury may be confused as well," Judge Bradbury stated. "Do not link your question to a verbal attack."

Controlling his frustration, Hilliard raised his eyebrows only slightly and waited.

"Only three times on the Job," Brian replied.

Hilliard then changed his direction. "You knew the hostage personally," he said. "You knew she was still being held. Yet that did not affect your actions on that day? Can you honestly tell this court that you did not wake up that day planning to kill Mr. Wilkes in order to free your 'friend'?"

"We do not shoot to kill. We shoot to stop someone, either from harming himself or from harming others," Brian answered, managing to keep his anger from showing.

"I submit that you made up your mind to shoot before you made entry. It was your chance – your 'shot' – at glory, wasn't it?"

"I don't seek glory. I'm not even certain what it is."

"Officer Davies, you gunned the suspect down!"

"Inflammatory," Courtland objected.

"Indeed," replied the judge.

"I'll rephrase," Hilliard said, barely managing to conceal his distaste. "You shot him dead. In a display of excessive force."

It wasn't a question. Brian remained silent. And as he had anticipated, Hilliard's cross-examination was combative, not conversational.

How did Brian maintain his composure under the prosecutor's attack? Beth wondered. She wanted to scream and hit at him with her fists. She glanced at Simon Casey, seated on one side of her, and at Neil Goodwyn, seated on the other. Only the priest's hands were relaxed.

"You aimed at Mr. Wilkes, did you not?"

"There wasn't time to aim. I used directional firing."

Courtland winced. Don't elaborate, she thought.

"And that is – ?"

"Discharging a weapon without aiming," Brian explained.

"You were eager then?"

"No, not eager. Willing to do my job if called upon."

"Irresponsible, wouldn't you say?"

"No. Delay can be irresponsible. I was prepared for the necessity of firing. It's always a possibility, and we can't shrink from it."

"Was firing truly a necessity? Couldn't a nonfatal method have been utilised?"

"No. On occasion our response needs to be faster than a weapon wielded by an offender."

"And yet you fired twice! Contrary to current procedure!"

"Yes. It's a matter of achieving energy sufficient to stop the threat."

"Are you telling me that one shot wasn't enough? That you had to ensure that death would result?"

"My lord! Officer Davies has already addressed this issue in testimony!" Courtland objected.

"Indeed he has. Move on, Mr. Hilliard," Judge Bradbury replied.

"Officer Davies, are you a racist?"

"That's an insulting question!" Too late, he recalled his barrister's instruction not to become upset. It can offset your testimony and weaken your case, she'd explained.

"Asked and answered during my examination-in-chief," Courtland said, rising quickly.

"Not directly," Judge Bradbury clarified. "Officer Davies, I agree that the question can be construed as insulting, but you must answer."

"No, I am not." Brian watched Courtland reseat herself.

"I put it to you," Hilliard continued, raising his voice slightly. "You chose power and dominance over peaceful resolution. In fact, your testimony is a fabrication, a desperate attempt to defend yourself because you killed an unarmed man. Is it not?"

"We are tested for visual acuity," Brian said, trying to remain calm. "A knife was clearly in the hand of the hostage taker. I was called upon to act before he could use it to kill the hostage, which he was threatening to do."

"Visual 'acuity'?" Hilliard mocked.

"I have good eyesight," Brian said firmly. "My personnel records will confirm it." And good vocabulary as well, he thought.

"Your shots killed Mr. Wilkes. The medical examiner has confirmed that," Hilliard said slowly, stressing each word. "Can you truthfully assert that your actions – which took a human life – were reasonable?"

If he hadn't already been standing, Brian would have risen to his feet to add strength to his answer. "I will always assert that an action that protects an innocent life is both reasonable and lawful. The hostage taker was presented with other options and did not choose to avail himself of them. The use of a firearm is a last resort but sometimes the only way to resolve a critical incident. If your life were at risk, Mr. Prosecutor, I would come even to your rescue."

Hilliard threw up his hands and turned away.

"Redirect, my lord?" Courtland asked.

"If you can do so briefly," Judge Bradbury counselled.

"Officer Davies, it is your sworn statement that the hostage taker Roy Wilkes was holding a knife at the time you made entry into his flat. Yes or no?"

"Yes."

"Were you aware prior to making entry that a knife was on the premises and had been used to wound the hostage?"

"Yes. Firearms teams are apprised of any information which may affect our actions should entry become necessary."

"Thus in your view was it a logical and reasonable conclusion that the hostage taker would be holding it whilst threatening the hostage's life?"

"Yes."

"Did you warn the hostage taker that you were armed?"

"Yes."

"Did you direct him to drop the knife?"

"Yes."

"Did he step back or lower the knife?"

"No."

"Did he turn away before you fired?"

"No."

"Did he, in fact, take any action that would have indicated that his intent to kill the hostage had changed?"

"No, none."

"Could you be mistaken? As you and others have testified, things happen very fast."

"No. The hostage taker had already shown he was capable of violence. The situation had escalated. There was no question that the hostage's life was in danger. His action in fact determined my action."

When Courtland sat, Judge Bradbury stood. His eyes swept the courtroom briefly. "Tomorrow morning at 10:00, members of the jury. Until then, court is adjourned."

Brian took a deep breath, wondering how long the air of liberty would be his. The days in court had been difficult, but he had known his turn was coming. He had wanted his testimony to be heard. Now it was over. He could take no further action to defend himself. Had it been enough?

He could ignore the predictable press headlines – "Trigger Happy Cowboy Cop Testifies" and the like – and hope that Beth did not see them. Her smile had already lost some of its bounce, and his reassurance of her would seem hollow. He could trust that his character witnesses, who would begin their testimonies in the morning, would have a positive impact on the jury. However, closing arguments by both barristers would follow, and he could see no way that defence counsel could counter what the prosecution would say. They would all then hear the judge's instructions to the jury and wait for the verdict.

Lives could be broken here. Was the law the only entity that survived intact?

CHAPTER THIRTEEN

WHEN BRIAN ARRIVED AT COURT, escorted to the dock by his two custody officers, he was surprised to see both his Federation reps, Henry Lloyd and Roderick James, and his solicitor Arthur Wheatley, in an intense discussion with his barrister Fiona Courtland. Judge Bradbury entered, and Courtland immediately requested permission to add a new witness to her list. Brian allowed himself a quick glance at Beth, knowing they were both wondering what new development could possibly have taken place.

The prosecution barrister objected, citing the rule of discovery and accusing the defence of grandstanding.

"Your charge is premature," Judge Bradbury stated. "Miss Courtland, I'd like to hear a bit more about the reason for the delay in naming this witness."

"It's a matter of new evidence, my lord," Courtland replied, "which is critical for achieving justice in this case. Prosecution will of course have the opportunity to cross-examine the witness, and I would not be averse to a short recess if my learned colleague would like to review the data which will be given in testimony."

"You've piqued my curiosity," the judge decided. "But I'd advise you to show relevance quickly or we will proceed with the witness list as previously disclosed. Mr. Hilliard?"

"No recess requested at this time."

"The defence calls Vincent Lisle," Courtland said.

A slim individual with a slight stoop entered the witness box, smoothed his tweed suit, and was sworn in, adjusting his glasses on his nose as he read the words on the card.

"Did I pronounce your name correctly?" Courtland asked.

"Yes, Lisle rhymes with trial," he volunteered, smiling.

A happy witness? Why? Brian thought. No one is ever glad to be interrogated in court.

"Please give the court your occupation."

"I am an associate professor of criminology at the University of West London. I teach in the School of Law and Criminology."

"How did you come to be involved in this case?"

"I was approached by two members of the Metropolitan Police, to be specific, two Metropolitan Police Federation representatives. They requested my assistance in performing a series of scientific experiments regarding the disposition of a knife in a hostage rescue scenario."

"Professor Lisle, what was the purpose of your experiments?"

"To solve the discrepancy between the forensic data in this case and the statement of the police officer who rescued the hostage."

Judge Bradbury turned to the prosecuting barrister. "Mr. Hilliard, please remind the court of the forensic data just mentioned."

Hilliard stood. "My lord, the knife which Mr. Wilkes was alleged to have held was found over ten feet from his body. We conclude from this that he could not have been holding it when Officer Davies entered his flat and killed him."

"Miss Courtland?"

"My lord, we have always believed the statement of Officer Davies, who has sworn that a knife was in the hand of the hostage taker when he made entry."

"I trust we are all more clear then?" the judge said crisply, directing his question to the jury but not waiting for any to respond. "Proceed, Miss Courtland."

"How did you assist the Police Federation officers, Professor Lisle?"

"They had performed two experiments which did not dispel the forensic findings. I was able to identify the flaws in their process. I then designed and conducted two further experiments and completed an official report."

"My lord, I have that report." She handed a copy to Hilliard and to the usher. "May I enter it into evidence?"

It was duly catalogued.

Courtland resumed her questions. "Why two tests?" she asked.

"It is important to show that the results of an experiment can be duplicated," he explained. "Hence I led two."

"Please continue."

"In the previous experiments subjects were told to hold the implement, a rubber knife, in one hand above their heads and then to strike a pillow – which they held waist high – with their other hand. The pillow was intended to represent the hostage, although the participants were not advised of this."

"And the problem with this was – ?"

"Participants did not utilise the full range of motion. I asked Officer Lloyd, one of the police representatives, to demonstrate their experiment. I then saw that the test was static and the motion was incomplete. May I?"

"Yes," Judge Bradbury and Courtland agreed at the same time.

Hilliard shook his head in frustration, knowing any objection would be overruled.

"First," Lisle said, "the hostage taker restrained the hostage." He bent forward and wrapped his left arm round an invisible person. "Next, he straightened and prepared to stab her." He raised his right arm high before bringing it down. "Did you see?" he asked. "There is an arc, a trajectory. When an object is held high, above one's head, for example, there is a backward movement before the object is brought down. It may be so small as to be nearly imperceptible to the human eye, but the movement is there nonetheless."

"What conclusion did you reach following this observation?"

"That if Officer Davies' bullets hit the hostage taker when the hostage taker's arm was in the farthest position, then the expected – and I emphasise expected – trajectory of the knife would have carried it backward some distance. In other words, the knife would not have just fallen out of his hand and landed nearby. Nor would it have fallen forward. Indeed my experiments confirmed this."

Brian was on the edge of his seat. Hope. The professor's testimony held hope. He turned and saw Beth gripping Neil Goodwyn's arm.

"In my first experiment we had twenty participants. In the second, since it was necessary to confirm the findings of the first, we used forty. We asked each to mimic the entire procedure, restraining an imaginary hostage – the pillow – and then stabbing it. Our subjects were men between the ages of 35 and 45 who were inexperienced in close combat. The upward – or you may wish to say backward – movement was greater than we anticipated, reflecting, I believe, the desire to have maximum downward momentum and therefore maximum force. We gave the individuals a push at the critical moment."

"Where – " Courtland seemed to have difficulty finding sufficient breath to complete her question – "did the object fall?"

Brian held his breath in anticipation of the response.

"The implements hit the wall and dropped to the floor. We measured the distance from the hostage taker. In each case, it was more than eight feet. If there had been a sofa in our demonstration room, the knife would have been close to it, not close to the hostage taker."

"Is there anything else you would like to add?" Courtland asked.

"Yes," Lisle answered. "I believe that not only did the hostage taker have the knife in his hand, but that he intended his movement to give him power sufficient to result in a killing blow. If his movement had been tentative, the knife would not have fallen so far away from him."

Brian felt his muscles relax. He watched Courtland pause for several moments before thanking the witness and sitting, evidently unwilling to release the witness to cross-examination. There wasn't a sound in the courtroom.

Hilliard also moved slowly. "Only a few questions, my lord," he said. "Professor Lisle, where were the tests conducted?"

"At the police training centre in Gravesend."

"Was the room where you held your experiments similar in size to the sitting room in Mr. Wilkes' flat?"

"Yes, the police officers provided the dimensions, and we duplicated those in our choice of setting."

"Would the items of furniture in Mr. Wilkes' flat have made the room seem smaller?"

"Yes, of course," Lisle nodded, his greying hair swinging forward and back.

"Was the room you utilised carpeted?" Hilliard enquired.

Hilliard was being careful not to attack the witness directly, Brian noted, simply to raise doubt about the conditions and his findings.

"Yes, although our carpet was not as worn as the carpet described in the forensic report, meaning, of course, that in our tests the knife would have been less likely, not more likely, to slide."

"Did 100% of the subjects give you a positive result?"

"No, in the first test six percent did not. In the second, seven percent."

"The second test was thus less successful?"

"From a statistical point of view, both had the same degree of success."

"What did you regard as a negative result?"

"Incidents when the implement fell four to six feet from the hostage taker. None of the implements fell close to him."

Hilliard took a moment to digest Lisle's answers. "Certainly," he said, "you were unable to simulate the impact of Officer Davies' bullets striking Mr. Wilkes, were you not?"

"You are correct. We could not push them hard enough. Rounds from a firearm would have increased the amount of force but correspondingly the distance covered by the knife."

In the silence that followed, Judge Bradbury spoke. "Mr. Hilliard? Miss Courtland?" he queried. "My turn now?"

Neither responded.

He turned toward the jury. "Usually at this point I tell jurors what the law is regarding the crime, as a way of guiding your deliberations. That brings us to the current day. We human beings have created a system to deal with the injustices of this world. However, since we as human beings are less than perfect, any process we create has an inherent possibility of error. Today is one of those occasions. I do believe, our defects notwithstanding, that our system is better than most and far, far better than none."

Courtland stood, wanting to hold the CPS accountable for their rush to judgement. Although theirs had been an attempt to take advantage of the current anti-police sentiment, she knew that that accusation would be both inflammatory and unnecessary. She mentally rephrased. "My lord, if I may, this prosecution has been based on a questionable interpretation of Officer Davies' past performance and an equally biased reading of forensic results. I respectfully request that the charges be dismissed."

"Mr. Hilliard, I am waiting for your submission." Judge Bradbury squeezed the bridge of his nose with his fingers.

What did the judge intend? Brian wondered. Would the case not be given to the jury?

The silence in the court was absolute, although Judge Bradbury had not declared it. All eyes were on the prosecutor.

"My lord, the prosecution recognises that there is no case to answer," Hilliard said quietly.

"Officer Davies," Judge Bradbury nodded, "your actions are thus found to be lawful. You are hereby freed from all charges. I'd like to see you reinstated – back on the Job, as you would say – with immediate effect. Jury, you have discharged your duty. Court is adjourned."

Brian stood, stunned but relieved. He had no feeling of triumph. He hadn't won; he simply hadn't lost. He stepped out of the dock, the custody officers not accompanying him. The suppressed exclamations or rustle of others' movements didn't register. Only the words he'd waited over a year to hear rang in his ears: reinstated with immediate effect.

Courtland reached him before he left the courtroom.

"An unusual conclusion," she said, "but a good one. Not one witness spoke against you personally. It was the evidence which was on trial, and with the new empirical data to explain it, you are free and clear. CPS doesn't prosecute cases unless they believe they have a good chance of winning them, and even they can see that in these circumstances they do not. Live your life. This case is over."

Beth entered, her tears illuminating her smile.

"Did you know about the experiments?" he asked Courtland.

"Until today, only about the failed ones. Here's what I did know – I believed you from the outset. Mrs. Casey was a most sympathetic witness. We had reason, if not proof, on our side. It was a challenge, I admit, and there were some rocky spots, but I've always respected your sort. I was glad to do my part."

"Is it truly over?" Beth wanted to know.

"As you may be aware, the coroner's court will reconvene in the near future. I will be present, although there is no cause for concern. The coroner's scope is narrow. He'll be objective, seeking the facts only of the case, and his verdict cannot be inconsistent with that of the criminal proceedings which concluded here today."

"Will Jenny be called?" Brian asked.

"Yes, the coroner can call witnesses, and they must appear. The coroner himself will lead the questioning, but there is no cross-examination. In fact, since the aim of the court is to establish how, when, and where the death occurred, not who is responsible for it, the roles of prosecution or defence do not apply. It will be anticlimactic at best. A required part of our judicial process but in this case inconsequential." She left them.

Brian and Beth exited the courtroom together, engulfed by family members and firearms officers. Chief Superintendent Brierly and Chief Inspector Denison stepped forward to shake his hand.

"Until Monday week," Denison said with a broad smile. "At that time we'll do what the judge instructed, beginning with our post incident procedures."

Brian nodded. He'd be required to attend a two-week "back to ops" course, to requalify him on his weapons and to undergo a series of shoot/no shoot scenarios.

He saw Casey, mobile in hand, wave at him. He'd let Jenny know. How would he tell her? Brian was not certain how he would have framed the words. He felt exaltation and exhaustion at the same time. He laughed, leant on Beth, and was escorted past the clamourous press.

CHAPTER FOURTEEN

BRIAN ANSWERED EVERY RING of the doorbell. He'd already welcomed Neil Goodwyn and a number of his firearms mates, who had arrived in twos and threes, all bearing liquid refreshment. He peppered his two Federation reps with questions when they entered.

"We never gave up," Lloyd stated.

"We knew we had to find proof," James added. "Something that would guarantee an adjudication in our favour. I wish it hadn't taken as long as it did."

"I wish I had a recording of it all, particularly the judge's words," Brian said. "I'd play it until it wore out. Until I can accept that it's not just a dream."

When Jenny stood outside with an uncertain smile on her face, he drew her in.

"Simon didn't tell me much," she said. "Only that you were free and to meet here."

He embraced her and then explained about the new evidence. The Federation reps added detail. "Do you recall when we interviewed you? And you said that the hostage taker didn't stab you right away? That there was a delay after he raised his arm? We think we now know why that was. He was moving his hand farther back to gain maximum force for the blow. The experiments proved it."

She shivered. "That's scary even now," she said.

"Then the judge challenged the prosecutor," Brian said. "And that was that."

"I wish I'd been there to see him get his comeuppance!" she exclaimed. "What did he do? Melt onto the floor like the Wicked Witch in the Wizard of Oz?"

"Almost! He was speechless for a moment though," he laughed, remembering. "When he found his voice, he was forced to dismiss the charges."

She laughed with him, realizing it had been a long time since she'd heard him laugh. He was a big man with a big laugh, and he had been silent. "What was it like in court?"

"Subdued excitement in the courtroom and cheers outside. No one was expecting it."

"This calls for champagne, doesn't it?"

"Not for you," Simon said, joining them.

She looked around. No one had brought food. "Brian, aren't you hungry?"

"Ravenously," he admitted.

"Me, too. Simon, let's call every restaurant in Hampstead that delivers," she suggested.

The pizza came first, followed by Chinese, French, and Italian as well. Simon and his mates settled every bill. Neil Goodwyn stepped forward to bless the food.

"Are we thankful?" he enquired with a smile.

"Yes!" they shouted, all in high spirits.

"The sun is a bit brighter and life a bit sweeter for all of us," he concluded. "Amen."

They tucked in, and the priest found a place next to Jenny. "I'm proud of you," he said. "You stood tall in court. When challenged, you rallied. You were motivated by love and not by fear."

"I had strength I didn't know I had," she admitted.

"That's a sign of God's presence."

"My anger at Roy," she added. "It burned so brightly for so long, but now only embers are left. In a sense he destroyed himself. But the consequences were so serious, both for me and for Brian."

"I'm reminded of something C. S. Lewis wrote," Goodwyn said. "'You can't go back and change the beginning, but you can start where you are and change the ending.' I believe that you will and that Brian will also."

Brian revelled in the reassuring sounds of a normal activity. The gathering would have been more raucous, of course, if Meg and Robbie hadn't been there, but there were still occasional loud bursts of hilarity between bites from some of the men. He didn't want the day to end, but with the alcohol and release of tension, he felt a wave of fatigue.

"A few words before we go?" Simon asked, his arm round Jenny's waist. "She's craving a milkshake at that American diner on the High Street." He smiled. "I always find it difficult to tell her no."

"Brian, I don't think I'll ever tire of hearing the story of today," she said. "After so many months of uncertainty. One blow after another. We both lost part of ourselves this past year, but now we've been restored."

"Casey – Jenny – Hampstead has been a haven. I'll always be grateful that you provided this refuge for us."

"Glad to do it," she said, hugging him. "See you soon."

"It'll stay with you for a while, Davies," Simon cautioned.

Brian nodded, knowing that Casey was referring to more than the trial experience. "I expect so," he said.

Others began to make their way to the door. "What's next?" was their question.

"I've been given a week's leave," he said to all of them. "I'll be back on the Job after that. We're packing up tomorrow and going home. Perhaps there it will seem real."

He and Beth corralled the children and began the bedtime routine, their parents assisting for the last time amidst his heartfelt thanks for their support.

When he and Beth were alone, he sat down on the edge of the bed and took her face in his hands. "Bethie, I've thanked everyone else except the one who matters most to me. I thought my future was going to be – limited. Now that we know it's not, I want to tell you. I agree with you. I'd like very much for us to have another baby."

CHAPTER FIFTEEN

"GUN COP VINDICATED," "No Verdict Forthcoming" – better headlines than previously, but Casey was glad that even these had been replaced on the front pages with other news, and none of the bylines belonged to Lionel Hodge. He had printed information that was illegally obtained, hence both he and Croxley were liable for criminal charges. "Traitor Cop Arrested and Charged" would make for good reading, but he had little faith that the Crown Prosecution Service would proceed. They seemed to lay charges against innocent coppers like Davies and then neglect to follow up with guilty ones.

The two weeks since the conclusion of the trial had been productive. Davies and his family had moved back to their home in Rickmansworth, and he and Jenny had been able to arrange for a final cleaning of the Hampstead flat before putting it on the market. Davies was well into the post incident procedure drills which would allow him to return to full operational duties.

However, Jenny's morning sickness hadn't eased significantly – which he found worrying – nor had her need for naps. He'd still not allowed his father to visit, although Martin, his brother, had been on leave recently and had seen no signs of paternal aggressiveness. It was perhaps too soon to declare a victory – or even a cease fire – on his dad's battle with alcoholism and abuse, but it was a start. He'd sent MacKenna to Portsmouth to discover information that could either confirm or deny this. Whilst he waited to hear from him, he'd follow Goodwyn's advice by continuing to set boundaries and watching to see if they were respected.

He smelled the aroma of Italian spices when he entered the home in Chorleywood. There'd been a nip in the air, and he liked stepping into the warmth and receiving Jenny's embrace.

"Spaghetti soup," she smiled, "with mini meatballs. It's simmering. Our salad's already chilling in the fridge, and I'll heat the Tuscan bread just before we eat."

"We have a few minutes then?" he asked. "Because I have something for you. Sean MacKenna completed another assignment for me – to find the rest of the story about your World War I VAD." He handed her a small packet.

She opened the flap, drew out the pages, and read silently for a few minutes.

"There were clinics all over England and Scotland following the war," Simon said. "It took Mac awhile to find the one where Elspeth had served. As you know, she planned to take nurses' training when the war ended, and she did. She trained in Hampstead, as a matter of fact, but found Perry in a clinic in northern Scotland."

"He survived the war, and she found him! She must have taken care of him." Jenny was amazed at the amount of detail Mr. Mac had been able to uncover. "A clinic outside Glasgow," she noted.

"Now closed."

"How did he discover all this?" she asked, glancing at the sheaf of papers she held in her hand.

"Perseverance and good fortune," Simon smiled. "At the outset he had only her name – which we knew didn't change since she didn't marry – and the knowledge that she had been a nursing sister somewhere in Scotland. Fortunately we Brits are good at keeping records."

"So he went all the way to Scotland?"

"Yes, and it's a good thing he did. A local library had held a retrospective not too long ago on World War I. He persuaded the librarian to allow him to review the material, some of which had been held in storage by a local clinic. There were drawings by some of the clinic's residents who had served as well as poetry and needlework by some of the nurses. Elspeth was mentioned by name, and so was one of the artists, a Perry Sparling. His artwork depicted postwar as well as war scenes, but his drawing of a nurse – whom Mac believes is Elspeth – was the only one he completed in colour."

"She died in 1975, the year I was born," Jenny mused.

"And Mac believes that Perry died in the clinic. His date was listed under his drawings."

"1932," she read.

"It's reasonable to conclude that he never recovered fully from his head injury. We know from her diary that he wasn't disfigured in the war, but his sight, speech, hearing, and memory were affected. If he had been able, he would have pursued a trade. There's no record of that."

"So – some handicaps must have remained," she said.

"Long-term memory and mobility are the two most likely, according to Mac," Simon stated.

"So he might not have remembered their relationship and how deeply loved he was," she concluded. "How sad."

She put the bread in the oven and set the table for their salad and soup, putting the pages next to her place. When the bread was hot, she tossed the salad and ladled the soup.

"Simon, listen to this," she said between bites. "'Uniforms stiff with sweat and fear / I stand on hallowed ground. / A land torn open, a bloody bier / I stand on hallowed ground. / Called Somme, Ypres, and Passendaele / I stand on hallowed ground. / Once-beating hearts now lie still / I stand on hallowed ground.'"

Usually he finished his meal in half the time it took for her to finish hers. Tonight, however, he was pausing to hear and to reflect.

"And here's another," she read. "'Here, e'en here / A world away / I hear the guns / All night and day. / I see their faces / Their stumbling strides / They hear them too / On every side. / What's past lives on / It hasn't died / Pain lingers long / No peace abides.'" She ate a little more soup and frowned. "Simon, shall I add another spoonful to your soup? Mine's cold now, and another partial serving will heat it up."

"I'll do it," he said and watched whilst she turned the pages over.

"She's no Owen or Sassoon," Jenny said, "but her verses are very moving. I'm glad to know what happened to both of them. Thank you for this. It gives me a new perspective."

Reseating himself, he added, "There's something the report didn't mention. Perry – it seems that I'm related to him. Several generations back, of course. On my mother's side of the family."

"Really? You're related?"

He nodded.

"Doesn't that make you want to know more about him?"

"He left home early to find work, so no one remembers much about him."

"Not even what happened to him in the war?"

"He served with the British Army, as so many did, but Mac found no record of visitors or correspondence when the war ended. Somehow he was lost to them. Elspeth was truly all he had." He paused. "By the way, you should know that Mac refused payment for any of this work. I think he's rather fond of you."

"I'm fond of him." She took a tentative taste of the renewed soup. "Simon, we're so fortunate, aren't we? In spite of everything that's happened to us. It doesn't get any better than this, does it?"

He looked down, a smile playing at the corners of his mouth. "Better than salad, bread, and – "

"Cold soup," she added, laughing. "Still, we're okay, and we have a future filled with hope."

"I've had a think on that, and I hate to admit it, but some things are beyond my strength. Like providing hope. And I've concluded that it comes from somewhere or something – outside us."

"Or Someone," she added. "Simon, why do some people have it when others don't?"

"Some take it in and make it a part of themselves. Sometimes others have to show us how to do that, and then it becomes a resource we can use when we encounter circumstances we can't control."

"We've had too many of those." She smiled at him. "Simon, that's downright theological! Neil Goodwyn would be impressed."

CHAPTER SIXTEEN

SIMON CASEY FROWNED, puzzled by the notice of an incoming call from Jenny on his mobile. He was at the police training centre at Gravesend, on a break from supervising training exercises for his team. Should he answer? The last time she had rung him on the Job, she had been in trouble. What could the reason be today?

He decided to accept the call but remain silent until he knew its import.

"Simon! Simon! Are you there? I have some wonderful news!"

"Yes," he croaked, tension and relief colliding.

"Simon, we're having twins! The doctor confirmed it. He heard two heartbeats!"

He could not manage to say anything.

"That's why I've been so sick. 'It's not unexpected when there are two,' he said." She was laughing her words. "Not unexpected when we're expecting!"

She was talking so fast he couldn't get a word in, but it didn't matter. He was over the moon.

"Simon, are you there? Have you heard all this? I think Someone's been looking out for us, don't you?"

Yes. Oh yes.

"I know you can't take a long call, but I have a little more news. He's recommending bed rest – modified, not complete – and not for long, just until my next checkup, because of our family history, even though I'm stable so far. As a 'precaution.' Isn't that funny? He sounded just like a policeman! And won't it be great if we have to have a cook? Then we won't have to eat pizza every night!"

He laughed aloud.

"I know it'll be a while before you can come home, but you know where you'll find me."

"Best news ever," he said, controlling the tremor in his voice but stumbling a bit in his words. "See you soon. Love you both. No, all."

He closed his phone. No one was about, and he wanted to tell the world. "I've had a call from Jenny," he told Davies when he appeared.

"Is she all right?"

"Better than," he smiled. "Twins, Davies! I'm going to be a father twice." He repeated the news to Howard when he joined them. Others gathered round, slapping him on the shoulder and ribbing him about his prowess.

All were happy for him, but Howard had the best response. "Head home now, mate," he said, "but don't set any speed records. I'll finish up here with the lads. Give Jenny our best."

He rang her back to let her know he was on his way, wanting to hear her tell it all again. Wanting to see her face whilst she did. Wanting to pepper her with questions. How was she? Even short term, she would need help. She was small; could she carry two babies safely? When would they know if they were having boys or girls or both? What would they name them? How could he ensure that the next months passed without incident? Would they allow him to be with her during delivery?

Perhaps the answers to these questions weren't most important today. What mattered was letting her know how happy he was and how ready for their next adventure.

THE END

ACKNOWLEDGEMENTS

I NEVER INTENDED to write a book. I lived on the Mississippi Gulf Coast and was happy with the pace and activities of southern life. Then came Ivan, with hurricane force winds and the fear of loss. A year later Hurricane Katrina brought the fact of loss.

What better way to communicate the life lessons learned from the traumas of these storms than to write a story?

Thus was born *The Witness,* a crime-suspense novel set in London and focusing on the trauma of violence. My protagonist experienced the elements of trauma and took the steps necessary to recover.

But the story wasn't over. When *The Witness* ended, the characters were still alive to me. Further challenges awaited them. Hence *The Mission* came into being, which examined the trauma of grief, and to end the trilogy, *The Hostage* detailed the trauma of injustice.

These three books have a common element: hope. My experiences taught me that healing is possible. Never simple, never easy, but worth the struggle that true healing requires.

The following individuals helped me to navigate through the process of police and legal procedures in *The Hostage:* Bill Tillbrook, Chief Superintendent (Retired), Commander, Specialist Firearms Command, London Metropolitan Police Service; PC Ian Chadwick (Retired), Specialist Firearms Officer, London Metropolitan Police Service; and Tom Gede, Attorney at Law, Morgan, Lewis & Bockius, LLP. For generosity and expertise beyond the call of duty, I thank them.

Anna Hall-Zieger, Professor of Creative Writing, Texas A&M University, made valuable constructive comments about literary issues in the manuscript. My son Jeff Gottlieb made unusually perceptive conceptual observations. The involvement of both necessitated areas of rethinking and rewriting, which improved the effectiveness of the story. My stepson Paul Kryske helped in traversing the arcane digital world.

My husband Larry suffered through all the painful early drafts and provided endless encouragement during the changes necessary in the creative process. Where I was weak in the marketing arena, he was strong.

Any inaccuracies, if present, are mine, not theirs.

Where one journey ends, another begins. My next trip will be a stand-alone novel set during the Cold War and entitled, *A Casualty of War.* Buon viaggio!

ABOUT THE AUTHOR

NAOMI KRYSKE was educated at Rice University, Houston, Texas. She left Texas when she became a Navy wife. Following her husband Larry's retirement from the U.S. Navy, she lived on the Mississippi Gulf Coast until Hurricane Katrina destroyed her home and caused her relocation to north Texas.

The Hostage is the third of a series of novels set in London (*The Witness* and *The Mission* are the first two), involving the Metropolitan Police, and exploring the themes of trauma and recovery. In 2008 she was awarded a grant from the Melissa English Writing Trust for *The Witness,* the first novel in the trilogy.

Naomi has been a Stephen Minister in her church and sings in the Chancel Choir.

Visit Naomi on the Web at www.NaomiKryske.com and on Pinterest at www.pinterest.com/NaomiKryske.

CPSIA information can be obtained
at www.ICGtesting.com
Printed in the USA
BVHW082010030921
615989BV00007B/115

9 780578 9445